THE GLASS WALL

Goran Baba Ali has written and published various literary and journalistic works in English, Kurdish and Dutch. *The Glass Wall* is his debut novel in the English language. As an ex-refugee, originally from Iraqi Kurdistan, he has personally experienced some of the protagonist's hardship in this novel, including a few weeks living in a desert. Since he left Iraq in 1994, he has lived in various countries. He studied sociology in Amsterdam, where he was also the editor-in-chief of *exPonto Magazine*. After fifteen years living in the Netherlands, he moved to London in 2012 and has since spent most of his time writing, including a part-time freelance job reporting news from Iraq for the English language outlet *Insight*. In 2019, he completed an MA in creative writing at Birkbeck, University of London.

For more information, you can visit his website:
www.goranbabaali.com

This is an unforgettable novel. Its theme is the dark adventure of the refugee, driven to flee from her or his native country, living an isolated half-life of exile between memories of a lost homeland and the calm indifference of the 'safe' world around.

As a Kurdish writer, with a full experience of war, flight, uprooting, the kindness of strangers and the hostility of foreign border guards and bureaucracies, Goran Baba Ali has seen and felt the worst of the exile condition. But he has turned it into an almost Kafkan allegory which runs all through the book, the sustained image of a glass wall. Immensely high, transparent and yet impenetrably thick and strong, it divides a scorching desert landscape from a 'normal' prosperous world where grass is green, families picnic beside pretty lakes and shops are stocked with food and cool drinks. But the transparency is only one-way. The thirsty refugees who stumble out of the desert and collapse at the foot of the wall can see the happy world beyond. But they can't reach it, and the inhabitants of that world can't see them or hear their cries for help.

This is the story of Arman, the young refugee who finds himself at the foot of the wall at first without food, water or shelter from the burning desert sun. His efforts to find a way through the wall (there are certain heavily-guarded crossing points) and to build some sort of refuge for himself develop into a narrative which is never monotonous, a fascinating struggle for survival, a tortuous negotiation with the elderly guard at a crossing point, a slow discovery that his only secure possession is his own past reconstructed in dreams and memories. And, as the novel continues, great dramas arise which begin to shake and transform that complacent world beyond the glass.

The powerful central image carries the book through to its poignant conclusion. But the metaphor of that giant one-way wall of glass, segregating the scattered of this world from the settled, will stay with the reader as long as fear and flight torment this 21st century.

Neal Ascherson
Author of *The Death of Fronsac* and *Black Sea*

THE GLASS WALL

Goran Baba Ali

Afsana Press
London

This paperback edition is first published in 2024
by Afsana Press Ltd, London
www.afsana-press.com

All rights reserved
Copyright © Goran Baba Ali, 2021
The moral right of the author has been asserted

This is a work of fiction. All characters, places, events, organisations and institutions in this novel are either products of the author's imagination or are used fictitiously.

Typeset in Minion Pro by Afsana Press Ltd
Printed and bound in Great Britain by Clays Ltd, Elcograf S.p.A.

A CIP catalogue record for this book
is available from the British Library

ISBN paperback: 978-1-7399824-1-6
ISBN hardback: 978-1-7399824-0-9
ISBN e-book: 978-1-7399824-2-3

To all those who are facing a glass wall.
Or those who have the feeling they are facing one.

1

He must have arrived at the sea again, for the young man saw a thin, grey streak come in sight, rising just above the horizon. Had he been wandering in a circle all the time through the desert? For three days, or four? He had lost count. He took a few more steps, dragging his bare feet through the sand, and the strip rose higher. The heat slapped his face and his bare arms. Clad in only a T-shirt and worn trousers, his head wrapped in a rag, he looked round, dazzled by the gleaming sun high in the vast cupola of the blue sky that enclosed the desert from all sides.

He pushed himself forward, hobbling. Tired, hungry and thirsty; a water bottle in his hand, with only a few sips remaining. The faint line was now higher up in the bright sky. He lingered, staring at it, eyes wide open, dizzy from the sun. There was no sea. Only the air between the horizon and the line. But wait! What was that glassy layer? Its tone slightly different from that of the sky. Oh, it was glass, indeed. A huge piece of glass rising from the heat haze that emanated from the sand. But just what was this immense glass pane—a barrier, a fence, or something else besides? It was a wall of glass. Oh, no, no, no... This is not happening!

He gathered his strength and limped forward, clutching the plastic bottle. The strip rose higher and higher, the glass wall gaining magnitude all the while until the young man came close enough to observe the tops of buildings and trees emerging far in the distance behind the glass.

It was there, a stone's throw from where he stood in the sand. Grand and glorious, reaching high into the sky, the glass wall stretched the length of the desert.

Unbelievable! Truly unbelievable! How can they do that to him? Oh, no, please! They can't do that! He is imagining it. It's one of those mirages. It must be.

He took a few more steps and his jaw dropped: some two hundred metres behind the glass, a vast lake shone serenely. An oasis of vegetation, above which, behind a few green hills and rows of trees, protruded dozens of buildings. Ivy-covered towers, copper roofs and gilded domes, terracotta brick façades, skyscrapers with shiny glass glistening in the sun. Several cranes rose into the sky, hovering over the skeletons of new buildings.

Tiny and frail in front of that giant monster, the young man looked left and right at the colossal wall of glass expanding over the desert; each end melting into the shimmering heat haze of the horizon.

He knelt in the sand and squinted in the bright sunlight at the city behind the glass. Tears blurred his sight. He could feel a lump growing in his throat and a heavy weight pushing down on his chest. He closed his eyes and sighed deeply.

A moment of desperate ire, and deep down wretched; fists tightly clenched in the sand, bending forward. The plastic bottle crunched in his hand. If it wasn't for the blistering sand and the heat of the sun in the back of his head, he could be sure he was dreaming.

He straightened up, wiped his eyes, then turned round and looked back at the desert. A trail of his footprints stretched in the sand to a vanishing point at the horizon behind him. Litter spread everywhere around. Worn shoes and sandals, torn clothes, sticks, twigs, long tree branches, a few large stones half-sunk in the sand, here and there holes filled with ash and charcoal, empty plastic bottles, rusty crumpled tins, abandoned bags and suitcases. Beside each of these, a small hillock of sand had grown. Nothing more except a vast, expansive desert behind him, utterly silent.

He looked at the water bottle, the last of anything he had left now. He drank the remaining sips and tossed the empty bottle away. Into the litter.

He stood up and hobbled to the glass wall, leaning on it with both hands. Exhausted, perspiring in his ragged clothes, he peered at the town on the other side. Honestly, this can't just be true.

A gust of wind blew sand over him, clattering against the glass. He wanted to shout out but his lungs felt weighed down and nothing came out. He started panting in the heavy, dry desert air.

He stared at the wall that rose high in the sky above, and banged his head on the glass. The sharp pain reminded him of the wound on his brow; from bumping his head on something hard. A few days ago, in the boat. There were other people as well. Then a splash. He had fallen in the water. Splash. But what had happened before that? He couldn't remember. His sight turned black. He held to the glass and sat down at the foot of the wall.

Eyes firmly closed, teeth clenched, he removed the rag from his head, put his sweaty palms to his forehead and felt a burning sting. He clenched his teeth harder until the pain slightly eased.

Opening his eyes, he rested his hands on the glass again and stared at the unreachable landscape. The town seemed even further away. Right behind the glass barrier, just in front of him, stretched a wide asphalt road, behind which the lake. On its far side, several boats, some with masts and sails, were moored in a semicircle. Shadowy human figures moved about on the boats and on the promenade, their presence barely noticeable. From one side to the other, willows, magnolias, maples, shrubs, reeds and bullrushes encircled the lake, and far, far away, to the left, a vast forest filled his view. The lush reflection in the lake of the buildings, the hills, the trees, the clean blue sky and the moored boats, made the world behind the glass even more enticing.

He pressed on the glass with all his strength, then banged on it vigorously. No trembling. Not even a slight quiver in the hard glass. Only a dull clang resonated as if it was made of iron. He raised his fists again, but overtaken by a wave of nausea, leant on the wall, his head resting on his forearms. Pounding wouldn't help anyway when there was no one on the other side to hear him.

'Nothing will help, boy! Better to go back,' shouted a harsh, metallic voice from nowhere.

The young man flinched and turned, searching for the source of the voice. Nobody was in sight.

'I wouldn't waste your time here—better go back home!' cried the voice again, sounding as if it came from a radio buried somewhere in the sand.

The young man jumped up and limped along the glass wall towards the voice, frowning. The man spoke his language in a strange yet comprehensible way. His voice clanged as if he was speaking into a tin. It was clear that it was not from a native speaker, so it must have come from the other side of the glass.

About five metres away, there was a small cement hut right behind the glass wall, with an iron door to the street.

Another few steps and the young man came upon a hefty older man in a white shirt, sitting in the hut behind the glass at a desk, peering into a large computer monitor. His grey eyes looked small behind his thick glasses that drooped over his nose. One hand clasped a mouse whilst the fat fingers of his other hand spread over a keyboard.

The young man took another step forward and put his forehead on the glass, careful not to hurt his wound again. The old man was surrounded by three bare walls and a low ceiling, with the iron door to his left. On the wall behind him, stood a small white air conditioner. The fourth wall of the hut was the glass wall standing between them. A set of blinds was rolled up under the ceiling.

The man behind the glass addressed the young man without diverting his eyes from the monitor. 'I would of course not want to meddle in your business but I'm warning you, whatever you try, you will not succeed. It's impossible to get in.'

The voice reached the young man through pinprick holes in the glass, arranged in perfect order within a circle with a diameter of no more than fifteen centimetres. On the other side of the glass, behind the holes, a bowl-shaped speaker was fixed with a microphone dangling from it. Under the holes, there was a horizontal slot, about thirty centimetres long, but so narrow that only a single sheet of paper could slip through. The young man brushed his fingers over the holes and along the slot, bent his head and held his ear close to the apertures.

'Listen, young man!' said the old man, his metallic voice coming now directly to the young man's ear, which made him recoil. At the same time, he heard the old man's own voice inside the cubicle, muffled, and in another language.

'The only way to be let in is to have a good story,' the old man continued.

The young man lifted his head and stared at the older man. What did he mean?

'Here is the procedure,' the old man added, releasing the mouse, bothering at last to look at the young man. He took off his glasses and said, 'You tell me your story. I type it into this computer and send it on to the authorities. It's up to them to decide whether you pass or not. If they allow you to come in, I open the door for you.'

The young man looked more closely at the glass between them. There was indeed a rectangular outline in the glass about two metres high and less than a metre wide. It was a glass door, held by a thin metal frame, hardly visible. No lock. And the glass was about five centimetres thick. He pushed on it, but the door did not move. How was it possible? How could it be locked without any lock? He hammered on it with all his strength, but in vain.

'Don't get agitated, boy. It's set to lock magnetically and can only be opened electronically. Only when your asylum request is granted, will I get a code with which I can order the computer to open the door for you. But it's impossible to break it open. I'm telling you.'

The young man took a step back and saw his own, faint reflection in the glass. Dishevelled hair and a beard of a few weeks covered his bony chin and cheeks in a disorderly fashion. His tanned face was as dark as his arms, which stung from sunburn.

The old man stared at him from the other side of the glass, as if waiting for some reply.

'And when you're through the door,' the man started again, as there was no response from the young man, 'you're not in yet.' He leant forward and pointed to the space in front of his desk. 'Don't you see that you'll end up inside the turnstile?'

The young man looked. There was indeed an enormous iron turnstile right behind the glass. Why all this? Why don't they just let him in and then ask him questions or whatever they wanted?

'Only me, with a push of this button...' the old man said, moving aside, allowing the young man to see the large red button on the wall behind him. 'You see it, don't you? Only I can open it for you. But before that, I need permission, of course. So come up with your story, I suggest.'

The man paused and scratched his almost bald head. He straightened, then slumped into the chair which rolled back on its wheels, his large stomach dangling in his lap. He squinted at the young man, then continued, 'You look like you want to try it anyway, my advice notwithstanding. Come on, try it then. Tell your story.' He rolled himself forward on the chair back to the desk and bent over the keyboard. 'But I warn you; it's really a waste of time. You'll see... And boy, do something about that!' He nodded at him, pointing to his wound.

The young man pulled a dirty handkerchief out of the pocket of his worn trousers and wiped the blood from his forehead, looked at the handkerchief, then wiped his brow again.

'Your chin too,' the Guard said, nodding.

The young man watched his own reflection in the glass again

and wiped his cheeks and chin, then returned the handkerchief to his pocket. He looked left and right. On either side, the glass wall stretched as far as the eye could see. Did he really understand what the man was talking about? Should he believe him? Did this man behind the glass really mean what he said, or was he laughing at him? Why would he? He might have said all of that to discourage him from trying. Or maybe he was just a confused old man whose task was only to guard the gate. Surely there must be someone else who could allow him through, if this old man had indeed no authority.

'Listen, boy!' the Guard said in the metallic voice. 'I actually don't want to listen to you today. You have no idea how tired I feel.' He then released the mouse and looked at the young man who wearily leant against the glass, his body already drooping with exhaustion.

'You know,' the Guard continued, 'I spent last night up till late, drinking, and now I can barely keep my head up. Let's do it tomorrow. But we can do the first formal intake now and register you as an asylum seeker. If you don't give up and go back, that is.' He turned his gaze back to the screen.

The young man said nothing. He didn't even know what to say.

After a short silence, the Guard peered at him again, then said, 'You must be the last of your sort, boy. It's been over a year now since anyone has come here. They all know about this wall. How come you never heard of it?'

He stopped for a moment then started again, 'Don't you see the glass? You see it, don't you? You really can't go over it. People have tried to penetrate this fortress, but no one has succeeded. They camped here for weeks and months, waiting to be let in, but their stories were rejected. They got angry and tried everything to get in. Look around. I don't know where they got all those huge rocks from or how they extracted them from the endless desert. They tried to break the glass. But... Oh my, oh my!'

The young man turned his head and looked at the scattered litter and the stones. The wind had now dropped. The heat even stronger. He looked back to the man. How was it possible that he spoke his language so well? It was actually the loudspeaker talking to him. But to hear a stranger speak his mother tongue... But what was his mother tongue? And mother? Who was his mother? No answer came to mind. Only a dizzying gap inside his head.

'It was pathetic,' the Guard continued, 'though sometimes it was amusing to watch.' He smiled. 'Then they tried something with really long tree branches. Where the hell they found those, I don't know. I think they had tried to make ladders so that they could maybe jump over the glass wall, you know. That was ridiculous but also sad. You know how high it is? It's a hundred and thirty metres tall. Who can jump over a wall of a hundred and thirty bloody metres high? And some others tried to dig under it, so they could tunnel themselves through to this side. But no way! The glass, let me tell you, is planted five metres into the ground and fixed to a concrete base.'

The Guard turned his eyes to the monitor briefly, then looked back in the direction of the young man, 'It's unbreakable, really. You know, when they finished building it two years ago, they tested it by crashing it with a bulldozer at high speed. That didn't cause even a scratch! They showed it on television, and it was everywhere in the papers and on the internet. How come you knew nothing about it? You cannot get through, boy. No way, really!'

The Guard paused for a few moments, resting his chin in his hand and advised the young man in a calm voice, 'I would go back before you become exhausted, as you already are. How, I don't know! But you have survived the desert coming here, so you can maybe return... Oh, and by the way, even this vast desert, even this is man-made.'

The young man turned and stared at the desert behind him again. He had spent a few long days and nights walking through it. What does he mean, 'man-made'? What was this old, mad man talking about?

'Oh, what a project!' the metallic voice rose again behind the young man, making him turn to the old man again. The Guard's own subdued voice sounded more sarcastic, amused almost. 'You know how long it took them? And... Oh, yes, and the mastermind of all this...? You see that billboard over there?' The Guard nodded towards his right.

The young man took a few steps to the left. There was indeed a huge billboard on the other side of the road, picturing the smiling face of a man: his blue eyes sparkled; his light-blond hair looked dyed. And what would that sentence say written in large letters over the poster? Was the smiling man in the picture probably welcoming visitors to the City?

'I'm really worried about you,' the metallic voice continued through the perforated circle of holes in the glass. 'Soon you'll be hungry and thirsty. I can't help, as you see. How long have you been on your journey, boy?'

The young man limped back and stood in front of the hut but

said nothing. He stared at his own reflection in the glass again. The appearance was strange to him. He could not remember he had ever looked like this. He frowned. It didn't feel right. He put his head in his hands, pressed his fingers to his temples. He could not raise any thoughts. Could not even think of a reason why he was here. But he had to go to the other side of the glass wall. That he was sure of.

'Listen, young man!' the Guard said, lifting his head up. 'You look like the type that never gives up. No problem with that. I like guys like you. But I feel I have to warn you: there is no point in making an effort. And don't try to manipulate me with that sad look of yours. Because I really can't help. What can I do for you, do you think? Nothing. Really nothing. I can't even give you a piece of bread. Not even a sip of water.'

The young man sighed, closed his eyes and put his head onto the glass.

'The only thing I can and must do,' the Guard continued, 'is listen to your story and type everything down and report it to them. To the authorities, you know.' He paused.

The boy opened his eyes and stepped back, staring at the old man.

'But not today,' the man said, leaning forward on his desk. 'No, I'm really not in the mood for that. Sorry! I don't feel so well.' He grabbed the mouse and looked back at the screen.

The young man wanted to shout at him. What did he mean he was not in the mood? He wanted a story; he will get one. But surely, he was not going to leave him to die of hunger and thirst behind this wall? How could he? Hey, you old man! You're going to open this damned door. Did he just shout that, or was it only…? Oh, and did he actually have a story? He should think harder. There must be something he could remember.

'And what would your story be about anyway?' the metallic voice rose, making the young man jump. 'I think I can guess. How did I know where you came from, you think? And you see I speak your mother tongue, right?'

The young man looked at him then at the speaker behind the pinprick holes.

'Ah, I'm joking.' A faint laugh inside the hut. 'No, actually my speech is simultaneously being translated by my computer into your language, and it will translate yours back into my language. When you finally say something, I'll hear you through the speakers. But I knew where you came from the minute I saw you arriving. How do I know that? Oh, that's my job; I can recognise many various folks who seek asylum here. Or used to, I must say. I mean in the good old times when we were allowed to let other people in. I know, son, there is often war in your country. I know all that. You probably had to serve in the army at an early age; maybe even as a child. You probably had to murder other children, their parents and even neighbours and relatives or members of your own clan. And now you've probably deserted the army and you're now being hunted and... How old are you anyway?'

'I don't know,' said the young man, hearing a subdued rasping metallic voice inside the hut. So that must be his words in translation. His own hoarse voice sounded strange to him. He had not spoken for three or four days. But stranger still was the Guard's question and its meaning. Besides, all that the Guard had just summed up, things that were supposed to have happened to him, none of it made sense to the young man. He felt dizzy.

The old man smiled and looked into the young man's eyes. 'I understand if you don't want to say it. But I guess you are the same age as my youngest daughter.' He paused, looked at his own hands and stomach. 'I know! A young daughter at my age! But it happened.' He shrugged, looking pleased with himself. 'Well, maybe you're a couple of years younger. She's twenty-four, just finished university and she is doing a Masters now. She even wants to go for a PhD; to get a doctor's degree and all that, you know? And guess what! It happens to be about your country. No, not exactly, but something like that. You know what I mean! Or maybe not.'

The Guard bent down and took a flask from his leather briefcase which lay on the floor by the desk. He unscrewed the lid and poured tea into a mug. Or was it perhaps coffee or... The young man thought about the words that had just flashed into his mind: 'tea' and 'coffee'. From a 'flask'. He vaguely remembered he had done the same: pouring tea in a cup; a glass cup; a *piyala*. He had drunk tea. But where and when? He thought, but the thoughts turned him giddy. But wait! A smile jumped on his lips. He still knew words. He knew the names of the things.

He looked into the hut again, rolling his eyes round, and thought about the names of all that he saw inside: the computer monitor, the keyboard and mouse, the desk, the chair, the flask, the mug, the bag, the walls, the ceiling, even the air conditioner, and the glass between them.

'Oh, sorry boy,' the Guard said after a pause and a sip of his drink. 'You're getting impatient. I know you must now be thinking how unfair it is. I know it is. But what can I do? Or what can my daughter do? Oh, she will be very interested in you, actually. She knows all about your situation and what's going on in your country and all that. Well, I mean in countries similar to yours, to be more precise. And she was one of the people who, when they constructed this wall, protested loudly against it. Oh, oh, I hope she'll not find out about your being here. She'll make a huge fuss, I'm sure. Now you might think, young man, what if I told her about you? No way! Absolutely not. That would be the end of my job. I must keep my mouth shut. So, what about your name?'

The young man wanted to say his name, but nothing came to his mind. He closed his eyes. He should try, as he must have a name. He has one. Yes, he was sure. So, he should try harder. But... He turned his back and took a few steps, limping, away from the little office. The shadow of the glass wall now stretched over a large area.

The man called him back, 'Listen, son. It's fine if you don't want to give away any information about yourself. But I would really reconsider the matter, if I were you.'

The young man squatted in the sand, staring into the vast desert, beyond the shadow of the wall. He bent down and drew his finger through the sand. What was the first letter of his name? He couldn't think of any. No name, not even a letter from any name. His finger deep in the sand, he heard the old man shouting behind him in the metallic voice, 'Go, sit somewhere out of my sight, boy, and try to think about it more clearly. But if you're stubborn enough and want to try it, come back tomorrow morning to share your story with me. I've just called in sick and written to tell my superiors that I'm taking half a day off.'

The young man stood up and turned to the hut. Behind the glass, the silhouette of the Guard was wearing his coat. Was he ready to leave?

'My bus is coming in a minute. I'd better go,' the old man said, rolling down the blind.

The young man limped back to the glass wall and sat down, staring at the other side. The Guard came out of his office, shut the iron side-door, and walked to a bus stop a few metres away, swinging his large black briefcase in his hand. He was no longer wearing his glasses.

Moments later, a bus arrived, covered with images of gorgeous people and luxury household appliances. Large and small text, in a language the young man could not read, was printed over the pictures in different colours. The passengers gazed out of the bus with blank stares, as though peering into a void. But the strangest thing was that the bus was driving in the opposite direction of that in his country. Shouldn't it drive the other way around or on the other side of the road? It came from the right heading left, while it was driving on this side of the road. The front door on the left side of the bus slid open. The old man got on and swiped a card on a small device beside the driver whose seat was on the right side of the bus, contrary to cars in the young man's own country. The door closed and the bus drove away. No engine sound could be heard. But the young man imagined its rumbling, in the silence that dominated this side of the glass wall.

2

Next morning, the young man woke half-buried in sand, perspiring. The sun, hot and bright, shone right onto his face. Where was he? He spread his arms, mustered his strength and dragged himself out of the sand hill. So here he was, at the foot of this immense glass wall. Oh, yes; and the City. He sat upright and looked through the glass. It lay over there, behind the trees, a wondrous sight. Many buildings glistening in the morning sun. Was it an illusion dreamt up by his fevered mind, or was it indeed real?

He remembered the Guard's admonition. A story was what he needed, wasn't it, to be allowed in there? He looked over to the hut. The blind was drawn down. What time was this Guard expected to start work?

Occasionally, a car drove swiftly, in the wrong direction, along the road behind the glass, or a bus would pass without stopping. A few little boats floated over the water, with triangular sails in various colours. Small groups of people or couples lay on sun-loungers at the side of the lake. Seriously? He was burning from the heat and they sought the sun voluntarily?

He waved to them, shaking both arms. But of course, who would bother to even to look over to his side! He banged on the glass. Would anyone even hear him?

Thirst unsettled him and staring at the water made his mouth feel even more parched. He looked round, but there was nowhere he could sit in the shade. The whole of his body ached. He bent over, rubbed the back of his right thigh and calf, then rolled up his trouser leg and removed a large piece of rag that had turned dark brown from dried blood. He stroked the scab. It had healed enough, so he tossed away the rag and rolled down his trouser leg.

He had sustained the wound during the capsize. He closed his eyes and tried to remember. Who was on the boat with him? And what had happened before the Splash? How could he tell any story if he didn't even remember his own name? He started panting. He would maybe get stuck in this desert forever. Breathe. Breathe. He must remember. Think, think. Of course, he had a name. Of course, something had happened before he fell overboard. Think hard, maybe something would come up. Something had happened. Splash. Something else. Something before that. But he only remembered the moment he fell into the water with a hefty splash...

On the water surface, above him in the dark, the shadow of a large floating boat. Screams and faint sounds and voices of people falling into the water all around him. Sinking into a vast darkness. Bright light behind his eyelids... Then waking up on a shore among large jutting rocks, his injured forehead throbbing with pain, his small rucksack still fastened to his middle. Gathering his strength, he had dragged himself upright and leant against a rock. Looking down, he had noticed blood draining from a deep gash in his leg into the surf. He had searched the bag and found three bottles of water, some biscuits wrapped in plastic-coated paper and bread that had now become a wet lump. He had taken off his coat and shirt, remaining only in a T-shirt. He had torn a strip from the shirt and bandaged his leg. Then swathing his head in the rest of the shirt, he had picked up the rucksack and left the shore.

He held his head in his hands for a while but could not remember more. Maybe he should now worry more about water and food. What was he going to do if the Guard didn't let him in? Beg him until he opened the door. That is what he was going to do.

He pushed himself up from the ground into a standing position and walked to the hut. He peered inside through a slit at the side of the blind. No, the man was not in there. Maybe he wouldn't come today? He said he was sick yesterday. What if he never showed up again?

He sat down, curled up, chin on knees, staring into the desert. Suddenly, a voice started him. Did a woman call him? He looked round but saw no one. It was absolutely quiet. A petrifying silence. The woman called again. It was his mother's voice. He looked round again; his eyes bulged. But the voice echoed inside his own head. Mother called him again. By his name. Yes, his name was something like… He bent and knelt in the sand. It was… Arman.

His name was Arman. He murmured it, a grin across his face. Arman. Yes, his name was Arman. He repeated it, laughing. Then repeated it, again and again, until it sounded strange—as if it were someone else's name. He began to doubt it. The more he repeated it aloud, the more it sounded strange. He stopped;

in case he might lose the name altogether.

Better find something to eat or drink. He went to the rubbish and rummaged through the remnants, hoping to find a bottle of water or some food. He dug under the sand hillocks, looking for more clothes and bags but found only a pair of worn shoes and a torn hat as well as a few dried beans and chickpeas. He bit them but couldn't break them, so tossed them away and abandoned his search.

He returned to the glass wall and lay down with his just found hat over his face to guard off the sun. Sleeping might ease the thirst and hunger. At least, he no longer needed to think of it. Nor about his lost memory. Regaining his own name gave him more control. But over what? What could he control now? Nothing, but maybe his own thoughts. Maybe if he tried harder, he would remember his mother's name, and that of his father and siblings. And of his grandmother too. Yes, he had a family, he was remembering now. Thinking that comforted him. He closed his eyes and curled up.

The hazy image of Grandma smiled at him. How amazing to see her now! Oh, yes! He could tell Grandma's stories. He had to try to remember her tales. That was what he needed most: stories. His fate now depended on stories. His life too, for that matter. At least this is what the old man had said.

He removed the hat from his face and jumped to his feet. Behind the glass wall, on the other side of the road, a man and a woman with three children got out of a car. A family.

The youngest boy of about seven or eight years ran to the glass wall, crossing the road, towards the very spot where on this side Arman stood. A dog jumped out of the car and ran after the boy. When they came closer, the little boy started laughing while pointing at the glass. At him maybe. Did they think he was funny, with his...? He looked at his clothes and ran his fingers through his thin beard. He put his hat on, smiled and waved to them. No response from the boy who unzipped his flies and urinated on the glass. What? How the hell could he be so rude to pee in front of him? Almost at him, were the glass not between them.

The dog stood there with its head raised, wagging its tail, staring at the boy. No sooner had the boy finished and zipped up his flies than the dog ran to the glass, sniffed, then raised its hind leg and peed near the same spot as the child.

The boy ran to the bus stop and sat on the metal bench, swinging his legs. The dog followed him and jumped on the bench, barking, though Arman could hear nothing. He raised his fist at them, then started pounding on the glass.

The child and the dog turned simultaneously, staring at the glass wall, and walked towards it in careful, orchestrated steps. The little boy started pressing on the glass with both hands.

Arman banged again on the very spot that the boy's hands were exploring on the other side of the glass. Did the boy and the dog even see him? Did they hear him?

The boy seemed to have heard Arman's pounding on the glass, so was now banging too, and Arman heard muffled thuds. The boy put his ear to the glass. It seemed clear that he couldn't see Arman. But how was that possible? He could see the family clearly himself, almost as if the glass didn't exist between them.

He took a few steps back from the glass wall and stood there looking at the whole picture. Was all this confusion meant to frighten him away? Or maybe they wanted to test his patience and perseverance.

Arms hanging to his sides, staring at the scene in front of him in disbelief, Arman sat down in the sand, away from the wall.

The boy knocked a few more times on the glass before running back to the car, followed by the dog who was barking madly, without being heard. They all got in the car and drove away, going North, then went along the lake and disappeared behind the trees. Also this car's driver seat was located on the right side of the vehicle. How weird!

Arman remained sitting for a while, pondering what he had just seen. Why would they do such a thing to him? He straightened himself up and sat cross-legged, hands resting in his lap. How would that please them anyway? He scratched his unshaven chin, thinking about the behaviour of the boy and the dog, and of the passengers of the bus who peered into the void as if they were looking at themselves. Didn't that mean...? Wait a second!

He stood up and shuffled back to the glass wall, shaking his head, fists clenched. He leant with his face pressed against the glass and remained standing in that position for a while. What should he make of his revelation? It was now clear: from the other side, the glass must be a mirror. People on that side saw perhaps only the reflection of themselves, of the City and the whole picturesque landscape behind them; their own reality, nothing more.

He hammered on the glass with both fists and kicked it hard. Aaaaaaaargh! He then hit the glass with his head and the wound on his brow started bleeding again. He took out his handkerchief and wiped it, turning his back to the wall. He collapsed to the ground, and remained there in a heap, the shadow of the glass wall looming over him.

Early in the afternoon, when the sun had shifted to the other side of the wall, Arman woke up. The heat clawed at his face and his bare arms. It even pierced through his T-shirt. Or perhaps he had a temperature. He felt the wound on his forehead. It was no longer bleeding, but it was swollen.

He looked over to the hut. The blind was still rolled down. Wouldn't it be better if he went to sit there in the shade to save his energy until the Guard came? Maybe he would pity him, as he surely must see the hunger and thirst on his face. He would beg, then shout at him if that failed. Actually, the old man was resolute in his explanation that he could not help. He was clear about the rules. He was honest. What if he *were* honest? If he in truth could not let him in? A story was all that was needed to be allowed to cross. But what if his memory never came back?

Wasn't it better to just give up the idea of trying to invoke the pity of the old Guard and leave? To walk along the wall to its very end. There must be an end point to this wall, or a passageway somewhere. But which way should he go?

He stared in both directions. Maybe he should go to the left, to the south. After a few steps he turned, looking to the right side. What if he went to the north? Would it matter anyway? Perhaps it might.

He looked again to both sides a few more times. Nothing in sight, except the colossal glass wall stretching into the haze. It seemed lower the closer it was to the horizon. And there was a pool of water over there, at the end, southwards, where the glass melted into the shimmer. But he was sure it was only one of those mirages he had seen the days before, while walking across the desert. He finally took the left and determined not to look back.

After he had walked for about an hour, no change had occurred in the glass, except that every few hundred metres, there were vertical lines that indicated that separate panels of glass had been fitted beside each other. He turned to the bright reflection of the sun shining on the lake that was now behind him on the other side. The road bent following the curve of the lake, undulating over small hills, vanishing into a distant expanse of trees in rows. The City had now disappeared, and right where the lake had ended and the road had bent, a forest filled his sight behind the glass wall.

With each step he took, huge trees came into sight one by one. A multitude of them. After a few moments, there were only trees, leaning against the glass wall. As if the world on the other side was falling and being held up by the glass.

In another half an hour, he was still walking by the forest, perspiring. Was there no end to this? He sat down facing the forest. The shadow on his side was now much deeper, expanding over a wide area into the desert. And it was also much cooler where Arman sat beside the glass wall, peering into the murky wood on the other side. Despite the complete silence on his own side, he imagined how chilling the quietness could be among those tall, thick trees so close to each other, with their dark-brown barks. Some were covered in ivy all the way to their massive branches. The speckled spots on their huge, outstretched roots and the dirt patches between them made the forest even eerier. But if he were to be in there, he could maybe hear birdsong. Maybe in there it was not so quiet and terrifying.

He raised his head: there were no birds among the foliage. He put his hands and his brow to the glass and peered deeper into the forest. He had been in woods before, at times in his life. If he were now in that forest rather than here, in this dry never-ending desert, he might find some fruit or nuts or even a spring of fresh water.

He stood up and resumed his walk, now faster, dragging his feet through the sand, his neck turned to the glass, looking into the forest. He had to get to the end of this wall so he could enter the wood. Surviving in a forest must be so much easier. And he could finally find his way to the City. Maybe this was all a kind of trial. He had to win his right to enter the City.

He came to an abrupt stop, for he was very far from the hut and there seemed to be no end to the wall. It would soon be nightfall with only the vast desert on one side of the wall and the forest on the other. He recalled the awful feeling of being lost in the desert before eventually coming upon the glass wall. What if he were not to find any entrance, any opening in the wall, nor even another hut with a Guard? He would then never again encounter another human being. At the hut, he at least had the chance that the Guard would eventually pity him and let him in.

He hurried back. Run. Come on, run before it gets dark. He shuffled through the sand, panting. He actually didn't need to hurry. Why should he? What waited for him?

He spotted something glistening about a hundred metres

from the glass wall, in the desert. He staggered towards it and picked it up. It was an old, rusted tin with no label left on it. He scratched the rust carefully from the bottom but could not make out the writing or the expiry date. He took it and wandered round for a while—maybe he would find other tins or things to eat. A sudden gust blew away his hat. He ran after it, but it rolled further into the desert. When he at last turned his head, only the top line of the wall was now visible, about to merge completely with the horizon. And the hat was swirling in the sand many metres away. He sighed, then ran back to the wall and resumed his route beside the glass, back towards the hut.

Slanting down, right above the City and the trees, the sun was now a glowing yellow ball that had lost most of its blinding-hot brilliance. The sky was gradually turning pink and orange, bathing the low clouds, the buildings and the tops of the trees in a delicate hue.

Arman turned to the desert, leaning back on the glass wall, shivering in the cold evening breeze. He could still taste a subtle sweetness through the bitter aftertaste of the contents of the tin. He had smashed the tin against one of the large stones and devoured the viscous, sticky, black substance without even knowing what it was. It could have been jam or molasses. But it had certainly gone off. And he had now become even more thirsty.

He drew his knees to his chest, curling into a ball. The breeze brought with it a recognisable smell. The same smell as when he sat in the boat with so many other people from different countries. They also had wanted to come to this side of the world. He rested his chin on his knees and stared in the void, seeing the scene before his eyes in vivid detail.

More than thirty people had squatted or sat in the small boat, among them a few families with children. In the dark, they could see only each other's shadows. All were curled up against one another, feeling sick from the rocking of the boat and the briny tang of the sea. Arman had felt the sway in his guts and in his head. Squeezed between four other bodies, he was barely able to move. The hood of his coat stretched around his face, covering his head up to his eyebrows. His rucksack stuck to his back, with straps tightened around his shoulders and a belt at his waist. A life jacket covered the whole of his chest and stomach.

Just shortly before they had boarded, he had bought the life jacket from a man for twice the market price. But who would fight over the price of a life jacket amidst such life-threatening mayhem, in darkness, among bushes on a scary, rocky shore?

Hiding among the shrubs, more than fifty people crouched down, waiting for the boat to arrive. Arman was among them, sitting beside an old friend from his own village. They held hands, shivering in the dark. Two men ran round from group to group, exhorting them to remain silent. The children especially were difficult to keep quiet. So too the angry young men who were infuriated by swarms of fiendish, invisible mosquitoes, intent on biting them on every bare spot of their bodies.

When the boat arrived and silenced its motor, the people stormed onto it, shouting, swearing and crying as it was not certain everyone would find a place on such a small boat. For some it was not the first boat they had tried to board. Arman did not even know how he succeeded in getting on; it must have been the sheer pull of the crowd, which propelled him forward onto the boat. His friend was left behind.

Hours steering through the cold night, plunging over the waves, the small boat felt as if it were a swing pushed back and forth by a hidden strong power. As though a giant demon were playing with them, throwing the boat from one hand to another. Arman was drenched from the water that poured over them again and again, when the boat slid down a huge wave before being lifted up by another, swamped. He had been sick a few times. Children cried and shrieked. Women prayed and recited religious verses. Men swore. Stinking water washed the vomit from their clothes, ran down the boat, rising up to their ankles.

How long he had been asleep, Arman didn't know when he was jolted awake and heard a huge splash. A piece of metal or something else, he could not see in the dark, hit his forehead. He was thrown over to the side. The back of his head hit the edge of the boat. Another sway and he fell overboard with a backward somersault, plunging down into the cold sea. Bubbles escaped his mouth, as he rose in the dark to the surface.

He stroked the scab on his brow. It had healed well. The taste of the fishy tang of the sea overcame him as he felt the breeze of the desert, bringing back the horror of that night. But now the cold air was even more excruciating. It had darkened. The blinking stars seemed closer than ever. He looked back at the City. The sky had also darkened over there. Far off, hundreds of lights now shone in the buildings and on top of the huge cranes, reflecting in the murky water of the lake.

He rubbed his shoulders and chest and hugged his knees tight. He should maybe try to sleep. But he was remembering.

3

Arman raised his heavy eyelids, with a splitting headache, his stomach in knots. Two hands were shaking his shoulders. The face of a stranger, a much older man, bent over him, saying something in a language he could not understand. He turned his head with difficulty to the hut. The blind was down. The pain made him clench his teeth, roll on his side and curl up, pressing his legs firmly into his stomach.

The stranger said something else and rubbed Arman's back. He helped him to sit upright, then took a small plastic bottle of water out of his deep pocket which he quickly opened and put to Arman's lips. The moisture in his mouth comforted him; worth more than anything else in the world at that moment. He used all his strength, lifted his head and took a large sip, followed by a few more gulps. The man put the bottle away, took a piece of hard bread out of his other pocket which he broke in two, pushing one piece into Arman's hand. Then grabbed Arman's arm, helped him to stand up, and led him to the shade by the glass wall. He said something else accompanied with signs, apparently trying to make clear that he was sorry he had only a little bit of water and bread and now he had to go. He said goodbye and walked off, to the right, going north.

Arman, now much encouraged, waved to him, put the bread

in his mouth, took a bite and started to chew. The sun had already passed to the other side of the glass wall, where in the sky masses of cloud had gathered. It must be past noon and the Guard was still absent. For a second day. Or even longer maybe? How long had he been sleeping? It seemed ages. He looked back to the stranger, who was already a hundred metres away. Should he not follow him? Maybe the man knew somewhere better. But in this state, he wouldn't be able to walk. He waved to the man and mouthed, 'Thanks!'

In the heat of the early afternoon, he woke again, hearing himself talking but could not make out his own words. He was lying, trapped between the glass door of the hut and a small sand hillock, with the familiar intolerable cramps in his stomach and a dry mouth. Fever burnt all over his body.

He crawled towards a place at the glass wall where he could see the other side. Had he been dreaming or did that man indeed feed him? His mouth was still dry, and his lips chapped.

A pleasant breeze blew but could not bring down his body heat. Were his mother now here… No one else could nurse him as Mother had whenever he was ill. Only putting his head in her lap was enough for him to be soothed into a healing sleep, while she massaged his shoulders. Or was it Grandma? Grandma could also heal him just with a mixture of herbs or sometimes with her sedating stories. But it was his mother's soup which would work the real magic. That soup! A broth of vegetables and lamb or chicken. Cauliflowers and lentils. That is what he needed now so desperately. But in this heat? No. Water; he needed water most.

His mother resembled Grandma so much that Arman usually

pictured Mother's face whenever he thought about Grandma in her younger years. Both women competed to bestow their love on him. But Mother was right here with him now. The warmth of her hug. She was smiling to him in the haze of the desert.

Arman smiled back. He was now remembering his family. And their names. Also his siblings. His sister and two brothers, who were all much older than him. They had been devastated when they heard that Arman had decided to leave. His sister had grabbed at his coat, crying, begging him to change his plans and find another way. 'Let's go back to the village,' she had said, sobbing. She had promised to go with him. They could live there with Grandma. But had that even been an option?

Maybe if his father had tried… Oh, but Father's face was nebulous. Present but so far away; out of reach. Also Mother's smile was changing gradually, her lips quivering. She was now crying. Her face was as vivid as it was then, when she had hugged him and begged him not to leave. While the smuggler was shouting, calling Arman to hurry up, his mother had tightened her arms around him, and kissed him over and over again. He remembered the taste of her salty tears in his mouth.

Now, he tasted his own tears. He wiped his cheeks, swallowed down the sorrow that had accumulated in his throat and tried to think of something cheerful. But Mother did not let go. She was crying and yelling. Her voice echoed. Or was it only in his head?

He stared at the moored boats, at the City behind the hills. Was all the effort, the risk, his mother's woe, and his parting from his family, was all of that for nothing? Only for getting stranded in this senseless desert?

He turned to the desert. He should probably collect his

courage and go back. But even if he were not to get lost in the desert and were to find his way back, he would end at the coast again. How would he ever cross the sea to return home? The thought of it, and the heat, made him retch, not helped by the awful cramps which had him writhing on the ground.

He remained curled up until the pain faded. A soft breeze made his sweat feel icy, comforting him. His wet T-shirt stuck to his skin and now lowered his temperature, albeit a few degrees. He wiped the sand from his face and neck and struggled to sit up but to no avail. He collapsed again to the sand.

Around noon the next day, a continuous clatter on the glass wall and the pitter-patter of rain on the sand all around him, jolted Arman awake. The rain pelted down on his face and his body. Drops of water slipped into his mouth. He smiled and turned his head left and right, watching the spattering of the water around him. He spread wide his arms and legs and burst out laughing; his sore lips hurt when he opened his mouth. He rolled himself in the puddles, drenched his face in the water, sipping it, while breathing in the cool air.

He stood up and ran around, arms wide. He put back his head, his face towards the sky, and opened his mouth to the rain to swallow what he could collect, careful not to choke.

Dancing round, he jumped from one puddle to another. The rain poured down and soon there were puddles everywhere. Some of the holes were almost full of water. Through the wall, the City, the lake, the hills and the trees undulated behind the rain that dribbled down the glass.

He ran to the wall and put his face to the glass. It rained there too. The large raindrops made the whole lake ripple. The ducks, geese, gulls and coots fluttered over the water surface, rejoicing at this sudden bounty from the sky.

As soon as the rain stopped, the birds returned to the surface, floating in pairs or small groups. The raindrops disappeared and the glass cleared.

Arman turned. The puddles were vanishing as fast as they had emerged. The sand sucked in the water so fast that almost at once no trace remained, except for the damp sand. Oh, no, no, no. He hadn't drunk enough of the rain. He stamped to all sides, drenched, his feet squelching in his wet shoes. He ran to the litter. There was still murky water inside the bags and among the folds of the abandoned clothes. Quickly, he cupped his hands and drank some. But soon all the water escaped through the holes in the bags and clothes into the sand.

He went to the wall, took off his shoes and leant against the glass. He had cheered up, now shivering from the chill of his wet clothes. But how stupid of him not to have thought of a way to collect rainwater. He turned his shoes upside down and drained them.

The sun had come out again, warming him; his clothes dried up. And even though it had now crossed to the other side of the wall, its heat was once more becoming scorching. He pulled himself in, sticking more to the glass so that his head was in the shadow, waiting for it to grow wider and cover the rest of his body.

That evening, he woke, perspiring from fever once more. The cool breeze made the drops of sweat on his neck and forehead feel like hail pellets.

He turned his head towards the glass; the sun was disappearing behind the buildings and the trees on the hills, bathing the lake in gold. On the other side of the road, a flood-light projector lit the billboard of the Welcoming Smiling Man with shining teeth.

The next morning, Arman arose from under the old clothes and bags and stepped towards the hut. The blind was half drawn, spreading its shadow over the upper half of the old man who sat at his desk, holding his large glasses in his hand, elbow on the desk, staring at him, head askew, as if to check that this was the same person he had seen a few days ago.

'Oh, thank goodness! There you are again,' the Guard's interpreted metallic voice came out through the holes in the glass. 'Oh, boy, you know how worried I was about you? I was sick in bed all the time since I left you.'

Arman reached the hut and stood there, looking at the Guard. He was going to beg him to be let in.

'I struggled with a terrible fever,' the man continued. 'I was sweating, and I think I was hallucinating and dreaming about you, you know? After each fever attack, my wife and daughter told me that I was muttering about a young intruder whom I was afraid hadn't a story good enough to let him in.'

He paused. Arman wanted to talk, but the man continued, 'I'm sorry, boy, but I denied your existence. I had to swear, you know, that there was no one. It's been more than a year since the last refugee appeared here, I said. Because that would otherwise cost me my job. If they had found out about you and told other people, you know. I'm very sorry! What would an old man like me want a job for? Oh, I promise you, I can't do without it. But come out now with your story. I feel fit and am all ears. I'm listening, boy...'

'I have no strength to tell any story,' Arman said, putting his head to the glass. 'I have a fever as well. Let me in, please. I just need something to eat and drink. That's all.'

'Oh, I'm afraid I can't, boy. I told you, didn't I? Even if I want to sacrifice my job for you, I can't open the door. We must first write down and send your story. Everything depends on it, young man.'

'I am tired. Please!'

'Listen, boy. Let's at least begin with the registration and the first interview. That would give you the right to food and drink,' the Guard suggested, putting on his glasses, straightening himself behind his desk.

Hearing this, Arman also straightened up. If only there could be some food and drink. The rest was not important.

'Have you remembered anything of your identity?' the Guard asked, putting his hands ready on the keyboard.

'My name is Arman.'

'Oh, great! We have a name now. Nice name! I like it.' The Guard started typing. 'Arman who?'

'I don't know. That's all. I remember my mother hugged me tight and cried. Her salt tears flowed into my mouth when she kissed me. Then when I broke from her arms and left, she called after me...'

'Okay, let's hold the sentiments for now,' the old man said, gently motioning with his hand, bringing Arman back to the present moment. 'What else do you remember? How old are you?'

'I think I am nineteen. Going on twenty,' Arman said, putting his head to the glass again.

The man typed something else too. Then opened a drawer, took out a small camera and came to the glass between them.

'Would you stand straight and look at me, Arman? I'm going to take a picture of you.'

Arman straightened himself, head upright, and looked directly into the lens.

The man returned so quickly to his desk that Arman wasn't sure if he had even taken the photo.

'And so, what's your story?' said the Guard as soon as he had sat down and put the camera on the desk. 'Tell me in short. Just in a few lines.' His fingers were on the keyboard, waiting.

'The people... They put me on a boat with...'

'Which people? Wait, I don't want you to tell me about how you came here. Not at this stage. They might ask you later on. But now...' He paused, staring at Arman, waiting.

Arman looked back at him, not knowing what the old man wanted; he seemed to be asking him for his story, yet didn't want to hear it!

'We know all of that, you know. The routes and all that. But what's your own story? What have you done in your homeland to be...?'

'I haven't done anything,' Arman said, still lethargic, staring at the man.

'I mean what is the reason you decided to leave your homeland in the first place?'

'I don't know. I can't remember.'

'That is a problem, you see!' The old Guard leant back in his chair, withdrawing his fat hands from the keyboard. He took off his glasses. 'So, you don't have a story,' he said, staring at Arman. 'And in this case, I'd really advise you to go back. There's no way...'

'Would you please stop saying that?' Arman shouted at the man, banging on the glass with both fists.

The Guard clenched one hand tight around the arm of his chair, his glasses in the other hand, staring at him with wide open eyes.

'Where the hell would I go back to? And how? I don't even know where I am. Don't know how I ended up here. I survived a bloody sinking boat. And it took many days to reach here. That's all I know. And you want me to go back to that hell of a sea?'

'Calm down, boy!' the Guard stood up and waved to him with both hands, brandishing his glasses. 'I understand. I know, I know.'

Arman threw himself against the closed glass door and dropped down to the sand, where he stayed prone, his face against the glass. The Guard's shoes came closer. The old man crouched in front of him, on the other side of the glass.

'Listen, boy! We have no other way.' The Guard's own voice was now much quieter and more subdued. But even in the mechanical, clanging sound of the translation, Arman sensed the compassion he needed in order to regain some strength.

'Come on, I want to help,' the Guard said. 'Nobody has affected me as much as you. But I can only help if we have a good story, you know? Come on, we have no time to lose. *You* have no time.'

Arman turned his head. From his position, the old man's bald head looked smaller over his large stomach. The man smiled at him, put his head to the glass and peered into Arman's eyes.

'Listen, son...' he said, sounding soothing even in the metallic voice. 'Your life depends now on this story. Because once the authorities receive it, they will send you some food and drink; so long as you wait on the decision. So come on, get up.'

The Guard stared for a few moments through the glass at the desert, then stood up and resumed his position behind the desk. He put on his glasses and typed some more lines. Arman could hear the chugging of a printer coming from under the desk, then the swishing of paper going through. A drawer was opened and shut. The Guard filed the paper away in a brown cardboard folder, closed it and put it on the desk.

'Alright, boy,' the Guard said, standing up. 'You are now officially an asylum seeker. I messaged through your request, saying you don't remember anything yet. And here is your dossier.' He lifted the folder, looking at Arman. 'Now I leave you to rest and hope you will soon remember some more concrete facts.' He came to the glass door again. 'See you tomorrow, Arman.' He rolled down the blind.

After a few moments, Arman heard the muffled sound of the door opening then shutting. He closed his eyes. The little strength and energy that he had retained was vanishing. He imagined how the bus was now arriving, taking the Guard, then departing. He imagined the sailing boats and the ducks floating on the surface of the lake; the sunbathing couples; the promenade; the green hills and the town behind them.

A metallic shriek above his head, chop-chop-chop, woke Arman. He covered his eyes with both hands, his thumbs in his ears, and squinted through his fingers in the bright sun. The large blades of a descending helicopter filled the air with a pulsating loud swish.

He sat bolt upright and leant back against the glass wall. The huge flying machine swayed from side to side, balancing itself about two metres above the ground, scattering the sand in all directions.

A hatch opened and a man, heavily clothed, wearing a helmet with goggles and a microphone in front of his mouth, dropped a large wooden box, right behind the stones that stuck out of the sand. The man raised a thumb to Arman and shut the hatch.

Arman remained still, his back stuck to the glass. Just as the helicopter ascended again as high as the glass wall, its whizzing sound diminishing, he finally waved.

Another metre above the glass wall, the helicopter veered with a swift turn, its whirring fading gradually in the distance. Silence reigned once again.

With deafened ears and a sense of disbelief—how had all this happened in a few minutes, or had it happened at all?—he stared at the large army-green box, then stood up and ran to it. He knelt in front of the box and opened it. Laughter grew in his chest, bursting against his ribs. All that food, drink and equipment! His grin hurt his lips. But how could he suppress his joy?

He ripped open a pack of orange juice and drank half of it in one gulp. Then searched urgently through the box and found a nylon bag full of apples. He tore the bag and took out an apple, bit into it, then, with the apple between his teeth, fished out a pack of fruity nut bars. He threw half of the unfinished apple into the box and took out a bar, which he bit into. Mmmm! Another bite. Nothing had ever tasted so delicious.

He rummaged through the box again. Water! Four packs of them. One, two, three… He counted six bottles in each pack. Twenty-four large bottles of water!

He tore the plastic around one pack and took out a bottle. He leant back on the box and drank half of the water. He poured the rest over his head and face and threw away the empty bottle. The breeze rolled it away over the sand.

Having quenched his thirst, he searched through the box again and discovered a large pack at the bottom which he took out. What? This couldn't be happening! He stared at the picture on the packaging. A tent? No, no… This couldn't be real. He shouted and dropped the pack which almost hit his foot. Unable to contain his excitement, he started to jump around.

When he had calmed down, he knelt in the sand to open the bundle. But wait! He dragged the bag towards a spot where there was less rubbish, just a few metres from the hut that erected over there behind the glass wall.

He tore open the plastic packaging and pulled out the tent with all its iron rods, spikes and poles, and an instruction booklet with illustrations showing step by step how to assemble the tent. He set about the task immediately, grinning so widely that it hurt his chapped lips.

After about ten minutes, he went back to the box, took out another bottle of water, drank some, then picked up the half apple. He found a baseball cap in the box and put it on his head, then, biting on the apple, walked back to the metal structure he had put together for the tent.

Two hours later, he had managed to raise the back of the tent above the ground. The wind made it hard to secure the poles to the canvas. He hammered the pegs deep into the sand with the mallet he had found in the box. Now protected from the wind, he lay down under the half-pitched tent, putting his hands under his head; the rest of the tent's canvas covered his legs.

He lay there for a while, eyes closed. He had now more vivid images of his family. Father would spend most of his time listening to the radio or reading every single news article in the papers, whenever he had no work. He worked in construction. And had his father not also been in the desert? He had been indeed, when he was sent to the front during one of the wars that had ravaged his country.

Was it not amazing that he now could remember those details? Arman was not even born at the time. That desert and that war had been exactly ten years before he was brought into this world. The regime at that time had invaded a small country in the south, trying to annex it, and had conscripted most men, even those in their mid-forties, and sent them to the southern deserts to defend the occupied territories against international ally forces that had gathered in a neighbouring country, just over the desert border.

Arman's father had also suffered hunger and thirst with his regiment when their IFA military truck had broken down and remained without water and food for three days in the middle of the desert, before they had received help.

A few hours later, Arman awoke with pain in his stomach and looked left and right, confused. Aha, he was under his half-pitched tent. He smiled and crept out. Also the large box was still there, a few metres away.

Pushing his stomach hard with both hands, he stood up and went to the box. After a few steps, he bent and vomited. He took two more steps, then knelt in the sand and was sick again. He put his hands on the ground to steady himself and remained on all fours until he felt better.

The sun was already behind the buildings on the other side of the glass wall; the evening was settling. At last, he made his way to the large wooden box and moved it around to drag it to the tent. But it was too heavy. He took out an armful of its contents which he carried to the tent. Then another armful. What a rich man he now was: two blankets; a pillow; a spongy thin mattress covered in thick rubber; sheets; a small gas stove; a pot; a set of saucepans; two plates; cutlery and utensils. He stared at his belongings and smiled. He must learn to cook.

There were also packs of rice, lentils, chickpeas, tea and sugar; six packs of pitta bread; cans of tomatoes; cheese in easy-to-open tins, and other groceries—he would have to find out later what they were. Oh yay, even tomatoes and salad in a plastic bag and a few large cucumbers wrapped in nylon. Cucumbers! He put one under his nose and inhaled deeply. Mmmmm!

He rummaged through the last contents of the box and laughed; they had even provided him with a camping lamp. In a smaller package, he found a folding knife and put it in his pocket. Then he dragged the empty box to the vicinity of the tent and repacked the scattered items.

He remembered Grandma's pantry in her large house in the village. A small windowless room under the stairs that led down to the stable. Whenever he would go downstairs from the veranda, he would open the door to the pantry before going on through a short corridor to the stable. Arman marvelled at how Grandma had arranged all those items in order in such a small room. So many cartons, wooden boxes and sacks of food of various sizes; barrels; tubs; casks; plastic and tin containers. Grandma had six or seven of those containers for storing rice and flour. She had put them on cement blocks or bricks and had piled the boxes and small tubs and casks upon each other or on shelves on the walls. She used to say, putting her hand on Arman's head, that her pantry was even richer than that of the Royal family at the time her mother was their maid and she herself was only a little girl.

Arman drank some more water, opened a cheese tin and ate a large piece with bread. He actually should take it easy in order not to get sick again. He switched on the light, put it on the box and went back to erecting the tent. After a few minutes, he was sick once more.

Later into the night, Arman sat beside the glass wall, with a cup of strong, sweet tea, watching the lights in the buildings across the wall and their reflection in the dark lake. He turned and looked at the little tent he had now pitched perfectly, with the dim light gleaming inside.

Back home, his family might have started sleeping on the rooftop already, as the spring air must be pleasantly warm now. He would, on summer nights, lie down on his back on the bed, under the dark sky, counting the starts until he fell asleep, hoping for a breeze to cool down the dry, stuffy night. For most people in his country, sleeping on the flat rooftops of their houses was one of the most pleasant, if rather inevitable, activities in the hot nights of the summer months. Arman would position his own iron bed frame with a thin cotton-filled mattress on it in a corner, far from his parents and siblings.

The joy of rooftop night life was a special happening each year in the summer season. Although in recent years, fewer people enjoyed the pleasure of outdoor sleeping, especially those who could afford air conditioners. Arman would sometimes take upstairs a portion of watermelon to eat in bed or while leaning on the ledge of the waist-high parapet that ran around the roof, chatting with one of the neighbours. Or he would, during the midday heat, when no one was to be found on the rooftops, hide behind the parapet for a glimpse of one of his neighbours; a girl a few years older than him, washing her house's courtyard, her dress folded up to her thighs. One day Father caught him and beat him to the point of absolute regret. He would never dare go near that part of the parapet, at any time. At least not without great vigilance, that is.

During still, muggy nights when there was not a puff of wind, mosquitoes would attack. Rooftop sleepers would then resort to mosquito nets, if they could afford one. Mother would sew them by hand, using cheaper chiffon. Inside his enclosed gazebo, Arman would enjoy his solitude, daydreaming, until the whizz of an infiltrating mosquito woke him up.

Here, in the desert, however, there were no mosquitoes. And an abundance of seclusion he had now in the vast, calm wilderness. The tent was his shelter. He smiled and looked at it again.

A metre from the tent, embers still glowed in a hole, left from the fire he had kindled in the evening with all the tree branches and twigs he had collected from the litter around. A small, soot-covered pot of tea was still in the ashes. Another, larger pot and a saucepan lay beside the fire pit. In one of them there remained some rice. He had tried to cook tomato sauce with rice, though it had been a failure—overcooking into a large sticky lump. The tomato sauce was tasty though. But nothing compared with his family dinners, or Grandma's delicious rice and special lamb stew.

4

Arman came out of the tent, the baseball cap on his head and a roll of toilet paper in his hand. He rubbed his dried, chapped lips that still stung, and looked round. The blind was drawn down at the hut and over there, behind the glass wall, the City shone in the early morning sun. Smiling, he sighed. He had just had some cheese and bread with orange juice for breakfast and had drunk enough water, so felt energetic and full of life. A different man. His mind clear, he now remembered almost everything of his life. The memories flowed smoothly. As if at once he perceived everything differently. Things that had happened to him or of which he had heard. With a new sense and significance. He was ready to tell his story.

He walked into the desert and when he was far enough to see only the top of his tent, and the glass wall seemed so much lower, he crouched behind a sand dune and dug a small hole. He pulled down his trousers and underpants and crouched over the hole, the toilet roll in his hand.

This was his first successful attempt to defecat since he had jumped onto the boat. A big relief. He was not sure whether he should better use the tissues or the sand to clean himself. In Grandma's village, he had learnt to clean his bottom with stones whenever they were in the fields or in the mountains and he needed to release his bowels. Washing with water was certainly the best way whenever it was possible, but he would in no way waste any of his drinking water for that. He wouldn't even wash his face anymore; something he always used to do first thing in the morning.

Some fifteen minutes later, he returned, but closer to his tent, he froze: a small animal, resembling a dog, dashed out of his tent with a large piece of bread in its mouth. He ran after it for a few metres, but the animal scampered over the sand and disappeared into the desert. Was that not a wolf? Or maybe a fox. Certainly not a dog.

'I see you've got a buddy, hahahaha,' the old Guard laughed inside his cubicle, the metallic voice imitating even his laugh. 'Never mind, boy. It's good to share! Now you've got a dwelling, you will get some company.'

'What was it? Not a wolf, I hope?' said Arman, walking towards the hut.

'Oh, don't worry! It's a jackal. They're scavenging around for food.'

Arman had seen jackals in Grandma's village. But this one ran away so fast that he couldn't even make out what it was.

'Good morning!' he said, now in front of the glass. 'Thank you for all this!' He pointed to the tent and the wooden box with the hand holding the toilet roll. 'I don't mean for this,' he shook the roll, smiling. 'For the whole thing. Look at my tent!'

'You don't need to thank me, Arman,' the Guard laughed. 'This is how it works. And don't worry, you'll get more food. Every fortnight. But now you have to tell your story. We only have three days for that. That's the rule.'

Arman stood there, in front of the glass door, looking at the man who was searching in the drawers. He had rolled down the blind halfway, so the sun only shone on his desk and the lower half of his small office.

'I love telling stories,' Arman said.

The Guard lifted his head, removed his glasses and stared at him, smiling.

'I was brought up with stories,' Arman continued. 'My grandma and my father, and sometimes my mother, told us stories all the time. They'd also heard those stories from their parents and grandparents.'

'But, listen, young man,' said the Guard with an interrupting gesture of his hand. 'They are interested only in your personal story. In what has happened to you, yourself.'

'These are also my stories. You see, Grandma's stories were all about our family and our folk,' Arman said, then sat in front of the hut, put the toilet roll down and leant back on the glass door, his head right under the small circle of holes in the glass.

'I remember when we were kids, we would sit with my brothers and my sister, listening to Grandma's stories, looking at the burning wood in the fireplace: a furnace, which was a large tin cylinder, placed in the middle of the room. It was fascinating to stare at the smouldering coal in the hearth and the smoke rising, going out through a pipe that pierced into the adobe ceiling. By then, we had moved back to the village. I adored Grandma. She would tell us that—'

'Wait Arman. Wait, boy. They really want to hear your own story. What made you flee and seek refuge here. They want to know—'

'I can only tell you what I remember,' Arman interrupted the Guard. 'I remember Grandma always said if you wanted to respect people, you should listen to their stories. "If you want to become friends with them and know them, you have to know their life stories. To know the world, my little sweetie," as she used to call me, "you should listen to people's stories, so now stop interrupting me" she would say. "Just be patient and listen." So I listened.'

He paused, lifted back his head and checked up on the Guard.

The old man had put back his glasses; his fingers on the keyboard, ready to type. 'Alright, I'm listening,' he said.

Arman lowered his head again, turned the peak of his cap backwards, put his chin on his knees and stared into the distance, deep into the vast ocean of sand. The sun shone directly on his face.

Grandma's stories, he began, were the most intriguing. 'They were about her family and the history of our nation. About the village she had left at an early age and had returned to more than half a century later.' Grandma was born about a hundred years ago in the village, and she would talk about herself just as one of the other characters in her stories, Arman explained.

'Once upon a time...' Grandma always began her story this way, Arman said, hearing the clicks on the keyboard behind him. She would tell about a little girl who was brought up by her grandmother, as her own young mother was a city girl who could not adapt to life in the village, so had returned to the city. Unlike her mother, Little Girl would run down the stairs to the stable under their house, the very first thing she did every morning when she woke up, to be with the sheep and with her dead father's black horse.

The horse would caress Little Girl softly with its large head and Little Girl would pet the horse, stroking its massive neck. She would then spend most of the day with the black horse in the stable during the winter months if it was raining or had snowed. And in the spring and summer, she would mount it and trot into the orchards to pick fruit from its back. She picked the sweet figs, the ripe yellow pears and the pomegranates that ripened at the start of each autumn.

Grandma wouldn't reveal the girl's name. Everyone in the village called her just Little Girl, she would say. And some had named her Daughter of the Horse because of her always being with the horse, growing up without her own father.

But mind you, Grandma would say, Little Girl's father was a warrior who at an early age had become an officer in the army of the legendary King of our People. And more than that: the Warrior's father had been himself a warrior during the Great War.

When our young Warrior was only fifteen, his father had ridden among the thousand horsemen led by the King, who wasn't yet king by then but a religious rebel leader who fought against the Colonialists. These foreign troops had occupied large swathes of land they had won in the Great War from the Ottomans.

The horsemen, our Warrior's father and many other men from the village with them, rode south to help drive out the Colonialists. Only a few men remained in the village, most of them elderly. So, women and children ploughed the ground, sowed the seed, harvested and carried the heavy crops back to the village on their backs and on the backs of their donkeys and mules.

The village, spread over the slopes of a huge rocky mountain, consisted of around one hundred houses at that time, built with stones and mud. Most of the families were related. The valley at the foot of the mountain was filled with trees, grown close together for miles along a rocky stream. Looking down from the village, the groves of pomegranates, pears, walnuts and almonds looked like a forest of fluffy green balls of wool. The stream flowed behind them, following the lie of the hills and the mountains. That year most of the fruit remained on the trees or fell uncollected at their feet. Also half the crops of wheat and barley remained unharvested.

Only a few men would return from that battle, surviving the crushing defeat of the cavalry at the hands of the Colonialists who by then had artillery and aircraft. From the father of our boy, the warrior-to-be, only his rifle came home. When he received it from his uncle, his mother's brother who was one of the few men to return, the boy kissed the rifle, crying, and swore to devote his life to avenging his father and the rest of the slain men of his Folk.

So the uncle would soon start teaching the boy how to hold the rifle, open the bolt, place a cartridge and press it into the magazine, close the bolt again, brace the butt against his shoulder, target and shoot, just as his father had done from the back of his horse during his battles.

The Warrior's uncle, who beside his own wife and children now also took care of his sister and her children, would tell the boy all about the bravery of his fellow horsemen, who had broken into the barracks of the enemy and into the strong forts the Colonialists had built in the southern deserts. And he would tell of the terror of their falling cannon shells, exploding amid the galloping horses, killing several men and horses in one go.

During the Great War, which lasted four years, people of the village had lost most of their cattle. They had either slaughtered them for food, or the animals had died of hunger and diseases. Poverty had spread over the rest of the country and no trade had come in or gone out of the village.

By the end of the war, the Colonialists had occupied the entire country. The rebel leader had taken over the rule of the city and most of the province, in a pact with the Colonialists. He would soon declare himself King.

By that time the little Warrior was nineteen and had become a true warrior. He was already a young man who had learnt from his uncle all the secrets of life that a young soldier needed. But foremost, he was obsessed with war and gallantry. With becoming part of the King's horsemen to avenge his father.

He had learnt to handle a rifle as a real warrior and to ride so skilfully that he could gallop at full tilt over the rocks behind the village, riding to the jagged pass that led to the summit of the mountain range. From these heights, the young Warrior could enjoy the view of the valleys and the orchards. He would then dismount from his black horse, sit on a rock, holding the rifle between his legs, looking at the village below, thinking about his long-cherished ambition: to make his father's dream come true. To defeat the Colonialists and to enjoy the Independence of his People.

'I loved the mountains,' Arman said, as he stood up, turned to the hut and looked at the Guard who stopped typing and lifted his head to stare at Arman inquiringly.

'I even liked the mountains more in Grandma's stories,' Arman added. 'By the time I lived in the village myself not so much green was left. Nor any of the birds and wild animals she talked of.'

He turned again and leant on the glass with his back to the Guard. 'From the other mountains on the other side of the valley, the village looked like hundreds of cubes set beside each other in long curving rows; each row behind the other, one level higher, like an enormous stair for a giant to step over as he headed for the top of the mountain. Grandma said that when she was a child, the village was then much rougher but was surrounded by trees, until, years later, people and rebels cut and burnt most of them down, because no other fuel was available. And again, when years later they discovered crude oil in the vicinity, the whole area became—'

'Let's stay with the time the young man became a real warrior,' the Guard interrupted Arman. 'But actually, it's lunch time. Let's have a break first, shall we?'

Arman looked at the old man who took off his glasses, put them in the pocket of his white shirt, then took out a lunch box and a bottle of orange juice from his bag and put them on the desk. Arman smiled, staring at the large man with a small sandwich between his fat fingers. He then turned and went to the large wooden box, his pantry, beside his tent. He grabbed a few nut bars, an apple and a bottle of water and went back to the glass door.

As yet, the Guard had eaten only half of his sandwich.

'You know, the Warrior was my grandma's father,' Arman said, biting on the apple.

'Wait, Arman, wait,' the Guard said, sipping his orange juice.

'We were supposed to be having lunch first.'

'I thought I could just finish the story while we're eating.'

'But I have to type it, right?'

'Oh, yes, I see,' he turned to the Guard. 'I was just saying that he was—'

'Arman, please! Just wait...' the Guard said, gulping down the juice. He then stood up and hurriedly removed the lunch box and the rest of his sandwich from the desk. No sooner had he sat down again and put on his glasses than Arman started to speak, sitting down, leaning back on the glass.

So at the age of nineteen, Grandma would say, the warrior-to-be left the village for the city to make sure his wishes would come true. And to avenge his father. In those days, people were still so pure and clean in their souls that their prayers were accepted. Their wishes came true. "In those days, my dears," she would say, "people could do magic. Life itself was magic".

One day, the warrior-to-be sat on the rooftop with his mother and uncle facing the mountain on the other side of the stream; the rooftops and terraces of other houses were beneath them. He was talking about his wish and his mother was trying to dissuade him. At once, the three of them turned their heads towards the narrow dirt road that extended out of the orchards into the village. A man, wrapped in bandoliers—shoulder belts with little pockets full of cartridges—a rifle across his back, was galloping into the village, where he went directly to the house of prayer.

From the rooftop, they watched people gather around him. The young warrior-to-be ran down the ladder, jumped from a rock beside their house and sped down the mountain, through the narrow rocky alleys, to join the crowd. He heard the man announce that he had come to collect men for the King's army and anyone who agreed to join, would be given food and accommodation in the city, and a monthly salary. The ruler had announced himself King, against the will of the Colonialists and now urgently needed men to fight for him. The boy enlisted himself.

After half a day's riding, the new Warrior arrived in the city on the back of his exhausted black horse, with seven other recruits from his village and other villages, the Royal recruiter at their head.

The Warrior saw the famine and the war in the faces of the men and women who were strolling in the streets. Children with bare feet, and in shabby clothes, looked hungry and lethargic, lingering in the alleys rather than playing, retreating with their backs to the walls when the horsemen passed.

He saw Asian soldiers who were brought from the Empire, and levies that the Colonialists had formed out of locals and tribesmen disloyal to the King, wearing bandoliers, armed with rifles, guarding the buildings they had occupied in the centre of the city.

The atmosphere felt so very different in the city from that in his village. People in the village could at least grow food for themselves and their animals and were much more energetic and happier than city folk. But soon, he would become accustomed to the ways of the city.

Arriving at the barracks that evening, the Warrior heard all that he needed to understand of the situation. The Colonialists were desperate, for they didn't know what to do with an influential tribe leader and religious man who had declared himself to be

King. They needed him to keep order and so they promised him and his People that they would allow them to establish their own independent state, but in the meantime they were also trying to divide the local tribes and to incite some of them against the King. The Colonialists had sent a hard-liner to the city as their Political Officer, a Major who did everything to undermine the King's authority. The King therefore had decided to revolt, and the young Warrior couldn't wait to take part himself.

The Warrior soon became part of the King's personal guard and met a young maid in the Royal household. They fell in love, and took every opportunity to exchange gazes, smiles or words, and were sometimes able to meet in the kitchen. After only a few months had passed from his arrival in the city, the Warrior married the Royal Maid.

When the battle started, the Warrior had already been promoted as an officer of the King's own Legion. The Colonialists were driven out of the city at an uprising, while the colonialist Major was away. Several of their men were detained by the King's men. The Major had collected a force from the most powerful units of the Imperial troops and installed these men at the borders of another town less than a hundred miles away, ready to be deployed to take back the city. The King decided to advance on them first so taking them by surprise.

The Warrior's horsemen were the first to face the Imperial army. This force, beside cavalry and an infantry that consisted mainly of the heavily armed Asian soldiers, also included artillery and military vehicles and aerial support from planes whose roar above the battlefield had at that time more effect than their bombs. Several of the Warrior's horsemen fell dead and many were captured. The foreign soldiers decapitated some of the dead bodies with their curved machetes.

When the rest of the regiment retreated, they met the King and other horsemen at a mountain pass, where they had taken positions behind large rocks waiting for more warriors who had decided to support the King to arrive from other tribes.

The King's forces were unable to withstand the cannon and aerial bombardments for long, so had retreated after two days fighting. The King ordered the Warrior to ride back to the city to warn the inhabitants and remaining troops with the news of the imminent return of the Colonialists. The King demanded the whole Royal family to abandon the city for safer areas controlled by his own clan.

From the top of a hill, shielded by a tree, the Warrior watched how the wounded King and one of his top officers fought from behind a huge rock with their last bullets until their capture by the Colonialists.

That night, when the Warrior reached the city, half the residents had already left. At dawn, he heard the clatter of the Imperial cavalry trotting through the streets. He put his young wife, the Royal Maid, on the back of his horse and galloped back to his village.

'Oh, I'm sorry, Arman! My bus is coming. Shall we continue tomorrow?' the metallic voice said.

Arman was pulled out of his story, turning to the hut, confused. The Guard had stood up, hurriedly putting on his coat. He turned off the computer, put his glasses in his inside pocket, came to the glass wall and before he rolled down the blind, waved goodbye.

Arman smiled to him, then turned to his desert, hearing the muffled sound of the iron door shut behind him. He curled up, put his chin on his knees and stared back into the distance.

5

As soon as the Guard had arrived the next morning and was ready to type, Arman picked up his grandmother's story: The Warrior returned to live the life of a villager. That was when something happened that would shape Little Girl's destiny, Grandma had said. The Warrior stayed at first with his wife in his mother's house, hiding from the Colonialists who were searching the villages and small towns for anyone who had fought in the King's legion. They had arrested the King, who was for them no longer a king but a rebel leader, and sent him to exile in India. They imposed their own rule on the city and all surrounding towns.

At first, the Warrior would climb up the rocky mountain on his horse to hide in the sanctuary of the woods. He would stay for days and only come down to the village to pick up some food and pay visits to his wife. They were expecting a child and had planned to have several. So after a while, when there was no sign of a search, he was reassured and returned to live in the village. He built a house of his own and started, with his wife, to cultivate land for the family.

One early morning, his wife woke up and searched everywhere but found no trace of him. In the stable, she saw two large eyes shining in the dark. As she approached, she flinched and froze where she stood. She saw the black horse standing there, peering at her with a familiar, but sad look. It was tacked up, the Warrior's rifle dangling from the saddle. Staring at the horse for a few moments, she hugged its large head and cried.

Later in the morning, she understood that the Imperial troops had arrived late at night and encircled the village. Some of the villagers had seen through the small windows of their houses, horsemen and dozens of infantry levies marching silently through the village. But no one had seen them entering any house or arresting anyone. No one knew what had happened that night and there was no trace of the colonial troops, nor any sign of the Warrior. There was only the saddled horse in the stable with the chickens and the sheep.

Months later, when the baby girl was born, the first thing the Warrior's widow did was to walk down the stairs to the stable, with the newborn in her arms, to show her to the horse. The black horse had become the only companion of the former Royal Maid who still felt herself a stranger in her new family.

'And the baby was to become Daughter of the Horse, wasn't she?' the Guard said, interrupting Arman's story.

Arman winced and turned to look into the Guard's little office.

'So that baby was going to be your grandmother, right?'

'Yes,' said Arman, standing up with a grin. 'And she was brought up partly by her own grandmother and partly by the horse, as Grandma herself used to say. That's why the villagers called her...'

'Daughter of the Horse,' said the Guard again. 'Yes, I've got it! But I suggest we leave it there. That's your great-grandfather's story, isn't it? So what has happened to you to make you flee your country, dear Arman?'

'Maybe that was the reason I am here now. You want my story? This is my story.'

'You're not telling *me*. You have to tell *them*,' the Guard said, nodding up to the ceiling. 'I'd love to hear your stories. But it's not for me, Arman. It's for them. Do you want them to let you in? You have to tell them why you're here. So, simple as it is.'

'But it's not so simple. They have to hear all the reasons that forced me to leave my country and to understand why I am… And that's what I remember, man! I am telling you what I know.'

'Okay, let's hear what you know. And I hope you'll soon…'

Arman had already sat down again with his back to the glass door and started telling. Soon the clicking of the keyboard resumed in the office behind him.

Only a year after the disappearance of her husband, Little Girl's mother went back to the city. As a twenty-year-old city girl, she could not get used to life in the village and taking care of their field and the orchard, as well as a house and a horse and a stable, while raising a baby as well. So she had left her baby daughter with her mother-in-law, the Warrior's mother, and went back to her life as a maid; a maid for the Royal family.

The Colonialists had allowed a few members of the Royal family, especially the women, to come back to the city from their hiding places in remote villages or over the border in a neighbouring country. They were thinking about also bringing back the King himself from exile to help put down rebellion that now started to emerge everywhere, in every form and manner. There was now mayhem in the absence of the King. Not only in the city, where people had had enough of the harsh ruling of the

Major, the colonialist Political Officer, but also in the villages and small towns of the province and in other cities. Tribal leaders fought, in the footsteps of the King, intending to push out the Colonialists or at least convince them to deliver their promise to help the people establish their own independent state.

One of those who returned from exile was a cousin of the King. She was a young woman in her late twenties who was already a prominent lady, adored by many. The colonialist Major respected her greatly and had regretted her absence from the city, so had sent a personal invitation to her to come home.

The lady and her sister, the King's wife, came back to their parental home. They now needed a trusted maid, so they enquired as to and learned the whereabouts of the King's former maid. They adored her and had known her for such a long time, as she had started to work for the King's household at age twelve, long before the King had become a ruler.

The colonialist Major admired the Lady for her knowledge of the history and both the politics of her region and of its warfare, as her father had been an Ottoman general. She was educated and well read, and encouraged other women to be so too. As the colonialist Major spoke the local language like a native, the two of them used to have amusing tea-time conversations.

On one occasion, the Royal Maid overheard them talking about the King's return from exile. The Lady had asked the Major why it was so difficult for the Empire to accept the demands of her People. She said that all that the King wanted was for his People to be left alone to themselves. "I'm doing my best, believe me," the Major had said. "And I truly think you deserve that." But there were other forces that refused to accept that, and it was possible that the leaders of the Empire might listen to them rather than to a Major who served in such a small place that even the Colonialists' own monarch at the heart of the Empire did not know that it existed, he had explained.

The Maid had realised that the teas were getting cold on the tray in her hands, standing behind the veranda door. She had hurried into the garden and served the tea with a little pot of milk and a few pastries on a small plate.

'And what about her husband?' the Lady had then asked the Major, nodding to the Maid. 'Any news?'

'I've asked everywhere. I hope I can deliver some good news soon,' the Major replied, smiling at the Royal Maid.

'Let's hope he's still alive,' the Lady said, holding her maid's hand, also smiling at her.

The Major had a history known to the people of the city. Disguised as a local, he once had operated as a spy for the Empire, well before they invaded the area. He had been visiting the region even before the Great War had started. His identity had come to light only by chance once when he was playing backgammon with a tribal leader. He had apparently been forgiven by the tribes, as he was much admired for speaking their language so perfectly, for knowing them so well.

After the King was exiled, and the Major had gained the upper hand in the city, he had tried to restore some stability by providing food and better services. He had also developed an ambitious project, which was soon to be praised by the Lady and many intellectuals of the time, though he continued to be hated and feared by many others.

'The Major established a weekly newspaper in our language,

can you imagine?' Arman said, lifted his head and looked at the Guard who was hunched over the keyboard, typing. Arman knew about that, he explained, from his father who was even more obsessed than himself with the history of their nation.

Father had read a memoir written years later by the King's Treasurer. According to that memoir, the Major's newspaper included news about the city and the province, and of course also about new political developments in the region. All the stories in the paper were from the Major's own perspective, which contradicted that of the intellectuals and most of the tribal leaders and all those who struggled for Independence. They for their part saw it as another way to control the People; this time through their minds.

The newspaper included a lot of advice on how to lead a better life, and on manners. But it also encouraged the nation's own culture and language. Many writers and poets admired the Major for knowing the People's language better and for caring about it more than the native speakers did. It was the Major who had started efforts to clear the language from influences of the other languages of the neighbouring peoples, especially those spoken in the recently collapsed Ottoman Empire.

That Major had in the past been a journalist himself and already had experience of publishing a newspaper. He had brought a large old printing machine from the south of the country and trained the locals to operate it. He had hired local writers and anyone else who was literate and well-enough educated to write in the language of their community for his weekly paper.

'When I was still a child, my father found copies of that

newspaper in a library and used to read them to Grandma,' Arman said, looking into the hut. The Guard was busy typing, prodding the keys on the keyboard so hard that it reminded Arman of the traditional men who typed letters and applications on large, ancient typewriters for illiterate people in front of his city's main Court and other government institutions.

Arman leant on the glass so that whole his body was now in the shadow of the glass wall, while the sun shifted to the other side. He looked at the old man, who relaxed deep into his chair, his large arms dangling along the chair's arms, his stomach drooping over his groin. He seemed to be happy to take a break.

'My father would also read from the King's Treasurer's memoir to Grandma. I'd sit beside her and listen. Sometimes I'd lie down and put my head on her lap and soon fall asleep with the stories in my ears.'

'What about her own mother? Grandma's mother. The Royal Maid, I mean,' the Guard asked, putting his hands back on the keyboard. 'Did she tell her daughter about her own life in the city? I mean she had left her baby and she was—'

'Oh, yes, sure,' said Arman, sitting down again in front of the hut. Upon arrival, he said, one early evening on the back of a mule, the Royal Maid, accompanied by the Royal family's messenger on his horse, had found the city feeling sober and empty, except for the presence of many more colonialist guards. They trotted through the alleys, some lit by oil lamps hanging on wooden poles, but most of them dark with lamps unlit, neglected and left covered in dust. Others were broken or long ago blown away. Despite Major's efforts to feed the locals well, the city looked gloomy, and the mood of the people was even gloomier, as the Royal Maid would soon discover.

Later, she would explain to her daughter, the Little Girl, that her People wanted their own country and king, as did all the other peoples of the region. Some of the colonialist majors who ran the cities and smaller towns, hoped that the dream of the People for Independence would one day come true, while others, probably out of animosity for the locals, were planning to divide the tribes and incite conflict among them. The Colonialists were busy, with other colonial powers, dividing the region into smaller states. But worst of all, Royal Maid would explain, other powerful colonialist officials, especially those serving in other parts of the Empire, began to yield to pressure from the surrounding nations who demanded that her nation should be split up and the people should be assimilated within the other communities inside the borders of those countries.

'From all sides, these foreigners were trying to prevent our nation from succeeding to realise the dream of self-rule. To have our own Independence,' Arman said, standing up, putting his hands to the glass, looking at the Guard. 'Perhaps this was because we were the largest nation in the whole region and we could become very powerful,' he said, dreaming away.

He then turned and leant back on the glass. By now, he explained, the People had lost all faith in the Colonialists and had no idea whether the Empire in its own capital had plans for or against them. Therefore, the rebellion was growing locally day by day.

To help ease the situation, the Colonialists had finally decided to bring the King back from exile and allow him to rule once more, no longer as king but rather as a simple ruler.

'You sound tired, Arman,' the Guard said, interrupting him. 'I can hear from your voice how thirsty you are. So let's end it here for now. My bus is arriving in a minute. Shall we call it a day?'

'Oh, don't worry, I'm now used to thirst and hunger. Let me just tell you—'

'I'm so sorry Arman,' said the Guard, putting his coat on. 'But if I miss my bus, it will cause me lots of trouble. You don't want that for me, do you?' He came to the glass, passing the turnstile. He looked closely at Arman, smiled at him and said, 'See you tomorrow, boy.'

'Goodbye,' said Arman.

The Guard rolled down the blind, and Arman ambled back to his tent.

6

The King ruled, to the dissatisfaction of the Colonialists, said Arman, continuing the story the next day. The success of his rule was in fact beneficial to both sides. At least for some time until the Empire had found out what to do with the whole region. For the Colonialists, this man—who looked not much different from most of other men of his clan, wearing his traditional turban with zigzagged patterns, braided tassels hanging from it over one shoulder, his dagger tucked in his knotted thick cummerbund—could not be more than a ruler of a small part of the country, as he could hardly gather the support of more than a few other clan leaders in his own region.

Unfortunately, said Arman, closing his eyes, putting his chin on his knees, for the Empire, he said, the main country and a strong central government was more important than the wishes and aspirations of the various communities. Arman opened his eyes, stared at the desert and continued: The Empire wanted to force all the Folks, including my People and our King, to integrate into the new state that they were about to establish. They wanted them all to submit to a new king; a handsome man, as Grandma used to say, they had brought from some foreign country in the depth of the deserts south—far south from our own region—and installed him as Head of State for the new nation.

Grandma knew all this by heart. She would meet the King with the dagger in his cummerbund later in her life and would work in his household. But she had learnt about most of the preceding events from her own mother, the Royal Maid, who had overheard the stories first-hand from the King and other officials and Colonialist officers who used to visit the King or the Lady. A maid such as she could overhear and note all that happened in the Royal household, she had explained to her daughter, my Grandma. Even all that happened in government offices and in the barracks, she had said. For how many times had she not overheard the Lady and the Colonialist Major talk about these matters over afternoon tea in the Lady's garden? So she had told her daughter—when she was older and could understand these worldly matters—all that happened in the city and in the rest of the country, even in the Empire.

Far away, in other parts of the Empire, an Imperial Minister of War and a woman who was obsessed with the region and had become a political officer herself, had planned the fate of our country and had decided to force us become part of the new state. That Colonialist woman, Grandma would explain, that fervent traveller who knew the region better than anyone else in the world at the time, had brought the new king, the handsome man, with her and she herself had sat down to draw the map of our new country. Despite their promise to our King—that we would finally have our own autonomous state—these foreigners had invented a country for us and made us a part of it. For now, to keep everyone quiet and going about their own affairs, the Colonialists withdrew their forces and left our city, handing back local government to our own King.

The Royal Maid, who served in both the Lady's house and that of the King himself, had many times overheard the Major trying to convince the Lady and the King that the Empire he served would, of course, eventually grant us the right to establish our own independent state. But the Major now had less power than before, as it was our King who ruled in our city and in the rest of the province, wherever he could enjoy the loyalty of other tribes beside his own.

Our King didn't trust the Colonialists, nor did he believe all the promises they had made, not even those from the better foreign administrators who showed him some appreciation and loyalty. As for the Empire and its Minister of War, their intention was to unite the newly made country under the rule of one national king and a central government. And that new king had to be that young handsome man from abroad. For the explorer woman, who had by now become an administrator in the new country, this was a holy mission that had to be executed perfectly, no matter what happened to anyone or any resisting group in the country. And the War Minister? He was a man whose obsession at the time seemed to be finding the most efficient ways to set in motion all the war machinery available to him to achieve these goals: his Empire's goals. He was a minister of war, after all.

This Minister of War, who years later would become the Prime Minister of the Empire's home country, had once said that it was cheaper for his Empire to bring someone from a foreign country and make him king in our invented country, than to try to make a king from the local people themselves. A local king, he had argued, might not be accepted by all the different tribes and religions who did not even share the same language.

So, the War Minister had agreed to the choice of the Colonialist woman, the instigator of the map; she who had determined to import the Handsome King from a country far south of ours. Rumours had gone that she was in love with that man who was many years younger than herself.

It was that very same Minister of War who finally decided it was also cheaper to bomb our city from the air than to deploy an army to remove our King.

Only a year after they brought back our King from exile in India, the Colonialists bombed our city to alarm the people and cause trouble for the King and his followers. One house was hit, and an entire family was killed. Most of the people immediately left the city. But the revolt became even stronger.

To demonstrate his power to the Colonialists, our King left seven hundred armed men to guard the city and on horseback, at the head of an army of five thousand men, he set off to take over another significant city from the Colonialists.

Again, air bombardment managed to defeat the King's army. Even time-bombs were dropped, which blew up unexpectedly, close to the fighters or even near to civilians in the city, and in some villages where there were rebels. A man from one of the targeted villages had already become a legend at that time for dismantling the bombs with a simple pair of pliers.

A few months later, the Empire's Air Force bombed our city once more. This time, they also hit our King's own house, though he, himself, was not at home. The city went empty. Almost all the inhabitants abandoned their homes and took refuge in the villages. But because the Lady had refused to leave her home, the Royal Maid stayed with her. She was to see an empty city, as it had never been before. A ghost town, she would describe it later to her daughter, Grandma.

One day, the King's driver took Royal Maid out for a ride in the Royal car, as Grandma once recalled an anecdote from her mother. The young Indian man had served a few years earlier as the mechanic for the Colonialist Major and had remained in the city, even after his boss, the Major, had left. The Driver gifted his own car to our King and so he himself became the Royal Driver. People in those days were like that.

The Indian man, who by then spoke our language, opened the door for Royal Maid, treating her for the first time in her life like a lady. After offering her his hand to get into the car and closing the door, he spun the crank at the front of the car to start the engine. The car crackled and rattled. He jumped behind the steering wheel and drove her through the empty city. The Royal Maid enjoyed her ride, without worrying that she would be seen with a stranger in the empty city. Though the Indian man, who spoke our language and was soon to marry a local woman, was no longer a stranger.

The Royal Driver had become famous and was much loved in the city after he had saved the King's son by evacuating him from the bombed Royal house and had driven him to safety outside the city.

A year later, the Colonialists again bombed the city. This time, even the Lady fled. So Royal Maid went back to her late husband's village and was reunited with her daughter, Little Girl, who was already about four years of age.

'And that was your Grandma herself?' the Guard enquired.

Arman flinched. 'Yes!' he said, turning to the hut. 'And when they were reunited, she came to know her mother for the first time. She had been brought up until then by her grandmother, the mother of her father, the Warrior, you remember?'

'Oh, yes! That must have been a major turn in her life,' the Guard said.

'Definitely!' Arman confirmed, standing up to lean on the glass door and look into the hut. 'Grandma often said that although her mother stayed for only a few weeks, those weeks were the most memorable and precious period of her childhood. Even though she was just a small girl, she fondly remembered that time and cherished those moments for the rest of her life.'

'What about the King?' the Guard asked, lifting up his head to stare at Arman.

'Well,' said Arman, 'the Colonialists soon took over the rule of the city once more and again they put aside our King. They helped the Central Government of the Handsome King, you know, to become more influential and stronger; heavily armed, even with planes. But at that time, the Lady had also become more important in the city, and my great-grandmother, the Royal Maid, came to know all the prominent women of the city and many women from other cities and towns of the country. She even met Colonialist women.'

'And now we both deserve a break, don't you think?' the Guard stopped him there.

'Absolutely!' Arman agreed and returned to his tent.

After a short lunch break, the Guard asked Arman why he thought the King had refused so often to agree with the Colonialists instead of making a pact with them, allowing both sides to have what they each wanted. Arman said he didn't understand the politics of that time much, but Grandma and Father, both knowing much more of these matters, had often repeated their belief that no other country in the region would have agreed to their People obtaining Independence, so the Colonialists had only used this issue to further their own goals. They had found oil in the country and as that was essential for fuelling their war machinery and their aeroplanes, they'd had to remain in charge. 'As for our King,' Grandma always said, 'he wanted above all to know that his own People would be respected. The Colonialists looked down on us. And our King could not accept that.'

Even after the Colonialists had taken over the control of the city and most of the province, as well as other towns and cities, the King was involved in several revolts and uprisings, Arman explained to the Guard. Until yet again, the Colonialists bombed the city and other areas of rebellion. They captured the King once more and sent him again into exile. However, this time he was sent to the south of the country. Nine years later, he was to take the opportunity of a revolt in the south against the Colonialists and return to his own village.

Grandma herself had often seen the King when she had moved to the city at the age of twenty-one to serve along with her own mother at the Lady's house. But she always regretted that she was not in the city when the King died in a hospital in the capital, fifteen years after his escape from his second exile. When they brought his body back, most of the citizens of the city lined the streets or attended the Royal burial. By that time, Grandma was in her mid-thirties and had returned to her own village with her husband and now-elderly mother.

The clicking on the keyboard stopped. Arman turned and saw the Guard stand up, putting both his hands on his desk. The metallic interpretation of his voice said, 'I think this is a good point to stop at. Although you still haven't told me your personal tale.'

Arman said nothing. His thoughts were still with Grandma and her stories. He noticed that the sky had turned darker, and it was raining. He stood up and turned to the Guard who was behind his desk staring at Arman.

'I have another suggestion,' the Guard said. 'I'm going to leave you to think and to remember your own story. But we have to submit this application today. I only need one concluding paragraph.' He sat and put his hands back on the keyboard. 'Are you claiming that what the Colonialists did to your country was the reason you left?'

'I don't know,' Arman said, putting his hands on the wet glass. 'Don't you think it was bad what they—'

'Listen, Arman. It's not about what *I* think. We can't use my words. *You* should tell me about it. You should give me a statement. Now, try it!' The Guard was now blurred from Arman's view behind the raindrops that dribbled down the glass.

'I remember we were in the village... On wet days like this we would all gather at Grandma's house...' Arman muttered, his voice almost silenced by the pouring rain. 'I would sometimes spend time in the stable with the... Grandma had no horse anymore at the time. But she had lots of sheep and cows and... And whenever it rained—'

'Let's leave it there, Arman. You must be drenched,' said the Guard and stood up again, came to the door and wiped the condensation off the glass. Arman saw the old man's huge silhouette behind the dribbling drops of rain.

'Go back to your tent, Arman. I'm going to submit your claim and call it a day. See you on Monday.'

'And what day is it today?'

'It's Friday, boy.'

'Are you going to have two days off?'

'Oh yeah. And now we've done this, I think I can finally have a peaceful weekend.'

Drenched in rain from head to foot, Arman stood in the middle of his tent, his head bent forward, right under the tent's low ceiling. He tossed away his wet cap and took off all his clothes and his shoes. His scrawny body shivered in the cold. He ran his fingers over his ribs that now protruded as never before. His sunburnt arms had become much darker compared to the rest of his body.

He ran out again and stood in the rain for about ten minutes, rubbing his hair firmly with his fingertips. He then scraped his body with the sand and washed it off.

Now that he'd had a proper shower and cooled down, he went back inside, grabbed the towel and dried himself quickly. He wished that they would send him some new clothes if they were ever going to drop him another box. Even if they wouldn't be to his taste and nothing like his own wardrobe in his room at home, he would appreciate them. He had selected his clothes so eagerly. When he went shopping, he would spend hours looking for just the right jeans or the one T-shirt that would at once catch his eye. He used to wander through the bazaars, searching in almost every shop until, among hundreds of shirts, the right one would shout at him. He smiled and looked at his worn-out T-shirt. Its picture and text had faded so much that he could no longer remember what it had shown.

He spread his wet clothes over the floor and sat on the mattress, naked, waiting for the weather to dry up again. But actually, it would be better if it wouldn't get dry too soon. No, let the rain go on and on, long enough for the... Oh, but what about the food box? His pantry. He ran out to check. Luckily, the top of the box was one solid piece of wood that covered the rest perfectly: waterproof. So, he ran back into the tent, dried his hair and body again, lay down and covered himself with the blanket, enjoying the drum of the rain on his tent.

7

The two days Arman had to wait until the Guard came back on Monday, felt the longest that he had endured since he had arrived at the wall. He finally had caught up with the days of the week. But it was more unsettling now he knew he had to wait for two whole days. For most people in his country, the weekend took only one day, Friday, and the new week began on Saturday.

Yesterday's rain had cooled down the desert. The night was freezing, but the morning was fresh and the sun warming and comforting. Yet soon, before midday, it would once again scorch his skin. On the other side of the glass wall, in contrast, it was still cloudy and grey, and occasionally rainy.

Would they let him know on Monday if they were going to allow him to enter the City or not? He should have asked the Guard how long it would take to decide on his request. Just wondering about it made the time pass even more slowly. So better not to think about it.

Not thinking about Monday and the decision on his request for asylum did nothing to make time pass more quickly, however. He was now thinking more about his family. He had never missed them so much. Not even when he was in prison nor when he was among the rebels in the remote mountains. Then, there had at least been other people around. And lots to do. But in this empty desert? He sat inside his tent, with nothing to do but eat and drink. And ponder.

Now and then, he would go and sit by the glass wall, staring at the City in the distance, remembering his own city, his own home and his room. And friends. Though he didn't have many. Most of the time, he was engrossed in fending for his family, along with his father and brothers, spending his precious teenage years among adult workers. But his rebel comrades were his friends, weren't they? At least, he considered them friends; though most of them were of a different calibre. Or was it all a mistake? Maybe he shouldn't have joined them in the first place. He thought about his girlfriend. It was a short relationship, but the richest experience he had so far in his young life. And most poignant. That someone could disappear out of his life just like that. So unforeseen and unanticipated. Though he knew it was not a courtship that would last forever, the way he lost her... That was what hurt the most. Would he ever meet her again and hear any explanation from her side? Or was it the case that he, who had disappeared out of her life suddenly and without warning, was to blame? But she must have understood that it was not with any intention. It was maybe just fate. One unfortunate moment that determined the rest of their lives. Eventually, he had come to accept it. But heartbreak is heartbreak. No matter whose fault it is.

Once he heard a howl and ran out of his tent. He saw the jackal far off, on the top of a sand dune, its forelegs spread wide apart, looking at him, as if waiting to be chased. Or was it challenging him?

As soon as Arman raised his hand, the jackal ran away to

stop much farther off. Arman retreated to the entrance of his tent and the jackal went back to its old place, still peering at him.

Arman crept a few steps towards the menacing animal that was now baring its teeth, but before he got closer, the jackal ran away again to its same far-off spot.

Arman went inside, brought out a piece of bread and tossed it to the persistent beast. It landed somewhere between them both. Arman took a few steps back and the jackal dared to sprint to the bread, which he seized and ran quickly away with, to disappear once more in the desert.

Should he be worried? He had heard stories of jackals attacking people. Or jackals that had excavated bodies. In Grandma's village, they would sometimes appear late at night, unnoticed, to steal whatever they could find, or snatch chickens and attack other livestock. He had only once seen one from the rooftop at midnight, sniffing in the garbage.

A few hours later, the jackal appeared again and howled. This time, Arman also threw him a piece of apple and a small cube of cheese. The rest of the time, he waited for the animal to return, running out of the tent whenever he heard a noise or imagined having heard something.

In those two days, Arman noticed more animals in the desert, some of them in the colour of the sand. Until now, his own condition in the desert had prevented him from paying attention to anything other than food and drink. The thought of looking for an animal or insect to eat had not entered his mind for even a second. But the desert provided food for any species that dared to prey on another.

Only once did he see a small bird, resembling a sparrow, swoop down on the sand and pick up a sand-coloured beetle and fly away as fast as it had arrived.

On another occasion, he noticed a little yellowish mouse sniffing round his pantry box, rearing against the box on its hind legs and tail. It then crept into the tent and found a few crumbs. In Grandma's house in the village, dozens of mice nested in the mud roof that was constructed with large wood battens and joists. The mice were heard all the time scuttling over the beams and the plastic sheets that covered the ceiling. Sometimes a small baby mouse would fall through a hole in the sheet into the room, causing a commotion and screams.

When the mouse sensed that Arman was watching him, crouching at the mouth of the tent, it scampered quickly round all sides of the tent but could not find a hole in the canvas through which to escape. Arman didn't want to torment the frightened little creature anymore, so he sat back, giving it room to escape. The mouse took the opportunity and legged it so nimbly over the sand that it wasn't clear whether its feet even touched the ground.

On Sunday afternoon, when the shadow of the glass wall had covered a larger area, Arman went to clear the litter that now seemed too close to his tent. Now that he had told his story and had abundant food and drink, he could pay some attention to his environment. Father often used to repeat a saying that goats make themselves comfortable even for one night. They flatten and clear the place to lie in, clean beasts that they are, he would explain. And it was true. Arman had noticed that unlike sheep who seemed never to care about their wool being matted with dung, goats always cleaned themselves and their beds. So better be a goat and clear the litter. Even if it was just for one day, or maybe a few days, touch wood, before he would achieve asylum.

He took an armful of torn clothes and bags some two hundred metres away from his tent. And that was good for now. He would later dig a hole and bury them. But when he was back, what a surprise! A few green shoots stuck out of the sand behind one of the stones. He knelt down and looked at them. They must be from the few beans and chickpeas he had thrown away the other day. Rain does miracles. The seeds had benefitted from two showers and now look at them! His grin filled his face. Soon he would have fresh chickpeas. And beans.

He ran to his tent, brought a bottle and watered the young plants. He should be thrifty with the water though. He took a sip and screwed back the top on the bottle. He sat down, cross-legged, put the bottle on his lap and stared at the shoots. If these were to grow, he could grow more. He could ask for some seeds to be delivered to him with the next relief box. He will ask the Guard if he was allowed to order anything. That way, even if they wouldn't let him cross the wall, he could take care of himself. At the end of the day, he was a farmer's son. But better be hopeful. He might not need to start farming in the desert.

He ignored the litter. Why bother? The sand would cover the rubbish anyway. And the wind would uncover it again. He went and sat at the wall. It was a sombre, grey day in the world behind the glass.

On the other side of the road, a bus passed, heading north, without stopping at the bus stop at which the Guard would get off. Just as the bus turned at the bend with the lake, a group of people appeared. A dozen men and women in their mid-thirties or forties, coming this way. They were hurrying as though on a mission, wearing clothes Arman had only seen in movies. Loosely hanging T-shirts; baggy trousers; huge trainers and military boots.

Arman stood up and put both hands on the glass wall. What was going on on that side?

The rushing women and men were coming closer; some with large rucksacks on their shoulders. Two of the men carried baseball bats; others held large wood sticks or iron rods; a woman swayed with a pair of nunchucks, like those used by karate fighters. When they reached the spot just across the hut, they suddenly swarmed to this side, crossing the road, running and shouting, though unheard. Most of them had their neck or bare arms fully tattooed; some with rings lined up on their eyebrows, ears and lips.

At the hut, those with a rucksack took out spray paint bottles and started hurriedly writing in large letters in their own language on the iron door and the walls of the hut. Some wrote a few lines on the glass wall as well.

Arman started thrashing around, running from one side to the other, stumbling in the sand. He waived to the angry vandals. 'Hey, maybe you should smash the glass with your bats. How could your writing even help me?'

He banged on the glass, shouting at a woman with a large metal rod, 'Hey, maybe you should bash the glass with that. The bloody mirror on your side. Please!'

Suddenly one of the men began hammering on the iron door to the hut with his bat, lifting it steady with both hands. Arman could faintly hear the thuds. But not even a dent occurred in the harsh metal of the door. Then another hefty bald man—wearing tight-laced boots, and large silver rings in one of his earlobes—jumped in the air and while landing on his left foot, he kicked the door heavily with his other.

'Yes!' shouted Arman. 'Hit it! Break it! Come and get me out of here, please! Hit it! Break the damn door!'

The man jumped and kicked again, and again. But nothing happened. Did they hear him?

'Hey, guys, do you hear me? I'm here, please! Come and get me!'

Just as a police car emerged from where they had come and halted, with its flashing lights, behind them, the woman with the rod started hitting the glass. Arman heard its reverberation and felt a subdued trembling in the glass. Then when four officers jumped out of the car, and two of them with truncheons swooped on her, she threw the rod at the mirror and ran away, following her companions who now had run into the road, metres away, brandishing their bats and rods at the two other police officers who were waiving batons at them. The woman with the nunchucks came forward, holding one of the sticks in her hand, swaying the other with the chain in the air, around her own head and shoulders.

Arman, holding his breath, put his hands and forehead onto the glass and silently watched the tension that was unfolding in front of him.

As another police vehicle arrived with its flashing lights, the group made a run for it. The police officers burst out laughing, while swinging their batons at them. The two officers who earlier attempted to apprehend the woman with the iron rod, now stood in front of Arman, behind the glass. They were also laughing when they turned to the wall, peering into Arman's eyes. They were, of course, watching themselves in the mirror.

'Hey, do you see me?' Arman shouted, banging on the glass. 'Hey, please, do you even care what's going to happen to me behind this damn wall? Do you even know I am here?'

He sat down and leant his head against the wall, watching the officers getting in their car, lurching after the other vehicle that was driving slowly behind the running group. In a split second, the road was empty again.

A while later, Arman woke up beside the glass wall. On the other side, a fire engine-like vehicle was splashing foam and water at the wall, while two men were scrubbing the mirror with large wipers on long wooden sticks. Another two men and a woman were scouring the iron door and the hut's walls with large scrubbing pads.

On Monday morning, the Guard again appeared for work, rolled up the blind, took his glasses out of his pocket and put them on. He took off his coat, hung it on the back of the chair and turned on the computer—all without looking at Arman who was already standing by the glass door to the hut.

The old man didn't appear cheerful, at least not so talkative as he had been before. Would it have anything to do with what happened yesterday? The man didn't seem to have even noticed anything when he got off the bus earlier and crossed the road to his office.

'Good morning, sir,' Arman said, smiling.

'Hello,' the old man replied without raising his head.

'Do you think they might answer my request today?'

'Would you please go to your tent or somewhere else?' the Guard said, still not looking at him. 'Just leave me for a bit, would you? Mornings are not the right time for me, you know. Especially Monday mornings, man.'

From the sudden heat in his head, Arman was sure he had blushed. He looked round, shrugged, reversed the baseball cap on his head, walked away and went to the place where he usually sat by the glass wall to stare at the lake and the City.

A group of men and women were walking north on the other side of the road. They looked different from other people he had so far seen there behind the glass. They looked more like him; probably they were also refugees who had been let in, maybe years ago? Some of them had rucksacks on their back, some had equipment in their hands. They were probably builders. Or gardeners. Or they were going to work in the fields, perhaps.

Arman had also worked in the fields as a child, alongside his father and the rest of the family, when they lived in his grandmother's village. Though Arman was born in the capital, when his family had moved there seeking a better life, they had left just three years later to return to live in the village. Arman was to grow up in that village until he was nine years old. He had then preferred animals to plants, but he knew enough of farming to be able, one day, to work in the fields on the other side of the glass wall. He had also learnt a great deal from the rebels. Although with them he was more a construction worker. A builder. As his father had been. That was actually their profession. They were good builders. So, if he were to be let into the City, Arman could work on construction. There must be lots of work over there. Look at all those cranes all around the buildings, Father would have said if he had been here. There you go Arman. There is your place. So much work laid ready for you!

'Hey, Arman, would you come here, boy?' the metallic voice startled him, as if it came from the past; from his father.

'Arman, come here a second!' It was the Guard calling him.

Arman hurried back to the hut and saw the old man standing there at his desk, behind the glass, with a paper in his hands, his face still morose, frowning.

'Listen, Arman,' he said, looking down at the paper. 'The authorities have taken a decision on your claim. They just sent it. I'm going to read it to you. I have to do so, as per law,' he stated in an official tone—even the metallic interpretation of his voice revealed that. Arman heard the Guard's own voice inside sounding hoarse and bereft.

The old man started reading:

Dear Arman,
We have received your asylum claim and examined it. Although we acknowledge that the 'Colonialists' to whom you are referring in your claim were predecessors of the present generations in our country, we cannot compensate you for any losses that might have been inflicted on your predecessors as a result of any act that might have been conducted indirectly, or even directly, by our men and women in your country at the time. It was a different era, about a hundred years ago, therefore, our government cannot be held responsible. And the fact that you personally were not involved in any of the events described in

your claim, means that you are not entitled to refugee status, without which you will not be allowed to enter our country. Thus, the gate cannot be opened to you. You are advised to go back to your country of origin. However, our law grants you the right to appeal against this decision within one week. You are allowed to submit a new asylum claim on new grounds. During the period of your appeal and your new claim, you will retain the right to humanitarian aid to be delivered to your current location at regular fortnightly intervals.

Arman stood there frozen. Speechless.

The Guard stepped forward and passed the paper through the slot, waiting for Arman to take it.

'Listen, young man. I'm really sorry about this. But don't worry. You can submit a new claim. We will. We are going to work on it.'

Arman stared at the paper in the slot. What should he do with it? He could not even read it. His breath was slowing down, his eyes closed, shoulders drooped. What now? What should he do, or say, or think for that matter?

'Would you take it, please, Arman?' the Guard said, nodding to the paper.

Arman grabbed the paper sheet, pulled it from the slit, without looking at the Guard, and turned from the hut.

8

Arman crumpled the rejection paper, tossed it away and staggered into the desert, stomping in the sand, his head in his hands as he went. The Guard shouted after him, trying to comfort him; his voice and the metallic translation of his voice faded in the back.

A few hundred metres away, he knelt in the hot sand and stayed there for more than half an hour in the sun, giving himself up to the memories that came back first slowly and in order, before they flowed into his head. But all the events, all the thoughts led again to this place. This very glass wall, behind which the Colonialists in Grandma's stories really lived in flesh and blood. Or rather their descendants. So he had arrived at their very door.

He stared into the void, in the vast sea of sand ahead of him, shaking his head. Did he now even want to enter their world? He was not welcome. Not even pitied. Or maybe he should. Maybe he could one day discover the secrets concerning the disappearance of Grandma's father, his own great-grandfather, behind this glass wall. More reasons for trying even harder now. So, anger would not help him. Perseverance was needed. But what if none of his stories were good enough to earn him entrance to the City? And should he be telling them about his family? About his own folk? Was he not betraying them?

It didn't feel right. But his life now depended on it. And if those people behind the glass wanted him to share his life, they really should listen to the whole story. What did they want for God's sake? His personal stories? Well, that's exactly what he was not going to tell them about. One thing he was not going to do was vilify his own nation. He had fled great injustice, that was true. But what was the reason for keeping him behind this wall until he told them what they demanded?

He walked back to his tent, failing to look into the Guard's office. Noon was approaching and the sun had become unbearable. Perhaps having lunch might cheer him up and keep him from worrying. He took a handful of pitta bread from a pack in the box with a tin of cheese and an apple. He had only four apples left. He also grabbed a bottle of water. Then quickly counted: there were still fourteen of them.

Inside the tent, he ate a bite of cheese and bread, then lay down, trying to stop the flow of thoughts. But how could he? How could he stop these thoughts when all was he felt was…? He sat upright and banged his head with both fists. Unfair! Really unfair! How can they just… Aaaaaaaaaargh! he shouted; his fist raised against the wall. Actually, no way could he rest in this state inside his tent. He jumped up, put on his baseball cap and rushed out.

He walked along the glass wall northwards to put some distance between himself and his tent and the hut, and particularly the scene on the other side of the glass wall. But most of all he had to calm the storm of thoughts in his own head. He remembered now so much of his life, so sharply and in so much detail. Never had he felt so conscious of the past.

He was walking while glimpses of his life and the stories of his family mingled with worrying thoughts about his asylum request, so that everything eddied in his head. Filled with dread of the unknown that was to come, doubts and suspicions pierced his thoughts. How did this all develop this way? The way the Guard had hastily wrapped up his claim and sent it. What should he think of the decision on his application? Maybe they were right. Why should they care about his family's past? Or the history of his People. He was not here because of what had happened a hundred years ago, was he? Maybe he had better tell them all about why and how he left his own country. But wouldn't it have been unfair to the Warrior, his great-grandfather, and to his grandmother, to ignore their stories? To let them be forgotten. Unfairness that had struck his family through generations. It was now happening to him at such a young age as it did to his great-grandfather. When he was telling the story of the Warrior, it felt very much as if he were talking of himself.

He had walked away from the hut for about an hour. The landscape had now changed on the other side of the glass wall. The City and the lake were no longer in sight. Only hills, and meadows with cows in them, cornfields and orchards, or small shrubs. Far away, in the middle of the fields, farmers worked the earth.

He sat for a while. He needed to take a rest and concentrate on his memories. And to try this time to enjoy them. Staring at the hills and the cornfields at their feet brought him closer to his family. He had watched them working the fields, when, as a small child, he would try to carry a large fork to help. His father would run to him to help lift the fork and stand behind him, holding the wooden fork handle, thrusting it, together, into the furrows. And when the tomatoes ripened and cucumbers grew, he would help to pick the harvest.

Grandma and the rest of the villagers had returned home and rebuilt the village a few years after it was blown up and destroyed by the former regime. All the orchards had burnt to the ground. The water springs dried up. It would take another few years before the returning families restored the village to the glorious beauty of its past. Though it would never feel the same, Grandma always said. But for Arman, who was growing up there as a child, there was nothing else like it.

The village in Grandma's stories was only a fairy-tale place that Arman saw in children's books and magazines. Whenever Grandma talked about it, Arman would imagine a collage of huge, fabulous mountains drawn in watercolours, pricked with various trees and flowers, and all kinds of animals glued to it. Deer; parrots; elephants; tigers; lions. All the animals and birds Arman liked. And, of course, the Warrior's black horse.

The real village, however, was the one where Grandma's house provided the safest dwelling, the warmest hugs and the hottest fireplace in the winters. Though none of those animals and birds he used to imagine were there. The old village was God's own chosen place on earth, Grandma used to say. Although in the winter snow would cover everything and life would become harsher, the warmth in the houses kept everyone cosy and content. And the animals had enough fodder to graze happily through the cold months. In the spring, the village, the orchards, the mountains, and the whole area would go through a rebirth. Magical and mysterious.

Arman looked round and the vast desert again reminded him of where he was. He was sweltering under the scorching sun, and thirst had started to disturb him. But the old memories did not fade. Grandma's face was still so vivid in the shimmer above the sand.

The reality of the desert and the hard glass, and of the rejection he had just received on his asylum request and the betrayal he now felt from the Guard, all roused his rage again. He jumped to his feet and started to run round in the desert, shouting, 'Grandma, these are the very people who took your father. The very people who tormented our King and ruined our dream of having our own state. Who bombarded our city and burnt our fields. The very people who destroyed your life even before you were born. And they decided my fate and made our history for us. Should I be ashamed, Grandma, now I'm begging them to allow me into their country? Should I Grandma? And yet they don't even let me in. Aaaaaaaaaargh!'

He kicked the wall and banged on the glass until his hands both ached. Had the Guard been honest with him? Was he telling the truth about the wall? Was this man not actually also a part of the system? So Arman had been fooled, fobbed off. Maybe all that the Guard had told him of the wall and the desert was just a lie. He was trying to discourage him from looking for a way out. That was the man's job, wasn't it? To deter anyone from coming to the City. Of course, he would not let him in. He is not allowed to. What a disappointment, old man! Oh, what a sordid business!

He started to dig madly in the sand at the foot of the glass wall. He dug and dug until the earth became too hard for his fingers to go any deeper. He looked round but saw nothing to use as a tool. He took out his folding knife and tried that, but it didn't help very much. It would take months to dig a hole five metres deep and a tunnel wide enough for him to pass through with this little knife. If not a year. And then to have to dig himself out on the other side as well. But what about the concrete base? And that is if the Guard was telling the truth. Must be true. Otherwise, what could possibly support this monstrous glass?

He was now thirsty. Why didn't he take some water with him? Actually, he should have just taken a bag full of water and food and walked off. There must be an end to this wall. To this farce of a wall. 'Hey, you are all such brutes, so heartless... How could you think of this bloody glass?' Arman yelled. But would shouting and swearing be of any help? It might, actually. 'Oh, and you, old man. You're such a phoney. Such a dishonest, brutal man.' The Guard must have been laughing at him. 'Liar...!' Arman shouted again. 'Aaaaaaaaaargh!'

He stood there for a few moments, his arms hanging at his sides, his head on the glass. The thirst was unsettling. He then walked back to his tent, dizzy and dazed from the sun. His thoughts and the stream of memory had become anything but calm.

As he approached the tent, he stopped and took a deep breath, shaking his head. The jackal ran out of the tent with its muzzle full of bread. He ran after it, shouting, 'Hey, you bloody beast, give it back. Why do you rob me, even though I feed you?'

The jackal disappeared in a blink. A few bites of the pitta had fallen from its mouth. Arman collected them, listless and languid. He staggered to the box, put the bread inside and took out a bottle of water, of which he gulped down half. Then took off his cap and poured some over his head.

It was approaching the end of the afternoon, the sun was now in the sky on the other side, above the distant City, and shone on the lake. The Guard had already gone and rolled down the blind. With the bottle in his hand, Arman went to the little plants and watered them. He then walked back, went into his tent, took off his shoes, lay down, knees to his chin, and started to cry.

The Guard came in. His huge body filled the tent. He immediately put a black sack on Arman's head and pulled it down. Arman could no longer see. He started panting, gasping for air. Thrashing around, he tried to shout but could not. The Guard's hoarse, loud voice echoed, shouting, 'Don't panic Arman! Don't panic boy! I'm just stifling those voices in your head. Don't panic, son! Don't panic! Breathe! Breathe…!'

As he flinched and woke up, panting and shivering from his dream, Arman opened his eyes and saw in a blink the jackal run out of the tent. He quickly got to his knees. His right arm was numb, so he crawled to the opening of the tent on his knees and his left hand, and shouted at the jackal that was running away, 'Get the hell away from me! You've never had enough, you little bastard!'

He remained there for a moment; half his body crept out of the tent. It was getting darker now. Against a red glow of the sunset that was reflected on the trees and the hills, the buildings were dark shapes with a golden aura outlining their contours. Remembering his dream, he smiled. Actually, the Guard was maybe not even allowed to come over to his side.

A cold breeze made him shiver. He shook his arm until the numbness was gone. He then grabbed a blanket, wrapped it around his shoulders and went, bare foot, to the glass wall. He sat there, staring at the reflection of the sunset in the lake.

At this time in his city, young people would sit on the benches in the main public garden, cracking sunflower seeds, joking and laughing. Shy couples would curl up under a tree in the less exposed spots with an arm around each other's shoulders, as Arman himself had sometimes done with his girlfriend. In his poor neighbourhood, children were still outside playing with whatever they had found in the unpaved alleys that were strewn with rubbish. His own mother must be cooking now, anticipating that Sister might arrive from work any time soon and run straight to the kitchen to help. Father has already taken a nap on a thin mattress in the garden porch after a day's hard work. Grandma in the village has made a fire in the corner of her patio to prepare a simple meal for herself; the smell of burning wood has filled the place, blending with the pleasant aroma of the smoke and cooking of neighbouring families. The jingling bells ringing throughout the village from the herds of sheep and goats returning from the pastures; shepherds bellowing commands and herding dogs barking, droving the animals in the narrow alleys.

Later that night, Arman lit a fire from some twigs he found hidden in the sand, and the rags and worn clothes he collected from the litter. Maybe better to burn them than to bury them. The wind last night had blown some back nearer to his tent. He wanted to cook just as he remembered from the time they lived in Grandma's village. Or the way his rebel comrades had done in the mountains. But the fire was so feeble that it could not resist the wind and was soon blown out. He then put on his shoes, took out all the groceries, utensils and the other items from the large wooden box, stored them in a corner inside the tent and zipped down the flap. He broke the box to pieces, kicking it and using the mallet, and fed the fire with the wood.

After dinner, he rearranged his stock inside the tent, hid the food among the other items or inside the saucepans. Now this little bastard would not be able to find them. He then made tea in a small pot and wished they had provided him with a teapot as well. With his cup of tea and a fruity nut bar, he sat beside the embers in the fire pit.

Unlike the previous nights, he was now wide awake. His memories did not allow him to sleep, despite the exhaustion from the long, distressing day. He spent the whole evening alternatively going into the tent to lie down and try to fall asleep and coming out, returning to the glass wall, or walking round, before going back to the tent to try to fall asleep, but in vain.

Well after midnight he was still awake, sitting at the mouth of his tent. A gentle breeze had started. The desert felt peaceful in the moonlight.

A howling woke him. He sat upright, shivering. So he had finally fallen asleep in the cold. Did he really hear something or was it a dream? He lifted his head. Over there, on the top of a sand dune, two small balls glistened in the distance. Glowing marbles. Wasn't it the very place where the jackal would wait for him? Oh, yes, it was the jackal!

Arman crawled into the tent, rummaged among his groceries, and took out a pitta bread. He tossed a small piece to the usual place. At once the jackal ran and picked it up, remaining still. Wow! It didn't run away this time. He tossed another piece nearer to himself. The jackal exposed its fangs, growled, then crept forward slowly, lowering its body further to the ground, putting its chin on the sand, wagging its furry, black-tipped tail, staring at Arman, then at the bread.

Arman retreated to the tent's mouth, ready to crawl back in and zip down the tent's flap if the beast would attack him.

Suddenly, the jackal leapt for the bread, tucked into it and ran off, jumping, in a wide semi-circle, then stopped, looking back at Arman.

What should he do? Toss him another piece, this time even nearer? Maybe the animal wouldn't want to attack him. Why would it? He was feeding him. But what if it thought Arman wanted to hunt him? Why would Arman want that? He's got all this food now. But the beast didn't know Arman's intention, did it?

The jackal continued staring at Arman for another moment, then scurried away, lowering its head, and disappeared behind the sand dunes, in the haze of the dawn.

9

The next day, Arman zipped up the flap, got out of his tent and stretched his arms up towards the scorching sun overhead. Behind the glass, over there, the blind was fully rolled up. The Guard's silhouette sat at his desk in the shady office. A metre from the tent, yesterday's fire pit was already half filled with sand. A hillock had risen beside it.

Arman went straight to the back of his tent, barefoot, hobbling on the hot sand. He pushed off the sand that had gathered on his tent and was weighing it down, by sweeping his arms across the blistering sand.

As he wobbled back, he heard the metallic voice shouting, 'Hello Arman!'

Arman only raised a hand and entered the tent without answering the Guard's greeting. The voice shouted again. Arman didn't respond but sat down, drank some water and made a snack of pitta bread and small cubes of cheese. Biting on his sandwich, he lay down. What should he do now? Should he just leave this place, or should he go to the Guard and tell him why he was really here? But after the way he had been treated, how could he trust this man anymore? But did he have any other option? He did not. There was no choice to make. There was only one option: Go and tell your story!

If he still had his mobile phone with him, he could talk to his family. He had lost it in the capsize. The last time he had used it was on the boat, calling his father to tell him they had finally left. Half an hour after they had steered into the darkness of the sea, the connection was cut. He had put his phone in the pocket of his coat, or maybe his trousers. He touched both his pockets, groping for the phone. Instead, he found the folding knife. That was all he had now in his pocket. Of course, it was silly. How many times had he searched and searched again for that phone? The very next thing he had done when he had woken up by the shore, after rescuing the biscuits and the lump of bread, was to search every corner of his rucksack for the phone. No, he was certain he had lost it.

If he had still had it, he could have told his family where he had ended up. But would they believe that? Even if they believed it, they would certainly have entreated him to return home. Father would promise to do everything to get things right for him this time. But that could only have been wishful thinking. His father would not have been able to make anything better. If that had been possible, he would have done it in the first place. Well before Arman would have had no way out but to escape from the country. Poor Father! Of course he would have done everything to prevent anything from happening to his youngest son and the child most adored by all the family. Also his older brother, who had a wife and a son and daughter of his own, would have done his very best for him. Anyone who had enough significance and money would have done everything possible too. And his uncle, and of course Grandma.

Most of the time, he found it stifling being the centre of

attention of the family he loved. All of whom wanted the very best for him and longed for his success. And for his part, he'd had to do his very best not to disappoint them.

Mother would say sometimes in an amused way how unbelievable it was that 'this piece of happiness' in the family was in fact an unwanted child. 'How could we even think of getting rid of this bunch of love?' Father would say, holding him tight, pressing Arman's face to his chest, almost smothering him.

His parents and siblings had only just moved to the capital in search of a better life and job for his father when Mother had found out that she was pregnant with him. At the age of forty-two, taking everyone by surprise, Mother always said. Her laugh and that of her husband had frozen on their faces, turning gradually to disappointing frowns, when the doctor announced their good news.

'Or, is it bad news, I should say?' the doctor had asked as he slouched back in his chair. 'I'm sorry to hear that! But there's always a way. You are now in the capital.'

'Oh, no, no...' Arman's father had said. 'No, I mean... The thing is—'

'No, no way!' Mother had added. 'But at this time?'

'Why don't you go home and think about it?' asked the doctor, suggesting the obvious.

This was at the turn of the millennium. Life had been the hardest for Arman's family in their own city during the ten preceding years but now the capital at last held promises for them. It had apparently marked the start of a prosperous new life. Arman's uncle, his father's brother, who had already lived for many years in the capital, had now started a trade in the main bazaar and needed help. Who could be better than his brother and nephews? By that time, Arman's father was a middle-aged man, strong and active, but his older son was only ten. His daughter was eight and the younger son five. But everyone could lend a hand, Uncle had said. Even the five-year-old could be of some help in the huge warehouse. Only there was no place for his sister-in-law, Uncle had apologised. 'No place for women here in the bazaar. The young girl would be just fine. She could make us tea and sweep or so, you know?'

'So what is the problem with a newborn?' Mother had said. 'I can raise another child just like that. Actually, it's better to have something to do, if I have to be sitting at home all day on my own,' she had reasoned.

The only misfortune with the newcomer would be that for now the whole family, the five of them, had to live in one single room, sharing with two other families the kitchen, toilet and bath. This house was ancient, now falling into decay. But Uncle had reassured them, while helping them to settle into the room, that they would soon be able to rent a house of their own and who knows, maybe one day, when business was flourishing, buy their own house.

'And let's be hopeful,' Father had said. 'Every child will bring their own livelihood with them.'

Apart from the start-up difficulties, housing conditions and the news of an awaited new family member, of which the children were told much later, the family was happy and looking forward to a better life in the capital. They were indeed enjoying every facet of life in the large city, which was so different from their own hometown, even with the little money that they had.

Arman was conceived by his parents' euphoria of their new life in the capital, for, though he himself had no memory of it, he often heard the stories from the rest of the family.

'We have made him with love, honey,' Father had said his final thought about the matter. 'Haven't we become so much younger and more energetic here in the capital?'

'Oh, you definitely have, love,' Mother had said, laughing, stroking her expanding belly.

Arman crawled to the entrance of his tent and looked over to the hut. The blind was drawn down. The sun had just passed the glass wall into the sky on the other side. Perhaps the old man had felt bored and had left early. Or was he disappointed in Arman, who had ignored him? Or maybe he needed to go to do something else for his bosses. He had probably received an assignment from the authorities. At the end of the day, he was their instrument, wasn't he? Or maybe he had called in sick again. Such an old man! Why did he not retire and spend time with his family? But even if he did, what difference would that make to Arman? Someone else would guard the gate and block his entrance to the City.

So no matter who guarded the gate, Arman must finally tell his story. He must tell them the story they wanted, if he were to have a chance of getting into the City. Thus it was that he decided to do that very thing tomorrow. Depending on whether the Guard showed up and did not disappear again for a few days. Oh, hopefully the old man would not become ill again.

But no, Arman changed his mind. No, he would tell the stories he wanted to tell, and in the way he chose. They should listen to him. They must hear his stories. How could they be so rude and callous as to tell someone that they only wanted to hear what they decided? Do they really have no sense of respect for other people's lives? Did they really not care what had happened to him, and to his family and his People? They wanted to know why he had left his country and why he was here? Well, that was exactly what he was going to tell them, right? And he would certainly do it in his own way. He decided to be resilient. He will be.

Oh, if he had now some books, or even just one book which he could read and read over and over again. Or at least a notebook. He could then write down some of his thoughts. His memories. Or maybe poems. Now was the best opportunity to realise his dream of being a poet. In fact, he was not bad at writing poems. But not as good as Grandma. Had he not learnt from her? Not only was she an amazing storyteller, but Grandma was also a great poet. Arman used to write down her poems for her, as she was illiterate.

Arman and his siblings would also read for her from classical poetry books or folk tales and history, before they got bored and asked her to tell them more stories. Before they had started to read for Grandma, their parents, especially Mother, Grandma's own daughter, used to do that. Actually, any book anyone had read in the family was intended to be for Grandma. Arman smiled, realising that now.

Grandma could only write her own name and that of Arman and a very few other words. She had learnt in the school of the Lady when she had come to the city to join her mother, the Royal Maid. Sometimes she would make a shopping list, misspelling Tamatos; Cucombers; Onin; or Meet, for Arman to run to the grocery shop in the village. That was during the time they had moved to the village to live with Grandma, after the capital had been bombed by international forces that were trying to topple the country's regime and drive out the dictator. But Arman was only a few months older than two years and did not remember any of that, nor anything else of life in the capital.

Arman's memories started from the village, where he grew up close to Grandma, until the time when his family moved back to the city again when he was nine. This meant that Grandma was the most meaningful influence, if not the only one, on his early childhood. 'Come, put your head on my lap, little freak,' as Grandma would call him whenever he was naughty. She would then start to sing him to sleep with her own poems as lullabies.

If she tried hard, Grandma could also read some sentences letter-by-letter before she got tired and said, 'Ah, I'm too old for this! Leave it. You read to me now, would you, my love?'

Of course he would. That was the most pleasant thing Arman could do for Grandma once he was old enough to go to the village school at the early age of four. He was the youngest in the class. Every time she asked, Arman would happily lie down on the thin mattress covered with flowery fabric, his head on a large cylinder cushion in a corner of Grandma's living room and read to her. Grandma always sat beside him, holding the top of a wooden spindle in one hand, the thread between her fingers, while spinning with gentle slaps by her other hand to twist and wind thread from a mass of wool in her lap.

Grandma used the woollen thread to knit loofahs, bathing cloths. Like most children, Arman used to hate being washed with a rough woolly loofah and stopped using them as soon as he was old enough to wash himself. But now, he missed the feel of the rough thread on his back. And indeed, he felt his back itching from just the thought of Grandma's loofahs.

A voice shouting in the distance woke him from his daydream. He strained his ears. No, he was not imagining it.

'Hey, is there anybody in there?' the voice shouted again, in a language Arman could understand but not speak very well. A man's voice from one of the neighbouring countries to his homeland.

Arman stood up slowly, looking round for something inside his tent to defend himself with. Maybe the mallet? But put his hand on the folding knife in his pocket and crept out cautiously.

A thin man in his mid-fifties, or maybe early sixties, sunburnt, stood a few metres from the tent, in shabby clothes. A large backpack on his shoulder. His long, grey hair bushy; a large moustache, also grey, covered half his face growing down over his thick, grey beard; his head wrapped in a worn-out colourful shawl.

'Don't be afraid! I wouldn't hurt you, young man. I'm unarmed,' the man said, as he put his backpack on the ground, opening his hands and arms wide. From this gesture and by the way the backpack fell on the sand, it was obvious that it was almost empty. The man stood there still, frail and gaunt, making no attempt to step forward.

Arman stared at him for a moment, not knowing what to do or say.

'Can I crash here to rest for a couple of hours?' the man said, nodding to the tent.

'Oh, yes, of course! Come in please!' Arman said, making an

effort to speak the man's language, and stepped aside.

The stranger picked up his backpack, came closer with weary steps, bent and entered the tent, looking at Arman from top to toe.

Arman followed him. 'I'm sorry, it's very small. But please sit on the mattress,' he said in a hospitable tone, welcoming the stranger in his own language.

The man tossed his backpack to a corner and sat, stretched his legs, took the shawl from his head and leant back on the pillow.

'Goodness! How lucky I am to find you! I haven't sat on a mattress for a very long time.'

'Would you like some water?' Arman asked his guest, bending to grab a bottle from the grocery pile in the other corner of the tent.

'That would be terrific, Arman!'

'How do you know my name?' Arman turned to the man, eyes wide open, while kneeling by the food, reaching for the water bottles.

The man put his hand in his pocket, pulled out a folded, crumpled paper and held it out towards Arman. 'I found this over there.'

Arman gave the bottle to his guest with one hand and took the paper from him with the other, unfolded it and saw that it was his own rejection letter.

'Keep it, young man! You might need it one day.'

'What for?' Arman said, still standing, his head bowed under the low roof of the tent.

'I don't know. Maybe we'll establish a union for all the rejected in the desert one day! I have all my papers still in my backpack,' the stranger said, unscrewing the top of the water bottle quickly.

Arman smiled, refolded the paper along its creases and put it in his pocket, asking the man, 'Do you speak their language?'

'Not too badly. I was a university lecturer in my country, mind you!'

Arman stared at him for a moment, still smiling, then asked, 'And what is your name?'

'Ah, just call me the Wanderer,' the man said and gulped down the water.

Arman folded one of his blankets, put it on the ground and squatted on it opposite the man. 'So are you just arriving or you were…?'

The Wanderer snorted, 'Do I still look so fresh?'

Arman was not sure if he understood his remark but smiled politely. 'I mean are you…?'

'I'll tell you later what I'm doing here,' the Wanderer interrupted Arman. 'But tell me, how did you manage all this?' he said in an envious voice, nodding to the tent and all the items in it.

Arman sat cross-legged and began to tell the stranger how he had struggled to tell a good story, the reason for his seeking asylum, and how he was rejected and no longer knew what his next step would be. But by that point the man was about to fall asleep.

'Maybe I can tell you later what to do next…' the man said in a hoarse, sleepy voice, as his heavy eyelids shut, and he started to snore.

10

It was becoming dark when the Wanderer came out of the tent. Arman was making sauce, mixing a tin of tomatoes and one of beans, reheating them in a pan on the gas stove.

'I thought you must be hungry,' he said, looking at the Wanderer who was stretching his arms, yawning. His long grey hair, fuzzy and fluffy, dangled over his shoulders.

'That's so kind of you, young man!' the Wanderer said, brushing his fingers through his beard, then came closer to Arman and bent over the saucepan.

'I also have some rice left from yesterday,' Arman said and lifted the lid from a pot beside the little stove. 'Sorry! It was not a success, as you see.'

The man smiled, crouched beside Arman, pinched a bit of the rice, which stuck to his fingers. He looked at Arman and suggested, 'What do you think if we just threw it away and I cook some more? That way you could learn how to cook rice the best way.'

'I'd love to,' said Arman and ran inside the tent and brought out the pack of rice, of which about half was left. And the lamp. The man was away with the pot of yesterday's rice.

Arman put the pack of rice grains down beside the stove, turned on the light and put it in front of the tent. It lit a large area.

'That's amazing! You're really a king here,' the man shouted, coming back from where he had thrown away the old rice. 'Get me the oil, King of the desert. I hope you have some?' he said, while squatting again at the stove.

Arman smiled and ran inside, brought out a bottle of oil and handed it to the Wanderer.

The man carefully poured some oil in the pot and asked Arman to crouch beside him to watch.

No sooner had Arman done so than the oil started sizzling and the Wanderer said, 'Give me a bottle of water!'

Arman fetched a bottle and handed it to him.

The Wanderer waited until the oil was well heated, then added about two cups of water to the pot. The oil sizzled more aggressively, spattering around.

Arman winced.

The man laughed. 'Don't be afraid. Just keep clear when doing this. And get me some salt.'

Arman again ran inside and brought a sachet of salt.

The man took a large pinch and added that to the water. 'Give me a spoon.'

Arman ran inside again, laughing, and brought a spoon.

The Wanderer, also laughing, started to stir the water. 'Come and sit. I'm not going to send you for anything else.'

When the water began to simmer, the Wanderer asked Arman to pay attention. 'This is the most crucial moment. You stir the rice very gently. Only to separate the rice grains so that they don't stick together,' the man explained, shaking the spoon between the clotted grains of rice and slowly stirring until all the grains settled in the boiling oily water.

Arman, squatting by the pan, watched the water as it was absorbed by the rice, leaving bubbling holes.

The Wanderer then lowered the fire, put the lid on the saucepan and stood up. 'Now, we're going to leave it for twenty minutes to steam. Have you got a ball?'

Arman, stood up, staring at the Wanderer, eyes wide open. Did he hear him properly? 'A ball?' he asked, snorting. 'Where would I've got a ball from?'

'I don't know. I thought you had everything here, King! Let's have some fun. I've got an idea,' the man said and ran to the litter that scattered round the sand hillocks. He gathered some of the torn, worn-out clothes, sat on one of the stones and started to wrap the pieces of cloth around each other.

Arman went closer and stood watching him.

The Wanderer pulled the bits of rag, knotting them together, then stretched them and wrapped them again and pulled and knotted and stretched and wrapped again and again until there was a medium-size ball in his hands.

Arman watched him, his hands on his hips, giggling, then burst out with a big boyish laugh.

The Wanderer jumped up and kicked the ball high in the air. 'Hoo-ha!' he yelled, running after the ball. 'Let's play Arman. Let's play, man. What are you waiting for?'

Arman ran after him and shouted, still laughing, 'Yay! Let's kick!'

The Wanderer kicked the ball to Arman so hard that the sand flew from his feet and he fell backwards to the ground.

They both laughed and as soon as the man stood up again, Arman kicked the ball into the air.

The Wanderer ran and kicked it before it reached the ground and fell again. Another wave of laughter. The ball had nearly hit the pot of rice on the stove.

The man stood up and ran to the pot, lifted the lid, pinched the rice, tasted it and put the lid back on. He turned off the stove and ran back to his place, shouting, 'Kick it! Kick!'

'But the sauce is cold now,' Arman shouted, while kicking the ball.

'Put it on the stove then,' said the Wanderer, kicking back.

Arman picked up the ball, tossed it in the air and kicked with all his strength.

When the ball reached the Wanderer, it burst into pieces and landed on his head; the strips of cloth slung over his face and shoulders, decorating his long grey hair and beard.

They both burst into laughter again, putting their hands on their knees, as they bent forward, panting.

The man then shook the rags off his head and sauntered back to the tent, exhausted. 'I'm getting old, man! This desert is killing me.'

Arman looked at him and snorted. He took down the pot, lit the gas stove again with the last match in the small box, tossed the box away and put the saucepan on the fire.

'Was that the last matchstick?' the Wanderer asked, panting. He sat in front of the tent.

'Don't worry, I've got another box,' Arman replied and stood up. He went to the tent, brought out two plates and another spoon. At the stove he found that the fire was out. He went to fetch the other match box.

'Come on, no need. Let's eat!' the man said, raising his hand.

Arman returned to the stove, took down the saucepan, served the rice and sauce and put one plate in front of his guest who sat to one side of the tent's entrance. He then sat down at the other side and put his own plate on his lap and began to eat.

'This is such good rice! I feel I'm home now. How did you learn to cook so well?' Arman asked, trying to make the sentences as correct as he could in the Wanderer's language.

'Well, at my age, you could imagine...' the man said with a full mouth, gobbling up the food. 'And the sauce is not bad at all,' he said after a pause.

'I'm glad you like it. Let me get some juice,' Arman said, put down his plate, stood up and entered the tent.

'I feel bad,' Arman heard the man say behind him, his mouth full. 'I don't want to eat up your food and drink.'

'Oh, don't worry. I'll get more in a few days, I hope!' Arman said, coming out of the tent again.

The Wanderer, who had now almost finished his helping, had abandoned the spoon and was eating with his hand.

Arman gave him a small pack of orange juice, then went to the stove and brought the saucepan and the pot. He served all that was left of both the rice and the sauce onto the Wanderer's plate.

The man didn't say anything. He only stared at Arman with an expression of thanks.

Arman smiled. It was so nice to have a companion. 'You can stay here if you don't have a place somewhere else,' he said, then sat down again in front of the tent and resumed eating.

'Thanks for the offer! But, no, that's not for me,' the Wanderer said and wiped the plate with his hand, gathering what was left of the rice and beans. Dirt had gathered under his long nails.

Arman looked at his own nails. They were as long and as dirty.

'Do you have some bread?' the man asked, looking at his own greasy fingers, then back at Arman. He shrugged, smiling.

Arman crawled inside the tent on all fours and took out the last piece of pitta he had hidden in the cardboard box that had contained the saucepans, then crawled back out of the tent.

The Wanderer was still waiting with his hand in his plate.

Arman looked out for the jackal. There he was. Its eyes glistened in the distance, where the Wanderer had thrown the rice. Arman smiled. At least his failed rice would be enjoyed by someone. He pinched a piece from the bread and gave the rest, the larger piece, to the Wanderer.

'Thank you, Arman! What an amazing host are you!' the man said, tore a piece of bread, scooped up everything that was left on his plate, and crammed it into his mouth.

Arman stood up, tossed the other piece of the bread to the jackal and sat down again.

The jackal sprinted for the bread, then ran back and disappeared in the dark.

The Wanderer stared at Arman with a surprising frown, still munching the large mouthful.

'That's my little friend,' Arman said, but immediately corrected himself, 'Well at least I'm trying to become friends with him.' He took a spoonful from that was left on his own plate.

'Don't trust those little devils,' the Wanderer said, munching. 'They steal from you, whenever they can,' he mumbled, choking down his last morsel. 'And you really can't tame a jackal. No way! Are you crazy? They would eat you up if they were really hungry.'

Arman scrubbed his plate and spoon with the sand, put them

aside then also scrubbed his own hands in sand.

'It's actually good to leave the grease on your hands for a while,' the Wanderer said and wiped his plate with the last piece of bread which he pushed into his mouth. 'This dish is all clean,' he said, then put aside the plate and began to rub his hands together.

Arman went inside the tent, poured water in a small pot and added a handful of tealeaves. Then put sugar in two cups, picked up the new matchbox and went out again. He lit the gas stove and put on the pot. 'Let's have some tea,' he said as he sat down.

'This is really the best hospitality I could possibly expect from a young man like yourself, King of the Desert,' the Wanderer said with a friendly grin. 'But tell me, Arman, have you sandbathed yet?'

Arman stared at him, lifting his eyebrows.

'Actually, that's the best way to bathe in a desert,' the man said, starting to shiver. He rubbed his own arms. A cold breeze had begun.

Arman jumped up and rushed into the tent and brought out the two blankets, gave one to the Wanderer and wrapped the other around his own shoulders and sat again, still staring at the man, with his head askew.

'Thanks, boy!' the man said, wrapping the blanket around his body. 'In the mornings, when the sand is not yet too hot, just dig a deep hole, jump into it and cover yourself with the sand. You can also rub your hair with it. Really… It's even better than soap.'

'I'll try it. It sounds terrific. Never thought of such a thing,' Arman said, chuckling.

'You can wash your clothes with the sand as well. Just rub them with it then shake them out well. I'm sorry to tell you this, but you stink a bit,' the man said, without looking at Arman.

'I'm sorry about...' said Arman, crumpling under his blanket. What a blunt man!

'Ah, don't worry!' the man reassured him, now looking at him with a smile. 'Maybe I do too. But the sand bath will help, really.'

The lamp started to dim slowly until it died. Arman grabbed it, tried to relight it. But it was idle.

'We don't need it,' the Wanderer said and curled up, hugging his own knees.

The moon was now high in the sky, illuminating the desert.

Arman put down the dead lamp, went to the stove, put out the fire, brought the tea and poured two cups.

'Amazing! Thanks, young man!' the Wanderer said with a smile and started to sip his tea at once. 'Delicious! The best tea! But do you have some more sugar for me?'

Arman shuffled inside, holding the blanket tight, brought the bag of sugar and a spoon and gave them to the man. 'Sorry, I've got no teaspoons.'

'No need, King. Please sit down,' the man said. He put a spoonful of sugar in his cup and started to stir skilfully, tightening the blanket around his shoulders at the same time.

Arman wrapped himself with his blanket once more, sat down and curled up. He sipped his tea, staring at the Wanderer.

In the moonlight, the man was a scrawny shape under the blanket that wrapped around his whole body, with only his head sticking out. His long grey hair fluttered gently in the wind.

Arman touched his own hair. His too was growing long now, though he had cut it short before he began his journey a few weeks ago.

The Wanderer was now staring at the glass wall, behind which the lights in the buildings twinkled far away.

For Arman, the scene had now become so familiar that it no longer moved him.

'Have you been to other parts of the desert, Arman?' the man asked without turning to him.

'Only for a few hours in each direction,' Arman said, nodding to left then to right. 'And all the way from the sea to here.'

The Wanderer, still looking ahead, told Arman that there were other people in the desert, apart from themselves. If Arman had continued walking north for about two days, the man said, he would have found another glass wall right-angled to this wall, and if he had continued to walk along that for another day, he would have arrived at the sea. 'So the same sea you came from.'

'I still don't know how I found my way here,' Arman said. 'But, yes, I came from the sea as well. I must have walked for three or four days,' Arman told the man, now almost shouting over the sound of the wind that had become stronger.

'You see, that's what I mean,' said the Wanderer, shouting back. The wind ruffled his hair and messed with the stray, long wisps of his beard. 'You must have been wandering. Lost. That's what I have been doing for longer than a year. Just wandering through this desert, getting lost, finding my way back to the glass, then on to the sea again, for a swim to somewhere else.'

'Somewhere else? Is there somewhere else here?' Arman shouted, holding the blanket tight on his head and around his body.

The wind now blew clouds of whistling sand, hitting their backs, the tent and the glass wall. The tent shivered in the wind, but stood steady, as its edges had sunk well into the sand.

'Let's go inside. This is getting crazy,' the man shouted, stood up, swaddling himself tight in the blanket, and entered the tent.

Arman stood up too and rushed to the stove. He picked it up, while still clutching at his blanket that fluttered and was about to be blown away. He pushed the stove inside, then ran and fetched the saucepan, the pot, the plates and the spoons and ran back into the tent.

'You can sleep on the mattress. I'll be fine on the ground,' Arman said, while zipping down the tent flap. Now it felt quieter inside. And darker.

'Ah, don't worry,' the Wanderer said. 'I have my own sleeping bag.' His silhouette in the hazy dark took a sleeping bag from his backpack and spread it to one side of the tent where behind him Arman had stored the groceries and all his equipment and utensils.

Arman lay down on the mattress and covered himself with the blanket and suggested to the Wanderer that he might use the other blanket as a pillow.

'No need, Arman. Don't spoil me,' the man said inside the sleeping bag, while zipping it up. 'So, yes, they have divided the desert in different parts,' he said and started to explain how.

Arman listened flabbergasted, not sure if he could believe all that this stranger said. The man sounded and looked very much as though he was a confused, totally lost wanderer.

Outside, the wind howled through the rattle of the sand against the tent, but inside, the man's hoarse, sleepy voice comforted Arman, who listened drowsily, forcing himself awake so not to miss any of the Wanderer's stories.

11

Arman woke up with the satisfaction of having enjoyed a good and peaceful sleep. It was a quiet morning. He stretched and turned to look at the Wanderer. He was not there. Nor was his sleeping bag. Arman jolted and sat upright. Also the tent flap was open. He looked round. No trace of the man. Oh, and the food and drink. He rushed on all fours to the food corner, rummaged in the clutter of the utensils, the saucepans and plates, but found only a bottle of water and three nut bars left in a small pack. Even the matches were gone.

He dashed out of the tent and looked to all sides. He walked around the tent, then stared at the horizon, his hand on his brow, shading his eyes. No trace of the man. Not even footprints. Did he leave during the night and in the wind? Arman ran back into the tent and looked at the scattered pans and utensils again. He shook his head, sighed, his lips trembling. Unbelievable! How could this man rob him?

He went out again and looked to left and right, then ran further into the desert. Then a few more metres, jumping over the little sand dunes and looked behind the larger ones. No trace. Nowhere.

'You bastard... Aaaaaaaaaargh...' His shout echoed muffled over the desert, in the warmth of the morning sun that shone over the golden sand.

He then went back and sat in the shade in front of his tent, his hands in his lap. What a nasty thing to do to him. Why had he not just asked? He would have given him what he wanted. He would have given him as much food and water as he needed. He had seemed to be such a good man.

Arman remembered in a flash all that they had done together yesterday. Oh, how happy this strange, mad man had made him for half a day. Or a ghost of a man. He vanished so surreptitiously as if that day had not happened. But yet, perhaps he was still a good man. Robbing Arman didn't necessarily make him a bad man. He knew that Arman would soon be sent more food. So maybe it was fair after all. Arman had seen much worse in life, so why should he be so distressed about it? But the man didn't know anything about Arman's past, did he? Maybe he thought that Arman was just a young boy who had not yet seen any of the difficulties of life. So what? Did he want to teach him a lesson? Just as he taught him how to sandbathe and cook rice?

But maybe better not to be angry with him. It would be much better to go to file his appeal, wouldn't it? But the Guard was not there yet. Should he take a sand bath now? The Wanderer said mornings were the best time. He put his hands deep in the sand. It was not yet warm enough. Maybe later in the morning. Or would late in the afternoon not be better?

He went into the tent, sat down in the food corner, looking at the empty space left by the food and drink he used to have. So what now? Was he going to go through the hunger and thirst again? He closed his eyes and stifled the sensation in his throat and chest. Sobbing wouldn't help, would it? He wiped his eyes with the back of his hands and grabbed the three nut bars. He put two in his pockets and tore the wrap from the third bar to one side and took a bite. Then a second bite. He picked up the bottle, paused for a moment, then unscrewed the top and took a huge gulp. He put the top back, put down the bottle and had another bite from the nut bar and stared at the last bit. He must not eat all of it at once. Better to ration his food and water. 'Huh, food and water!' he snorted. 'I'm left with only one fucking bottle of water,' he shouted, and the last bit of the dried fruit and nuts fell out of his mouth.

He picked up the half-eaten lump, brushed the sand off it and put it back in his mouth. Then closed his eyes and chewed again, scowling, feeling the sand between his teeth. He remembered the hardship of the first days. Now, he was back to square one. He looked at the last piece of the nut bar again and pushed it into his mouth.

He then lay down on the mattress, put his hands under his head and thought of what the Wanderer had said about the desert last night before they, or at least before Arman had fallen asleep. So, there were many other people in the desert. But to meet them, as the Wanderer had explained, Arman should walk north for two days and then walk down east along another glass wall that stood at right angles to the main wall for another day, until he ended up at the sea. He could then swim a metre or so and go ashore again on the other side of the glass wall partition and walk up, back westwards for another day, then continue along the main glass wall again for about another three days to the north to reach those people.

They were more than thirty people, among them two families,

the Wanderer had said. They had been waiting for months at a hut, similar to his own, for a decision on their asylum requests. Most of them were rejected three times so had no more chances for new claims. The Wanderer had stayed there for a few days. They had three large tents; the two families in one tent and all the single men in the other two. They still received aid periodically. They had tried for months to dig a hole under the wall to tunnel themselves to the other side. However, when the Wanderer had left them, they had not even gone three metres in the hard ground under the sand.

It would take Arman seven days to reach them. With a bottle of water? And two nut bars? 'With one fucking bottle of water?' he grumbled. 'Minus a gulp already.'

What if he now had the Warrior's horse? His great-grandfather's black horse. He could get there in a day. But he would need water and food for the horse as well, wouldn't he? If he were a warrior like his great-grandfather, if he had a rifle, shoulders wrapped with bandoliers with pockets full of cartridges, and a dagger in his waist, he could possibly force himself into the City. He could threaten the Guard. 'Huh!' he sneered. But how could he smash this damn glass with bullets if a bulldozer couldn't even scratch it? What if he had shot through the tiny intercom holes in the glass door? Maybe the bullets could crack open those little holes and penetrate the glass.

Hold on! He got an idea and rushed out to the hut. He knelt down at the glass door and started scratching the edges of the pinprick holes in the glass with his knife. Only a millimetre of the knife's point went through. Not even that. But try as he might, as hard as he could, turning the knife, it didn't even scratch the glass. He pushed harder and the tip of the knife broke.

It was already hot and the morning sun on the back of his head dizzied him. He stood up, kicked the glass with all his strength. Ouch! 'Bloody bastard!' He limped back to his tent, lamenting, and lay down again.

But what if he were a horse himself? He could freely trot and gallop through the desert. And they would even allow him into the City, he was certain of that. They would, in fact, chase him to catch him and take him into the City. But he would not even have had to leave his country in the first place, if he had been a horse. Oh, how he wished he were a horse!

And another problem: it would make no sense to walk south, as according to the Wanderer, if Arman had continued walking for two days in that direction, he would have noticed that the glass wall bent slightly and that the forest behind it ended. High hills would have appeared on the other side of the glass, and then vast fields and farms; sheep or pigs or cows would have grazed in the meadows. And occasionally a glimpse of a farmer. Then there would be another forest covering much higher hills, to end abruptly, after hours' walk, at a high cliff that looked out to sea. And there the glass wall ended as well. Right on the cliff. A cliff as high as the glass wall, rising up straight from the water, so it would not permit him to walk along the shore. Nor could he climb the cliff. And now to push back any boats or dinghies carrying refugees that was heading for that coast, the local authorities had installed large, old boats equipped with machinery and huge air ventilators and pumps that produce great artificial waves in the sea. The Wanderer had seen with his own eyes, he had said last night, how a boat was capsized when it tried to ride those waves.

Could that have also caused his own boat to sink, Arman had asked. But no, for the Wanderer had said that the boats, such as the one Arman came in, usually sank because the shores were mainly rocky, causing eddies and strong waves.

The Wanderer had also said that he had once swum along that cliff for about an hour, avoiding being seen by the guards on the boats, but had not seen an end to the cliff. What came after that, he didn't know and could not say. So he had swum back and walked into the desert again. He had asked Arman if he was a strong enough swimmer to go even farther than he had done to discover how it ended. No, Arman had said. He could swim, but not very well. He still didn't know how he had survived the capsize and reached the shore. His life jacket must have helped. Then he had told the Wanderer of his own wandering in the desert.

Arman had been lucky to chance upon this place, the Wanderer told him. He could have met his end wandering around in circles until he ran out of water and energy. He said he had seen several skeletons or decomposed bodies of refugees who were lost in the desert and dead from hunger and thirst or heat. But the Wanderer himself had learnt how to find his way through the desert and obtain water and food.

'Ah, of course! By robbing people,' Arman mumbled, shaking his head. Or maybe it was unfair to assume that. The Wanderer had actually explained how he managed most of the time. Whenever he was tired of wandering, he would settle down somewhere near the coast, using makeshift shelters or temporary hiding places inside discarded boats. He would try to fish, which was extremely difficult due to the rocky shore and the heavy waves. Other species such as crabs were easier to catch, he said. He would filter the sea water using the sand and bottle them. But what made life at the coast arduous was, beside the harsh weather, the numbers of marine police and coastguard patrols there, almost continuously, searching for boats or surviving refugees. How many times had they not destroyed his hiding holes after he had managed to escape and run back deep into the desert?

If he still had had all that water and food, Arman could maybe have made it to where the families were. Or he could have walked together with the Wanderer if he had only stayed and not stolen the food and water. There had been enough for both of them. They could have joined the rest of the refugees and have had a better time all together.

But then again, why should Arman believe that man for all that he had said about the desert, the coast and the families; he who robbed him? Maybe all his stories were lies. Had he just wanted to impress Arman? Or he was confused. He must be confused. Wandering for more than a year in this damned desert, of course it has maddened him. It will madden Arman too. He is just wasting his time here. The Wanderer was at least right about that. He had told Arman not to trust the Guard. This guard was just fobbing him off, as the Wanderer had warned Arman. Maybe he only wanted to keep his job, this old man. If no one were to claim asylum here anymore, the authorities might close down this gate and the Guard would lose his job. That is how these people are, the Wanderer had said. 'They don't want you to move on, to enter. They want you to stay until you die of hunger and thirst.'

But Arman had not told them yet his own reasons for leaving his homeland. So maybe if he did... It would not matter, the Wanderer had said, trying to convince Arman that they would reject him anyway. 'Oh, no, they would give you food and drink,' the Wanderer had corrected himself. 'But the sun and heat will kill you. The summer is coming, man. And you will see then that real hell is here. You know why they have laid this desert and built this wall, Arman?'

'No, but it's absolutely insane!' Arman had said in a drowsy voice late last night, forcing himself to stay awake as he was curious to hear all that the man had to say from inside his sleeping bag in the dark.

The Wanderer had said that a few years ago a megalomaniac, power-loving President on the opposite side of the sea had tried to bully the countries on this side by threatening to send them more than a million refugees if they raised their voice against the dreadful things he had done and was still doing to his own people, and to the people of his neighbouring countries.

The Wanderer had explained that this horrendous man, who thought of himself as a Caliph and was dreaming of an empire in the region, had invaded parts of the countries that bordered his own and assaulted other nations, bombarded them, burnt their cities, displaced whole populations, and cut down thousands of trees to clear their mountains for the movement of his troops and prevent his opponents seeking shelter there. He had used the refugees and displaced people from those countries to bargain political deals or to alter the demography of those regions. He had kept the displaced people in camps and also allowed other refugees from outside to come into his country. To silence this side of the world, he had started playing a game. 'He used refugees as a commodity of trade, can you imagine?'

No, Arman did not understand what this mad man was talking about. Not at first.

A few years earlier, the Wanderer continued, before the Megalomaniac President started his new threats, he had allowed thousands of the refugees and displaced people to go through his country and cross the borders to head for the countries on this side of the sea; 'Where we are now,' the Wanderer had explained. That caused mayhem over here. The governments of these countries had then been obliged to accept anything that President was planning in his region. In addition, these governments had to pay him to keep his gates closed, no matter how viciously he treated the refugees in his own country.

'You know nothing about how anxious these people over here get about the thousands of foreigners arriving at their cities, Arman. I mean we're trying everything to get to this side of the world, but do you think we're welcome? Imagine what they might have done when before they recovered from the first refugee crisis, they heard these awful threats again. So, when they heard that a million foreigners were about to invade their cities again, they built this wall.'

Arman had told the Wanderer that he wished he had known about all these important facts before he had left his own country. He had vaguely heard something on the news, and he knew that the Wanderer was talking about the same President who was still persecuting many of his own people. He knew also it was the same President whose fighter jets were bombing the areas in Arman's own Region, where the well-known guerrillas were based; those who were fighting the Megalomaniac. He knew that those were the same planes that had once killed one of his own rebel comrades. But he had never paid particular attention to the urgent refugee problems, because he was entangled in his own issues. And when in his own turn he had to leave, he was told by the smugglers that on arrival, after the boat was moored, he should walk for about one hour before he came to a checkpoint where he would be received, interviewed and soon be allowed to enter the City. Yes, he did know there was a wall. But they had not mentioned that the wall was made of glass or that it was such a high, colossal wall. They had talked about some kind of fence, but they never mentioned a desert. Nor did they warn that the boat might capsize, or that he would be the only survivor who had to make the rest of the journey on his own.

It was now all chaos and muddle in his head. As if an old, scratched CD was spinning inside his skull. He was recalling the events and all that the Wanderer had said or what the Guard had claimed. He didn't know whom he could now trust. The Guard or that confused man; that thief. But did he have a choice? He did not, in fact. He would be thirsty and hungry again and he was not at all sure that he could survive the heat of the desert a second time. So he had to try to obtain more food and water before even deciding whether to stay or leave.

12

When Arman came out of the tent and walked over to the hut, the Guard was already sitting at his desk; his face and the upper half of his body in the shade of the half-drawn blind. Only his plump hands were in the sun, moving over the keyboard, typing.

'Good morning Arman,' the Guard said, lifting his head to look at him, smiling. He took off his glasses, put them on the desk and continued, 'I thought you might be furious with me and would have nothing more to say to me.'

'Let's get this thing done, please!' Arman said lethargically. Was the Guard's wide smile fake? But then the sparkle in his eyes revealed that the old man was delighted to see him. That was reassuring.

'Great! So you do want to file an appeal?' the Guard said, sitting back into his chair and taking his hands from the keyboard, so that they too fell into the shade, on his lap.

'Whatever you call it. I need food and drink. How long does it take until…?'

'Are you running out…?'

'I've been robbed.'

'You what?' the Guard said, leaning again forward over his desk—his belly kept him a small distance from it. He stared at Arman and asked, 'What do you mean robbed?'

'A man was here yesterday and stayed the night. But when I woke up this morning, he had gone and had taken all my food and water.'

'All of it?'

'He only left one bottle of water and two of those sticky nut and fruit bars. Three. I already ate one.'

'Listen, Arman,' the Guard said and grabbed the computer mouse. 'Let's file the appeal. But I don't expect that they will send you food before the weekend. Usually on Sundays.'

'And today is Wednesday, right?' Arman asked.

'It's indeed Wednesday. So you have to be very sparing with your water.'

'But that's what, Wednesday, Thursday, Friday, Saturday, Sunday, five days? How can I survive five days with only one bottle of water?'

'I'm really sorry, Arman! I can't do anything about that. That's the rule and they will not adapt it.'

'What kind of a rule is that?' Arman shouted, raising his fist. 'You let me starve and die from thirst and you call that a rule?'

'Listen, Arman,' the Guard released the mouse and leant back again, putting his hands on the arms of the chair. 'You are a smart boy. So you should understand—'

'Understand what?' Arman interrupted him, yelling. 'I'm going to die of hunger and thirst, man!' He pounded on the glass.

The Guard winced. 'But you should be able to see it from our perspective as well. There are procedures. If there weren't—'

'I don't give a damn what your side is. I say I'm going to die. I'm already thirsty, man!' Arman shouted, as he bashed the glass between them and yelled again, now harder, 'So that guy was right. That's it. You want to scare me off. You want me to give up and… I mean he said—'

'And you listen to a man who robbed you?' The Guard bent forward, putting both hands back on the desk, in the sun again.

Arman tried to calm down, concentrating by looking at the man's hands. They were so clean and smooth. So soft for his age. He then drew back his own bony and sunburnt hands from the glass, bent his head, looking down at his own bare feet. The sand had become much warmer now, almost burning. And the heat from the sun on the back of his head was unsettling. He lifted his head and looked again at the Guard who was still staring at him. He then looked at the small air conditioner on the wall behind the Guard, just under the ceiling.

The Guard shrugged, with a subtle smile that Arman thought was from embarrassment, or maybe pity.

'I'm going to put on my shoes and cap,' Arman said and hurried to his tent.

Inside, he slipped on his shoes and looked everywhere for the cap but couldn't find it. 'Goddamn you, man! Even my cap?' He wanted to scream, but he had shouted enough. What's the use of it anyway? Better to accept everything and save his energy. He looked at the bottle of water. 'Minus a whole gulp,' he mumbled. He grabbed it, sat cross-legged and held it with its bottom against his skinny belly. One and a half litres. Minus one mouthful, he corrected himself. Five days. No, actually four. Sunday doesn't count. They might, hopefully, deliver the aid early in the morning. And today was by now approaching noon. He had already had his morning gulp. He took off the top, took another sip and closed it quickly. So this was the morning ration.

He then divided the bottle in virtual lines with his finger. The whole bottle was 150 centilitres. Half was 75 centilitres. So, 37.5 centilitres per day. What if he were to drink a good gulp three times a day? A large gulp was maybe better than taking several sips at regular intervals. That would not satisfy his thirst. No, a good gulp, roughly what he has already had so far; so about 12.5 centilitres. That is what he is allowed per meal.

He was good at maths when he was still at school. If only he'd had the opportunity to finish his education, he really could have become something. Someone. But what? Perhaps an engineer, or some such expert? His mother had hoped that he might be an engineer one day. But his father thought a dentist was much better. That's where the money was, Father always said. 'But the boy is good at maths, dear,' Mother would argue. 'Even so,' Father would say in agreement. 'He still can aim for dentistry. Maths always comes in handy. Even to a dentist.'

It was true. It had come in handy just now! What about his nut bars? That was easy. He only needed to divide each into two pieces and ration each half per three meals. That was ridiculous! Only a small cube per meal. He regretted that he had already eaten a whole bar. Anyway, that must be it for today, or at least until the evening. And he would do the rationing again tonight, to ensure food for the rest of the remaining days.

He hid the bottle under his pillow and ran out of the tent. He should not run, actually, but save his energy. So he slowed down. Oh, what about the plants? He walked to the litter pile and crouched near the stone where the small shoots were growing. They had already withered. There couldn't have been enough water for them all. Either for him or for the plants. They would have needed time anyhow before they would have fed him.

He stood up, shaking his head, and went back to the rubbish heap. He searched among the discarded old clothes and found a shabby, torn shirt. He rubbed it with the sand, remembering the Wanderer's advice. 'The fucking thief,' he grumbled. He then shook off the sand from the shirt and wrapped his head with it.

Back at the hut, he saw the Guard lift his head, remove his glasses and stare at him with surprise. Arman then looked at his own faint reflection in the glass. If he were not so angry, he would have roared with laughter. He would have laughed at his own ludicrous headwear, with the pocket at one side sticking out of his loosely wrapped turban and the frayed collar drooping from the other side. One of the sleeves dangled over his shoulder and the other stuck out at the top of his head. He snorted, then chortled and no sooner had he had another quick look at his own reflection in the glass than he burst out laughing.

The Guard stood up, still staring at him. He too started to laugh. Arman looked at him disapprovingly, but he could not stop laughing. The Guard sat down again with a bump in the chair that rolled back and hit the wall. He slouched and laughed some more. The computer's metallic voice shouted hahahahaha through the pinprick holes in the glass; the fucking pinprick holes which he could not even scratch. The metallic laughter made Arman laugh even harder, putting his hands on his knees. His own laughter was then translated through the computer speakers into the hut. The Guard had another fit of hefty laughter. Arman knelt on the sand and pressed his fists on his own stomach; his laughing was becoming more of a wheeze. He laughed and laughed until his laugh faded and became a groan.

'Hey, wait Arman! Did he take your hat too?' the Guard said, standing up and came to the glass. 'Are you alright, boy?' He wasn't laughing anymore.

Arman nodded, pressing harder on his stomach until he had controlled his laughter. He looked up and saw the man had put his head to the glass, watching him. Arman rose to his feet, still giggling. Now he stood close up, face to face, to the large old man whose enormous belly was squashed up to the glass between them. By now the Guard had fully rolled up the blind, so part of his face was in the sun. His shining teeth looked too good for his age. Maybe they were dentures. Arman wanted to laugh at his posture but didn't have any more energy.

'Listen, funny boy,' said the Guard. His lips weren't in sync with what came out of the speaker in Arman's language, while the man's own voice was faintly heard in the background, just as in an old, dubbed film. 'I've already typed up your appeal. Do you have anything to add before I send it off?' the Guard asked.

'Add to what? What have you written?' Arman said frowning, his translated metallic voice ringing inside the hut behind the Guard. He then took a step back as he suddenly felt uncomfortable to stand so close to this huge man, frail and small and skinny in front of him, on his own side of the glass.

'Ah, formalities, you know?' the Guard said. 'Just that you disagree with them rejecting your claim. I mean, for now the most important issue for you is that aid should come. I've applied for that as well.' He went back to his desk and sat down again with a thump. The chair rolled back a short way.

'But I think you should also write down how wrong I think they are,' Arman said, stepping forward again, putting his hands on the glass. 'You know when my Grandma talked about Little Girl, which was she herself, you could hear the grief in her voice all the time. "Little Girl, who never knew her own father," Grandma would often describe her so when talking about her. And your people can say they're not responsible for killing my ancestors?'

'Well, Arman, listen,' the Guard said, straightening his large body in the chair. 'It's not about responsibility. It's—'

'So what is it about?' Arman slightly raised his voice.

'It's about...' the man posed, then rolled himself forward with the chair and put his glasses on the desk. 'You know, they say—'

'You mean you say...' Arman corrected him.

'Not me, Arman. No, I don't have any say in this.'

'That's what you want me to believe. But you're just part of them. Don't try to—'

'Listen, son—'

'Don't call me that, please! I'm not...' Arman again raised his voice.

'Okay, deal! Just calm down. Let me explain it to you.'

'I don't need any explanation. It's all clear. Just let me tell you my stories.'

'Exactly! That's what I want to hear. As long as you tell your story, your own story, you'll have a chance to be let in.'

'No, I want to tell the whole story. You should listen.'

'That's great as well!' The man now relaxed in the chair.

'Those stories are the reason I am here. Yes. You call them history, but for me—'

'Not me, Arman...' the Guard said, sitting upright again.

'Okay, not you. Whoever. Them. Your superiors who think

this is only history. It was about my great-grandfather. Grandma's father. It's not so far away, you see? He was my grandmother's father. And she herself is still alive. So for me, it's all so recent.'

'I see, Arman. But—'

'What but? She never saw her own father.'

'Arman, boy, this is—'

'No! Just please listen to me,' said Arman, and his voice quivered. 'I know your people are not responsible for all that happened. But what about this? I remember once Grandma said that the Warrior, so her own father, had overheard our King once asking the Colonialist ruler, the Major, you know, that hardliner of a Political Officer, what they were doing in our country. The King asked that. And the Major replied that they were working for the future of his own country, the Empire. "All I'm doing is to ensure a good life for my children and their children," he had said. "So am I," our King had answered.'

The Guard was typing, his fingers running over the keyboard as if he were playing the piano. His glasses were back on, sagging over his nose. 'I'm listening,' he said, lifting his head to peer into Arman's eyes, while pushing back his glasses with his finger.

'That's all. I mean... So I'm here to hear about the fate of my great-grandfather. Grandma's father. What did you do to him? What did *they* do to him? Your ancestors.'

The Guard moved back from the keyboard, slumped in his chair and took a deep breath, which Arman heard even at his side of the glass.

'Listen Arman. This is a complicated issue. Please let's keep it simple. For your own sake. I mean we already tried to claim that in your first application, didn't we?'

'I know. That's too complicated for your country. But not this...' Arman spread both his arms, indicating to the glass wall. 'And this...' he turned to the desert; his arms still stretched out. He remained with his back to the Guard.

'Look at me Arman,' the Guard demanded. 'I'm going to rephrase what you just said in a more formal tone and submit your appeal. Alright?'

Arman looked back at the Guard without saying anything. He watched the man typing, now and then pausing to think; his head bent over the keyboard. He pushed his glasses back over his nose and continued to type. After a few minutes, he said, 'Done!' and leant back in his chair. 'And we can start with your new application right away, if you want.'

'Thanks for the appeal!' Arman said in a calm voice. He looked away, staring at the end of the glass wall that merged into the horizon in the distance. A cool gust made him feel refreshed; the crisp air brushing his face. But the midday sun shone right over his head, about to pass over the glass to the other side. He fumbled with his turban. It actually had helped with keeping the heat of the sun from his head.

'Yes, let's start!' Arman said, nodding, while looking back at the Guard.

The Guard rolled himself forward again to the keyboard, spread his fingers over it, ready to type Arman's new asylum claim. His whole office was now in shade.

Arman sat down in front of the hut as usual, leant back on the glass and started to speak.

13

I spent my childhood between Grandma's village and the city. I was only two when my parents left the capital for the village, escaping the chaos of bombardment and airstrikes. International troops had invaded our country to remove the regime. They caught the Dictator in a den under the ground and three years later, after being on trial for two years, he was hanged. This time, most of the people had welcomed the war and the demise of the Dictator who had brought nothing for them but misery. My father was one of them. He had finally found satisfaction and a feeling of justice in seeing a video of the hanging. That was, for Father, enough revenge for the death of his entire family, which had been my family as well. They were killed, eighteen years earlier, along with more than a hundred thousand others. Only my father and his brother had survived. Father escaped by a miracle, and my uncle lived at the time in the capital, far from the massacres.

But the invasion and the chaos that followed the fall of the regime meant that my uncle's wholesale business in the capital collapsed, so my father lost his job at his brother's warehouse. Father left the capital with Mother and their five children. I was one of them. Just a baby of two. My family couldn't even afford to pay the rent of a single room in the house we shared with two other families.

I don't remember any of that. But I know every detail of every part of it. My parents and siblings often talked about those three years they had spent in the capital as if they were talking about other people's lives or they were reciting a film or stories from a book. Each on their own way. Each of them described a different part of that life in a way that even surprised the other members of the family. 'Hey, do you remember the day...' And I had to turn from one to another of them and listen attentively so I could put the puzzles together. And when they talked about me, they talked about 'the baby' as if it weren't me!

Father told the stories in a different way, though. Those three years, despite the fact that they had been very special for him as well, were only a small part of his rich life. When he talked about his own life, it felt as if he talked about the whole world. Everything was in it. So many wars and catastrophes and... His stories were almost as rich as Grandma's stories. Except that Father himself was always a significant part in his own stories. I couldn't believe one man could have seen so much. He was born in a...

'Wait Arman, boy. You're again drifting away from telling your own story. You're now talking about your father. And that's—'

'Didn't we agree that I could tell my stories the way I want?' Arman stood up and turned to the Guard. 'Don't you realise that my father's stories are also mine?' he said, putting his hands on the glass, looking into the Guard's eyes.

'Okay, boy. I'm just saying. Because I know if... Okay, never mind. Go on.' The Guard gave in and returned to the keyboard.

'Thanks!' said Arman, then sat again and continued: Father

was born in a village so far from that of Grandma that there was no prospect nor any reason for him to meet my mother if both villages had not been destroyed, and all the villagers taken to concentration camps. Father's village lay in the desert-like plateau, far south of our city in the warmest area of the region, while my mother and Grandma lived in a village in the high mountains in the coolest part, far to the north.

My parents often said they had married at a late age considering the custom of their time when most people, especially in the countryside, married in their teenage years. Mother was thirty and Father thirty-three. Though Grandma always said that she also had married at thirty-three, but that was even decades before them.

'But that was just because of your unfortunate life,' Mother said. 'Otherwise, a beautiful woman like yourself was impossible to be left alone by men. Come on, you finally robbed the heart of a poet, didn't you?'

'Oh, shut up, you!' Grandma would say. 'Don't embarrass me. Your father was just a man with a good heart,' Grandma always told her daughter, and I had heard this kind of argument between them so very often.

When Grandma was twenty-one years of age, she left the village for the city and stayed with her mother, the Royal Maid, serving the Lady. By then, the Colonialists had left a long time ago and our King had just recently escaped his second exile and lived in his own village. Now, the grandson of the Handsome King ruled the whole country, including our region. Grandma then began to learn to read and write at the Lady's school for girls. But that didn't last for long, as her mother often became sick, with serious back problems, so Grandma, being a healthy young woman, took over more of the chores in the large house. There was no longer time for education.

Some twelve years later, something changed her life forever. A poet used to visit the Lady in her garden along with other writers and artists to read poetry or talk about politics and all other matters of the world. He attended many of those gatherings and the young maid, my Grandma, who wasn't considered young in those days, would catch his gaze whenever she served them tea or cake and sometimes dinner. The man, though also only thirty-three, was often looked at askance for not yet being married. As for Grandma, who would have dared to look at a member of the Royal household? Except for that brazen Poet.

Once, the Poet caught the young maid in the kitchen with his poetry book, struggling to read his poems, letter by letter. He had taken the book, read the poem to her and while she was blushing and lowering her eyes, he had asked her whether she would like now and then to hear more poems from him? She had stuttered, 'Ye, ye... Yes!' The man had bowed and proposed, 'So would you marry me? I'll even write poems for you.'

The Lady herself had blessed their marriage. That had been only a few months before the Lady died, so the newly-weds were able to move back to the village, with Grandma's own mother. It would take them five years to have a baby girl, who was to be my mother.

As for my father, he had been married to another woman before he married my mother. That was two years before the pogroms began. Whenever Father told of this part of his life, he would get a lump in his throat and tell the story in tears. Even years later. No matter how many times he told this to reporters and TV programmes or justice organisations and the courts. His young wife, a girl from his area, and their baby boy of a few months were among those who never came back from the concentration camps. Nor were their bodies found in any of the mass graves that were discovered and excavated years later, after the fall of the Dictator.

Father was born in that remote village in the harsh plateaus and said that he had never wanted to leave. Since his childhood, he had been in love with the soil there and wanted nothing else but to work in that rough earth with his own hands. When I saw those very fields for the first and last time, I didn't believe anything could grow there. The village, after it was rebuilt, was just a large patch of hard, rocky earth spread over that arid terrain. There were about twenty dry, simple adobe houses with ceilings barely higher than the inhabitants. The only thing that fascinated me was the small rhombus-shape holes in the walls all around the house, some ten centimetres above the floor, which allowed draughts in to cool the house, better than any air conditioner. And during their short winters, they would simply close the holes with a piece of rag. I don't remember if I saw more than one or two trees in the village, when I visited it some five years ago with Father.

Not all the houses had been rebuilt in the village. Also the ruins of my Father's family house were still standing. It had been a large house with many rooms; actually, three houses built beside each other, where the whole family had lived. I walked through them or jumped over the remains of some of the fallen walls, thinking of my half-brother, his mother and my grandparents and aunts whom I never met and would never know. There were not even any photos left of them. I touched the stones and the mud bricks, but they were eroded and soulless; too old and battered to feel the presence of my family in them. As for Father, when he had cried enough in every bit and corner, he never wanted to go there again.

Working the land, that rough soil, used to be the purpose of his life before the village was destroyed, Father often said. He loved that more than anything else. But it was taken from him. I could always see the grief in his eyes. Always.

The first time he was sent away from the soil was by his own father for schooling, as he wanted a different life for his children outside of that village. None of Father's three sisters had had more than a few years schooling in the primary school in a larger neighbouring village. But he and his older brother had finished secondary school in a nearby town. Later, when my uncle went to university in the capital, Father wanted to remain in the village to continue the life of a farmer, just as his parents and everyone else in the village had done. But my grandfather had persuaded him at least to go to college in the city. Even after he had fulfilled his father's wish and had come back to the village with a college degree in Mechanics, Father still wanted to farm. Nothing else.

So coming back to the village with a certificate, Father found a job at a garage in the nearby town and, in addition to helping his parents in the fields, he earned a good living for a while as a mechanic. But soon, when our Dictator started a war with a neighbouring country, he had to join the army but instead joined the rebels.

He was now an army deserter and a rebel. That was his

father's nightmare come true. Grandpa had himself spent two decades in the armed resistance, or the liberation movement as they themselves had called it. When the movement was forced to end and the fighters had surrendered, Grandpa had settled back in the village, but that was only about six years before the next war had begun.

So now, my Father was fighting for the freedom of our People and dreaming of our own state. Just as everyone else did. And as my great-grandfather had done. They never stopped dreaming about that, and still do. As I do.

People in the village and thousands of other villages sheltered the rebels, at least at night, fed them and bolstered the movement by sending their own sons to fight. Any boy, and even sometimes a girl, who wasn't ambitious enough to attend university or college, joined the resistance.

Father's village was one of the villages that had grown and become hubs for the rebels, and the regime had had to give up trying to control them. So Father had come back with his Kalashnikov and settled down again. He built a small house of his own beside those of his parents and his older sister with her husband and children and married a young woman from the village. Farmers and rebels, and the daily life and rebellion had become one. Most of the trade and the economy of these areas relied on the neighbouring country that was at war with ours. Traitors they were, these villagers, in the eyes of the regime.

At some point the Dictator was fed up with that. Especially after all the hard blows and defeats in the eight-year war with the neighbouring country. So the Dictator planned a great campaign to root out the resistance once and for all: destroy the villages and all their fields and orchards, water sources and their animals, and annihilate the villagers themselves so that the rebels would have nowhere to go, no alternative but surrender or flight to the neighbouring countries.

When the troops came to my father's village, after destroying hundreds of other villages in other areas and bombing some with chemicals and nerve gas, Father was with Grandpa in the fields, down from the village in the valley, digging furrows by hand, using only spades, to divert water from the narrow, shallow river into the fields. They had heard about what had happened in other areas but thought their village would not be attacked, just as other areas had assumed too.

The few men who had brought the news to the fields were fleeing southwards and advised Father and Grandpa to do the same without returning to the village. But Father ran as fast as he could, leaving his father to walk at his own pace, back to the village. Halfway there, he encountered dozens of other people, then hundreds, then thousands. Men and women, young and old, and children too all swarmed through the fields and barren soil, hurrying on all sides, as no one knew in which direction was safest to go. Like a stormy sea, people flowed in waves into each other. Those coming from the east would suggest they all should go westwards, but others just arrived from the western areas said they had fled their villages last night as the troops arrived, so maybe the south was safer, they had thought. Some said they had fled their areas in the south, but north was not an option as the northern villagers had just arrived saying their villages had already been attacked two days ago.

It was mayhem, Father said, whenever he recalled that day.

The military had apparently tried to hunt down the villagers in the region and gather them all in this vast area so that they could take them away more easily. The locals were now trapped and with nowhere to go, with barely any possessions and whatever clothes they had on when they were attacked. Many were even barefoot, especially children. Yet some people had managed to take their sheep and cattle with them. The animals spread through the crowd, getting lost, bleating and mooing. People had seen that the troops had already started forcing groups of families into military trucks. And all those who had fled in their tractors or any other vehicle they could find, were lined up on the main roads, surrounded by the soldiers.

Father struggled to reach the village, elbowing himself through the frantic crowd, but saw some people from his own village saying that most of the families were already taken and the troops had now started to blow up the houses or destroy them with bulldozers, and burnt everything that was left. He saw smoke rising in far all around.

He had tried to find his family among the crowd; his wife and baby and his mother and sisters. His uncles and cousins. Anyone. Just someone. Walking round and round through thousands of people and animals, asking any acquaintance he encountered, but no one had seen them. He couldn't even find Grandpa and didn't know if he had gone in another direction or had just decided to stay in the fields.

It had now started to rain, and people struggled moving through the mud, losing their shoes and sandals. The evening was falling, becoming colder by the minute. Finally, a few young men from the village met Father and told him they had seen his whole family along with their own when they had all been persuaded to board the military trucks. Father agreed to try to reach the mountains with these men, and to hide there. The only hope they had was that the government troops were honest when they said that they would not harm women or children or old people.

Father spent that night in a cave with several other young men and a number of families but left early next morning to try to sneak through the mountains into the city. Months later, he learned that a few days after he had left, the troops had found the cave and shouted at the people, giving them only five minutes to come out and surrender, before they shot hundreds of bullets into the cave, followed by hand grenades, then stuffed the mouth of the cave with twigs and tree branches and set it on fire. The smoke had suffocated anyone who was still alive in the cave.

After leaving the cave, Father was found a day later by some soldiers while he was asleep in the bushes, not even close to safety. They took him with several other men in a truck to one of the country's large military bases in another town, where they separated the men from the women and the young and elderly from the rest and sent them to different camps or death trenches. When the truck that carried Father reached the gates of the base, it was diverted, as the base was already packed with people from other villages.

Father was put temporarily in a school until there was room in the military base itself. Men and women were crammed separately in the classrooms on the second floor. All the windows were sealed, and the doors guarded by special forces. When, after much begging, Father was allowed to go to the loo, he had taken the opportunity when two women were arguing with a soldier distracting him from guarding the door, so he had managed to sneak into the classroom full of women and children. He had looked round quickly but caught no sight of any of his family or anyone he knew. He then noticed a few women jumping out of one of the windows they had broken. Glass lay shattered around their feet. Without wasting a second, he ran to the window. There was a ladder by the windowsill, which was held firm by a man in the narrow little alley behind the school, waving to the women to come down quickly. Not all the women took the risk to try. But some of the younger ones succeeded. The moment Father had jumped down the ladder, a young woman slipped through the window behind him, shouting with fear, freeing herself from the clutches of a soldier. She fell over, shaking the ladder, and just as the man at the bottom had let go of the ladder to run off, Father landed in the alley, the woman on the top of him, and the ladder now in pieces. The soldier loaded his Kalashnikov and shot, but Father had just reached the corner and escaped into another narrow alley, dragging the woman behind him. Both ran through the alley, then another alley and another without knowing what direction to take, hearing shots behind them, until a door opened, and hands pulled them into a house.

That family would shelter them for about a week, hiding them in a small secret space behind a cupboard whenever there was a search, as there were for a few days after the escape. Security forces searched every single house in the neighbourhood over and over again. Then, when it was safe to do so, the sheltering family managed to contact the family of the woman in the city and they came and took her to safety. They also arranged for

Father to sneak into the capital so that he could at last stay with his own brother.

Only about six months later, when the campaign was over and the regime had released those who had survived the concentration camps and had issued an amnesty for all members of our Folk, wherever they were, to surrender and start a new legal life, Father went back to the city and found the woman with whom he had escaped. She now lived in a room with one of her acquaintances in the city, with her mother who had also survived one of the notorious camps. Father found a job with a mechanic and rented a small house for himself in a poor suburb. He now and then visited the two women. About a year later, my father married that very young woman. She and her mother moved in with Father. That woman was to become my mother and her mother my grandmother.

'What a lovely outcome from such horrible events, Arman,' the Guard said, ending the rhythmic clicking of the keyboard.

Arman turned, tears blurring his sight. The undulating silhouette of the Guard behind the glass had leant back in his chair.

As he stood up and wiped his eyes, he now saw the Guard more clearly: the man had rested his elbow on the arm of the chair, his glasses in his hand, his huge stomach bulging over his crotch.

They smiled to each other.

'I bet you're hungry and thirsty now. Do you want to take a break?' the Guard said, bending over, putting both hands on the desk, beginning to fumble with his glasses.

'Yes, I'm hungry and thirsty. But what do you think is waiting for me? A sip of water and a little cube of nuts.'

'I know it's awful to ask, but do you mind if I have my own lunch, while you might take an hour to rest in your tent?'

Arman smiled, nodded and sauntered in the scorching sun to his tent. Inside, he took a huge gulp of water, then ate his small ration of the nut bar and lay down.

Arman woke up in the dark and in a cold breeze. Where was he? What had happened? He sat upright and looked round in the tent. He had overslept. It was already dark outside. He crawled to the entrance. The Guard had gone home. Of course!

He sat in front of the tent for a few moments, then wrapped his shoulders with a blanket and went to sit at the glass wall. He stared at the twinkling lights of the City, far out of reach; his lips pursed, quivering; feeling overwhelmed by his own desolation. The City's reflection rippling in the lake looked so peaceful and calm. But what was the use of it to him? He peered at it, pouting. No, it was not even bewitching anymore. Rubbish!

He stood up and walked back to the tent, pulled down the zip and closed himself in. He took his evening ration of water and nuts and lay down again.

14

The next morning, Arman opened his eyes and flinched. The jackal was right in his face, sniffing. He sat upright quickly. His roar and abrupt movement startled the animal who sprinted to the mouth of the tent and escaped through a hole at the entrance, as the flap was still zipped down. It had apparently tunneled itself in under the flap. It stank inside the tent. An excruciating, pungent smell.

Was the animal trying to bite him or it was sniffing around for food? It can't just eat him up, just like that? This little beast! He was now calmer, so crawled to the tent's opening and unzipped the flap.

'Hey, Little Friend,' he said, sticking his neck out. 'Did I scare you off too?'

The jackal remained there, a few metres from the tent, staring at him, its muzzle lowered over the sand.

'You hungry as well? I know you are. But I don't have food for you. Not even for myself. I have nothing, okay? Don't try to manipulate me with that sad look of yours.'

The jackal bared its fangs and snarled.

'And don't threaten me with your fucking teeth. I can kill you as well, you know?' He jumped up and thrashed his arm in the air. 'Now, get the hell out of here.'

The jackal ran away and disappeared behind the small dunes.

Arman yawned and stretched. He had a headache and felt dizzy. He went back inside and ate one ration of the nut bar, a small cube, crunching it slowly, enjoying the taste of each nut and each bit of the dried fruit separately. Then, a large gulp of water.

He went out again and sat at the entrance of the tent. There was no sight of the jackal. Wouldn't it be amazing if he could tame him? He would at least have a companion. But was it even possible? In this doomed desert! The Wanderer said it was impossible. He was a wise man and experienced. So he must know better.

Arman once had a rabbit, which he had taken from the village when they moved back to the city. His father had allowed that, because Arman could not be without a pet. In the village, he had grown up among animals and birds. Grandma had a stable full of sheep and goats and cows, and a flock of chickens, roosters, turkeys, geese, ducks, as well as a mule and a donkey. Arman visited the stable at least once a day, especially when Grandma or Mother went down to feed the cattle or to milk the cows and the sheep and goats. But the cat was more attached to Grandma and never submitted himself to Arman as a pet.

Arman would also mount the donkey and gallop through the village, in the orchards or over the rocks behind the village, pretending he was riding his great-grandpa's horse, which Grandma always talked about.

But Arman's favourite was the rabbit. A family in the village, who had a rabbit farm, had given it to him when it was but a newborn: a ginger rabbit with white spots. Although in the city, they lived in a small, simple house in one of the poor, newly built suburbs, the house had a large garden, where his parents had built a chicken coop and a hutch for the rabbit.

The rabbit had become the most important part of Arman's life, apart from going to school. He would go to have a look at him in its den first thing in the morning before school. He would feed him, play with him, chase him, hug him, stroke him and even take him inside and put him in his own bed before his mother could find out and force him to take the animal back to its hutch.

When his parents discovered that the rabbit had burrowed through the garden, and both their neighbours, to the left and to the right, complained that his rabbit had tunnelled through into their gardens as well, Father decided to slaughter the pet. He had brought Arman round by buying him a few children's books and promises of other things that never were produced. A pair of parakeets or even lovebirds, Father had promised.

One early Friday morning, Arman was enjoying his school holiday sleep in bed when he heard a woman screaming and thought something had happened to Mother. He ran out to the garden and saw Father with a large bloody knife in one hand and the rabbit's long ears in the other, decapitated. Blood dripped from it. The rabbit's headless body thrashed about in his own blood on the grass. Arman ran inside, sobbing, trying to calm and comfort himself with thoughts of the parakeets. Though Father had said they were not the same as parrots and couldn't of course speak or anything. But still. They would be fun, Arman thought. And if he were to get lovebirds, he would try to domesticate them so that they would not need always to be kept in a cage. He thought every bird could be domesticated if you loved them enough.

That noon, Arman could not even sit at lunch with his family who every Friday gathered together for lunch, just as many people in his country did. They were to eat the rabbit, with rice and some of Mother's delicious sauces.

'You missed it Arman. You know how yummy Mother makes rabbits,' his older brother had teased him after lunch.

'You had to hear him shouting like a human being. Just like a woman. I thought it was Mother,' Arman had explained, upset.

'Hey, Arman, are you okay, boy?' the metallic interpretation of the Guard's voice shouted.

Arman lifted his head. The Guard's large shadow waved to him from behind the glass, then went back to his desk.

Arman stood up reluctantly and shouted, 'I'll be there in a minute.' Then went back in the tent, put on his shoes, wrapped his head in a turban with the old shirt and went to the hut.

'How're you coping?' the Guard asked.

'I'm already thirsty and hungry. It's Thursday, isn't it?'

'It is,' said the Guard. 'I suggest you start telling your own story, though I have to say I'm now so curious about how your parents... But let's leave that for now and—'

'No, there's much more to tell before I come to that. Otherwise—'

'Alright, Arman. But you know that we have to submit your second application by Monday afternoon?'

'I know, but as I said—'

'Okay, boy. Let's get going then. I'm ready.'

Arman sat down and started to tell his family's saga since the marriage of his parents, giving details of his own childhood.

Only a year after their marriage, Father had had to join the army, leaving his wife with a newborn, Arman's oldest brother, with Grandma in the small house they had rented in the city. The Dictator had started yet another war. This time, he had invaded a small neighbouring country on the southern borders. Most of the men who were able to carry a gun were called up for military service, except for teachers, nurses and other essential government employees. Father was sent to the desert to defend the borders of that annexed country. After two months of hardship, he managed to take leave, but he deserted the service, although he knew that the punishment, if he was caught, was execution in front of his own house, which all his neighbours had to watch, while his family had to pay for the bullets.

He had spent three months in fear and hiding in the houses of various family and friends before international forces drove the Dictator's troops out of the annexed country and imposed heavy sanctions on the regime, which caused the mass uprising of the population.

'This stupid move of the Dictator was the beginning of his own fall and was the salvation of my People,' Arman said, turning to the Guard with a smile.

'I'm curious to know how,' the Guard said, looking back at Arman with a hesitant smile.

Arman, glad to see that the Guard for the first time was not trying to divert him from his story, continued. As soon as the war started in the south of the country, he began, the people in his region to the north revolted and drove out the Dictator's forces. They liberated large areas; three major cities and several towns and thousands of villages, including those that had been destroyed. So Arman's Folk finally established their own Autonomous Region, with their own President, Government and Parliament.

In the first few years, with support and aid from other countries, the Region started to thrive. Arman's parents settled in the city, raising a son and a daughter. Father had various jobs, always providing for them. Grandma also remained living with them in town until her village was rebuilt a few years later and she moved back there on her own.

After the Guard's shift ended and he had left, Arman spent that afternoon mainly in his tent to avoid the sun. Though also in the evening he had not much to do, except sitting either in his tent or by the glass wall.

It was raining most of the time on the other side, while Arman wished for a few drops of the rain to pass over the glass wall to his own side. But his part of the sky remained so clear that he could at night count the stars until he fell asleep, lying on his back beside the wall. Only the freezing cold of the midnight desert would wake him. He would then run back to his tent, shivering, wrap himself in both his blankets, and fall asleep again, with an empty stomach and dry lips.

The next day, early on Friday morning, Arman woke up hungry and thirsty. He crawled to the corner where he had kept the water bottle out of his own reach so as not to exceed his ration. He picked up the bottle and shook it. He had far exceeded his own ration. Less than a quarter of the water was now left. He put the bottle back in the corner and crawled back into his bed. He then tried his pockets. Only half a nut bar was there. Of course, it was not easy to keep himself to such strict rations. He couldn't even remember when he had eaten the rest of the nuts and drank the water. But they were such small amounts anyway.

He breathed, then breathed deeper. There was some moisture in the air. An unusual damp. Was he imagining it? He sniffed, then moved his head and hands round. There was something going on, for sure. It was humid, but pleasant. He crawled to the tent's mouth, drew up the zip and stepped outside, into a thick fog through which he could not see even the glass wall. The dull light of the morning, penetrating the mist, gave it a whimsical air.

Arman sniffed in the fog and felt a new freshness. But the moisture in the air was not so great that he could feel any actual fluid in his mouth. He walked through the mist to the glass wall and put his hands on it. It was wet. He wiped both his palms up over the glass and brought them to his mouth. Water! He found a few drops of water on his lips! He licked them. Could anything be more amazing than this? It was water. His mouth was now wet. He did it all again and achieved a few more drops in his mouth. Another move and more water. Drops of water, actually. But enough to moisturise his mouth, and after a few more times his throat as well. He then licked the glass. That way, he even got more liquid in his mouth. As though he were drinking water. Drops of water.

He then walked along the wall and wetted his hands by sliding them over the glass, then wetted his face with it. He repeated it a few times and dampened his neck and his chest. And his arms. He took off his T-shirt and rubbed his whole body against the glass. The City appeared behind the glass through the clear patches in the condensation; the trails of his hands and body. It was a vibrant morning on the other side.

He continued licking and wiping the glass, but soon the mist was vanishing. It became lighter and the air clearer. The glass dried up. The sun shone across the desert from the horizon. No water, no drop of water or moisture remained anywhere around. Except the bit left in the bottle. And that lake over there. Both out of reach. Not the bottle, though. He walked inside the tent, grabbed the bottle and stared at it. He was now even thirstier. One sip would work a miracle. So he took it. And a miracle happened indeed. It felt much better, he could tell by the lazy smile on his own lips. Eyes closed.

He then went out again, put his T-shirt back on and lay down beside the glass wall.

When at last the Guard arrived and settled into his office, Arman told him about the years before his birth. Just about five years after his People had established their own Autonomous Region, different political parties were entangled in disputes, as they could not agree to share power nor to find a way for the distribution of resources. This was when oil was discovered all over their Region. They began the infighting that would last for years, devastating what the various communities had built up in the first years of their self-rule.

In the meantime, Arman's parents had another son, but lived in poverty, until, ten years after the establishment of their self-ruled Region, Uncle encouraged them to move to the country's main capital and work in his warehouse.

All throughout Arman's story, the Guard had listened

attentively. But in the end, just before going home, he told him that he must now think about sharing his own particular place in these matters. The old man wasn't allowed to interfere in his stories, he said, but wanted to warn him not to miss this opportunity. 'You might even be let in and end your quandary all together!'

15

On Saturday, Arman came out of the tent, dizzy and disoriented. His chapped lips stung. His tongue felt rough and cracked. He walked to the glass wall and stood there for a few moments. It was a beautiful day on the other side. Oh, and now on his side as well: a cool breeze cheered him. Only for a moment. The sun was already becoming scorching on this side of the glass wall. And he had not even one drop of water left. But he only needed to endure this one day. Tomorrow, so much food and water would be dropped that he would be swimming in them. Well, if they didn't forget him. But what if they ignored him? Then only a rainfall could help. That mind-blowing torrential downpour that day in the beginning of his arrival. That was what he needed now more than anything. He looked at the sky. No clouds. Not even a single clump of cloud anywhere in the distance. Better go back to his tent and try to sleep.

Just as he was about to turn away, he saw a group of young girls and boys running on the pavement on the other side of the road, in sports clothes: shorts and T-shirts or tights and tiny tops or sports bras; headphones in their ears; water or juice bottles in hands. He pounded on the glass and shouted, 'Hey! Hey, please, can you hear me? Come here please!'

Suddenly one of the girls stopped, and after her another.

The first girl pointed to the glass wall and they both crossed over the street, looking cautiously to both directions, though no vehicle was in sight. When they reached the glass wall, they looked at the mirror.

Arman walked towards them and stopped where they were on the other side of the glass. He pointed to the water bottles in their hands and at a chocolate bar that was tucked to the edge of the first girl's bra. He shouted, knocking on the glass, 'That, please! Would you give me...?'

The two girls looked at each other, stopped for a second with their necks askew. Did they hear something? Of course not! They had their headphones on. 'Remove them, please, would you?'

The first girl pulled the chocolate bar from her bra and gave it with her water bottle to the other girl, then pulled down her bra, revealing both her breasts, staring at the mirror.

'Oh, no... No, no, no, no... Not that... What the hell are you doing?' Arman shouted. 'The food... I want the food. And the water.'

The girl touched her reddened nipples, then took off her headphones and asked her friend something Arman didn't hear. The other girl removed her headphones, letting them hang around her neck. She took a tissue out of her shorts and gave it to the first girl who tore it into two pieces and put each on one of her nipples and lifted up her bra over her breasts again. She grasped both her breasts, shook them a couple of times, looking at the mirror to where Arman stood on his side. She then took back her bottle and chocolate bar from her friend and returned the chocolate bar to her bra.

Both girls put the headphones back on their ears, took a sip of water and crossed the street, running back to the group that had also stopped, performing stretching exercises while waiting for them.

They all resumed their jogging.

Arman ran a few metres along the glass wall in their direction, shouting, 'Hey, please, can you hear me? You might toss some food or a water bottle over this goddamn wall.'

The group was soon far away.

Arman stopped and put both hands and his head to the glass wall and shouted again, 'Hey, you little bastards! Little, pitiless bastards! I am starving on this gloomy side of the world and you're watching yourselves? I need water and food and you show me your bloody boobs? Aaaaaaaargh!' His lips ached from opening his mouth so wide. He tasted his own blood, running his tongue over the sore cracks.

He then dawdled back to the tent, dragging his feet through the sand. Listless.

Around noon, he woke up with a strong headache, drenched in sweat. He winced from stomach-ache and curled up and pressed both fists as hard as he could in his tummy.

Writhing in agony on the mattress for some moments, he tried and sat upright, still curled up, his fists in his stomach. Could he actually stand the hunger and the pain in his gut? He could barely open his dry mouth or move his sore, cracked lips that were still bleeding slightly. But he had mentally accepted the thirst. Only the hunger pangs felt as though his stomach was about to turn inside out.

But wasn't it stupid to think about giving in to thirst?

Perspiring would waste all the water from his body. He could die only from that, couldn't he? But what could he do about it?

He waited a moment until the pain in his stomach relaxed a little, then crawled out of the tent. He lifted his head to the sky. There was not even the trail of a cloud. He looked for the jackal. There was no trace of him either. He hadn't seen him since yesterday. Of course, the little bastard had understood there was no food anymore.

Arman mustered his strength and stood up. He had an idea. He pulled out a pole from one of the corners of the tent at the front side. The canvas sagged down in that corner and the tent partly collapsed.

He then went to the rubbish heap, dug in the sand and found an old shoe. He took out the lace, then pulled up the drooped side of the tent and crawled in. He took the folding knife from his pocket, opened out the knife blade and fastened its handle with the lace to one end of the pole. He then wrapped the old shirt around his head, picked an empty saucepan, put a blanket on his head, bent down at the tent's mouth and went outside. Just like a warrior in a cloak.

A few steps from his tent, he knelt down in the sand, put the empty saucepan down, about two metres in front of him, and stretched his arms forward with the spear he had just made of the pole and the knife, pointing in the direction from which the jackal usually emerged. He waited.

He waited and waited, but there was no sight of the jackal. He was sweating, losing more water. The bright sand dazzled him, and even though he was in the shadow of the glass wall, the heat engulfed him. His scalp throbbed inside the rag round his head. But he only needed to be patient and wait. Would a warrior actually wait for his combatant or go out looking for his prey in its burrow? He was more like a hunter. A cowardly hunter who wanted to trick his prey. With a bloody empty pot. Yet wasn't his prey almost a friend?

The jackal emerged and Arman started shaking and sweating even more. The dizziness darkened his sight. What if the jackal attacked him? For the hungry beast must sense his weakness and fear.

The jackal was nearer, its image blurred by the tears in Arman's eyes, who felt sick from the convulsion in his guts. The closer the jackal ran towards him, the hazier its image became in his eyes, until the hunter-warrior collapsed, thrust the spear into the sand and fell on his face, sobbing and murmuring, 'I can't kill you, my friend. I can't.'

He woke up in the haze of dawn, feeble and foggy-minded, shivering in the cold breeze. The blanket covered only his head down to his waist. His bare feet and calves were in the cold. The jackal lay a few metres from him, its muzzle on the sand, staring at him. Arman made an effort and pulled out his arm from under his own body, languid and frail. The jackal darted away.

Arman managed to drag himself back to the tent, lie on the mattress and cover himself with both blankets. Oh, shouldn't he have zipped down the flap? The jackal stood there, only a few steps from the opening of the tent. But Arman had really no more energy to even crawl to the tent's mouth.

16

The deafening whirr of the helicopter awoke Arman. But could he gather enough energy to get up or even to be thrilled? And what was that smell that made him nauseous? A tangy, acidic whiff. Had he peed himself? It didn't feel like it. Oh goodness! It must have been the jackal. Ugh! It stank like hell. Disgusting! But the beast hadn't done him any harm. Well, except for peeing inside his tent. Maybe the little bastard had crept into his bed at night, and now, terrified by the shrieking helicopter, had run away.

Amid the piercing, whooshing of the helicopter's blades and the flutter of the tent's canvas, Arman imagined the heavily clothed man with his helmet and goggles dropping a large wooden box, looking for Arman to raise his thumb to him. Or maybe he would not, as Arman didn't reply last time. Or maybe that was part of his job; he had to remain polite, no matter what. But what would he think if Arman would not get out of the tent to welcome the aid? Might he think that the refugee could have left and decide not to drop the box?

Wouldn't it be amazing if the man had jumped off the helicopter and paid him a visit? He needed some nursing. Maybe some medicine. A hefty headache spasm forced him to put his head back on the pillow. Maybe he wouldn't even manage to walk to the box, or even if he did, would he be able to eat or drink? He could barely open his own mouth. With great effort, he brushed his tongue over the broken cracks on his lips and licked the blood.

Suddenly came a muffled thud through the helicopter's roar. So the box was dropped. That was reassuring. And of course, he would manage to get there and feed himself. No time for languor and lethargy, now there was food and drink to pick up.

The whooshing sound of the helicopter changed in pitch and intensity and began receding, gradually faded and left only complete silence. And a box of food and drink, maybe?

He must have fallen asleep again, or rather fainted. When he woke again and remembered that they had dropped his food aid, he sighed deeply a few times and pushed himself to sit up. He stretched his shoulders gently and moved his head slowly left and right and cracked his neck. He stood up and managed to hold on the tent and walked out, stooping under the tent's mouth.

He stood for a moment in front of the tent, looking at the large box over there, about a hundred metres away, plunged in the sand. The jackal was circling it.

Arman staggered, barefoot, through the sand that had not yet become warm in the early morning sun. 'Hey, you, little bastard. It's not for you.'

That evening, Arman sat at the glass wall, wrapped in a blanket, beside a fire pit full of glowing embers, sipping his warm tea with his still-sore lips. He was another person compared to the last two days. Only his lips would bleed when he opened his mouth wide. He had put some Vaseline on them, which they had included in the box along with painkillers. They had included also a new baseball cap. And this time, there was twice as much food and water as last time. They had put food and drink in place of all the items such as the tent, mattress, blankets and the utensils that were provided the first time. And they had added a teapot, which now lay beside the ashes.

'Oh, God, I could open a shop if only other people were here to buy,' was the first thing he muttered when he opened the box this morning. Huh, that was a crazy idea. But wouldn't it have been wonderful if there were other people? Then a shop would have made sense, wouldn't it? He had always dreamt of running a grocery and envied his next-door neighbours; the two sons of the grocer, who worked in their father's shop. As for Arman himself, he'd had to work in construction, ever since he was thirteen, with his father and both older brothers, to help the family. Life in the city was much harder than in the village.

They had moved back to the city because Father had thought with the thriving economy of their Region, there was a lot to be done in the city. For all of them. But first they all had to work hard for some time to make a good start. To begin with, they had to manage to buy their own house before anyone could think of other opportunities. Just like his brothers, Arman had had to leave school temporarily, which he was never able to pick up again. The grocer's sons on the other hand, who were around his age, could both enjoy school and go to help in their father's shop in the afternoons. But that was not the reason Arman envied them.

Working in the shop, which was just down the road from their house, fascinated Arman. He would sometimes, if there was no other work for him, visit the grocery and help the boys to put things on shelves or sort out the fresh fruit in front of the shop from the bad; shine the apples; sprinkle the vegetable with water; and all the other small jobs needed in a grocery. Imagine if he had such a shop of his own. But why would anyone in this desert buy anything from him, when everyone would have received their own ration by helicopter every fortnight? Ah, come on, people would always want to trade and shop, wherever a large gathering gets together. And please, don't spoil the daydream.

Back to reality, he turned and looked at the twinkling lights of the City on the other side of the glass wall, behind the silhouette of the hills and trees. If he could finally manage to get in, he could have a shop over there. That would make much more sense. He was a hard worker and was sure he could make it so successful that the inhabitants would all hurry to shop there. Imagine if he now had a corner shop, just around the corner of those few high-rise buildings. All those lights in all those flats meant so many customers. He could stay open until this hour. Of course, by now, many of them will already have eaten and are maybe watching TV or preparing to go to bed. But maybe someone just came back home from work and wanted to cook a late dinner. What could be more practical than this shop? They could pick up just what they wanted on the way back. So close to their own homes. Wouldn't that be amazing? He would have everything in his shop. Just everything anyone at this time of night might need. Maybe some people even at midnight want some crisps and dips or whatever anyone needed at midnight. What about just being open all night? Just all day and all night and never closing? He could hire other people to work for him. And then he could just live in a room behind the till. Isn't this what he had always dreamt of? Aha, yes, a dream it was. Only a dream. Ah, come on! Again, he pulled himself out of his daydream. Maybe he shouldn't think too much. Why not just live life as if it were real?

He felt hungry again. He had not yet been able to eat much of all the food he had received because of his sore lips. He had a light breakfast and gave some food to the jackal too. He put the pole back in the tent's construction and straightened the sagged part. Then took a sand bath in the afternoon, thanking the Wanderer for suggesting this astounding luxurious pleasure that the desert offered. The very man who robbed him and forced him into such a critical condition, facing death.

After he had rubbed his hair and his whole body with lukewarm sand, he dug a hole, large enough to lie down in, and covered himself with the sand. He remained under the warm sand for half an hour.

As he got out of the sand, free from all the tension and all the pain in his body and all the tiredness of the last few days, he walked back to his tent, naked. At the glass wall, he suddenly winced. What if people over there can see him? He covered his groin with both hands. Okay, it was silly, of course. It was certain no one could see him from the other side. And no one else was around. Nonetheless, he looked round, just to make sure. And you know what? Why bother? He released his groin and opened both arms wide, lifting his head up to the glass wall.

'Watch me if you can. I don't give a damn, people. Watch me!' he shouted, and the cracks on his lips bled. He didn't care!

Then with a grin across his face, he ran to the place where he could see the Welcoming Smiling Man on the billboard.

'You don't want me in your City?' he cried. 'You want to see only yourself in the mirror?' he shouted, then grabbed his own penis. 'Now watch me!'

He began to pee on the glass in circles. Then he ran away from the wall and jumped in the air, dancing, spinning, and swaying with his penis. 'Yippee... Whoop... Watch me!'

When played out, he went into the tent, put Vaseline on his lips, then put on new, clean underwear, trousers and a white T-shirt, which they had included in the relief box this time. Also a pair of strong, comfortable trainers. He then washed his old clothes with the sand and put them folded in a corner of the tent. Half of the tent was now full of the food packages and tins and cardboard boxes.

This time, they had given him also a new gas bottle, batteries for his lamp and even more charcoal and matches. Even spirit to make kindling the fire easier. He would cook rice tomorrow, the way the thief had taught him. But let's not call him that. The Wanderer was a nicer name for him. And he was a real Wanderer and maybe stealing was just part of being a Wanderer. How could they survive if they were not to take food and things they needed from other people? And honestly, even if the man had asked for it politely, Arman wouldn't have given him much of his food and water just like that.

He lay down, tightened the blanket around his body, wishing the Wanderer would come back and stay for a few days. There was now so much food and water.

In the haze of dawn, a silhouette approached through the swirling sand. Arman leant back on the glass wall, holding tight a rabbit, the colour of the desert, in his arm. Where did this rabbit came from, he couldn't remember. Protecting his eyes from the sand with his other hand, looking through his fingers, he saw the nebulous figure coming closer, becoming clearer. A young girl, roughly his own age. Her hair blew in the wind. She squinted at Arman, standing there in front of him.

'Can I stay here?' she asked, nodding to the tent.

Arman looked at the tent, then back to her. 'Oh, yes, sure. Let's hurry inside.'

They both ran into the tent, the rabbit still in Arman's arms.

Inside, Arman zipped down the flap, invited the girl to sit on the mattress, then he sat opposite her on the ground.

'Can I hold him?' the girl asked, nodding to the bunny.

'Oh, yes, sure!' Arman said and put the rabbit carefully into the girl's arms.

The rabbit didn't resist but made himself comfortable in the girl's lap. She stroked him and groped its fluffy, white, round tail, then hugged him tight and looked at Arman.

'What's your name?'

'Arman. And yours?'

'Ah, just call me Lost Girl.'

Arman smiled, then frowned and held his head askew. 'Are you lost?'

'I'm not sure. But it doesn't matter, now I've found somewhere to stay, right?'

'Oh, yes, of course! You're welcome to stay.' Arman was not sure if he meant it. It was a lovely surprise, of course, but also uncomfortable. Why should he be, actually? He had been with girls when he was in the mountains. And he had even had a girlfriend for a year when he was only sixteen. And hadn't he hidden with a girl in a cave?

'You don't seem sure about it,' Lost Girl said, pulling him out of his thoughts.

'Oh, no, no. I am. But... Where do you come from? From your tanned skin, I can tell you've been in the desert for quite a while.'

'It's a long story. What was your name again?'

'Arman.'

'Yes, Arman. Strange name, isn't it?' the girl said, changing the subject.

'But seriously, what's your story?' Arman insisted.

'Now you become like one of them. Asking for someone's story. Why do I have to tell you everything about myself before you accept me?'

'Oh, no, it's not like that. I mean...' Arman tried to apologise.

'It's okay. Don't worry. It's just a long story. I hope we're going to have lots of time together so I can tell you all about it!' she said, with a seductive smile.

He also forced a smile to his quivering lips. 'But just tell me where you've been staying in the desert?'

'Sorry Arman, I'm done in. Can I get some shut-eye?'

Arman jumped up and grabbed a blanket, stuttering, 'Ye... yes. Of course. Have... have some rest.'

The girl lay down, with the bunny still in her arms.

Arman covered her with the blanket and stroked the rabbit's long ears. 'I'm going to leave you for some...'

'No, stay here, would you? It's windy outside.'

The wind had indeed begun to howl around them. So Arman sat back in his place and stared at this stranger who had insinuated herself so easily into his bed, making herself quite at home.

'I'm glad I found you,' Lost Girl said drowsily from under the blanket. 'I've been living with my family for months somewhere miles away from here. Then a few days ago, I couldn't stand my parents anymore, so I left.'

Arman looked at her, mouth wide open, waiting for more.

After a moment, the girl continued from beneath the blanket, 'I always hated them. Even in this fucking nowhere they didn't let me go out of the tent. There were only two boys our age in the whole camp and I was not allowed even to look in their direction. But I'm happy I'm here now.'

Arman kept staring at her, waiting to hear more. But the girl remained silent for some time. She must have fallen asleep. But she muttered in a husky voice, 'Why don't you come under the blanket?'

Arman froze in his place, suddenly sweating and panting. He heard his own heart pounding in the middle of the whining wind that was now battering the tent.

'Are you not coming?' her voice now hoarse and raspy.

Arman was burning in the heat of his own body. He crawled forward but stopped and closed his eyes. He retreated on his knees and sat in his place again.

'Honestly?' the girl's voice now croakier.

Arman winced. He opened his eyes again and crawled this time right under the blanket, breathing heavily. 'Where is the bunny?'

'You don't need him, now you have me,' the girl's husky, panting voice said.

She grabbed his head and kissed him, sucking the blood out of his lips. Or was she biting him? More like a jaguar wrestling with its prey. She then hugged him tight, almost breaking his frail ribs. In a second, they were both naked. Arman flinched, but his body was paralyzed. Out of breath, he heard both their hearts pound together over the clatter of the sand on the shaking, fluttering tent.

The girl flipped him over and pushed him with his back into the mattress and forced herself on him, pressing on his chest with both palms as she straddled his waist.

The tent shuddered and flapped. The wind shrieked through a torn strip and spattered sand over them.

Arman breathed more and more heavily, panting, gasping for air. His body rocked, a warm current went through all his veins, as a mighty gust ripped the tent from the ground and took it away in a whirlwind of sand. Still in the grip of the girl's thighs, he was turning his head left and right, looking for the rabbit.

Lost Girl held the flapping blanket in one hand, flailed her other arm in the wind, her breasts quivering in the dazzling sunbeams. Her hazy image gradually melted in the light, fading away.

Arman forced his trembling eyelids to open in the stinging sunrays of the early morning that pierced his eyes as he looked across the sprinkling sand. His tent was shaking over there in the wind, but still pegged to its own site. Arman himself was still lying down by the glass wall. The blanket had blown away and he was half-covered with sand. The jackal was trying to crawl under his T-shirt, scratching his stomach.

With a jolt, Arman sat bolt upright and leant back on the

glass wall. 'Get the fuck away from me,' he cried, pushing away the jackal from him.

The jackal scampered away into the sandstorm, screeching.

Arman looked round for Lost Girl, but there was no trace of her. He then touched his own wet crotch and regained the feeling he had just enjoyed. Oh heaven! It had been a long time. He smiled and his cracked lips ached. He carefully brushed away the sand from his bleeding lips, covering his eyes with his other hand. A cold gust again spewed sand on his face.

He stood up, shook the sand from his clothes and his hair and ran along the wall for a few metres and picked up the blanket. He then ran back to the tent through the sandstorm.

Inside, he zipped down the flap, then rummaged among all the items and new groceries until he had found clean pants. Luckily, they had provided a pair. He changed and took a few gulps of water, careful not to open his mouth wider than the lip of the bottle. He stared for a moment at the mattress, stroked it, then lay down and drew the blanket over himself. He rubbed his sore lips, trailing the traces of Lost Girl's teeth. He closed his eyes. Maybe he could dream it again. Outside, the jackal howled through the wailing wind.

17

How could it have been only a dream? She was so real. He still sensed her tight hug round his body. The touch of her skin against his, and her smell. Her sweat. He stood in front of the tent, closing his eyes in the early morning golden sunlight. The wind had fallen. The press of her palms still on his chest. Her thighs around his waist. Was she driving him crazy? The Lost Girl.

She so much resembled his girlfriend—Lady Artist. A young girl he had met about three years ago when he, with his father, was laying paving bricks for her family on the patio. The girl's father, being a nouveau riche tradesman, like most people in the last two decades, had renovated and expanded his house, converting more than half of the old garden that most of the houses used to have at the front. Now the man had decided to pave the rest of the garden into a patio, as he thought this was modern, reducing the garden to a rectangular strip of flowers around the patio. And now Arman and his father laid the multi-coloured bricks, fixing them on a bed of cement with huge rubber mallets. This had become the family business, and was, indeed, now mostly just him and Father. And they had become expert in it.

That afternoon, an hour before they finished the job, the man's daughter came home, a large folder under her arm, seeming amazed by the result of Arman and his father's work.

'Can I walk on it yet?' she had asked Father, although she was already in the middle of the patio. She then looked straight at Arman, now fixing her gaze on him.

The two men stared at her, astounded, as if she just had put a spell on them. Arman didn't know what Father was thinking, but he himself was thrilled by the ease and audacity with which this beautiful young lady talked to strangers. Two construction workers. That was the spell. Yes. Arman had not seen any other young woman so at ease with strangers. His own sister was more of a shy and quiet woman, especially in front of men. And what more enchanted Arman was the folder under the audacious girl's arm, displaying random sketches, giving her an even more nonchalant look. Arman was sold on the spot.

'Oh, sorry! Shouldn't I have stepped on it?' the girl asked when there was no response.

'Oh, no, no. Of course you can. Please!' Arman finally said, his eyes still fixed to the folder.

'These are my drawings. I mean what is inside the folder. Those on the cover are nothing,' she said looking at the sketches on the folder, then smiling to Arman. 'I'm an artist. Just come from school. The School of Arts, you know?'

Arman smiled, but didn't know what to say. He then said something like, 'Aha, an artist!'

'Okay, Lady Artist, can you now move on?' Father said, in rather a rude tone. 'You can't yet stand on it for long. The cement needs to dry first.'

'Dad, you can't talk like that to a lady. She's not a child,' Arman said, embarrassed. But maybe his father was just jealous that this beauty was interested in his son, a sixteen-year-old boy, and ignored him. He who had always thought he would never grow old, never stop whistling at women from construction sites. Arman hated that. Also his two elder brothers rebuked their father for his macho ape-like behaviour, though they always said that they loved the shit out of him, to take the reproach from their comments. But now, it was Arman's moment. He knew this was a once-in-a-lifetime opportunity. He had to act quickly. Now. Immediately. And he did. To his own surprise more than to his father's.

'Can I see them?' he said, standing up, almost running after her, but he held back.

The Lady Artist, as Arman would call her ever since, turned just before entering the house. She smiled at Arman. 'Of course, if my dad is not home. Is he here?'

Arman nodded.

'Then I think—' She heard her father approaching in the hallway, so shrugged and hurried inside, saying a quick hello to her father. Arman saw her turn to him behind her father's back and their eyes caught just before the robust man blocked the entrance.

'How is everything going?' the man asked and when he noticed Arman staring past him, he turned over his shoulder. But perhaps his daughter had already disappeared into the house, for Arman saw no expression of irritation in the man's face when he turned again to him, then to his father.

The next day, Arman begged Father to let him leave work an hour early and went to wait in front of the art school. When Lady Artist saw him standing with one leg bent up, foot on the wall, she gaped at him, eyes wide open. What a move! she must have thought, for that hesitating shy boy from yesterday to make. In their year long relationship, Arman would surprise her a few more times with bold moves like that. But it was mainly she who came with all the ideas for their secret dates whenever she found an excuse to be away from home for a few hours, provided that she was home before dark. And of course, whenever Arman could also get away from his father and work.

They used to meet in an out-of-sight corner of one of the many cafés and shisha bars that were emerging one after another in the city. Or in exhibitions. They then disappeared into the crowd of the covered bazaar in the old city centre, holding hands, jostling through the scent of spices, herbs and incense. They would always try to find a corner somewhere behind a shop or back door of a restaurant and stealthily steal a deep kiss from each other's lips; amongst the rubbish or behind the trash bins.

One place they had found, and were sure no one else would ever think of, was behind the huge iron gate of the bazaar. The two parts of the gate when opened in the early morning and held against the walls, created a small triangular space between the iron gate and the wall. Arman would slowly, cautious to ensure that no one would notice, pull one of the doors and hold it for Lady Artist to slip swiftly behind. He would then look round and sneak in, hug her tight and kiss. Just a short moment that felt for both of them as if it had lasted for hours. Ages. A moment of pleasure, angst, excitement. They melted in the fluid heat, heartbeat and sweat of love; in the fever of love.

Arman felt now the sun hotter above his head and the sand warmer beneath his bare feet. He had stood there perspiring in longing with a burning desire to be somewhere else. Anywhere with Lady Artist. They were in love; besotted with one another. A crazy love. More an obsession, in fact. They wouldn't talk about it or announce it or confirm it to one another every time they saw each other, like other teenagers in love. They just yearned for a cuddle, a kiss, a moment of being together; whatever was possible to bring them out of their own lives. Two different lives; worlds apart. They would text each other and delete their messages immediately. Call whenever Lady Artist found an opportunity. A fever; yes, a year of real, true fever. Just for a year. Until Arman was arrested. And he had anticipated many possible breaks to their fragile relationship but not that. He would never see her again.

Arman shook his head, tears glistening in his eyes, blurring the bright yellow of the wide desert and the light blue of the empty sky. A fuzz. Nothing else. Silence.

He wiped his eyes with the back of his hands and looked at the hut. The Guard hadn't showed up yet. He sat down in the shadow of his tent, a lump still in his throat.

Wouldn't it have been amazing if Lost Girl really had appeared just like that? But what happened in that dream was something he could only dream about again. Though, in fact, a girl like Lost Girl could possibly exist somewhere in the desert. She was the type of girl who housed a wild beast, caged inside her delicate body, long-suppressed. And in the meantime, she might sneak out and always find creative ways to evade the restrictions of her family, just as Arman's lover had done. Lady Artist. But when one day she rebels and the beast frees herself, she would scare off an entire tribe! Actually, Comrade Songbird was such a girl.

It was her, in fact, who turned Arman's world upside down. Who had gone much farther even than Lady Artist.

Arman knew Songbird only for a short time. No longer than six months. But that was a long life. Named by her comrades because of her free soul and her beautiful voice, she taught Arman the finest aspects of being. Made him look at the world and life itself as a substance: soft clay paste that he could shape the way he wanted. As for herself, she had kneaded Arman into a different person. At least that was what he came to realise afterwards. When everything was over.

A bus stopped on the other side of the street. When it moved away, the Guard crossed over with his black leather briefcase in hand. Arriving at his hut, he looked at the wall, certainly looking at himself in the mirror on his side. Arman could run, stand there at the glass and make faces right in the Guard's face. But he didn't. He now had more respect for him. He now genuinely missed the old man when he was away.

A moment later, the Guard rolled the blind halfway up the glass door of his office. Arman walked over to the hut and greeted the old man who answered his greeting in muffled voice in his own language, switching on the computer. He then took off his jacket, hung it on the back of the chair, then, while the computer operating system could be heard starting, he sat at his desk.

'How're you coping, Arman?' the Guard's interpreted metallic voice came out the speaker. 'Oh, boy, I was so worried about you. But I see you look like you've received food and drink?'

'Oh, yes, thanks! I survived this time as well.'

'I wish I could give you something for your lips. They look

so… inflamed. They must hurt. Do they?'

'Ah, don't worry! Not so much now,' Arman said, brushing his finger over his cracked lips. 'They have sent me some cream. It helps.'

'Oh, good to hear that. What about food? Did they deliver enough? And water?'

'Definitely. Enough for an army.'

The Guard laughed. 'That's good to hear. I like your optimism. I see you have new clothes. Did they send you what you requested?'

'Clothes as well, yes. And shoes. Actually, trainers.' He lifted his foot and showed the Guard his new trainers.

'Good,' the Guard said, put his glasses on, grabbed the mouse and keyed something on the keyboard. 'So, shall we start?'

'Sure,' said Arman, sitting in front of the hut, leaning on the glass door.

'Oh, and I wanted to remind you that we're running out of time. We have to submit your new story today, end of the day. You know that, right?'

'No, I have lost the count,' said Arman, looking up at the Guard. 'I'm going to…'

'Focus on your own stuff, I hope you were going to say,' the Guard said and typed something else, hunching over the keyboard.

'Yes, I guess,' Arman said, staring back at the desert.

18

Ten years ago, when we left Grandma alone in the village and moved back to the city, I was only nine. Our self-ruling Region was thriving. It was becoming the very best region in the country. People moved from other regions, and even from neighbouring countries, to settle in our Region, where they could be freer and have a better life. Even tourists would come and visit, not only from the rest of the country but also from various places in the world.

As for the people of the Region themselves, almost no one wanted to stay in the villages. Especially younger people. The construction business and all other development accompanying it attracted people to go to live in the cities. Higher and higher buildings were rising everywhere. And that was when my family, my father and brothers, wanted to have their share as well. So they decided to move to the city.

When they were still in the village, Father and my elder brother, besides traditionally cultivating the land for crops and growing vegetables and fruit that they could barely sell, also worked as policemen, sometimes in our village and sometimes in neighbouring villages. My family also had a small salary from the government in compensation for being survivors of the mass murder campaign by the former regime. But even all of that was not nearly enough for us to have our own house in the village. Moreover, Grandma thought it was stupid to build another house when her house was so big; with four bedrooms and a large living room. Upon return to the village, after the massacres, she had rebuilt her destroyed house as it was when built by her father, the Warrior, and as it was when she lived in it with her husband, the Poet.

Grandma's husband, my grandfather from Mother's side, had passed away about two decades before Father had met her and her daughter. So long before the massacres. After their marriage, the man had lived about eighteen years with Grandma, had written and published a whole collection of poetry about the village, but devoted his life with Grandma to farming and raising their only daughter, who later was to become my mother.

I resisted our move and cried for days, begging my parents to stay in the village. I was in love with every bit of it. Grandma's house; the animals; the orchards; the fields; the river; the trees in the valley around the river; and the mountains; especially the rocky mountain behind the village, which I used to climb with friends up to the top, in the footsteps of my great-grandfather. I also loved my friends. I loved the school, and our teacher. He knew everything about everything and taught us about the world and about our own Region.

Father promised me a bright future in the city; good education; a nicer and more comfortable life. But I begged for us to stay or just to leave me with Grandma. Or at least to take Grandma with us, if we really had to leave the village. But Grandma said, 'Over my dead body.' So I tried that too. I said, 'Over my dead body.' It didn't help. I didn't even know how to die to stay. My friends suggested I fake my death. But I was afraid they would bury me for real. Alive.

I cried for the entire journey by jeep to the city. We didn't have much to take with us. Village goods were not of much use in the city, my parents had said. Both my father and Grandma had agreed not to have anything modern and what they called city goods, unlike the rest of the people in the village. We had no fancy furniture and not even a television set. We would visit our neighbours and family if we wanted to watch a popular show. Or when I wanted to watch cartoons. Only a radio was on all the time in our own house; Grandma's house, to be more precise. The main reason though, was that both Father and Grandma had lost any trust in the world, they said, as they both had moved so many times and left their homes—either forced or by choice. They therefore anticipated that they might have to leave everything behind again. Who knew when the next war or another pogrom would happen? It was true. We were again moving out, leaving the village. This time by choice, though not mine.

Before we jumped into the jeep, Grandma kissed everyone for the second time. Father pulled me by one arm; my rabbit in my other arm, while all my friends waved me goodbye. 'But we will visit often, my love,' Mother repeatedly said. 'It's not that we are leaving the village and Grandma forever, darling.'

My family had pledged to do everything in the city to ensure that I would receive a good education and go all the way to the university. Someone had to become something in the family, they said. They had all missed out on every opportunity themselves and now had to work hard to put together a good life for every member of the family. And first thing Father did, he got us a small second-hand television.

My older brother was twenty and my sister eighteen, so they had passed the age of school. Although my other brother was still only fifteen, even he wasn't motivated to go to school anymore. He had finished the primary in the village three years before we moved, and had refused to attend the secondary school, which was opened in the village a year after he finished primary. And now in the city, it was too late, he said. He would be embarrassed to go to school with all those younger kids. Although by law he now had to be educated, he somehow managed to spend a year going to government offices and schools to register, then leaving the school and looking for another or skiving off and cutting classes. When he was sixteen, nobody cared anymore what he wanted to make of his life. So he joined Father and my older brother working in construction. Sister and Mother stayed home for a while until my sister found a cleaning job, mopping the floor of a hospital. She had plans to take evening classes, to try to finish the first three years of secondary school, then perhaps to attend a nursing college, but none of that ever happened.

My family did their best to adhere to their vows. They gave me all the love and attention I needed. All went well and in two years we did have our own house. Until bad things started happening. I was thirteen when terrorists overran large parts of the country. Although our Region was not attacked, this put us under constant threat. And the economy crashed, as oil prices dropped so rapidly that we heard almost nothing except gloomy news about crude oil. Yet our Region, and in fact the whole country, depended on it.

By then, my older brother had been married a year earlier

and had moved out. Now life became difficult again and as construction work had stopped, we were all falling back into poverty. But Father and my other brother had taught themselves to paint walls and lay paving. Even now some richer people wanted to pave their patios and repaint their houses. I used to help them in the holidays, especially in the long summer breaks. But by now, I had to join them to earn enough money for the family. So Father suggested I stopped school for a year, though I had only just started the first year of secondary school.

'So you became a construction worker yourself, at such an early age?' the Guard interrupted Arman. The clicking of the keyboard halted.

'Yes,' Arman replied, turning to him. 'I had to quit school and after that never—'

'I understand. But I'm worried that this, though awful of course, is not enough of a reason to leave your country and I would...' He paused, staring at Arman.

Arman stood up and looked at him with a feeling of... He didn't know what he felt. Was he wasting his time? Didn't this man want to hear his personal story?

'Listen, Arman. Of course, I'd love to hear all about your life. I'd even like you to tell me all the details. But it's not for me, you know? They want to see if something political, something more substantial has happened to you to leave your country; that lovely Region of yours.'

'But that lovely Region of mine had not much for me. Am I not allowed to look for a better life somewhere else?'

'Well, that's the problem, you see! Looking for a better life wouldn't give you the right to enter our country. I'm sorry, but that's…'

'The rule, yes?' Arman completed the sentence for him, then walked away from the hut.

'Hey, come back here, Arman. I was going to say that's the sad thing. But I haven't made the rule. I'm just warning you. Because I do know how they think about things.' The metallic voice was shouting behind him.

Arman went back and stood at the hut, leaning sideways on the glass, pouting, looking at the horizon, where a mirage of trees and hut-like shapes invitingly fluttered in the distance. Some nebulous figures resembled humans walking, perhaps in this direction. They could be animals or anything else. But they were nothing more than an apparition.

'Listen, boy,' the metallic voice brought his attention back to the Guard. 'I'm trying to help, with the little I can. I don't want to put words in your mouth. I can't make things up for you. And I'm not saying you should make things up. But think about it. There must be…'

'Something political. I got it,' Arman said in a lethargic tone, without looking at him.

'So let's finish your story, Arman. It's up to you how you want to tell it.'

'I'm going to drink some water. And maybe grab a bite as well.'

'Oh, that's a good idea! I almost forgot it was lunch time,' the Guard said, looking at his watch. 'Shall we take half an hour break?'

'Uh-huh,' Arman said and dawdled to his tent.

After having a small lunch, Arman lay down. He had to make a decision. He should perhaps now tell exactly what had really happened to him. But shaming his own government and people, his 'lovely Region', would be betrayal, if not treason. How could he shed a bad light on his homeland, for which his father and grandfather had fought? But also his great-grandfather. And in addition, after all that Grandma and Mother had suffered many years before they'd had their own Autonomous Region. If all the suffering of his people he had already described would not be enough to grant him asylum, how would anything else he might tell make a difference? No! Stubborn as he was, he was not going to disgrace his homeland.

He stood up, listless, got out of the tent and walked back to the hut. He waited until the Guard had removed the lunch box and leftovers from his desk.

'You know what?' said Arman, peering at the old man, who, eyebrows raised, waited for him to deliver his fatal message. 'Tell them that although your ancestors came to my country with cannons and aircraft, hurling themselves through our towns and villages and even our homes, I have come here in peace. So I beg you to let me in.'

'You want me to write this down?' the Guard said, sounding unsure if it was a good idea.

'Yes, please!' Arman said, still looking directly into the Guard's eyes. He then sat down and leant back on the glass door. The soft clatter of the keyboard behind the glass reassured him. It was good that the computer could not translate the clicking of a keyboard too. How would that sound if translated in his language? It was weird that sounds sounded the same in all languages. But actually, you needed to know an object to recognise its sound. And various countries have various sounds. But you don't need to know their language to understand the sounds of their things. You only need to see them and get familiar to their sound. So the language of sounds is familiarity, you could say? But the computer also translated the Guard's laughs. And the tone of it raised and dropped whenever the Guard or Arman were shouting or spoke calmly. That was ludicrous, wasn't it? Though thinking about it now, it made sense—somehow. How would he know otherwise that the Guard was laughing if he didn't hear him, for instance? And that was definitely significant. To know his mood; or for the Guard to know what Arman's mood was. So, this way, it was actually a smart system. And although the system spoke his language in a rather ridiculous way, it was almost perfect. But how could he make sure it was precisely what the Guard said or meant with each word and expression? And more crucial than that, how exact was the translation of his own words? Should he be worried about that now?

'Is everything alright over there, boy?' the digital, metallic voice next to his ear startled Arman. The clicking of the keyboard had long stopped, and a total silence had ruled.

'Oh, yes, sure! Everything is alright,' Arman said, turning his head up towards him. 'I was just thinking. I mean the rest of my story is... Would you just give me another second, please? I have to think. I mean, can you not just say he cannot remember any more? I had this memory loss, you remember?'

'I'm sorry, Arman, dear boy. But I can't become your accomplice. I said I'd love to help, but I really can't add a word from me. You have to tell me what you want me to write down.'

'I know,' Arman said, turning his head, staring at the distance, into the desert. He explained that the bottom line was that though his People had finally, after a struggle that had persisted for more than a century, achieved their ambition, this did nothing for him or his own family. It is true to say that the city was developing and becoming wealthier. But it was expanding around them, into a mega-city of smaller, elegant towns for those who could afford them. He now knew no one to visit in such neighbourhoods, which were protected with gates and guards. He would himself never be let in, except as a worker. Modern and fancy buildings replaced the old houses and even some historic buildings. Luxurious markets and malls replaced the traditional neighbourhoods and the old local markets and small, cosy shops. Father constantly complained about these changes, Arman said. Even though he himself was contributing to it as a construction worker. As did Arman too.

He told the Guard that he had never felt that he was becoming a part of the city. Never felt he was really living in it. He was there to help build it and to serve the people. But he was never seen as a genuine natural element of that city. Not even at school. He was never fully accepted or recognised as a city boy. No matter how hard he tried.

By sixteen, he had managed to master the local accent; his attitude resembled that of the majority of the people in the city. But there would always be something that revealed his origin. Was that a slip of tongue, just a word used, or missing a little finesse in local custom or an expression he used, or anything else quite unknown to him. People would ask him where he was originally from. He didn't really know, he would say. He was the product of two different villages, one in the colder mountainous region north of the city and another in the warmer plateaus in the south. He was born in the country's capital, which should have given him more prestige according to his parents, and he had grown up partly in a village and partly in a city. His father spoke in a very recognisable accent of his own region and his mother and grandmother another accent of theirs. 'So you tell me where I am from,' Arman would suggest, when asked. But that made his origin a riddle, and sometimes more interesting for some people, though it always meant he was not from the city.

His parents and siblings had apparently less concern with this. But even Father complained frequently about how people treated him in the city. Once he had tried to revive his old occupation and found a job at a mechanics in the industrial district on the edge of the city. Yet he faced rudeness and humiliation there, even worse treatment than before. So after a few months he quit his job and couldn't find another in the whole district. But it was actually because he had beaten up his boss before he had left. Besides, his obsolete knowledge of mechanics with the emerging new machinery and skills wasn't sufficient. And God, all those complicated new cars!

Also as construction workers, they would be paid less and less as they were considered to be less skilled, while the modern buildings and high-rise flat blocks were more and more built by foreign companies who brought with them their own native workers or hired skilled immigrants from neighbouring countries.

It was true that he and his siblings could still enjoy some of the developments: better food; more varied fruit and vegetable; mobile and smartphones; fashionable clothes; internet; Facebook and Snapchat with all the hassle of social media. However, not only did they not realise how to profit from these resources as the poorest segment, but life itself was becoming daily more expensive in the city while they became more poor. Poorer and poorer. 'We were becoming no one. We didn't even exist. And besides all this, the political situation remained the same as ever. The same rivalry and the same—'

'Sorry, Arman, but it's time,' the metallic voice startled him.

'Time for what?' Arman asked, frowning, turning his head up to the glass behind him.

'We have to submit your story now. Your asylum request.'

'Oh, I see,' Arman said, standing up. It was indeed the afternoon and time for the Guard to leave. The old man had stopped typing and was working with the mouse, clicking and sometimes prodding with one finger on the keyboard. He was obviously ticking boxes in a form or something that must be shining on his computer screen, as the man's eyes were screwed to it. Bluish lights flickered on his glasses. He finally pressed the enter key.

'Done!' the Guard said, looking at Arman. 'Don't worry. I think you have an impressive story. It has certainly touched me anyway. And I hope it will also affect them this time. So let's call it a day, mate. I wish you a very good evening!' He moved the mouse round again, apparently shutting down his computer. He then took off his glasses, stood up, grabbed his coat, put it on, put his glasses into his inside pocket, came to the glass wall between them, skirting the turnstile, waved and smiled at Arman, then rolled down the blind.

Arman, still standing there, leant back on the glass and heard the iron door shut with a muffled clang behind him.

19

For the few days before the decision on his second asylum request came on the following Friday, Arman spent time mostly sitting or lying down in his tent. Or he would sometimes go over to the Guard for a chat. The Guard worked shorter hours these days and explained to Arman that officially he was not supposed to talk to him much, as his only job now was to watch the gate in case other refugees showed up. Nevertheless, he was curious to hear more details of Arman's life, he said. Though he seemed now to be more interested in the rest of Arman's family or in the history of his country, which he had insisted, during Arman's asylum requests, weren't relevant. Both of those issues were not up to him to decide, the man explained again.

Every time Arman went over to stand at the hut for ten minutes or so, the Guard would ask him about an aspect of his and his family's life. But when Arman asked the Guard to tell of his own life or something about life in the country Arman himself was so eagerly attempting to become a part of, the Guard said he was absolutely forbidden to say a word about his side of the glass wall.

'How very unfair!' said Arman, kicking the sand at his feet.

'I know,' said the Guard. 'But anything I tell you, even about my personal life, can cost me my job. And before you ask why that would matter in my old age, I tell you: I'm not allowed to tell you that either.' He pursed his lips in a rather proud smirk.

'You told me about the wall.'

'That's true,' the Guard leant back into his chair. 'That I am allowed to discuss. Part of the rules. You have the right to know what your chances are and what you're standing against. But to be fair to you, I'll tell you something later about my own family, as much as I'm permitted. Not my job though. That's absolutely not allowed. But let's stay with your stories for now.' He then told Arman that he had decided to write a book.

'A book?' Arman exclaimed, taking a pace back from the glass door.

'Uh-huh!' said the Guard. Yes, he had already started and was writing right now! He would appreciate it, he said, if Arman would let him work on it in the hours in which he had nothing else to do. His daughter had encouraged him to write. To share what he has seen in the years he had spent working with people from the rest of the world. 'But to be honest, you inspired me, Arman. Your stories.'

'Am I going to be a part of it, you mean?' Arman asked, stepping forward, scowling.

'Oh, no, don't worry. I can't do that,' the Guard said with a smile. 'It will be more about my view of the things from this side of the glass. I mean I'd also write about the years before they built this wall. I'm trying to find the right form for it. I'm not a writer, you see!'

Arman would then leave the Guard alone and spend most of the time in his tent. He would sit for hours pondering. What should he do if they rejected him again? Shouldn't he have told them the real reason for his flight from his country? Would it have made a difference anyway? He had already made it clear how difficult life had been for him in that society where there was no real place for him as a young man. For most of the young people, actually. And that's how it all began. The horrible things that had happened. Events that shocked him. How could he feel safe in that country anymore? The horrors of the former regime and even the fratricidal infighting between the various parties in his own Region and the plundering, all those killings and atrocities of the previous century were stories of his parents and their generation and those before them. These were, for Arman, only stories that he had told the Guard as part of his asylum request. Those were dark times that were supposed to be over. He was born in a different era. At least that was what he had been told and promised constantly through all kinds of media by the leaders of his own Folk and those who governed the Region. But this different era did not seem so much better for him, nor for many others in his generation.

Arman himself had been busy helping his father and the rest of the family to make ends meet, but many others, especially in his city, had found the situation intolerable; they were about to stand up against the political establishment. Many people were ready to revolt, especially young people and intellectuals. In fact, almost everyone who could no longer endure the injustice of the few political forces. In practice, some families and clans dominated all facets of life, indulged in the pleasures of plundering the wealth, living in paradisal oases that they had created for themselves and their kin before the very eyes of the rest of the population who could only observe them living their extravagant, unreachable lives, as if they were watching a reality show. The people had just wished an end to it.

Arman at this time had been deeply immersed in the euphoria of his adventures with Lady Artist, but had also worked hard towards one day catching up with his education and the dream of the future his family had promised him when they took him away from the village. But at the same time, he was contemplating taking part in the people's opposition. Alongside those who were actively struggling for bringing about change.

Change had become the mantra those days. A political and social movement. They wanted to change the entire political system and the way the economy was driven; the distribution of wealth. But some also wanted to change the culture and traditions of their society. Some wanted more freedom, while others wanted a more central role for their religion. At some point when activism and talks and democratic efforts to create a strong opposition had not helped and had barely changed anything, demonstrations began. Each group would protest for greater rights and improvement in whatever sector they wanted to have changed. Teachers; nurses; civil servants; clerics; religious parties; and students. Also Arman's father had joined the demonstrations.

When the protests first began, Arman had just turned eighteen. Father had allowed him to keep half of his wage for himself, to save for whatever he wanted to do with his life when he had enough money to stand on his own two feet. Of this half, he saved half and spent the other on his secret adventures with Lady Artist. But he was also aware of what was happening around him. One recent event had shocked him so much that it had made him lose trust in everything.

A young student had been kidnapped in broad daylight in front of his university in the Region's capital city and was found later beaten and shot dead through his mouth. The boy had only a few days earlier published a poem about the President's daughter, whom he had never met. No one had met her, in fact. No one had ever met or seen the President's wife or daughter on TV or anywhere else, while his sons were everywhere. The sons already took important positions at early ages, while much older men were obliged to answer to them, even if they were senior officials and politicians themselves.

Except for their own followers, the majority of the people felt not only angry but also embarrassed to be ruled by a family known for not being at all intelligent. But what really saddened Arman, disappointed him in fact, was that a young man, only nineteen, had been shot dead just because he had fantasised about the President's daughter. He hadn't said he hated her. He had said in his poem that he loved her. Though of course this was never investigated nor was it ever clear why and who had killed that young man, many in the Region who could not trust the stories of the ruling family and their followers, knew why he had been executed.

Not only did the prevailing fear and injustice make Arman uncertain about his life and future, but also his precarious relationship with Lady Artist. As she was more informed and on top of things than he was, she had warned him that their relationship was not more than fun and games. Arman had to promise not to fall in love with her and to be prepared for a shock of any kind. If her father would, for instance, get a sniff of their courtship, she had said, that was the end of it, if not a disastrous end. Her mother covered for her, pretending that she believed her each time she made an excuse to go out or as to why she would be late home from school. Although she never had said anything about Arman or that she was seeing a boy, she was sure that her mother knew. And her mother also knew, Lady Artist said with certainty, that her daughter knew that her mother knew about her relationship.

But Arman was not only in love with her already, he could not even get to sleep before hours tossing and turning in bed, thinking about her. From the moment he woke up in the morning she was on his mind. Even when they were not together, he imagined she was with him. In his bed while hugging his pillow; at breakfast; on the bus; at his side when walking the streets; at work where he imagined her sitting somewhere safe out of the range of his own or his father's mallet and chisel when they were breaking stones or cutting pavement bricks. He would, every now and then, go over for a peck on the cheek. Father would sometimes notice strange movements or sentences murmured by his son, but never caught him with her. The most amazing trait of his imaginary girlfriend, his soulmate, was her invisibility.

The most difficult aspect of the real Lady Artist, though, was her visibility. And that of Arman himself. Lady Artist laughed when Arman pointed that out. They both then wished that they were invisible. They could then be together forever.

'But we're already trying to remain invisible,' Lady Artist would say.

'It's not the same,' Arman would say, pouting in thought.

'I'd love to walk with you freely in the streets and to kiss you wherever we wanted. And that can only—'

'Don't dream away, silly boy,' she would say, pulling him out of his pondering. 'Try to enjoy it as long as it's possible,' she would suggest.

And the day came when Lady Artist became a permanent, invisible fairy. An eternal voice in Arman's head; becoming his salvation at crucial moments during all that had happened to him ever since.

That day, he was supposed to see her after work. An early summer afternoon. When he went home with Father around four o'clock, he dropped the tools, took a quick shower, combed his hair, straightened his collar, went out again and took the bus to town to meet her in a café. The bus got held up in the traffic, as hundreds of protesters were marching in the street. Impatiently, he jumped out of the bus and walked down the street, elbowing his way through the protesters. Police were on the pavements on both sides, armed with long sticks.

On a spot across the street from the headquarters of the ruling political party of the Region's President, Arman pushed his way forward through the crowd. Suddenly, some protesters started to throw stones at the building. Heavily armed guards in civilian clothing shouted at the crowd, warning them to stop stoning. But more protesters joined in, now throwing empty bottles, tins and anything else they could find.

A group tried to jump over the fence. The guards on the rooftop started shooting in the air. The protesters scattered. Still, some tried to go over the high concrete fence. Arman ran as well but was held back by the rush of protesters who came towards to the building. This time the guards shot into the mass and injured some demonstrators.

A boy fell in front of Arman, thrashing around on the ground, blood oozing from his chest. Arman bent over and grabbed his shoulders, but the police had now intervened, laying about with their sticks, arresting protesters randomly. A stampede thrust Arman away. He fell and crashed under their feet. He saw through the running legs two of the guards in civilian clothes come out of the building, pushing their way into the crowd, passing Arman, pick up the dying boy and drag him into the building. Sirens were heard approaching. Arman managed to crawl to the roadside and lean back on a large oak tree in front of the building. Another guard lurched out of the gate, pulled Arman's arm and dragged him into the building as well.

In the garden, a few other wounded young men lay on the grass. The guards, Kalashnikovs in their hands, closed the gates. The sirens were now closer. Clearly in front of the building. Their blue lights swaying behind the wall. But the gate remained shut. There was a persistent banging on the metal door. But nobody opened the gate.

The guards, jumping around, nervous as they were, dragged Arman and all the wounded inside, abandoning the garden. Two guards holding both his arms, pushed Arman into a room and locked the door.

Minutes later, another man came in and treated Arman's wounds, on his face and hands. They brought in two other wounded victims to be treated by the man, who was apparently a nurse. Then the door was locked again.

Arman spent the night in that room. They had taken away

his mobile phone and begging them to call his family had not helped. They interrogated him a few times, wanted to know which political party or group inspired him and who had recruited him. Who had encouraged him to take to the streets. Why had he thrown stones and why had he wanted to get into the building. He swore and tried to convince them that he was just a passer-by, but in vain. He cried and begged them to release him. At one point one of the armed men punched him so hard in his cheek that one of his molar teeth broke, so that he almost choked on his own blood. The nurse, seemingly one of their own and not from the ambulances, intervened again and stopped the bleeding.

That night, they didn't give him so much as a bite of food. And the only water he was given was when the nurse washed his mouth and treated his tooth. It was not until the next day, early in the morning, that they gave him and another three wounded young men each a piece of bread and some sweet tea. Then they blindfolded and handcuffed them and put them in a closed van, driving them away. He could sense that there were also three guards in the van. He could tell from their voices.

After a few hours' drive, they halted somewhere and pushed them out.

20

On Thursday morning, Arman asked the Guard if there was any news on his asylum request.

The Guard moved the mouse around, his gaze locked to the screen. 'No, unfortunately, nothing yet. But don't worry, Arman. From my experience, when it takes longer, there is a good chance that they might accept your request. If they want to reject you, they'll do it quickly.'

'Thanks for the reassurance!' said Arman, smiling.

'But don't take that for granted. That's only my own observation,' the Guard warned, still looking at the screen.

'And how is your book coming along?' Arman asked.

'Well, I still have to find out. I'm going to start working on it now.'

'Ah, okay, I'll leave you to work then,' Arman said and walked off, languidly. What about him? What should he do in this bloody hot desert? Ponder? Yes, that was all that was left to do. Now his storytelling was over, and he didn't need to struggle for food and water, he literally had nothing to do. Not even any desire to eat. Days felt so much longer. And they had indeed become longer, with the summer arriving. But even the nights still felt long. It was hard to fall asleep. The stillness of the desert was stronger and poignant. Deafening.

He walked a few steps away from his tent, but the sun was already unbearable. Maybe he should get his cap. But why? Where to go? He looked for the jackal. Just something to play with. Anything.

He paced back and sat in the shadow of the tent, staring at the world behind the glass wall. Maybe if he tried, he could tame the jackal. Since he had been a child, animals had some kind of affiliation with him. They trusted him. But come on, a jackal? And that in a desert. If it was a fox, maybe. Arman knew that foxes could become your friend if you took care of them. Though they wouldn't let themselves be domesticated either. It was maybe all for the food.

Father used to say a fox was never to be trusted. But Lady Artist had said once that she would really love to have a fox as a pet, when Arman had told her his father's anecdote about how once his earlobe had been bitten by a fox. Before Father was sent to the desert as a soldier, his unit had bivouacked at a port town in far south of the country. The soldiers slept on the ground in the vast rough wasteland at the shore. Father had put some bread under his head. Late at night, a fox had tried to steal it from him. Father had awoken with a jolt, and the fox had nipped his ear and run off with a frightened shriek. The trace of its teeth was still visible on Father's lobe.

Laughing her head off, Lady Artist had said that her fox wouldn't bite her ear. Or anyone's ear for that matter. She would feed him too well. But Arman loved rabbits more, he had said. 'How can we reconcile them? How can we entrust my rabbit to your fox? So that we never wake up one day to see his head in your fox's mouth. Just as Father did with my rabbit.'

'Ah, that will never happen. They need never to meet,' Lady Artist said, grinning, then winked.

'You never know. Maybe one day... you know...'

'You can get that idea out of your head, boy!' She knocked on Arman's head softly with her knuckle.

Arman tried but couldn't quite bring her to life. He needed her in this desert more than ever. But he now only recalled her face vaguely. In the prison though, her invisible presence had been his only solace. They had not allowed him to contact anyone and had not even informed his family of his sentence. He apparently had just vanished without trace. For five months. Only later, would he hear about his family's suffering, as they looked for him, knocking at the doors of every official institution, political parties, or powerful people.

Arman never knew where he was held. And when he was released, they drove him again blindfolded for a few hours, back to his city and dropped him a few minutes from his house, in an empty narrow alleyway. They gave him a soft, polite shove out of the car; the guys who all the way through the journey had talked, joked and laughed and involved Arman kindly in their chats. Just as the vehicle sped noisily away and he had taken off the blindfold, he saw that it was a four-by-four with heavily tinted windows and windshields. It had turned swiftly into a side-street and disappeared.

He surprised everyone that late afternoon. The front door was open as usual, and he dawdled, worn out and defeated, through the garden, into the kitchen. His sister saw him first, as she lifted her head from sweeping the floor. She screamed, tossed away the brush and dustpan and covered her face with both hands. Out of joy and horror, as she said later. Disbelief, it was in fact. Shock. When Mother ran to the kitchen and saw Arman standing there at the sink with long hair and unkempt, patchy beard and moustache, a much older version of her son, she fainted, her scream stifled in her chest. That was joy, she would confirm every time she recalled the moment. Pure joy. Oh, but he was suddenly so very grown up. He was her little boy no more, she would say. And never became him again, she would add regretfully.

Arman had indeed felt that he had grown much older in those five months. Not only he had endured physical pain and sorrow, but he had also learnt a lot about the Region's recent history, through which he had lived but had never touched or felt directly. Now all the stories and anecdotes he knew, or news and gossip, all became real; personified by the real people he met inside the prison. Although some, like himself, claimed to have done nothing, most of the men, old, middle-aged and young, were detained for being a threat to the ruling party of the President. And they did not deny that. But they insisted they hadn't done what they were held for without trial.

Some were arrested for plotting the establishment of clandestine groups to overthrow the party and the President's family that, as they explained to Arman, was becoming a dynasty. Some were held there for years, without anyone knowing where they were. And they said they were sure there was a similar place where women were also held. Anyone who had been released, was made to pledge never to talk about it or to give information about the inmates still inside. This oath was of course not completely fulfilled, and many freed prisoners would pass on news to the families of other prisoners informing them that their son or husband, father or brother, sister, daughter or mother, were still alive.

One of the men Arman met had been there for more than seven years. He was in his mid-forties but already looked an old man. The inmates called him Doctor, as he had become the prison's medical aid. At age twenty he had studied two years of medicine and joined a guerrilla organisation. But when the President's armed men had raided the headquarters of the guerrillas in the Region's Capital, and killed all those who had resisted and arrested all the others who had not managed to flee the city, he had been injured but had been able to reach the rest of the guerrillas in the mountains. A few years later, on a visit to the Capital, he was arrested along two of his comrades.

The Doctor treated Arman's wounds in the beginning and helped him to cope with the pain and the injuries he had endured after each interrogation in the first few days of his arrival. He told Arman about the raid on their headquarters and how he and a comrade, who had been his childhood friend, had fled together but they were chased and shot. They lay there in their own blood in the rain puddles in the street gutters for about half an hour, both moaning and groaning, holding each other's hands, trying to crawl to the safety of the narrow alleyways. But his friend had been so badly injured that he couldn't continue. The Doctor himself survived but never heard again of his friend.

'I don't think anyone knows what happened to him. They

must have kept him in a place like this. When you're held here, you have vanished,' the Doctor told Arman. 'No one could ever believe even those released who say this place existed,' the man said. He explained that even if those freed men were to take the news of prisoners to their families and even if the families could do anything to reach their loved ones, whatever they did and whichever senior official they might know or bribe, no matter how much money they could pay, they would never find or be given a clue to where the prison was situated. Their loved ones were just missing, and that was an unfortunate fact, officials would say. And if a released prisoner were to dare to reveal the secrets of this place, the party would refer the families or any human rights or whatever organisation to other existing prisons. 'But of course, we are not there,' the Doctor said, while Arman stared at him for explanation. 'Finally, that poor man would be declared as confused and paranoid. Maybe he's traumatised from his time in prison, they might say. Or in the best case, they may brand him as a liar.'

Arman had promised that he would bring the Doctor's news to his family if he were ever to be released. The man laughed and said that was sweet of him, but it wouldn't change anything. Better that his family, who might already have given up their search, be left with their grief.

On the second day of his release, Arman hurried to the art school and waited until classes were over and the students came out. When most students had passed the gates and he hadn't caught sight of Lady Artist, he sprinted towards a friend of hers; one of her close friends who vaguely knew of their relationship. She told him that Lady Artist no longer lived in the city. She had emigrated to America.

'What do you mean emigrated? She was... America? How come America?'

'You don't know that she married?' the friend said and asked Arman if he would like to walk with her rather than stand there so stupefied in the middle of the road.

'But tell me, please! What do you mean she's married?' Arman said, scuttling to catch up with her.

'Married means married; engaged; ring, you know?' She made a sign of putting a ring in her own finger. 'Where were you? You don't know about this?'

Arman grabbed her arm and stopped. 'Please, tell me what happened. No, I don't know anything about it.'

'Listen, I haven't heard anything from her since, okay?' She freed her arm and continued walking. 'Three months ago,' she continued, 'this guy had visited from America. Some family of hers. A businessman or something. They met, fell in love and married and she was gone. Puff. Disappeared. All that in a few weeks. Really less than a month. I went to their wedding. But that was it. She didn't even visit the school anymore. Not even to say goodbye to anyone. Not even to me.'

'That's unbelievable,' Arman said and stopped again, holding his head in his hands.

'Are you coming?' the girl said, watching him over her shoulder, rolling her eyes.

Arman trotted after her, held her arm again and looked at her, whole his body shaking. 'Didn't she ever say anything about me? I mean since—'

'Not really. She was very secretive, man. She never told me

anything about you. I mean I knew something. But how would I know when she kept it all secret?'

Arman took a deep breath and let out a loud sigh. He looked round. The desert empty and quiet. It had now become much hotter. The sun was tilting towards the middle of the sky, shining right on him. He was sweating.

Should he go to the Guard and see if he could add something to his stories? Would that even be possible? But better leave it. It was maybe too late anyway. Instead, he went into the tent, drank a large gulp of water, then lay down and started fanning himself with a piece of cardboard. He should think about something cheerful. But he only remembered his prolonged grief and the void the news of Lady Artist had left inside him. Even her invisible presence had left him after a while.

Someone who had helped him to recover from the loss was Comrade Songbird who would gradually take the place of Lady Artist in his mind.

In the week before Arman was released from prison, he began to know a young inmate in his mid-twenties from his own city, and in a few days they had become friends. None of them expected that Arman would be released. At least not so soon. The young man even told him he didn't think he would ever be released, as nothing was more threatening to the ruling party than the young people. He himself had been arrested a year ago, accused of plotting against the party, and more specifically plotting to harm the President's family directly. This was true, the Plotter himself admitted. Part of it, he corrected himself. Not the family part, he said smiling, then immediately corrected himself again. Actually, part of that part was also true, he had said, puzzling Arman.

The Plotter explained what he meant, as he could now trust Arman. He said that he had observed Arman since the beginning and sometimes overheard him when talking to others and during the few times they'd had a quick chat or said hello. So he had proved to himself where Arman stood, and now knew his good nature, as he put it.

'One thing I'm exceptionally good at is seeing through people,' he had said, making Arman wince, though he tried his best to hide his unease.

'But don't feel intimidated. I'm not creepy. I just see through you, as you can see. That's all,' he had said, putting his hand on Arman's shoulder in the way an old wise man would do, scaring Arman even more.

Arman now stared at the strange young man and didn't even dare to swallow.

Because he now trusted Arman, the Plotter had said, he could tell him that a few years ago, when he was only just twenty, he had formed a clandestine group of youngsters, boys and girls, mainly students, as he then was himself. He was a second year Physics student at the university. 'You heard of quantum physics?'

Arman shook his head.

'I didn't think so,' the Plotter had said. But that didn't matter, he had reassured Arman. That had nothing to do with his plots. 'I just didn't think it was a sensible subject to study in this country. I already knew more than my teachers. Just from reading on the internet, you know. I was hoping that one day I could study abroad.'

The group, he explained, consisted of young students who thought that the current politics in the Region and all the intellectual talk and other efforts could not change anything. At least not for the young. Other kinds of action were needed. The best would be an armed resistance, just as the old times, as the present rulers had done in the past against the regime of the time, the Plotter explained. But as this was, of course, difficult these days, they were planning other methods to disturb the situation: to sabotage the course of events, so to speak.

'So you were actually rebels,' Arman said.

'Not exactly. Not yet. But that had to happen at some point. I don't know what they are doing now. I have lost contact, as you see.'

By the time he was arrested, the Plotter said, there were about twenty-five members, and the group was growing. But keeping the secrecy of the group was the most sacred thing that they all had to preserve. It must be with their lives, literally. As he had proven. He was tortured for weeks but hadn't said one word about anyone, he said, showing Arman the traces of some of his wounds. The Doctor had treated him too.

If he had told on one of his comrades, half of the group would have been in danger, he said. He then explained how he had structured the group so that he himself had contact with only two others, who also had contact with another two and those only contacted each another two, and so on. That way there were various clusters so that, if anyone were to be arrested and give way under torture, they could choose to tell on only one of their contacts and in that way bring danger only to one cluster. Each cluster had, at some point, to stop growing, so that the last person would have contact with only the one who had recruited him or her. He himself had the code names of everyone but only knew the two whom he had personally recruited. The three of them were the Leadership of the group, who had to decide about operations. Others could pass along information via their contacts or suggestions for action but had to wait until the Leadership had decided.

They had started with an operation that the Plotter himself wanted to carry out before he was arrested. The idea was to keep the group small until they had done a few operations, then they would head for the mountains where all of them would meet and begin the rebellion and, of course, recruit more members.

His plot, which he had planned with both his comrades, the Leadership team, was to cause a split in the ruling party. 'I know it might sound very ambitious for a bunch of teenagers, well I was twenty-four myself by then, but it could really work. We had planned it so very well.'

Arman had stared at him, waiting for him to explain what the plan was. But the Plotter must have thought he was not buying the story, for he started telling him about all kinds of things that perplexed Arman even more.

'Look, through history many physicists and other scientists have been involved with revolutions and defying dictators. You know, one of Germany's godlike scientists—oh, by the way, the very man who had thought of this quantum thing I told you about. His son was put in prison and tortured and finally executed for been accused of planning to kill Hitler. I'm not sure if his father's quantum theory had anything to do with that, but that's not the point. You see, scientists and their offspring can also become heroes and revolutionaries.'

Arman, still staring, nodded.

The Plotter smiled, paused for a moment, then explained how his own conspiracy had landed him in the soup. He was supposed to go to the Region's Capital and make a start with the plot. He was good with computers and a skilled hacker. The plan was to create several social media accounts for fans of a few of the most senior politicians in the party, including the President's son and nephew. These two were already rivals as was well known to everyone. Some senior leaders in the party were either affiliated or hostile to one of these two, or they were secretly at odds with the whole Family. The Plotter would run the accounts and make sure that they achieved large numbers of followers. He would then also create dozens of accounts for fake followers who would spread rumours about the politicians and stir disputes. After a year or so, they would think about the second stage. One option was to assassinate one of those senior politicians and then spread rumours that the other camp had done it. Or perhaps just fake an assassination attempt. This part of the plot was yet to be decided at the time that the group would finally be based in the mountains.

Arman was staring at the young man with his mouth agape. Was this guy bluffing or was he confused? Maybe all the beating and torture had made him mad.

'I'm serious,' he whispered, peering into Arman's eyes.

Arman winced. The guy really could read his mind.

'They caught the whole plan on my laptop,' the Plotter continued. 'I might read minds and see through you. And I was intelligent enough to put together a group of opposition to this powerful dynasty. Nonetheless, I was apparently so stupid that I hadn't been careful enough to keep the plot secret. And what's a plot if it's not secret? You know what it is? It means that I might well have to spend the rest of my life in this dungeon.'

'But how did they find it?' Arman asked, still perplexed about the whole matter.

'And as stupid as I am, I travelled to the Capital in a passenger taxi with the plot on my laptop. I had done a little quick work on it when we stopped on the way for lunch at a roadside restaurant and shut the laptop without turning it off or at least closing the Word document about the plot. When they stopped us at the checkpoint at the entrance to the city, they asked me politely if I'd open the laptop and log in. The first thing the officer saw, a clever guy, was the plot. He read it first out of curiosity, maybe. Then he came to the plans and the names of the Family and other politicians, and scrolled down… Yes! Then he was shocked.'

Arman thought he heard something. He crawled to the entrance of the tent. The Guard had already drawn down the blind and was walking behind the glass wall to the bus stop. Arman pulled in his head again and crawled back to his mattress. The old man must be happy. Maybe he had written a good deal of his book and was now going to share his excitement with his wife and daughter. They must be so proud of him. But here, Arman did not even have a pen to write down his thoughts. And even if he had a pen, he had no paper to write on it. Oh, yes, he had one piece.

He took out the rejection paper, unfolded it, and looked at it. If only he could read it. He could, of course, read the letters but could not make out the meaning of the words. He would do his best to learn the language when they finally let him in. They must let him in at some point. They must let him in. What else? He flipped the paper and stared at its plain back. He could use that if he had a pen.

21

Friday morning, Arman gave the Guard time to settle in and come out of his morning sulk. Though he had woken up very early, he remained in bed, wrapped up in both blankets. If there was a decision on his claim, the man would call him. Better to wait. But could he wait? Since the Guard had left yesterday afternoon, Arman had been waiting for the morning to come to run to the hut. Not only for news about his claim, but also a little conversation with the old man would have been heartening. The presence of the old man behind the glass gave him a feeling of homely comfort. Even when he was not allowed to interrupt him. And, oh, the weekend, he even didn't want to think about it. Better not worry about the two days he was going to spend in total isolation.

Actually, didn't the old man give meaning to his very existence in this secluded desert? He remembered Plotter had once tried to explain the importance and the use of this quantum mystery. He had said something like if no one saw him, he simply didn't exist. And it all made sense—he had tried to convince Arman of the logic of the theory, while poor Arman had to listen with his eyes wide open and his mind in disarray. The very prison they were in was the proof for the theory, the Plotter had claimed. The fact that no one saw them and didn't even know of the prison, meant they just didn't exist. Only for the outside world, that is, he corrected himself. Because the inmates, and the guards, did see one another and therefore existed for each other. But that was not the point, he had said.

So, now Arman was not more than particles and matter and all the stuff Plotter had said. He existed solely for the Guard who was the only person to see him.

The Plotter had made Arman as obsessed as he himself was about this theory, so much so that Arman had dreamt of release from the prison if for nothing else than to pursue his schooling and go to university to read quantum physics—which was the only word, the only thing that had lingered with him from all the fancy words and subjects Plotter and later his comrades in the mountains bragged about all the time.

But wasn't it actually better if he studied for space travel, were they to finally let him into the City behind the glass? There must be some schooling for that. For wasn't it better just to leave this planet and go one day to live on another? He had once heard or seen on TV that one of his favourite actors, Tom Cruise, had signed up to go to Mars. That meant that you either had to be super rich or study for it.

Hey, did he hear a muffled clanging? Or had he imagined it in the silence? Was the Guard perhaps leaving? Already?

He dashed out of the tent and saw the old man behind the glass wall outside his hut banging on the wall, and then again on the iron door of his hut. Arman heard or imagined hearing a very muffled clang again. What had made the man so upset? He was now kicking the glass wall; the mirror on his side. Then, when he seemed to be exhausted, the old man raised both his hands in the air and was clearly shouting. Just as Arman did sometimes when he was extremely angry.

He stood there observing the Guard, knowing the man could not see him. That was the first time he saw the Guard behave this way. Maybe he had heard some bad news. About his family, maybe? Or his outrage could just be because he was unable to write today. He was not a writer anyway. Did he expect it to be an easy job? Arman had so many times tried to write poetry but could never succeed half as well as Grandma. Actually, the task of writing down the poems of that illiterate old woman was much easier than that of thinking them for himself. It's not so easy, old man, is it?

The Guard now opened the iron door and entered his small office, shaking his head.

Arman quickly ran back into his tent. He waited another ten minutes, then strolled towards the hut and greeted the Guard.

The old man replied with a brisk glance and lowered his eyes to the keyboard. He wasn't typing though. He looked as though he was stuck with his story. It was so obvious.

'Shall I leave you in peace to…?' said Arman, turning to leave.

'No, Arman, hold on a second,' shouted the Guard.

Arman looked back at him, frowning. Did he want him to help with something? Or was it about Arman? Was there maybe…?

'The decision on your asylum has arrived,' said the Guard, still not looking at him.

'It's bad, isn't it?'

'Let me just read it to you,' the Guard said, now looking at him with a lazy smile, then closed his eyes.

'They've rejected me. I can see it in your face,' said Arman, frozen to the spot.

The Guard said no more, stood up in a formal way, picked up a piece of paper from his desk, pushed back his glasses on to his nose and started reading:

Dear Arman,
We regretfully inform you that your second asylum claim has been rejected. Although we acknowledge...

Arman breathed deeply, then sighed, sagging down along the glass, and sat listless.

...that you and your family have endured a significant amount of hardship and dire economic conditions, however, economic adversity and misfortune cannot legitimise political refugee status.

It wasn't even a human voice telling him. It wasn't the Guard. It was a clang, metallic gibberish nonsense; he wasn't even sure if it had been translated accurately. But did that matter?

And the fact that you personally were not involved in any of the events your father went through, as described in your claim, these events...

Arman put his head in his hands, his elbows on his knees. He knew what was coming.

...by no means entitle you to refugee status, without which you

will not be allowed to enter our country. Thus, the gate cannot be opened for you.

Arman breathed heavily, leant his head back on the glass and shut his eyes.

You are advised to go back to your country of origin. However, our law grants you the right to appeal against this decision within one week. You are allowed to submit a new asylum claim on new grounds. During the period of your appeal, you will retain the right to humanitarian aid to be delivered to your current location at regular fortnightly intervals.

After a few moments' silence on both sides, Arman shook his head. He remained sitting. Better not to be upset. He should control himself at least. What could the Guard do? Poor old man was himself angry about the decision. And hadn't he warned Arman so many times? He had really done his best. And he had kicked the glass wall, their own mirror, on his behalf, hadn't he?

'Can I at least make a request for some more stuff I need?' Arman finally said, standing up, looking at the Guard with a forced smile. 'I especially need a pen and a notebook.'

'Oh, of course! I'm going to write them down, right away,' said the Guard, and his face glowed; relief gleamed in his grey-blue eyes. He sat down with a bump in his chair and started to type. 'So a pen and notebook, and… Tell me your list, come on! And, oh, yes, I forgot. So we're submitting an appeal, right?'

'Well, I guess so,' said Arman, still numb from the bad news. 'I've actually still lots more to tell. I have—'

'Let's do the stories on Monday, Arman. I'll submit a short appeal now. Then the new asylum request on Monday, okay? So what else do you wish them to provide for you?' said the Guard, holding his head askew on his own great shoulder, staring at Arman with his joyous eyes. He looked like a huge fat, bald baby with glasses, waiting excitedly for Arman to reward him or to praise him for accomplishing a small task such as eating his fruit puree or forcing a laugh or something like that.

The old man had maybe not been happier than this in a long time. What did he think? He must have been worried that Arman… What? What could he do? Kick the glass wall? Could that make it better? Or maybe the old man was worried Arman would hurt himself? Why would he do that? There was no need for that at all. The desert heat will kill him sometime soon, anyway.

22

Waiting for Monday to come, that weekend passed the most slowly of all those Arman had endured confined to the desert. He spent the time mainly in his tent fighting the heat and in the cool of late afternoons he sat at the glass wall watching the world on the other side. Or he would have a jog along the glass wall. Then cook dinner and go through the evening, with a cup of strong tea in his hand, by the light of the torch or the ashes in a fire pit, contemplating life in the City over there, on the far side of the lake.

On Friday early afternoon, after the Guard had gone home, Arman walked away from the wall, past his tent, into the desert. When he was out of the shadow of the wall, he walked another twenty metres into the sunlight, then took off his shoes and clothes and dug a hole his own length. He lay down in the trench and covered himself with sand. He pushed his hands and arms into the sand and wriggled his shoulders until they were almost completely buried. Absolutely alone. Only his head and neck stuck out of the sand; all he could see was little sand dunes nearby with a few larger hills farther off. The vast sky above enclosed his view of the desert in the shape of a cupola. In the heat of the sand, in the middle of the celestial sphere, Arman imagined that he was stuck in a huge pan of broth covered with an azure dome-shaped lid. Spine-chillingly claustrophobic. And his breathing was becoming heavier under the pressure of the sand.

Just as he wanted to jump out of the sand and run away, back to the tent, a little black beetle captured his attention. The insect was struggling to clamber up the mound of sand that had heaped over Arman's body. He lifted his head a bit to gaze better. The little beast was moving backwards, with its forelegs on the ground and its hind legs lifted up, pushing a round ball of something... eww, it was dung. But of what? Aha, maybe it was the jackal's. Or... oh, gosh, was it Arman's own? Shouldn't he really jump out of the sand? But he now had company, why ruin it? Better wait and see if the beetle could manage to push the dung to the top. It was moving so easily.

Arman puffed as vigorously as he could and blew the little insect away. The dung rolled back down the mound. The beetle ran after it, jumped on it and rolled it until it found the right position, then started to push the dung once more up the hillock on Arman's body.

'I'm sorry, little shithead! I'll let you do your job now,' Arman said, bowing his head and cracking his neck that hurt from bending.

He lifted his head again. The beetle had reached the top of the hill. What now? Rolling down? And indeed, the little insect rolled down with the ball of dung to the opposite side of Arman's body. It then pushed its treasure away up to a small dune, at arms' length from Arman, but twice as high as the mound over Arman's body. The beetle started the upward push again. This time, it went with a bit more struggle, as the sand was less firm, so the ball became stuck. The insect needed to reposition itself and then push harder. But halfway up the dune, it rolled back down.

'Shall I give you a hand or do you want to try again? Come on! Try once more. Let's see.'

The beetle took its steady position anew and pushed again. Halfway up, it was struggling. So Arman put out his arm and gave it a little shove to the top.

'I would have squashed you at once if you had appeared in my room, back home. With the sole of my slipper,' he mumbled, watching how the beetle rolled down to the other side with its dung, and out of sight.

Staring at the dune and the sudden void the insect had left, Arman thought about the rejection letter, for the first time since the Guard had read it to him. Did they really think they had taken a fair decision? How could these people be so cruel? It's true that his own government and leaders were far more brutal, but had he been wrong to think that in this country they would pity him and give him a chance of a better life? Nothing more than a life a little more secure and safe. That is all he would expect from them. Honestly, what did these people think? Did all his misery and hardship, all that his family had endured, mean nothing to them? What did that suggest? Was it so much more grim, more dreadful, in their country that Arman's suffering was just an amusement compared to their own misery? Because otherwise... What was really in their minds? And it was true that Arman had not been a part of his father's adversity. But was it so difficult to understand that all that trouble had affected his own life as well as Father's? His eyelids got heavier and slowly shut. It was all a sordid business. A sordid business.

He woke up shivering under the sand that had now cooled down significantly in the extended shadow of the wall. What on earth he was doing here under the sand? Oh, yes, of course! Sandbathing. But now, time to go home.

He lifted himself out of his sand bath, brushing himself down as he stood up. Part of the glass wall came in sight far away. He scattered the sand out of his long hair and little beard and dressed quickly. He might as well go further, deeper into the desert. Just for a change. But what if he lost his way? Probably he wouldn't. By now, he could orientate himself fairly well in the desert. He looked into the dark sky and saw the shiny star that was larger than the rest, still low in the horizon. That was east and the City was in the west. So it was now still early evening. Around midnight, the star would come to the middle of the sky and then fade away, losing its brilliance amid a million other stars. It was then much more difficult to tell which way was east and which was west. But usually, he barely moved away from his tent at night, except a few metres for a pee or a hundred metres or so for a bowel movement.

The star had helped him orientate himself when he crossed the desert in the beginning coming here. That was one occasion all those stories he had heard from Grandma and Mother coming to his rescue. About young boys or girls taking on a perilous journey following stars.

Arriving at the tent, he took out the last bit of coal he had left, made a fire and cooked some rice and sauce from a tin. He should be trying to cook something else as well. All these beans and lentils that still remained. But he left them for next time.

After dinner, he wrapped himself in a blanket and sat beside the small pit with the glowing ashes, in the soft breeze of the evening, staring at the world behind the glass wall, sipping his strong, sweet tea. Hundreds of thoughts stormed through his mind, but none lingered. Until one did. Songbird appeared, almost visible, sitting beside him at the embers. He prodded the glowing coals with the fire tongs they had provided for him in the last pack. He lifted the lid from the teapot. 'Would you like some?' he asked Songbird's apparition with a smile, then poured himself another cup.

Three months after his release from prison, Arman had still not been able to work again with his father and brother, as he was still in grief over losing his girlfriend and was recovering from the ordeal of confinement and all that had happened to him. Until one day he remembered the Plotter's comrade, the Geek.

A few days before he was released, Plotter had given him the name and address of one of his comrades. He was a computer geek, as the Plotter had called him. 'But he's a real geek, I'm telling you,' he had emphasised. Arman didn't really know what that was, but never mind. He knew it was not as bad as it sounded. The Plotter had said that his comrade was not very good at human contact and relationships, but he was a genius at hacking and other computer techniques.

When Arman rang the bell, he was shaking and thought of leaving. He could actually run as fast as he could, so that they would never be able to call him back or follow him. What was he doing here, in such an up-market neighbourhood? Why would a boy from this rich part of the city even think about opposing the political establishment?

He slowly took a step back and was about to leave the doorstep when the door opened. His throat dried. His face burning from heat. A woman, maybe the Geek's mother, asked him who he was looking for. Arman stuttered. He didn't know how to say that name. And what should he say if she asked why he wanted to speak to her son? Luckily, at that point the Geek himself appeared behind the woman and asked Arman politely to step in so that they could talk in the garden.

A week later, Comrade Geek introduced Arman to a girl, only a year older than he. The Geek explained that the girl he was going to meet was now the second-highest in the ranks of the Organisation, as he called it. They sat in an isolated corner of a café, just as Arman used to do when meeting his girlfriend Lady Artist. Geek started to tell him about the Organisation, but suddenly raised his head and stared at the door of the café.

Arman was under the spell of this young woman from the moment she came in. Her gait and the confidence with which she arrived at the table and approached Arman captivated him— shoulders held back, head raised, her slender neck ornamented with a black leather choker with a small gold ring.

The Geek jumped up, and Arman followed suit.

'Hello Arman, please sit,' she said with a firm but elegant smile. 'I'm sorry, can't tell you my name,' she said, sitting down, followed by Geek, then Arman.

'None of our comrades knows it. They call me Songbird. Comrade Songbird.'

She ordered Arabic coffee, while Geek and Arman both had cola. Arman again told his story of the prison and of how he had met Plotter. Then, when Geek left half an hour later, Comrade Songbird told Arman about the Organisation and how it now worked.

Following Plotter's arrest, the group had suspended all activities. Then after a few weeks, when there was no trace of Plotter, the main person who had been his first contact and part of the Leadership, took over the role of leader, as he was the oldest. But they all preferred to call him the coordinator rather than leader, Songbird said. And so the Coordinator had suggested it was time for the group to take action and become more active.

The Coordinator had arranged for all the members, young men and women, to meet secretly somewhere in the mountains. He had contact with the guerrillas who had for decades enjoyed the sanctuary of the rugged terrain of sheer mountains and steep wooded valleys. Arman said he knew about the guerrillas and that he had even met one of them in the prison. This was the Doctor who had treated both Arman and Plotter.

'That's good then. You're up to date about things,' Comrade Songbird said, then continued with her story. There, in the mountains, somewhere hidden among the bases of the guerrillas, the rebellious girls and boys had met. They had stayed for a few days and had finally decided that the mountains were the place for anyone who could afford a gun and was convinced that fighting for their belief in revolution was more important even than family, school and comfortable city life. The Coordinator was, of course, the first to decide to stay.

By now, she said, there were about thirty of them in the

mountains. They had their own base, while some twenty underground members had been left in the city. They had also managed to recruit a few like-minded supporters in the Region's Capital.

As for Comrade Songbird herself, she had continued her university study of political sciences and coordinated the clandestine part of the Organisation in the city, using the same structure of clusters that had been planned by the Plotter. Arman must join the armed movement in the mountains, if he desired to be part of the Organisation, said Songbird, 'which of course you do, I bet.' She had decided for him already.

'Oh, yes, of course,' Arman said, still spellbound by this enchanting student in her lavender hoodie. Her jet-black hair was tightly tied in a simple ponytail, and she wore light make-up aside from bright red lips that left a ring of colour on her cigarette butt in the ashtray. Her fingernails were the colour of her lips.

'So let's leave. It's not good to be seen for long in public together,' she said, standing up.

Arman stood up, but Songbird stopped him halfway, indicating that he should sit down again. 'Better if you leave ten minutes after me.'

'Can I ask you a last question then?' Arman put both hands on the table and bent forward.

Songbird nodded, raising her eyebrows, waiting.

'Are they using the weapons to attack?' Arman whispered.

'Oh, no, don't worry! It's only for self-defence,' she whispered back, turning to leave.

'Are you carrying one?' Arman asked, still whispering.

Songbird turned her head and gave him a reproachful

over-shoulder gaze and walked off.

Arman sat down and watched her walk jauntily past the other tables. She gave the waiter a smile and waved goodbye. At the door, she turned and caught Arman's eyes, shook her head and mouthed: 'No!'

That night Arman experienced again the presence of Songbird as real as anything else in the desert around him. In fact, he now doubted the existence of the real things around him. The glow of the cinders in the fire pit. The moon, now at its height, brightening the desert. He couldn't believe that anything that was going on in the desert, or the wall itself or even the Guard, were actual and for real. But the aura of Songbird, the warmth of her proximity, was as real as the blood that flowed through his own veins. He tucked the blanket around his legs and closed his eyes. 'Are you staying for the night, Songbird?'

23

The next morning, Arman woke to a screeching and squeaking. It sounded like… birds. He listened more attentively, holding his head up, askew. They were indeed birds. He crawled to the tent mouth, zipped open the flap and rushed outside. Shading his eyes with his hand, he looked up. A swarm of birds high in the sky, twirled and swayed in a group. A thick grey mass, changing shapes. They then funnelled, in the shape of a tornado, plunging down onto the desert, then flew low, all together, skimming the sand. Hovering for a moment, they formed a mass again and looped in the air, coming closer. They were swallows. Arman heard the flapping of their wings merging with their screeching.

Suddenly, a falcon appeared in the sky above, floating. It swooped down on the birds, cutting through them. The swallows spread in stunning unison, veered off instantaneously, then looped higher in the sky, outflying the falcon. Many of them hit the glass wall. Arman's jaw dropped. He watched how the falcon took off again, without a catch, into the air and flew high up along the glass wall to perch on top of it. A dark threatening shadow high up there.

Some of the swallows had fallen wounded at the foot of the glass wall. God, so many of them! And the jackal had now appeared, jumping around, trying to catch a writhing swallow that struggled to fly away.

'Hey, cut it out, little bastard! Leave them. Let them alone,' Arman yelled at him and ran towards the injured birds. Some were apparently dead already, some thrashed around, chirruping.

The falcon dived down again, with its claws wide open, grabbed one of the birds and swooped high up into the sky. It disappeared just as swiftly it had come.

The rest of the flock had now gathered in the air. They twirled once, then veered and passed over the glass wall, entering the world of the other side.

The jackal tore another swallow apart and ran a few metres away from Arman to bite at the bird, trying to eat it. Then left it and jumped on another.

'You're just a fucking wild beast. You stinky little shit,' Arman shouted, shaking his head. He looked round, not knowing what to do. What would Grandma or Mother have done if they had seen this carnage? These were birds from heaven, they would say. Holy birds. Saints.

Arman was shivering, but made a move and picked up two of the injured birds, nestled them in the crook of his elbow and, while the birds thrashed in his arm, he picked another one, put it on top of them, then another one, and ran into the tent.

He put the wounded birds down on the mattress, then quickly made a nest-like loop with one of his blankets and put the chirping swallows inside it. He ran out to the rest of the birds, scared away the jackal with a hard kick in the sand, then searched among the dead birds for any left alive. He could find only two more.

Back in the tent, he poured water in a pan, then washed the

blood from the birds' heads and beaks and bodies. He held them one by one over the pan and let them drink. Only one really drank the water. They were fluttering and flapping, escaping his clutch, twittering, swinging their little heads around.

The jackal stood at the tent opening, staring at Arman.

'Hey, you stay away from them, you bloody wild beast! Otherwise, I'll deal with you. No friendship anymore!'

The jackal bared its teeth, snarling, but remained in its place, staring at Arman and the birds inside the blanket-nest. It then put its head down, closing its eyes, still panting from running around.

Arman took out a pitta bread and tossed a piece far away from the jackal, who snapped at it and ran off.

He then pinched little pieces of the bread, dipped them in the water, wet them, kneaded them into balls of dough and put them into the birds' beaks one by one. He had learnt that from Grandma, when she treated injured birds or took care of newly hatched chicks.

He rushed out again, zipped down the flap and went to search among the wounded birds. The jackal was jumping and leaping, biting the dead birds, flinging them around. It then picked up one and went, sat some metres away and ate the little bird.

Arman peered at him with a pout. 'I'm sorry for being so cruel to you. Of course it's okay for you to eat them or hunt them down. I'd have done the same if they had been other birds.'

Swallows were one of Arman's favourite birds. They used to nest in the ceiling of Grandma's house in the village. They would appear at the beginning of the summer, build their nests bit by bit with mud pellets between the wooden beams that held the adobe roof. They would then brood, raise their chicks until they were grown and able to fly, zooming through the house, build new nests and hang around while the parents bred again. They became part of life in the house and in the village. Until one day, in the fall, they would depart.

Grandma claimed they were the same birds who came back with the entire family every year to nest exactly in the very place they had abandoned the year before and the years before that.

She used to talk to them and ask them about heaven. When the birds left for warmer places far south, on the way they visited heaven, Grandma said. Their chirping all the time was reciting words from God, she explained. But when Arman or the other kids asked what the swallows said or what the God's message was, Grandma would say you only needed to listen with your heart to understand them. They are telling us that we should love each other, have compassion and stick together. Loyal birds as they are.

For the rest of the day, Arman was busy taking care of the wounded swallows. He had put some Vaseline on their wounds and used plasters from the first aid kit he had received with his last care package and wrapped the worst wounds with the gauze.

Later, he collected the dead birds, what was left of them from the jackal, and buried them a few hundred metres away from his tent, to the south. Twenty-seven of them had died. He sat near their grave, leant on the wall, recalling what had come to pass that morning. How quickly it all happened.

If only Songbird were here now… But she was here, actually. Didn't she sit beside Arman right now, mourning the dead birds, as she used to do in the mountains? She was so good with animals; knew everything about them. She had wished to become a vet. But her wealthy parents—her mother a university lecturer and her father a lawyer—had talked her into studying medicine. Then after a month of medicine, she had changed to studying politics.

Swallows had also nested in the ceilings of the adobe houses where Arman had lived with the young rebels in the mountains. Though he himself had always loved animals and had often owned various pets, he had learnt to appreciate animals and wildlife even more when he was among the guerrillas and his rebel friends. It was indeed the guerrillas who had made it possible for the group of young rebels to establish their base in the heart of the mountains. They supported the rebel girls and boys and taught them how to live in the wild. How to cooperate, train and exercise, become tougher and rougher and nourish ideas and ideologies that would ultimately enable them to become guerrillas themselves. And that was the ambition of Arman and his comrades.

When he had first arrived at the Base with Songbird, each on the back of a mule, Arman was mesmerised to see all those animals, domestic and wild, stroll in the courtyard and between the houses and even inside the rooms at the Base, which in itself appeared to be a small village. A village in which the inhabitants were only city girls and boys; this was Arman's first impression, anyway.

Songbird took him there. It was her idea that Arman would be more useful to the group in the Base than as a member of the clandestine part of the Organisation in the city, where he lacked the necessary sophisticated knowledge and skills. After their first meeting, they had met a couple more times until one day she told him to prepare for the trip.

They travelled in a local passenger taxi and paid the full fare to the Region's Capital, as they would have triggered the curiosity of the other three passengers and the driver had they said they needed to stop at a remote spot. They also behaved as if they didn't know each other and sat in the back row with an old man between them. In the front row, beside the driver, sat a young couple.

On the way, Arman told the old man that he was a construction worker who had missed every opportunity to finish school. There was in fact no opportunity to miss, he had said. And now, he was going to the Capital because there was more construction work over there.

When they arrived at a bridge that hovered high over a stormy river in the early spring, Songbird asked the driver to let her off, just on the other side of the bridge, where there was a narrow path that led to the villages hidden in the depths of the densely forested mountains.

'Are you going over to the guerrillas?' the driver asked through the clang of the wobbly old iron bridge under the tyres of his car that bumped over the rutted tracks. 'You already look like one of them.'

'Oh, no, I'm visiting family in this village...'

'Huh!' snorted the driver, interrupting her, while looking at her in the rear-view mirror. 'They all say that.'

As soon as the car halted, Songbird jumped out, put her small rucksack on her shoulder and hurried to the road.

Before the driver had a chance to pull away, Arman opened the door on his side and said, 'Actually, I'm getting out here as well.'

The old man stared at him stunned. Also the young couple turned to look at Arman.

The driver got out too, rushed to the back of his car, opened the boot for Arman to take out his large backpack. 'Take care you guys,' he said, while shutting the boot. 'I'm not sure if you've made the right choice. But, honestly, those guys are amazing. They're real, you know. They're real. Not like us. I'm working my ass off. For what? To feed three little bastards? My older son, your age, barely even calls me. And my daughter, I don't even know exactly in which country she's ended up.'

Arman put his backpack on his shoulders and said goodbye. Songbird was waiting for him impatiently at the narrow dirt road. As he walked towards her, the old man stuck his head out of the window and shouted, 'Hey, you little liar, you took me for a ride.'

The driver got behind the steering wheel, shut the door and started the engine.

The old man shouted again, 'I hope you two don't waste your lives over there. But you will. You will. I'm telling you.' He then rolled up the window, while the car lurched forward, roaring away.

Arman and Songbird shrugged, then turned and took the path.

On the way, Arman asked Songbird if people already knew about their rebel group. No, she said. The driver and the old man were referring to the guerrillas, she explained.

The guerrillas were members of Songbird and Arman's own People who lived in another neighbouring country in the north. The country of the Megalomaniac President the Wanderer had mocked. The man who was trading in refugees. But the guerrillas, that was the thing about them, they accepted fighters from any part of the nation. And that was also the reason many of the younger generation in Arman's own Region were eager to join them. To the discontent and outrage of the Region's ruling party and the Family, who sometimes clashed with the guerrillas and often helped the forces of the Megalomaniac President to attack them. The guerrillas had taken position in the most impossible, rough mountains of the Region for the past few decades, hiding in the many immense, robust caves and self-built villages that were well concealed in the thick green vegetation.

After an hour's walk over rough terrain, up the mountain, then down to a valley, with Arman bent under the weight of his backpack, they came to a large village where followers of the guerrillas lived in peace with followers of the autonomous Region's ruling party and other political groups. It had become a hub for trade between both sides and enabled shopping for the remote villages. The guerrillas would find anything they needed from the cities, and they sold in return many varieties of rare vegetables, or the best and cleanest river fish, to the villagers or city folk who visited the area. It was also the last local village with a police station. The rest of the villages in the depth of the mountains were in the hands of the guerrillas.

Songbird didn't want to be seen there, so she waited behind a little hill among dense bushes, just above a creek. She indicated to Arman to keep quiet, then scanned the area. When she was sure all was well, she beckoned Arman to follow, while she ran down the hill, jumped over a stone in the creek, then immediately entered a small house that was almost hidden among a dozen thick trees. Arman behind her, with his backpack bumping over his back. She took out her smartphone and made a call.

Half an hour later, a man with three mules, brought food. After they had eaten, they mounted the mules and rode on.

The sure-footed beasts knew their way instinctively, so did not fall from even the narrowest of paths that cut the mountain slopes high up, slithering down through the forest, to climb again another mountain. Arman didn't dare to look down.

'These animals are called mountain taxis,' Songbird said, riding on the mule behind Arman. She had probably noticed his fear. In front of them, the owner of the mules, riding his own animal, sat careless, smoking his roll-up in a hand-made wooden bidi holder.

After about five hours' bumpy ride over rugged terrain on the back of the mules, they arrived late in the afternoon at the Base. They tethered the mules in the shade. Arman took his backpack from the back of his mule and waited for Songbird to lead him in.

There stood a deer on its frail legs, its fawn beside her, staring back at Arman, perhaps recognising that he was a stranger. Arman couldn't hide his broad smile and excitement; his heart beating out of his chest. They had even domesticated a deer!

'She is a gift from the guerrillas,' Songbird said, holding Arman's arm, dragging him through the courtyard into one of the rooms to meet the group's leader, the Coordinator. She greeted the comrades who were doing chores around the court. Two of them, a boy and a girl, were busy kindling a large fire in a corner. Two enormous pots lay by the fire, utterly covered in soot. A metre from the fire, a girl sat on a tree trunk chopping tomatoes and courgettes; a basket of groceries beside her. The smell of burning wood welcomed Arman, who by now was starving from the long hours of bumping and jolting on the back of the mule.

Songbird stayed only three days. Enough for Arman to fall completely in love with her. She shared a room with three other girls, while Arman settled in with four boys in another room in one of the four houses at the Base.

The houses had been built by the comrades themselves, with help from the guerrillas and local villagers. The villagers and mule owners had also assisted them bringing their belongings and all that they needed to furnish their houses. All financed by the young rebels themselves. By their families, in fact.

The majority of them were sons and daughters of well-off families in the city, though there were a few less well-off supporters also. Arman one of them. But all that their families knew of their whereabouts was that they had joined the guerrillas. It was more acceptable for the ruling party that the youth of the Region joined the guerrillas to fight for a long-held dream of liberation for the entire nation than to form their own group to topple the party or undermine the rule of the Family.

None of the members had told their families or anyone else about their Organisation. Nor had Arman. All new arrivals had to hand over their mobile phones and destroy the SIM cards.

Only the Coordinator had kept a phone with an unregistered SIM card for essential communication, especially for contact with the members of the clandestine part of the group. The phone was also the means of contact with the few trusted villagers and mule owners who helped with logistics.

The rules were set by the Coordinator, who in the meantime had declared himself as Leader. It was he who had established and engineered the mountain wing of the Organisation with the ultimate aim to become an armed group.

The Leader was indeed a civil engineer; the only member who had graduated. He was now twenty-four years of age, so he was the oldest of all the comrades after the Plotter's arrest.

The more members joined the more rooms were built. All in the same design: each house consisted of two large rooms with a wide hallway between them. One end of the hallway formed the entrance, and the other was closed by a wall containing a large alcove for storing boxes of food and other household items. Each room had a small window looking over the courtyard, and a door opening to the hall. On the other side of the large courtyard, opposite to the houses, was a row of three toilets, two shower rooms and a kitchen with shelves and niches in the walls. Both open sides of the yard merged into the trees that spread densely over the mountain from the top summit down to the valley, so that the Base seen from the other side of the valley was nothing but a small fleck among the green in the middle of the mountain.

Every four girls or boys shared a room, sleeping on mattresses on the floor. By the time Arman arrived, there were thirty comrades in the eight rooms—one of which, the largest room, was used as the meeting hall. For now, Leader and his two deputies slept there. Soon two more houses were needed, which Arman, as the experienced construction-worker of the group, would help to build. Hence, he was given the pseudonym Comrade Builder.

Arman stood up and walked back to his tent, dragging his feet through the sand. He regretted so much that he had never dared to confess his love to Songbird. Of course, she knew he loved her. Arman was certain of that. And he was almost sure she loved him too. But he had to tell her that he really loved her. Like love, love. Like he was in love with her. Wanted her. Maybe if he had revealed his love and his yearning for her, they could have become lovers, then married and the horror might never have happened.

Passing the hut, he stopped and looked at his own reflection in the glass where the blind was drawn down, making the glass reflective. His hair and beard were now so much longer. So very different from the mental picture he had of himself. At the Base, he would shave once every few days and cut his hair every three or four months, just as most of his comrades did. Even in prison, they had let them do that occasionally.

He left his own reflection, walked away from the hut, back to the tent, still overwhelmed by thinking about Songbird. The smell of the birds and their droppings had filled the tent. He knelt down at the blanket-nest, stroked the swallows gently and noticed that two of them were dead. The other three began to defend themselves with their wings spread, screeching and threatening to peck.

'Don't be afraid, darlings. I'm not going to hurt you.' Oh, but where was the other one? Arman looked round and heard the fluttering of the missing bird in a corner of the tent, where the groceries were. The bird was trying to hide amongst them.

Arman crawled to the clutter and offered the bird his hand. Its claws were entangled in a net of potatoes. Arman carefully freed its toes while the bird was cheeping and pecking his hand. When the swallow was freed from the net, it jerked over the food and utensils, jumping and flapping, until it was at the mouth of the tent. Before Arman could reach it, the bird took wing. Arman, on all fours, half of his body out of the tent, saw the bird hover over the sand, then with a few swift flaps of its wings rise high, and higher, then loop far into the sky. In a moment, it was only a small dot in the vast azure.

Back with the other birds, Arman removed the two bodies, then fed the other three and gave them water, despite all the jabs and screeches. He cleaned the nest, then grabbed a bottle of water and went to the grave, far from his tent. He buried the two dead birds beside the others. Then walked further south along the glass wall, the water bottle in his hand.

24

On Sunday morning, a peaceful breeze brushed the desert, rippling the sand, blowing the tops of the dunes. It chilled Arman's face, as he sat beside the birds' mass grave, leaning on the glass wall. The last dew drops were evaporating from the glass. His baseball cap shaded his eyes from the languid sunbeams of the early morning.

He had just buried another two swallows. May the last one live. Miraculously, she was the one with the deepest wound, which he had bandaged with the gauze around its feeble chest. She seemed vital and active this morning. Yes, it was a female, he had noticed when he fed her and changed the dressing. These were barn swallows with long, forked tails and chestnut faces, the top of their heads and backs dark cobalt blue. The females had a shorter tail and a chest brighter in colour, while the males had a longer deep-forked tail and more of a yellow-beige chest. He had learnt from Songbird to tell the differences in birds.

Wouldn't it be amazing if the bird should stay and lay eggs, to fill Arman's desert life with the tweeting and warbling of swallows zooming in and out of his tent the whole day through? Maybe he should break his aid box and use a long bar of the wood as a rod, up to one side of the tent, under the ceiling. That's where barn swallows liked to build their cup-shaped nests. But maybe she will just want to fly over the wall to go and nest somewhere in the City. As for now, hopefully he would not need to deal with another burial soon.

The closest Arman had been to a burial of a human was that of one of his comrades in the mountains. Comrade Veggie. He had been hit in an airstrike by the jets of the Megalomaniac President of the neighbouring country, on the way back from shopping in a village half a day away from the Base. Veggie had gone with two other comrades and a mule to carry the supplies. The two other comrades, a girl and a boy, themselves also badly wounded, brought back his shattered body hanging over the groceries on the back of the mule.

Veggie had just turned eighteen, the son of a well-off construction contractor who could have anything he wanted in life but had skipped university to join the young rebels and enjoy friendship and life in the wild, as he used to say. He had sworn to never carry a gun, just as Songbird had done, but he would do anything else to help the welfare of the group. That spring and summer, Veggie had provided almost all the vegetables needed by the members of the group. He knew a lot about growing them, even how to use a greenhouse and how to recycle food waste as fertiliser. He was a passionate vegetarian who was trying his best to convert his comrades, without much success. 'Our society is just not ripe for this,' he would then say, giving up—but tried the next day nevertheless. One thing he regretted about life in this paradise of tranquillity, as he called it, was the lack of the internet and his computer. If he'd had these, he could have shown his comrades so many videos and read out for them so many articles about vegetarianism and how some other nations were making progress in practising it.

'Come on, shut up, spoiled boy!' some of the comrades would say. 'You think we're ignorant? Of course, we know what vegetarianism is, Veggie. Just shut up about it, would you? We have no time for that.' They had all had to give up their computers and internet and their books. No moaning about it. They had a purpose and that could only be achieved if they all focused on that one goal: topple the government before it would become an unbreakable regime. The ruling party. And the Family. Leader couldn't be clearer about that. He reiterated these objectives every day.

If he were honest with himself, Arman didn't understand them much. He knew the main aim of the Organisation and that was why he was there. Though it was more out of revenge, after the prison. But he didn't get the hang of their discussions or the various languages they spoke. Didn't even understand them talking in his mother tongue, especially their debates in the evening meetings. He and a dozen other less educated comrades. They were just listening, mouths open, head swinging from one to another of these geniuses who tried to explain the world to each other. But one thing Arman and his fellow uneducated comrades were good at, was doing as they were asked. They were practical and wondered how this bunch of intelligent school-boys and girls could take down the ruling party. Just a bunch of teenagers and a few in their early twenties, whose total by the summer had reached thirty-nine, after Songbird and a few more had also joined this wing of the Organisation in the mountains.

Before joining them, Songbird had visited the group several times during the seven months Arman was among the rebels. She would stay two or three days. As co-leader, she would discuss with Leader the plans for both the underground wing of the group in the city and the rebel wing in the mountains.

Sometimes, Arman would disappear with Veggie and Songbird for half a day among the trees, down in the valley. Spending time with two obsessed friends, one with plants and the other with animals, was the best entertainment Arman could have in those rough mountains. Listening to someone who knew so much about something, indeed about a lot of things, was mind-blowing for Arman; better than any schooling. These two could talk for hours on end about one single bird or plant, yet Arman would still want to hear more. They would look for eccentric plants and outlandish birds and animals. Though no bird or animal was so peculiar to Songbird and almost no plant was unknown to Veggie who had at least seen them in his encyclopaedias or on the internet.

Songbird would now and then sing sentimental melodies, her husky voice quivering in her throat echoed faintly among the trees and the mountain rocks. Arman could sense the vibration of her voice in his own body, sitting there on a rock, staring at her. 'This is why they named me Songbird,' she said the first time she surprised Arman with her singing. She laughed. And her laugh reverberated through Arman's... through his whole existence, as it felt to him.

The unbearable distance Arman felt in the closeness to

Songbird was especially hard when they were amongst the others. He could not show any admiration for her. He didn't even dare to look at her when the other comrades were around. In the evening gatherings, when after the long talks and discussions she started competing with other comrades who sang as well as she did, Arman felt himself shrinking, sinking through the ground, immersed in his own sweat. Only an occasional gaze and a smile from her would bring him back to this world. She saw him thus. And that was the most important thing for Arman in that remote Base, which even his own family didn't know about.

Just three days after they first arrived there together and Songbird went away, Arman buried himself in his bed and cried for an hour. Two of the girls tried to soothe him, reassuring him that it was normal to miss his family and said that each of them had been in that state in the first days. He couldn't say he wasn't crying for his family; though he would have done if he had not been in love.

Every time Songbird left after a short visit and went back to the city, Arman felt her absence in every corner of the place. And among the trees. It would take a few days before he would get used to life without her again, waiting for her next visit; sometimes three or four weeks later.

That was until the day Geek was arrested because of a stupid mistake he had made when he was hacking social media accounts of a group of followers of the ruling party. Now, Songbird could no longer stay in the city and had to join the armed mountain wing of the Organisation. That was towards the end of the summer.

It soon got colder and there would be snowfall before they

knew it. So they had to be prepared, the guerrillas had advised them. They had to collect wood logs and stock food supplies.

Staring at the desert, Arman breathed deeply. Was that not Songbird's particular perfume he was smelling? She was here, beside him. That was certain.

The sun had become warmer now, shining on his face and bare hands and feet. He crawled to the grave, stroked it for a moment, then stood up and went back to his tent. He knelt down by the blanket-nest and changed the dressing around the swallow's chest. This time, the bird didn't resist. No pecking. Not even a single sound. He cleaned the wound, then wrapped her chest in a new piece of gauze, fed her, gave her water, then sat cross-legged, put the bird on his thigh and petted her tenderly.

He remembered the silence that had overwhelmed the courtyard at the Base and the shock on the faces of all his mates when the two wounded comrades arrived with Veggie's smashed body on the mule.

A comrade had seen them appear from the trees and shouted, running towards them. Then a hubbub and murmur spread fast through the Base. When everyone had gathered in the courtyard, the talk turned into a hum, then a gripping silence dominated the place.

The Leader swaggered towards the wounded comrades and took the mule's reins. Then two other comrades rushed up to take down the body. Songbird and another girl hurried to the two wounded comrades and helped them to the main meeting room where they kept medicine and a first aid kit.

The rest, still petrified, watched in silence the two other comrades lower the body to the ground in front of one of the houses. Arman hunkered down, shivering. Also one of the girls crouched beside him and put her hand on his shoulder. Suddenly a comrade's sobbing broke through the silence. Then moaning and crying and shouting filled the air. The comrades encircled the body, kneeling to stroke and hug their lifeless comrade; Veggie, the most peaceful one of all. He now rested in utmost peace.

The young rebels stood distraught before the body. Then, three comrades wrapped him in a blanket and put him in the middle of a room for all who wanted to mourn him. But they had no idea what to do next with his body. They knew they had to put him in a coffin and bury him. But what were the rituals around it? And where should they find a coffin? They had to make one. The carpenter of the group, Comrade Sculptor—who was actually an artist halfway through his course at the Academy of Arts, but handy with carpentry tools—offered to make one. To start with, they had to cut some branches from the forest. Arman offered to help. But before starting anything, two guerrillas arrived with a shovel and mattock.

The guerrillas, who barely cared about any rituals or tradition, said to bury him as soon as possible. Watching a dead comrade would break the morale of the fighters, they told Leader. He should prepare a good speech and try to boost their morale instead. Mourning was nothing for guerrillas and rebels. And there was no need for a coffin. Martyrs didn't need any conventional or religious affairs, they said, giving the mattock and shovel to the comrades. They then found a good place a few hundred metres from the Base, among the trees, and told the rebels to dig.

Early in the evening, as the desert cooled down and the City on the other side of the glass was enjoying a clear sky in preparation for the spectacle of the sunset to come, Arman kindled fire with the pieces of the box to cook the way they did in the mountains. Still living with the memories of Comrade Veggie, who had also been good at cooking, Arman chopped a large onion and put the slices in sizzling oil. Songbird was there, sitting on the other side of the fire. Arman sensed her. For real. 'I hope it doesn't tickle your eyes as well,' he said, wiping his own tears, then peeled and chopped a few potatoes and fried them in the oil, with onions. He added tomato paste and water and put on the lid.

Where would the Wanderer be now and what did he do? He must be somewhere in the desert hunting wild animals, if there were any to find. Or maybe at the coast, trying to catch a fish, while chased by the coastguard. Or perhaps he had found, somewhere, another group of refugees and had settled in with them. But now Arman was more concerned with his own conundrum: what should he tell the Guard tomorrow? Which part of his story? Should he tell him everything and defame his beloved Region and the leaders of his Folk? But would that even be a good enough story finally to grant him the status of political refugee? Would they care about a bunch of delusional youngsters who thought they could overthrow the ruling party and the most powerful family of their Region? Was this a good enough story on which to risk his last chance? But what did these people want then? What was good enough for them? What did they want to hear? What?

The later it became and the closer he came to tomorrow, the edgier he became. The quicker his heart pounded in his chest. He didn't even enjoy his dinner, as he had expected to do when he so passionately made the fire and cooked in the spirit of Songbird and Veggie. Not even the warmth of the embers in the fire pit and the sight of the twinkling lights of the City could soothe him, as it usually did when he sat there, wrapped in a blanket. Even his strong, sweet tea did not.

The evening breeze was becoming stronger and colder. He wrapped himself tighter in the blanket and drowsily lay down beside the fire pit, with his head right next to the embers. The sooted teapot lay at his side. Sleep was the best strategy for suspending all his worries until it was morning and time to tell his story. He would then be done with it. He yawned and the tears in his half-closed eyes, under his heavy eyelids, blurred the embers into glowing, colourful marbles, topped with flickering little flames. The spitting sparks crackled through the sighing of the wind.

He heard muffled thumps of pounding feet, many of them, or maybe they were hoofbeats rumbling and drumming through… He opened his eyes and saw over the glowing fire the hooves of a dozen horses galloping in the distance, in the haze of dawn, with dust clouds at their legs.

He jumped up and crawled to his tent and stayed there at the entrance staring at the approaching horses. Their rumbling hoofbeats now stomped harder on the sand. He wished he had learnt how to domesticate a wild horse. He could maybe catch one. But it was too late; they were so close, their huge heads rocked up and down, their hooves smashed the sand back and forth as they galloped past him, shrouding him in their dust.

As the horses passed by, their thudding hooves farther and farther away, Arman saw through the sand clouds a huge lion stare at him, panting. Its long hair fluttering in the wind, its strong jaw dangled, baring its large teeth; its immense paws sank in the sand.

The lion made an abrupt move, perhaps to attack him instead of the horses. Arman ran into the tent and quickly zipped down the flap. The swallow was thrashing around inside its blanket-nest, frightened.

Suddenly a heavy blow on one side drew the tent in, but then released it and crashed on the other side. Arman, even more petrified than the bird, looked round but could think of nothing more than wrapping himself in the other blanket and lying down.

The thumping and blows on all sides of the tent became stronger, rocking the tent, until it was pulled out of the ground at one side, revealing Arman and the swallow to the desert and the wind and the sand.

Arman was rolling himself, wrapped in the blanket, still looking for the lion, when he jolted awake, sweating, and saw the silhouette of the tent behind him, with one side ripped out of the ground, fluttering in the wind and the eddying sand. Holding the blanket tighter around his body, he made a great effort to stand up and jump on the tent, just at the moment it was wholly uprooted from the ground, about to fly away.

The sandstorm blew harder and harsher, whining and howling, poured the sand over him and wrapped him up completely in the tent. He could no longer move his arms, nor even lift his head. The sand became heavier and heavier on his body, sinking him into the ground, or so it seemed to him, with his head inside the folds of the tent, hearing now only the muffled whistling of the wind.

25

'Arman, boy... Arman...! Are you there? Arman...!' A familiar voice was calling him, when Arman came round under a heavy weight in the dark. He breathed with difficulty in the cavity where his head had been caught.

'Are you there, mate? Where are you? Where's your tent?' Arman heard the metallic voice of the Guard calling him. But he could not answer nor even move. He must be buried under the sand. A constant crunching over his head, as if someone was removing the sand from him. He shouted, 'Hey!' but his voice was stifled and dead. He sensed the dull light gradually becoming brighter around his face in the small hollow created by the bit of the tent's canvas that wrapped his head.

He mustered his strength and moved his head. Then his body. One of the iron poles under his back and apparently one with its sharp end right at his hip hurt him. He cautiously tried again and managed shifting a little. Then he pushed and wriggled, swinging round until the sand became looser around him. He turned his head to one side. It became lighter inside his space and there was fresher air. The crunching continued, and there appeared two paws, coming in through the sand. Then its head. It was the jackal. Its eyes right into his eyes.

'Oh, Little Friend,' Arman wheezed. 'Are you trying to rescue me? Good boy!'

He breathed more easily now. Another push, moving his shoulders, and he stuck out his head.

The jackal lurched and leapt away.

Arman tried with all his might and managed, despite the poles that restricted his movement, to roll himself on his side, then his stomach. He bent his knees inwards and bowed his head down, then pushed his feet backwards in the sand and pulled himself up. He repeated the movement a few times, then when he at last was out of the sand mound, he rolled himself out of the blanket and the tent that had bound him.

Lying on his back on the blanket and the tent's canvas, panting, exhausted, he opened his eyes. The silhouette of a helicopter hovered very high in the sky above him. It looked much smaller and different from the one that usually delivered his aid. Its roar sounded as though from another world. The jackal was jumping around, sniffing in some of the foodstuff that had emerged.

'Arman, is that you, boy?' the metallic voice shouted again.

Arman looked at the jackal with a lazy smile and mumbled, 'Thanks, friend!' He then rolled on his stomach, and once more curled his knees, disentangled his feet from the blanket and bent his head down in a grovelling position.

'Arman, are you alright, buddy?'

'I'm coming,' Arman said as loud as he could, not sure if the Guard heard him. Or actually if the microphone could sense him. He then gathered his strength, stood up and walked towards the hut over the new dunes that had covered the whole area.

'Oh thank God, you're safe. I've been calling you all morning, madly. I was so worried, boy. No Arman; no tent. What happened?' the Guard said, standing behind the glass, staring at Arman, with a grin that showed the man was relieved. 'I even called Emergency. That helicopter was coming for you.'

Arman lifted his head. The helicopter had already disappeared.

'But before you wish you had stayed there under the sand so they might have landed and taken you up with them to the City, no, they were not allowed to do that. Well, maybe they could give you some treatment or something. But are you doing alright, son?'

'Thanks! I'm okay. I survived once again,' Arman said with a forced smile.

'Did he rescue you?' the Guard nodded to the jackal that was still sniffing around over there.

'He did, my Little Friend. That's what I call him.'

The Guard burst out in a laugh. The metallic voice interpreted it as a harsh 'hahahahahahaha'.

'Oh God, my swallow!' Arman said, turning from the Guard.

'What swallow?' the Guard shouted.

'I'll come back in a minute. I have to check… Oh God!' he said and ran back to where he had been buried a moment ago.

He quickly pulled the tent out from beneath the sand, spread it out hurriedly but only found some of the groceries and his mattress and pillow inside it. He started digging the sand frantically, just as the jackal was doing.

'Do you think she's in there, Little Friend? Under the sand? You must sense it. Do you?'

The jackal dug himself into the sand and gradually disappeared.

'You stay away from her!' Arman shouted and dug here and there, crawling around, but found no trace of the bird. Not even a feather. He found more food and bottles of water. He took a large gulp from one of them, then lay down on his back, panting.

The jackal emerged from the sand with a piece of pitta bread in its mouth.

'You couldn't find her either, huh?'

The jackal ran away with the bread to a safe distance.

'Are we friends now? Or you really don't care?' Arman said, watching the jackal eat the bread. Maybe the beast wasn't even thinking about the swallow, let alone about becoming friends with Arman. Why should it if it couldn't eat him?

Arman stood up, rummaged among the clutter inside the folds of the tent and found more bread and biscuits and tins of cheese. He took the pack of biscuits with a water bottle and walked back to the hut.

Leaning on the glass, Arman told the Guard all that had happened over the weekend. The swallows, the sandstorm and how he had been buried under the sand, wrapped in his demolished tent. He then asked the Guard to start his new asylum claim and sat down as usual, with his back on the glass, while crunching the biscuits, telling his new story.

The keyboard clicked inside the cubicle behind him, faster and more energetic, while Arman was telling about the bloody protests, then his time in prison. The melodious typing sounded as if the Guard had become more enthusiastic about this story. Then it abruptly stopped.

'Why have you been holding this back all this time, man?' the Guard said after a short silence.

Arman stood up and held himself up against the glass, staring at the Guard, who in contrast to Arman seemed lively, probably because Arman had now told a story that could have a chance of success. Was that what the Guard thinking?

'I didn't want to, and I'm still reluctant to badmouth my own people. My leaders,' Arman said, looking down at his own feet.

'But I don't think you need to feel in any way guilty about that.'

'I know,' Arman replied, then sighed, lifting his head. 'But still. It's not easy, man!' He sat down again, took a sip of water and leant back again on the glass.

'Can you tell me more about the prison? What did they do to you?' the Guard asked.

'They hurt me a lot. Really. Only the first few days, though. But it was enough to break me. Lady Artist, you know, my girlfriend, helped me with this a good deal.'

'Wait, Arman,' the Guard interrupted him. 'What do you mean she helped you? You said that no one—'

'Oh, no,' Arman sneered. 'I mean thinking about her. Whenever the pain became unbearable, I'd think about her. She was with me all the time. I mean I felt that she was—'

'Can I suggest something, Arman?' the Guard said. 'Let's keep this invisible girl out of your story, if you don't mind.'

'Oh, is she annoying you?' Arman said, looking up at the Guard with a hesitant smile.

'No, absolutely not. I love her the way you describe her. But it makes things confusing. And these people will look for any excuse, a contradiction or inconsistency to reject your story. You can tell me personally all about her later. But please not in your asylum request, for Christ's sake. Anyway, carry on.'

Arman said he was feeling exhausted and maybe it would

be better if he went to set up his tent again, now it was a bit cooler. The sun had slanted to the other side and the shadow of the glass wall had covered the area where his tent used to stand. The Guard agreed and said it was indeed better to call it a day, reminding Arman that they should finish the story and submit it tomorrow.

26

The tent now stood firm and taut. Arman had made a base ten centimetres down in the sand and erected the structure inside. He had strengthened the canvas all around with a mound of sand. He now lay on his stomach inside the tent, with his head down to his chest stuck out of the entrance. Elbows in the sand, hands under his chin, he stared at the City behind the glass wall. The early evening breeze comforted him under the silver light of the nearly full moon.

Tomorrow will be the day. Thinking and rethinking about what he was going to tell, made him more certain that he was going to win. If not with this story, what else? The Guard would be shocked. If his prison story made him so animated, what would he say when he heard about his rebellion? He had not only joined the rebels but had then also rebelled against the rebels themselves. The Guard would jump off his chair, really. He would throw himself through the glass, hug him, and would then take him in. Into his City, as a victorious hero. He would!

But why would anyone care in that City over there about his rebellion? A teenager. What had he achieved anyway? Okay, but if it were true, as he had heard, the world behind the glass was supposed to be more humane and peace-loving than his own country. If that were true, if they cared about human rights and all that they claimed, they should praise Arman for rebelling against the tyranny of his leaders and then rebelling against the violence of the rebels. Wouldn't that be fair? Was that not enough heroism? It certainly should be.

Songbird and Arman, with another two comrades, had decided to leave the rebels and declared their decision to the group in an evening meeting. They didn't want to agree to the violence that the group had started to practice.

Ever since Songbird had stayed in the mountains and become, as she was, a co-leader, Leader had changed. His arrogance and boasting had become more aggressive. Not only Arman and Songbird, but also several other comrades had noticed that the young man was revealing weakness rather than confidence. Songbird once told Arman that she didn't understand why this guy must contradict everything she said. 'I haven't done anything to undermine him. Have I said anything like…?'

'But you always come over as much more clever than he is,' Arman had said, blushing, feeling his own grin frozen on his face. He was burning, not so much from his nervousness, but from the warmth of her presence.

'I mean what should I do? Shut my mouth and just do what he says?' Songbird had said, grabbing Arman's hand. The softness of her hand, and the warm touch he felt in her grip, made him feel dazed.

'Come, let me show you something.' She walked into the trees, dragging Arman behind her.

'What?' Arman said, stumbling. 'I don't think you need to do anything more than what you already do,' he said, panting, then stopped when Songbird halted and let his hand go.

'What do I do?' she said, turning to him.

'Your opposition is important for all of us.' He grabbed her arm, staring at her for a moment. 'We need you, Songbird,' he added in a pleading voice.

Songbird stared at him in turn, then pulled him on again. 'Let me show you this.'

When they were near Comrade Veggie's grave, Songbird stopped, stood behind a tree and pushed Arman back to stand behind her. She nodded to a mule tethered to a tree, just a metre from the grave.

'That's for Veggie's body. They're going to take him tonight.'

'What are you talking about?' Arman asked, putting his hand on her shoulder, peering into her eyes.

'Let's go. I'll explain. But no one else should know about this.'

She then told him that she had overheard Comrade Baker and the mule owner who had brought the flour in the morning, talking about Veggie's parents being in the village, waiting for their son's body. The man had said it was safer to do that at night. So he had left the mule behind, planning to return at night. If the other comrades were to hear of this, and certainly if Leader did, they would accuse Baker of treason, she explained. So let them do what they had to do and get it over with.

That evening, there was no singing in the gathering. The meeting lasted until midnight. Songbird had brought a serious issue to the attention of all, which had to be discussed and decided upon. She warned them that what they had built would not last long and needed a stronger structure. An organisation that should be run more collectively, she demanded. 'But also,' she raised her voice to have all their attention, moving her head from left to right, 'we can't hide in secrecy forever.'

A soft hum rippled through the room.

She then explained that the best way was to keep the underground part of the Organisation in the city as such and try to expand it to other cities, especially to the Region's Capital. But the armed group could not be held the way it was now. 'Our parents would soon lose their patience and start looking for us,' she said, staring at her comrades. And of course the authorities would very soon track them down, she warned. It was just a matter of time before they started to bother everyone's family.

'You overthink things too much,' Leader interrupted her, standing stiff beside her. Arman could tell how much he was trying not to look much shorter than her.

'Worse than that,' Leader added, 'you're sowing doubt in the minds of our comrades.'

'But we have to doubt our methods,' she said through the murmur of the comrades, all present in the room, sitting on thin sponge mattresses, in a few rows, around the metal wood-burner in the middle of the room. Also the two guards who were on duty at that hour outside in the courtyard had come to the window, eavesdropping.

'Aren't we supposed to be self-criticising?' Songbird asked, running her eyes over the gathering. Her majestic elegance and the charm of her height, standing there, overlooking the sitting comrades and even the upright standing Leader, spread so much awe through the room, it spellbound everyone. Or was it only Arman who was under her spell?

When it was Leader's turn to address the comrades, he said

that actually he already had plans for the Organisation. He had agreed with the guerrillas that they would provide them with more weapons, and they had now gun for each one of the comrades who had not yet received one. Arman was one of them.

Everyone should carry a gun from the next day and they would receive training from the guerrillas, said Leader, looking at Songbird, smiling. Smirking was that, in fact, thought Arman, feeling it was the right moment to support Songbird. He had to say something. For once, he had to express his opinion.

'But I think we had all agreed to join because we were told there would be no fighting,' said Arman with a quiver in his voice, certain that he had blushed, but luckily he couldn't see his own face.

'Things are changing, and we have to act accordingly,' Leader said, raising his voice to douse the murmur.

'And if all of us are armed, would it mean that we are fighting when they come to us? Is that what you mean?' Songbird asked, without looking at Leader, but with a brief glance at the questioning eyes of her comrades again.

Not everyone was keen to fight. Not everyone wanted to carry a gun. But on the other hand, not everyone agreed to do things peacefully either. Some thought that it was all too naive to think that they could overthrow such a mighty party and such a powerful family by spreading rumours on social media.

'What about going home and finishing school?' said Baker suddenly, piercing through the chatter.

Everyone turned to him in the silence that followed his words.

'So if we all… I mean can we…?'

'What a disgrace you are, Baker!' Leader said, shaking his

head. 'What are you suggesting? We all go home?'

'No, I mean if we—'

'I think you should just go to…' Leader interrupted him, looking at his watch. 'Is it not late for preparing your dough?'

Some of the comrades burst out laughing.

'Look, I meant to ask if we were not at least free to leave?' Baker said, standing up.

'Would you just shut up, comrade?' Leader said calmly, looking round, maybe to sense the general mood in the room.

Arman, sitting in a corner, caught Leader's glance and could tell he was furious but was forcing himself to remain calm.

'Hey guys, just listen to me,' Baker raised his voice, turning his head left and right between the comrades, while sitting down again. His face was as red as the embers in the hearth of the round wood-burner in the middle of the room.

'I'm not just a baker,' he shouted. 'I was about to study politics if you hadn't convinced me to come here. I was—'

'Please!' Leader mouthed to him, his eyebrows raised, shrugging, giving him a sign to leave.

Baker jumped up and left the room immediately, shaking his head, murmuring something that Arman couldn't hear. But he saw Leader nodding to two of his closest armed comrades who sat near the door, to follow him. The two slowly sneaked out. Did anyone else notice that?

Leader shouted, regaining everyone's attention, 'Guys, listen please! We're not having this conversation, right? We're not in doubt, I assume. Because there's no way back. Is it even possible, do you think? We are all going to end in prison. We—'

'Not if we decide something reasonable on time,' Songbird

interrupted him.

Leader ignored her remark and continued, 'I appreciate everyone's opinion. But enough discussion! Now is the time for action. And for leadership. I've taken on this strenuous task and I'll perform it well.'

Shouting was heard outside. Leader made a sign to hold everyone still and looked through the window. He put his hand to the pistol at his waist.

One of the two comrades who had gone after Baker rushed in, shouting, 'He's gone. Baker's disappeared.'

Leader ran out, and after him went the two armed guards who stood behind him and Songbird.

Most of the comrades jumped to their feet too and ran out. Then out went Songbird, who at the door turned and caught Arman's gaze.

Arman slowly stood up and followed his murmuring comrades. The room was emptying.

In the yard, Leader shouted, 'Let's go find him. Everyone, into the trees.'

As soon as several comrades had rushed to the trees, Leader turned back and shouted again, 'No, not anyone without a gun.' He then himself vanished into the dark, among the trees.

Half an hour later, three of the armed comrades brought Baker back; one of them said that they had found him near Veggie's grave, which to their shock had been opened and the body removed. Baker had a small rucksack on him, full of food and water, which was apparently prepared earlier. They had searched his pockets and found a list of thirteen names of his comrades;

their full real names and a few addresses. Arman was on the list, with his pseudonym 'Builder' and his real name with the address of his family home. But neither Leader nor Songbird were included. Arman never even found out Songbird's real name.

Baker confessed that he had recently been in contact with the authorities via the mule owner who delivered the flour twice a week. Intelligence officials had promised not to prosecute him if he gave them information about the group with the real names and addresses of his comrades. He had also guided the mule man to the grave. He tried to convince the comrades that the authorities had promised not to harm anyone and had agreed to release them all after making them each pledge that they would never again be involved in any anti-state or political activity. However, no one could believe that, as they knew well what had happened to their first ever leader, the Plotter. Wasn't it Arman the hero who had brought the news about him?

The next day, after breakfast, Leader gathered the comrades in the courtyard and, standing at one side of the court, surrounded by a number of armed comrades, made a long speech: 'Dear comrades, today is the day. Our revolution has started.'

Arman looked at Songbird, who stood beside him in the crowd. She nudged him, warning him just to wait and listen.

'As we all agree, there is no way to rid ourselves of the Family and their party, or any of the dominant parties, by peaceful means. No political party would take notice of us, the youth. We have to fight for our future. And we must literally fight and take up arms.'

A murmur went through the comrades, many of whom stood

in the middle of the yard, while some leant back on the trees, and some sat around, listening to him as he summed up all that they already knew, and had discussed so many times, about how corrupt their leaders were.

'But just think about it,' he said, suddenly raising his voice, catching everyone's attention. 'Our parents fought and made sacrifices for the freedom of the Folk, and these thieves picked the fruit. They're stealing our wealth in broad daylight, before our very own eyes. And imagine, we're fed up with these corrupt leaders themselves, and they are already preparing a teenager, just our age, your age, to be the next President. As if no one else in this country deserves ever to achieve any high political position, no matter how serious we study, how far we have been educated and how hard we will work.'

One of the comrades shouted, 'Absolutely! That's the point. No matter—'

Leader interrupted him with a gesture of his hand.

Arman turned and saw that he was one of the few who were determined to fight.

Leader continued, 'Aren't we frustrated that our leaders don't even give a damn to find out what we are capable of? We, who so very differently from their generation, are aware of what is happening over the whole world. We, the generation of the internet and social media. We, who easily can see and hear how other nations go about their daily life and enjoy their rights and can participate in politics.' He halted, letting his eyes brush over the crowd, waiting for another wave of murmuring to calm down.

'They have already established themselves as a royal family, this mafia,' he continued. 'And kings you can't change, when they become tyrants. You have to cut their throats. We have to eliminate these tyrants and kick out their families and offspring, just as our parents did with the former regime. We have to root them out. But not today. Not tomorrow. It will take time. We must first undergo military training. Exercise with weapons. And that, we will start today.'

Most of the comrades clapped and cheered, 'We'll root them out! We'll root them out!' they yelled.

'Are we becoming terrorists?' a comrade shouted.

'Oh, no! They *are* the terrorists. And we'll root them out,' Leader shouted back, annoyed.

The crowd cheered again.

Arman looked round, and then looked at Songbird again, shaking his head.

'Don't worry!' she said, holding his arm. 'He's bluffing. He's scared right now,' she said, then shouted, 'What about Comrade Baker? What are we going to decide about him?'

'It's already decided by the Leadership Committee,' Leader said in a calmer voice.

'Leadership Committee?' said Songbird, stepping forward until she was in front of him. 'Am I not part of the Leadership? How come…?'

'Unfortunately, comrade, only the armed comrades can be in the committee. This is the six of us at the moment,' he said, nodding to the five armed comrades around him. 'So go and exercise, I suggest. Carry a gun, then you may—'

'That's nonsense! Madness!' Songbird shouted, turning to the comrades.

A murmur went through the crowd. Another twelve armed

comrades were standing guard all round the Base.

Arman elbowed himself forward and reached Songbird. He grabbed her arm and pulled her back. 'Please, don't let it escalate. Should we go down to the valley and reflect?' he said and left at once. He went to lean on a large walnut tree, staring at the crowd.

Some other comrades did the same. Soon everyone went about their daily duties.

'We'll discuss all these matters again tonight, comrades. Keep tight and see you later,' Leader shouted, his hand tight on the pistol in his waist. He then walked to the room across the meeting hall and went inside, followed by the five committee members with their Kalashnikovs on their shoulders. They closed the door.

From his position against the walnut tree, Arman read on a board that had been fixed to the door: Leadership Committee.

27

That night, Leader allowed a member of the Committee to explain to the comrades how the Organisation would be restructured after everyone had been armed. The comrade then changed the tone of his voice and informed them that the Committee had decided to execute Baker.

Angry mutters passed through the room. Some sighed loudly or groaned.

Arman shuffled on his place, sitting in a corner, and searched for Songbird's eyes.

The Committee member said through the hubbub that Baker was stripped of his Comrade title, and was now a traitor, kept in the dungeon.

The mutters gradually became a grumble, then some voices protested loudly, though not directly in the face of the Committee members.

Leader shouted, 'Comrades! Can we have some order please?' Then he waited, standing near the window, stiff as a military commander, holding his head up as much as he could. Arman was sure he was trying to look taller than he was.

Silence was now restored.

Leader calmly asked, 'Is there anyone who doesn't consider this man to be a traitor?'

No one said anything. Then Songbird stood up from her place in a corner. 'Look, I don't think we have any right to execute someone just because he has betrayed us. We're not—'

'That's disloyalty to the Organisation you're now manifesting,' the Leader interrupted her. 'Who takes that right from us? This guy has put all of us in danger. He was about to reveal the names of our comrades. Not you and me. But our beloved comrades. Even your lover, Comrade Builder.'

'Lover?' said Songbird through the commotion.

Arman squirmed, pressing his back to the wall.

'Oh, please cut it out. This is getting ridiculous!' Songbird said, turning left and right, looking each comrade in the eyes, amid the hums and mutter.

Arman caught her eyes and wanted to say something. But Songbird looked back at Leader and said, 'You know what? I'm done here.' She turned back to the murmuring crowd. Arman tried to catch a glance from her again. But apparently she was avoiding that.

The room was uncomfortably hot from the burning wood in the furnace and from all the heated anger of the young people.

'I'm gone, dear comrades. And for that matter, Builder is going with me too. And two other comrades as well.'

Another louder murmur went through the room. Everyone looked at each other. Leader stood there, hands behind his back, looking shorter than ever, glancing at the comrades one by one.

Arman no longer knew what to say. He closed his eyes to think of something calming. Something that could reduce the tension. But Songbird's voice startled him.

'Can someone put this fire out, please? How can you breathe

in here, people?' She stepped over a few comrades, opened the door and left the meeting room.

Later in the night, she, Arman and the two other comrades sat with Leader and the rest of the Leadership Committee to discuss their departure. Songbird, whom they had chosen to speak for them all, tried to convince the Committee that it was in the best interest of everyone that they should go. For there was nothing worse than having members in the group who did not believe in the objectives or principles of the Organisation. Then she owned up that she had already called—from a smartphone she had been hiding since the beginning—a mule owner to come the next morning with four mules.

She handed over the phone and promised not to reveal the secrets of the Organisation or even to talk to anyone about the whereabouts of the group. The four of them, she emphasised, would pledge never to confess that they had been members of any kind of political organisation, even if they were to be put under torture.

'You're aware that there is no quitting,' said Leader in a calm, confident voice, sitting beside the window on a thin mattress on the floor, leaning back on a large cylinder-shaped pillow, looking them each in the eyes, one by one, in the quivering light of the *fanos* that was suspended from a shaft in the ceiling. The four of them sat on the floor in the middle of the room on a rag, facing him, while the other five Committee members sat on both sides of their Leader, their Kalashnikovs on their laps.

Arman, bothered more than ever by Leader's arrogant manner of talking, wanted to tell him to shut up, for who he did think he was? That, however, would have made things more complicated, so he just bit his lip and kept quiet, waiting for Songbird's next effort.

'Let's not call it quitting. It's just better for the sake of the whole movement if we weren't part of it. Just expel us. I mean you can officially ban us from the Organisation. Is that not...?'

Leader interrupted Songbird, raising his hand as a sign to stop. 'We have to discuss that with all the comrades. Why don't you go to rest in the guest room? Right now, until we've made a decision, you're dismissed.' He nodded to his deputy, Comrade Admin, to go with them. 'Let them collect their stuff and vacate their beds. And you two,' he nodded to another two members of the Leadership Committee, 'would you go with them as well, comrades?'

Early the next morning, when the four of them woke up in the guest room to a commotion outside, they saw through the window that almost all their other comrades had gathered in the yard with their pistols or Kalashnikovs in their hands. And now almost everyone had a gun, Arman suggested they tell them that they had changed their minds and would stay.

'No,' said Songbird, pushing him and the other two comrades away from the window. 'It wouldn't work like that. We have to be firm. They can't hold us against our will. Pack your stuff.'

They quickly packed and went out of the room. Seven or eight of the armed young men came forward blocking the hallway, their Kalashnikovs pointed at them. Over there, on the road out of the base, Leader was leading away the stableman with his five mules; his friendly hand on the back of the man, who was much taller than him, apparently explaining to him that plans had changed.

'Listen, comrades, let's handle this peacefully,' Songbird said, putting her backpack down as she stepped forward, her open palm against the gun barrel of an armed comrade.

'Or what?' said one of the gunmen, coming between her and his comrade. 'What're you going to do? Shoot at us? With your…?'

One of the female comrades came forward, pushing down her comrade's weapon. 'Hey, hold back, comrade. No insults. Criticise yourself.'

'No time for that, comrade. These…' the young, agitated man said, pushing his female comrade away with his elbow. 'These are—'

'Traitors, indeed!' shouted Leader, elbowing himself through the primed squad. 'Who do you think you are, huh, Angry Bird?' he asked Songbird, looking up at her, holding her chin in one hand, his other hand on his pistol at his waist.

The armed comrades who had heard Leader's comment roared with laughter.

'Who hired you? You know what the punishment for treason is, don't you?'

'Please, comrade, let the guerrillas settle this,' said Arman, putting down his backpack and pushing Songbird back so that she wouldn't try to do anything herself.

'Shut up, you knucklehead. Guerrillas can't save your ass,' Leader said, grabbing at Arman's collar.

'Listen, comrade, you're making a huge mistake,' Songbird said, grasping Leader's arm, pulling him away from Arman.

The Leader shook his arm off, out of Songbird's grasp, and

slapped her face. 'You stupid bi… How dare you?'

Now Arman grabbed at Leader's arm, who swiftly turned to him, swivelling on his heel, and punched him in the stomach with his left fist. Arman crumpled to the floor, clutching himself with both hands.

'Please, comrade,' said one of the two other leaving comrades, coming forward. 'Would you just leave us to—'

Leader grabbed his hair and pulled him towards the courtyard through the prepped comrades with their pointed guns. 'Take them to the dungeon,' he shouted.

The armed comrades stormed into the corridor. Two of them picked up Arman from the floor; two led away Songbird, who writhed and struggled, shouting that they would all regret their actions; another two pushed away the fourth comrade, stripping him from his backpack, while one of them grabbed his neck, putting him in a strangle-hold.

At the underground cell, one of the armed comrades took out Baker, tied his hands behind his back and drove him away. Another three armed comrades pushed Songbird and Arman and the other two leaving comrades down the cell.

The three days they spent in the dungeon were, for Arman, the worst he had ever endured: to be treated that way by people whom he had thought were his friends. The most horrible of all, however, was that only half an hour after they were put in the dungeon, they heard the rattle of shots in the distance. They were not certain, but assumed it was Baker who had been shot.

For those three days in the dungeon, the four prisoners were each given only one piece of bread and a bucket of water to share, for each whole day and night. Even the ruling party's secret prison had not been as harsh as this to Arman. At least the food had been sufficient there.

It was, in fact, more shocking for Songbird and the other two young men: Comrade Baseball who was named after the baseball cap he always wore, and Comrade Jogger, so called because of his daily jog. The man had also organised a group of jogging comrades.

The dungeon was an underground room not larger than two by two metres with walls about three metres high, plastered only with mud. Humid and stuffy. Its ceiling raised about fifteen centimetres from the ground by bricks, with only a few small holes left between the bricks for ventilation. The entrance to the cellar was a small, square hole at one corner of the ceiling, wide enough for only one person, not too fat, to come through and down over the steep stairs that took up a large space at one side of the room.

Arman had helped his comrades a few months ago fit a heavy, thick iron lid on the entrance that could be bolted with a huge lock. Unbreakable. He was certain of that. At least not from inside. Even if the four of them were to push it together. Staring at it in the dim light, he regretted having done the job so successfully, as he usually did; an attitude he inherited from his father.

None of the comrades knew what this abandoned vault was used for in the past. But now, feeling the humidity and the piercing cold of the cellar, it reminded Arman of a similar cellar for curing tobacco he had seen once used by farmers in the area of Grandma's village when he was only about seven years old.

He told the story to his three comrades, who decided not to call each other comrades anymore. His cellmates. He remembered how nauseous he had felt when he had gone into the cellar with his father and walked between the rows of the tobacco leaves, hung on strings like on a clothes line.

That was all that they could do during those three long days and three long nights in the dungeon. Telling their childhood stories and jokes. Amidst the stink of their own urine and excrement, as they had to relieve themselves in a corner, digging small holes with their bare fingers in the hardened mud floor, then cover them again. Or they would sing, trying to ignore the stench. Of course, Songbird was the best. Even the comrades on guard—ex-comrades in fact—enjoyed her singing and complimented her through the holes up under the ceiling.

'Would they really execute us?' Baseball asked once in the dark. 'We haven't done anything.'

'Let's hope they'll come to their senses,' Songbird said. 'I mean Comrade Leader should. It's his—'

'They killed Baker, didn't they?' Baseball said, then added after a deep sigh, 'I'm sure that was the shooting.'

'He had a list of the names of most of us, dumbass!' Songbird reminded him.

'But killing him, come on! Most of us were against that,' Jogger said.

'The Leadership Committee voted for it,' said Songbird.

'Okay, they were only six people. What about the rest of us?' said Jogger. 'We had no say in it at all.'

'Dogshit Leadership Committee,' Arman sneered. 'Ridiculous! How could we all be so stupid as to believe in this nonsense?

We're bloody gullible kids.'

'Okay, guys, what can we do now? Too late. We agreed to leave, didn't we? So what's the point of arguing about it now?' Songbird ended the conversation and started to sing again.

Miserable and hungry as they were on the third night, more fainting than asleep, well after midnight, someone opened the vault lid, came down and woke them, warning them to keep silent.

'Get the hell out of here one by one and run down into the valley. Quietly. Come on, get up,' the young comrade whispered. Arman suspected, but didn't know exactly, who he was. In the absolute dark, he couldn't see him, but from the contours of his silhouette he knew he was wearing a balaclava.

First, Baseball crawled up the stairs and went out. Then Songbird. After her, Jogger pushed Arman up and said, 'Wait for me. I know the best way out.'

Sticking his head out of the hole, Arman saw in the dark the silhouette of another comrade at the gate, while the guarding comrade was tied up, crumpled at the foot of the large walnut tree beside the cellar. He was moaning faintly, sounding as though he was gagged. When he was finally standing up, Arman quickly hugged the comrade who stood there waiting for them. He also was wearing a balaclava.

'Thank you so much,' Arman whispered. 'You—'

'Run, run…' the young man whispered, pushing away Arman who could almost tell who he was, but again he was not sure.

Arman ran to the large trees and waited for Jogger, whose silhouette was running towards him.

'Hey, Arman…' Songbird called him in whisper from behind

the trees. 'Hurry up! This way.'

Arman slowly followed the direction of her voice, looking over his shoulder for Jogger.

'I'm coming. Waiting for Jogger,' Arman whispered and flinched when Songbird emerged in front of him, grabbed his hand and dragged him on, running down the mountain.

Jogger caught up with them, whispering, 'Guys, I know a way. Do you know which way Baseball ran?'

'I saw him running down, but I think he forgot his baseball cap inside,' Songbird whispered, panting, while cautiously floundering downhill.

Arman and Jogger laughed quietly, also panting.

'God, you're horrible! Even now?' Arman said, holding her arm, stumbling behind her.

That night, before dawn, they reached the valley and walked through the dense trees, along a creek. Then at a shallow patch, they crossed the water, jumping over large stones, holding on to tree branches, and continued up the opposite mountain, on a route that kept them far from any bases of the guerrillas who might arrest them if they encountered them.

By dawn, they were halfway up the mountain but then had to hide in a cave. They could have been detected if they had walked in daylight, as the rebels, their former comrades, and the guerrillas both had binoculars.

On the way, they had stuffed themselves with figs and pomegranates that had begun to ripen in the early autumn.

The next night, they walked as soon as it was dark, taking a narrow path leading high up the mountain. They held on to the shrubs or the stones of the mountainside, as their other side were the slopes. If they tripped and slipped from the path, they would slide down into the creek that had now broadened out into a river.

Jogger walked in the front, Arman in the middle, and Songbird behind him. As if she was taking care of him. He wasn't a child for God's sake! He could lead them. Except that he didn't know the way. Jogger knew. So that's why he was at the front. But why did Songbird always push Arman before herself? As if she were protecting him. Which she was indeed. But come on, she was only a year older than him. All the time, from the beginning, she had acted as his guardian angel. She was an angel. That's for sure. But *he* should be protecting her. So she should be walking in the middle. Yes, he *should* be protecting her. He would take a bullet for her, Arman was quite certain of that. But it was tonight or never. He had to show her his strength. His manhood. He had managed so much better with Lady Artist in this way. Why did he feel so weak towards Songbird?

He knew why, in fact. It was her courage and intelligence. Would Arman ever achieve that? When they decided to leave the group, Songbird had promised to support him if he had chosen to catch up with school. He could do that in the evenings, she had advised him. He would certainly do that one day. But now, he had to show his strength and courage.

'Shall I hold your hand?' he whispered, turning to Songbird.

'Are you afraid of falling?' she whispered back, putting her hand on his shoulder, and stopped for a moment.

'Oh, no, I meant to—'

'Guys don't fall behind, please!' Jogger turned in the dark, whispering. 'We just need to get past this bend and we're safe.'

Songbird pushed Arman gently and they both resumed walking, with Songbird much closer behind Arman. Maybe she was now trying to take better care of him. Had he blown it again? Yes, he had made it worse. That was for sure. But maybe it was a good thing. If it meant anything, it meant that she took care of him. That she...

At once, a sequence of sparks flickered from the opposite mountain on the other side of the valley and a series of whizzing objects hit the mountainside all around them with muffled thuds. Then a ratatatat echoed across the valley.

Arman froze in his place and was sure that both Songbird and Jogger did the same.

'Hunker down, guys,' Jogger gasped, his silhouette cowering down, as another rapid succession of sparks gleamed on the other side, and bullets whizzed all around them, followed by a rattle.

Arman threw himself on to the ground and felt Songbird's arms on his back. She also was lying down, half her body over Arman's.

A rustling and heavy breathing, and Arman could make out through the dark Jogger's silhouette that had slid from the path, struggling to lift himself up.

'Jogger, are you okay?' Songbird whispered behind Arman, trying to crawl over his back.

'I'm fine, trying...' Jogger whispered back, panting and groaning. Obviously, he struggled to keep a hold, trying to heave himself back up to the path. He needed a hand.

Arman pushed himself forward and crawled towards him, Songbird behind him.

'Hold on, Jogger. We're coming,' Arman whispered as loudly as he dared, as another wave of whizzing bullets went over their heads to hit the mountainside. Then a rattle through the valley. Ratatatat.

Just at the very moment Arman heaved himself up on all fours and stretched his arm to help, the dark shape of Jogger below slid down, moaning and whining through the rustling of leaves, and the crackling and crunching of twigs and gravel.

28

As Arman told the story of his time among the rebels, the Guard typed on, non-stop; the rhythmic clatter of the keyboard reached Arman faintly, but couldn't distract him from his memories. The Guard would only seldom interrupt him to enquire about a detail or ask for an explanation. They had to submit the application before the end of the Guard's shift at five o'clock in the afternoon.

When he came to the moment he and Songbird had lost their fellow escapee, Arman paused, then said in a brittle voice that he still could not forgive himself for not being able to help Jogger get back on the path. If only he had acted quicker. Just a few seconds earlier. He had missed his friend's hand by those few seconds. 'Only a few seconds, can you imagine?' Otherwise, he could have helped Jogger to lift himself up. At least he could help him hold on to the verge until Songbird had reached them and they could both have dragged him up.

'Listen, Arman,' the Guard interrupted him. 'That was not your fault. What could you do in a situation like that? I'm sure you would—'

'I know, that's true. But imagine if, instead of covering my head, I had jumped towards him, I could at least have lent him that hand.'

'And he could have toppled you over and then you would both fall down. But let's keep the emotion out for now. We can't include this in your story. Tell me what happened after that to you? And to Songbird.'

'So when Jogger rolled down the ravine and we no longer could see him or hear him,' Arman said, then paused. With him the clicking of the keyboard. He stood up and looked into the hut. 'Actually, we weren't sure whether he had died or not. Maybe he survived. Sometimes I comfort myself with this idea. Maybe—'

'Let's hope so, Comrade Builder. But please tell me the rest of the story. How did you and Songbird survive? We don't have much time.'

Arman sat down again and continued his story. As they were whispering how they should crawl down to perhaps find Jogger, another succession of gunfire came. So he and Songbird lay down again, holding their heads under their hands for a short time. Then Songbird whispered that it was time to move on. They couldn't risk going down the ravine.

Arman crawled for about a hundred metres in the dirt, over gravel and protruding stones in the path, Songbird behind him. When they passed a deep bend and they were sure that now the mountain on the other side of the valley was not the same as the one from which the gunfire came, they sat upright, leant back on the rocks and had a short rest.

After another hour's walk, they found another small cave and hid in it until next morning, in the agonising cold. They were lucky to have their thick military coats on. Both had several wounds on their hands and knees, and on their faces. A gash in Songbird's wrist was so bad it bled all night through, though they wrapped it with Arman's T-shirt, which he had worn under his sweater.

In the morning, they found an old pot in the cave. Arman took it and sneaked into the trees, down the valley. He ate as many of the figs and pomegranates as he could and stuffed all his pockets with more. He drank from the river, filled the pot with water and walked back up the mountain. The figs were paradise's very own fruit, Grandma used to say, Arman told Songbird when he emptied his pockets.

'Had she come back from the paradise, your Grandma?' Songbird sneered.

'No, the swallows told her.'

After spending the rest of the day hidden inside the cave, that night they took the road through the trees down to the valley, along the river, then up and down more hills, under the soft light of a crescent moon that later in the night shone over the valley, gently lighting their path. Early in the morning, they reached an orchard and knew that they had arrived at a village.

The villagers helped them to contact their families. First Songbird's parents arrived in the late afternoon and took her back home without waiting even a moment in the village. Then Arman's father and older brother arrived that night and stayed until the next morning, waiting for the rest of the family.

Arman decided not to go back to the city but to leave the country. Even though he had to spend the winter hiding in that village. His sister had suggested they went to live in their own village with Grandma. But Arman, and Father as well, thought that would be a risk. In the spring, they arranged his departure.

'Were you afraid that the rebels would follow you?' the Guard enquired.

'Not only them,' Arman said, looking up at the glass door behind him. 'I also couldn't fall into the hands of the state security again. Or I would... I'm not sure what they would have done to me. But after the prison, you know, I had promised never again to be involved in politics.'

'I see,' said the Guard. 'So you're saying that your life was at that time in grave danger?'

'Absolutely!'

Another rapid click-clank from the keyboard and the typing stopped all together.

'You nailed it, Comrade Builder! You nailed it, boy!' the Guard shouted, standing up.

Arman heard the old man's delighted voice echo inside his office. Even through the metallic interpretation, he could sense the Guard's contentment. Though his expression seemed rather strange to Arman; or the translation of it, anyway. He must have meant that he got it right at last.

That evening, Arman cooked a marvellous meal. His most delicious so far. After dinner, sitting beside the embers in the fire pit, a cup of tea in his hand, he stared at the City over there under a serene night sky. He turned to the desert and noticed how tranquil it was on his side as well. A dark sky studded with the blaze of twinkling diamonds, spread in a curve over the desolate desert. Under it was a lunar landscape with sand dunes lit by the blue light of the half moon, their dark purple-grey shadows extending far from them. He was going to miss his desert if they were to let him in to the City.

If only he could tell his family the good news—that this time the Guard was so buoyant about the chance of his story's success. One thing that gnawed at him all the time he had been here in the desert was not being able to tell any friend or family member about all that he saw, experienced, felt and went through since he had left home. But also one thing he had not told the Guard and could not tell, was that that night in the cave, he and Songbird had spent it in each other's arms, both moaning from pain. Then at dawn from pleasure. At some point, Songbird had put her hand on the back of Arman's neck and pushed his head down to her own. Then she pulled his hair and kissed him. He would never forget how the warmth of her body vanquished the damp cold in the cave. Both sweating, their soft skins sticking together, they wriggled over their clothes on the rough ground.

The next day, Arman had barely looked her in the eyes, when all day they both told stories of their childhood. Only when it was dark again, early in the evening, before they left the cave, had Songbird hugged Arman once more, whispering in his ear that they might never see each other again.

The thing he regretted the most was that he indeed didn't hear from Songbird again. Maybe one day he would.

29

The few days following his third and final asylum request, Arman gradually lost his ardour and spirit. The desert was getting hotter by day. The Guard was busy with his own writing or engaged in long games on his computer. Once, when Arman asked him what he did so eagerly on the computer when he wasn't typing his stories, the Guard had said that he was playing card games. If only Arman had also something to play with! Maybe he should try with the jackal.

By Friday, when no decision had yet come in on his new application, Arman told the Guard that he now had lost all hope. The old man assured him that he shouldn't be worried. It was only three days since he had submitted his request. He said at the times when there were more refugees, decisions on their applications took weeks and sometimes months. And in the era before the wall, it could even take years. He then rolled down the blind and left, leaving Arman yet again facing the horrible, lonely weekend.

Later that afternoon, Arman was cooking dinner in the shade of the glass wall. The jackal appeared behind a sand dune a few meters from the tent.

'Hey, Little Friend!' Arman shouted, standing up. 'Where

have you been? Come here! Want a piece of bread?'

The jackal sprinted to the next dune instead. Oh, wow! There stood another jackal, with only its head and forelegs to be seen, its ears erect.

Arman took a step, but stumbled, knocking over a tin of tomato juice. 'Aaaaaaaaaargh!'

Little Friend pounced on the other jackal and they started spinning around each other. It was certainly a female, as Little Friend was sniffing her butt.

Arman sat down, opened another tin of tomato juice and poured it into the saucepan on the gas stove, staring at the animals. Now that there were two of them, wouldn't it be even more risky to play friends with them?

Little Friend ran to Arman's tent, the female after him. They started spinning around the tent. Little Friend stood at the entrance, then turned and peered at Arman. This was becoming ridiculous. Maybe he should stop this friendship farce.

'Hey, you beasts, get away from my tent.' He brandished a spoon and ran towards them, kicking the sand.

Both animals scampered away; the female one much farther. The male, no friend whatsoever, stared at Arman, snarling, then ran to the female; or what Arman thought to be a female. They started spinning around each other again, then butt-sniffing, nuzzling one another's head, and suddenly the female jackal darted over the sand; the male one after her. In a blink of an eye, they vanished behind the dunes.

He should be vigilant, now there was more than one of them. Nonetheless, Arman spent the next day, Saturday, all day on his own in the heat of the desert, staying most of the time in his tent, fanning himself with a piece of cardboard. No sign of the jackal or any other beast.

On Sunday, a helicopter dropped another box of aid, larger than the previous two, with more water and a greater variety of food, and more coal and a bottle of gas for the stove.

They think I've run away from hunger. As if I had nothing to eat. Fact is nothing even comes close to what I used to eat in my country. Nothing tastes the same here, if it tastes of anything at all. They starve me then send me food to show their pity for me. It's killing me that they send a helicopter to drop the food, can you imagine, but don't allow me to enter their country. Wouldn't it be much cheaper just to let me in? It would, I'm sure. Much much cheaper. Really.

Thus began Arman's diary in the notebook they had included in the delivery. All day long, the grin of delight didn't leave his face. The butterflies in his chest lasted the whole day, from the moment he found the spiral notebook with a pen attached to it. After hugging it and holding it steady, staring at it for some time, he spent most of the day sitting in the tent, writing.

The next day, as soon as the Guard arrived, he ran to the hut to share his excitement with him. Holding the notebook with both hands, showing it to him, he said, 'Thanks for this!'

'Oh, you don't need to thank me for that,' the Guard said as usual. 'It's just how it works. But tell me, what are you going to write in it?'

'About my life. Here in this desert. And before that, in my

country. And all that has happened to me, I guess.'

'But that part, all about your troubles and your family history...' the Guard said, taking out Arman's file from the drawer, 'we've got it in here. I'll hand it over to you when you come in.' He produced the file.

'I see. Maybe I should write about the things you never let me talk about then? And things about my family. My siblings. My mother. Friends and all.'

For most of the rest of that week, both the old man and the young left each other alone, engaged in writing their own memoirs. Every day Arman waited for the decision on his new asylum request so he would ask the Guard about it as soon as the old man arrived in the morning.

The desert was getting hotter, forcing Arman to stay in his tent all day long until it cooled down close to sunset. He would spend the time struggling with writing, discovering how much harder it was than he had expected. To put all that he had in his head onto paper was very different from telling people the stories face to face. It felt as though his thoughts were traveling ten times faster than his hand could write them down in words and sentences. He needed to develop the skill to pause the thoughts, slow them down and allow them out word by word at the pace of his handwriting. He had to rewind and fast forward them back and forth all the time to get that pace right. But by then he had forgotten what he had been thinking. Other thoughts took over, then other memories of events or people or things he had heard. It was a hell of an endeavour. Not easy at all. And not all the time pleasant. He would get frustrated and put his pen and notebook down. Then he would get bored and pick them up again.

The heat made the whole process even more frustrating. In only his underpants, he would sit on the mattress, perspiring, trying to stop his sticky body from touching anything that could irritate him. Now and then, he had to put down the pen to fan himself with a piece of cardboard from the food packages, only to be soaked in sweat again within minutes. It became a competition with the heat to see how long he could go on. Each time the heat would win, of course. No matter how long Arman could endure the sweating, he finally had to pick up the cardboard again and fan his face and chest. And now and then a sudden gust of wind would blow the sand into the tent, seasoning his face and all bare parts of his perspiring skin, just like meat on a barbecue. So he was now seasoned and ready, and he could go to lie in the sun. He indeed did that once. He couldn't even stand it for one minute. He would have been barbecued. Literally. Was he going mad?

All this interfered with the writing. He would scrub off the sand and sit with his back to the opening of the tent. But the sand that stuck to his back wasn't much less irritating. Now, he had to scrub his back and that was a bit more difficult than brushing his sand-covered front. Nevertheless, the softer breeze now and then was so pleasant that it was worth risking the occasional sand-spreading blast for it. Zipping down the flap was no option as inside the tent became, within minutes, a stifling, heated oven.

The more water he drank the more he sweated. But the more he perspired the thirstier he became. Even a light lunch could make his thirst worse and lead to more sweating for at least another hour. So he would eat what was left of the salad and cucumbers. Oh, the cucumbers tasted so delicious and refreshing.

He wanted to run to the hut and shout at the Guard about how unfair it was that he was sitting writing in a cool office with an air conditioner, but of course, it was not the Guard's fault. Arman was now sure that he was on his side. He was convinced the old man would love him to be accepted and open the gate for him. And the man seemed confident this time that they would let him in.

What angered Arman though, was that on the other side of the glass, people seemed to be able to enjoy the sun. They lay half-naked in their boats in the lake or at the lakesides. But they did that, because there the sun did not shine so fiercely on them every day. Unfair to the people on the other side, maybe? Well, you can't have everything! Arman would also have welcomed some rain. But would his wish be granted? No!

On some days it would rain all day and night on the other side of the glass wall, even though the summer was now here. Just the sight of rain, in the middle of a hot day, would give Arman some comfort, as he imagined the cool drizzle brushing his face. He would close his eyes and envisage the zephyr from the world behind the glass blow over his face. Until at last the dry, hot breeze would blow him back to reality.

He didn't want to think any more about the riddle that had most perplexed him. Even the Guard had no answer. How come it rained so hard on the other side, while not even a sprinkling spattered over the edge of the glass wall on this side? Come on, that was not too much to ask! He would have run to stand there at the glass wall with open arms and head thrown back to be splashed with it. Though the raindrops might perhaps have evaporated in the hot air before reaching his face.

That weekend, it seemed that almost the whole population of the City had come to the lake and spread itself around. The lake could not have welcomed one more boat. Boats, floating over the water, full of half-naked people partying or lazing in chairs and sun-loungers. Some under parasols, drinking or reading newspapers or books. Children playing or bending over what seemed like smartphones and iPads, or fishing lines.

People did the same all along the shore. They lounged on the narrow sand beaches in the sun or under the parasols. Or swam in small, marked zones. Played with balls or drifted on floats. Hundreds of others picnicked among the trees around the lake. Many would also walk or jog in shorts and bikinis along the road behind the glass, directly in the sun, while on his side, Arman didn't even dare to step out of his tent.

Both Saturday and Sunday went by in almost exactly the same way, on both sides of the glass wall. While for Arman this was a burning hell, the people on the other side were trying to absorb as much sun as possible. As if they had heard that the sun was about to vanish forever. They must have known that it would be raining for the next days so they made the most of the weekend, staying out until way after midnight in and around the lake.

Indeed, on Monday it did rain all day in the world behind the glass. Rain and wind. Such strong gusts that Arman was worried the trees would be pulled out of the ground. But wouldn't it be amazing if the wind blew away the billboard with the Welcoming Smiling Man?

That morning, as a bus drove away from the bus stop on the other side of the road, the Guard crossed hurriedly in his raincoat, under a large black umbrella that seemed to fight with the wind. He opened the iron door to the hut quickly, stormed in, holding his umbrella outside with one hand and shaking off the raindrops before pulling it inside and shutting the door.

Arman went straight over to the hut and waited until the panting old man rolled up the blind. He had taken off his raincoat and hung it on a hook in the wall behind his desk. When he saw Arman, he nodded.

Arman said hello. But the Guard did not seem to have heard him. He turned on the computer, took out his glasses and put them on, took off his coat, hung it on the back of his chair and sat. He grabbed the mouse, staring at the monitor.

The translation device got to work, crackling, then interpreted the Guard's words: 'I'm sorry, Arman! Still no decision.'

'Why do you think it's taken so long this time? Is that a good or bad sign?' Arman asked, knowing already what the old man's answer might be.

'Let's hope it's a good sign. Maybe there's lots in it for them to digest, hahahaha! It is a bit heavy.'

'Is that a good or a bad thing?'

'If you ask me, must be a good thing.'

'I'm asking you.'

'So a good thing, let's hope.'

30

Tuesday passed the same as the day before, except that it was less wet on the other side and more hot on Arman's. But on Wednesday morning, he stepped out of the tent and was startled to see so many people behind the glass wall. On the pavement; on the road; on the other side of the road; all along the wall from right to left as far as he could see. Men and women, mostly young, in their twenties or early thirties, maybe? There were a few older and younger as well. Some Arman's age. They were demonstrating. That was obvious from all the banners and posters they raised. Only he could not hear what they were shouting. But he would not have understood them anyway. He could not even make out any of the words on the banners.

He went to the wall and stood there staring at them, with both hands on the glass. So close to those who were leaning on the glass, which was to them a mirror. Suddenly, a wave of turbulence rippled through the crowd, as a bus stopped on the other side. Only the top part of the bus was in sight, above the heads. It must be the Guard, for it was his time to arrive. And it was indeed him, holding his black leather bag tight to his chest, elbowing his way through the mob. The men and women blocked him from reaching his hut, pushing him back or pulling at his coat from behind. He thrust his way through them, forcing his hefty body and large belly into their angry bodies, hitting them with his bag, shouting at them. God knows what. But Arman could tell he was swearing at them. Although he managed to reach this side of the road, the young people in front of the iron door to his office pushed him back. He then hurled his sturdy body at them and started hitting them with his bag. But the young protesters shoved him again into the mob.

Arman shook his head and started floundering. Why did they do that to him? Poor man!

'Hey, you, bunch of... hey, leave him alone!' Arman shouted at the people, pounding on the glass. But of course, no one heard him, as even he on his quiet side could not hear their uproar. He strained his ears, holding his head askew, and heard a very faint hubbub. Or maybe he imagined it.

What was going on? What were these people angry about? Why don't they let the Guard get to his work? What if there was a decision on the asylum request?

'Hey fuckers, that's my life you're ruining. I'm waiting every second and you're now... Hey, let him get in! Let him. Please!' But, of course, no one heard him. And were they to hear him, they would not understand a word of what he was saying.

The Guard made another effort to reach the door to his office, but the protesters pushed him back again into the crowd that sucked in and absorbed the hefty old man. In a short moment, he disappeared among the angry mob.

Arman ran along the glass—maybe he would catch a sight of the Guard through the arms and shoulders of the protesters. But there was no trace of him.

'Hey, you ruined my life. You bloody bastards!' Arman shouted again, kicking the wall. Then he unzipped his flies, took out his penis and peed at the glass. At the people behind it, swinging from side to side. 'You're ruining my life! You're ruining my life,' he said with a lump in his throat, pulling up his zip.

He sagged down by the glass wall, just a metre from his own pee, leant back, put his head on his knees and started crying. What bad luck for him that these people had found no other day or place to protest. But why were they demonstrating here anyway?

He wiped his eyes and stood up again. He went a distance from the glass wall. The crowd extended to both sides as far as his eyes could see. Strange people. Some were facing him, looking at themselves in the mirror. And hold on a second: the large photo of the smiling blond man with the white shiny teeth, the Welcoming Smiling Man, over there on the other side of the road, high above the crowd, was now crossed out in red paint. That man was the designer of the wall. Were these people angry at him? Maybe they were protesting against the wall again. Or could it be... really, could it be that they were protesting against keeping Arman in the desert behind the wall? That was possible! Wasn't the Guard worried in the beginning that if people were to get wind of Arman's existence, they would cause trouble? But how they would have found out? Maybe the helicopter men had revealed the secret? Or the Guard's own daughter? Could she now also be among the crowd? If she were, she would have helped her father. But how would Arman know? How would he know from this doomed side of the world? He shouted and kicked the wall.

'Hey, can somebody explain to me what's going on? Please!'

But of course, no one heard him. Of course. 'Aaaaaaaaaaaargh!'

He ran into his tent, took off his T-shirt and trousers, grabbed a bottle of water, poured half of it over his head and sat in the puddle. Then he gulped down the rest of the water. It was all a sordid business. 'Hey, you shitheads, you're driving me mad, you fuckers!' he shouted and knew that no one heard him. He picked up his pen and notebook, put it on his bare, wet thigh and started to write. Better to keep his mind busy and prevent himself from going mad. For no one would hear him in this doomed desert. No one would ever hear him again, if they would never let the Guard come to work again. What a sordid business!

Hours later, in the afternoon, Arman saw the police and other heavy-uniformed units, with shields and sticks, push into the crowd, forcing the protesters to disperse. Two immense armoured vehicles with water cannons were now at work. He put on his cap and ran out to stand there and watch, in only his underwear. The heavy stream of water hit some of the men and women and hurled them over the road that was now empty. The water also cleared the hundreds of bottles and cans and all the waste that had been strewn along the road and pavements.

The two vehicles drove slowly along the road, clearing everyone and everything in their way as they passed—even the barricades that the protestors had put up at some parts of the road. The crowd was now divided into those on the other side of the road and those on this side, both groups extending to the left and right of Arman and the hut.

Some of the protesters ran back onto the road behind the two vehicles, but the water cannon at once turned on them and shot them off the road. A young woman was now hit by the water and was pushed up to the glass wall. She was glued with her back to it, until the cannon moved on to other protesters and the woman fell to the ground. Arman ran to see that she wasn't wounded. She lay there examining her own head for injuries and when she was, maybe, sure that she was okay, she rose to her feet and ran out to the road again.

Although he now stood in the shadow of the wall, Arman felt the heat on his bare back and shoulders, hopping from one foot to another in the hot sand. He returned to his tent, put on his T-shirt, grabbed his trousers, took out the knife and carefully cut both legs just above the knee, fashioning a pair of shorts for himself. He then put on his trainers and went out again.

One of the vehicles had now passed and was about a hundred metres from the hut to the south, shooting water at the protesters. The other one was sweeping the northern side. Two police cars were parked in the middle of the road across from where Arman stood. Their search lights flashing. And although a number of officers and several other armoured troops stood in rows at both sides of the road, hundreds of the protesters were already back on the road again, shouting and waving their fists in the air. They had picked up their wet banners, lifting them and waving them, some smeared with mud.

Arman sat in front of his tent watching the scene that now amused him; as though he sat in an outdoor cinema. All to himself! A non-stop cinema for that matter. But a silent movie.

In the evening, the protesters bivouacked on both sides of the road, setting up makeshift tents with tarpaulin, canvas or sheets.

Armoured vehicles and police cars with flashing lights drove along the road back and forth. Their sirens were heard very faintly. They had put a strong barricade around the hut, with an armed guard in front of the iron door.

The tents on this side of the road mostly leant on the glass wall; a mirror to them, used as one of the walls of their tents. Arman could see inside them. All over the pavement on both sides, fires were kindled, burning wood and cardboard boxes.

Most of the tents were crammed with young people. They didn't look like they knew each other. At least, many of them did not. Some seemed to be couples or friends. Girls and boys mingled; some took off most of their clothes. Even the girls. But why did these people, so much the opposite to the people of his own country, take off their clothes so easily in public? Was it maybe because they enjoyed the sun? That was understandable, given how little the sun shone through the clouds and how it rained for much of the time in their world. Completely opposite to his side of the wall. But, oh, how easily some girls took off their blouse or even their trousers in front of those men and without hesitation, just as was happening in front of his very eyes! In those tents! Would he get used to it when he was on the other side?

In one of the tents, a young man, half-naked, in only a pair of shorts, started to play a guitar, muted though it seemed to Arman. A group of men and women around him. Suddenly a young woman came in, sat in a corner, between two men, took off her T-shirt and remained in her bra. Arman stayed for a few moments watching them, then went along other tents and looked inside those with an open side to the glass wall, or those that were no more than open tents, without any walls at all.

He walked backwards and forwards along the glass wall, staring at the people, forgetting even to eat. Shivering in the cold breeze of his desert. When he could no longer stand the hunger and the cold, he went back to his tent and put on the sweater he had received in the last delivery. He then broke his last wooden box, made a fire, cooked, and had his dinner watching the protesters in their sit-ins behind the glass wall drinking, eating, singing and dancing. The non-ending silent film. As time passed, they seemed getting drunk; hugging, kissing, getting more and more out of their clothes, or lying and falling asleep.

Later at night, most of the fires on the other side had gone out and his own had turned into ashes. He walked along the glass wall, observing the young men and women lying inside the tents like sardines in a tin. Some were completely naked; some had their legs across the backs or stomachs of others. Some with their heads on others' chests.

In one of the smaller tents, under the dim light coming from the streetlights through a slit into the tent, a young woman and a man lay naked in each other's arms, their legs entangled, rolling to one side, then back to the other. Arman looked round, then lay beside them on his side of the glass and put his hand into his trousers.

A while later, he woke up, shivering from the cold of early morning. The man and woman beside him on the other side of the glass had fallen asleep in each other's arms. Naked; without any worry that someone might enter their tent. And so oblivious to their surrounding as if it weren't them hours earlier being shot with water cannons. Such a peace of mind!

Arman jumped up, ran into his own tent and wrapped himself in both blankets.

The next day, the protest grew stronger. More people had arrived. Most of the makeshift tents, except for a few large ones, were now removed. Parts of the glass wall were smeared with writing. The Guard had not come in. His office was still barricaded, guarded now by a few more armed police. Tyres and wooden boxes were set alight in the middle of the road. The two armoured vehicles with water cannons had come back. Mayhem. Fiercer than yesterday. The security and the riot police, with helmets and shields, pushed the protesters away, beating them with truncheons, while the protesters threw stones and all kinds of bottles, tins and litter.

As it was getting hot on his side, Arman went back in his tent, watching them from there. His own battle with the heat began anew. While trying to write up some of his impressions of the protest, he fanned himself; caught by surprise each time a sudden gust covered him with sand. He would brush off the sand from his face and chest, swearing at the wind, but then wish for more. He would wipe his sweat, pour some water economically on his face and chest, and try to control his anger.

In the afternoon, two helicopters appeared, hovering over the crowded road on the other side of the glass. Their whirring sounded far off. They would now and then swerve into the space on this side of the glass wall, sounding louder.

Suddenly, a large crane drove through the crowd towards

the glass wall. The protesters made way for it. It steered nearer to the pavement with its huge chain track wheels, then stopped and directed its jib mast to the wall. Were they trying to break the glass?

Arman crawled to the entrance of the tent and watched as the inner mast slid out of the main jib, extended upwards, higher and higher until it reached the top of the glass wall. He stuck his head out into the scorching sun and looked up. The crane's hook passed the top of the wall, coming to this side. A huge black box was fixed to it, swinging. It hit the glass wall and was immediately pulled up and swung over the top of the wall to the other side and vanished behind it. He looked down and saw a dozen policemen scuffling with two protesters on the top of the crane cabin. Inside the cab itself, two other policemen seemed to have taken over the control of the crane, as the cab turned, and the mast veered off the glass wall towards the middle of the road. The police officers, holding tight to the two protesters, jumped from the top of the cab and the crane moved away in a thick cloud of smoke.

Arman pulled his head back inside the tent and remained there on all fours watching the protesters disperse all over the place, running to the pavements, covering their faces. Many had their backs to the glass wall. Some ran into the few tents that were still standing. A canister flew over the heads of some protesters, leaving a trail of white smoke behind. It kept spinning in the middle of the road, spreading a cloud of smoke. The young men and women covered their faces with shawls, or shirts, or sank their heads in their collars and ran through the smoke and fire. Another canister flew into the crowd. And another one.

In a short time, the whole area was clouded in smoke, through which the security forces, wearing military gas masks, advanced and took control of the pavements. The crane drove away. A fire engine splashed water on the fires through the smoke. The whizzing helicopters flew in circles over the area. Now, the protesters either stood or crouched down along the glass wall, hundreds of them, blocking Arman's view of the road.

That night, while service vehicles and dozens of street sweepers were clearing the road and the pavements, hundreds of protesters set up new makeshift tents, lying inside, resting, cleaning themselves, their clothes and their banners. They ate and drank, or again played music and sang, muted. In the road, police cars drove busily up and down with flashing lights. A helicopter hovered high above, its constant faint whirr reaching Arman.

Over there, on the other side of the road, where the billboard was, under the bright streetlight, two men on ladders, one on each side, took a new clean copy of the large poster of the Welcoming Smiling Man with the shiny teeth and rolled it over the version covered in red paint. Just when the two men descended the ladders and picked up long roller brushes and started to roll them over the poster, a few protesters ran across the road with tins in hand but were restrained at the edge of the pavement by shields of the riot police.

One of the protesters threw his tin at the poster, but it fell behind the police officers without reaching the billboard. The officers pushed the protesters with their shields so hard that this time three of the protesters fell backwards onto the road; a tin of red paint spilled on the road and another one went all over the face and clothes of one of the protesters. The others ran and helped him get to his feet, while the officers, heads inside large helmets, stepped forward, step by step, pushing them back with their shields, until they had cleared the road.

Arman walked along the glass wall, looking into the tents. Some of the young women and men were gathered around a laptop watching something attentively. But the laptop screen was not visible. He passed another two tents and stood by one where a few men and women were staring at a laptop held by a young woman who leant back on the glass wall, her laptop screen facing Arman. They were watching the news. It was showing scenes of the protest. It looked even fiercer than anything Arman had witnessed for himself over the last two days. Then they broadcast a vague, blurry, shaky shot taken from the sky. The camera zoomed in and showed down there in the desert a small tent. A little head stuck out of it. An indistinct face. It was him! Arman. He looked more closely at it, but the shot changed. They now showed how the crane was pulling away from the glass wall.

A presenter came into the picture. She said something Arman couldn't hear, though he wouldn't have understood it anyway. Suddenly, the woman with the laptop and all those in the tent lifted their arms and shouted. Hurrahed, maybe? Then they jumped up and the young woman shut her laptop, put it down, and jumped to her feet as well. They all started dancing, shouting and rushed out of the tent.

Arman ran along the glass wall, watching them. Also all the other protesters were now hurrying out of the tents, onto the pavement or into the road, dancing, clinking their drinks. They were clearly shouting, and probably singing. Whatever had happened, Arman could not tell. But it must have been some good news. He imagined that it could be that the demands of the protesters were met. Whatever they were. Were they going to let him in? That was possible, wasn't it? Didn't they show his picture? The whole fuss seemed, in fact, to be about him. Or maybe better he shouldn't give himself false hope?

When he went to bed, wrapping himself in both his blankets, there were still some protesters hanging around, though most of them and almost all the police had left.

31

Late next morning, on Friday, Arman woke up from a deep sleep, perspiring under the two blankets. Though groggy and out of breath, drenched in his own sweat, he felt rested after two days of following the protesters on the other side of the wall, while fighting the heat on his own side or keeping himself warm from the freezing nights in the desert.

He quickly kicked off the blankets and took a deep breath. His body still sluggish, he made an effort and sat up, stretched until his bones cracked back, then crawled to the opening of the tent. The protests had indeed ended; the road looked cleared and clean; all the paint and writing removed from the glass wall; and the Guard had showed up for work.

Arman crawled back in, put on his shoes, then his cap, drank a large gulp of water and sprinted in one go straight to the hut. The sun was already high in the sky and the heat heavy and sultry.

The blind was drawn up halfway. The Guard sat morose, pouting, staring at the monitor, his glasses fallen down his nose. The upper part of his body and the upper half of the room were in shade, while the rest of his body and the room were in full sunlight. He obviously ignored Arman. He couldn't have not noticed him, certainly.

'I'm glad to see you again,' Arman said, waiting for the Guard to finally acknowledge his presence. But no response.

'I thought... What has been going on for the last two days?'

The old man at last looked at him, still pouting. 'It's a bit complicated to explain, Arman.'

'Well obviously they were protesting against something. Did it have to do with me? I saw a picture of myself. They had tried to film me.'

'You did?' The Guard peered into Arman's eyes, holding his head askew. 'How is that possible?'

'I saw it on someone's laptop in one of the tents. You know, they had pitched their tents all around—'

'Yes, I also saw that. Of course!' the Guard interrupted him. 'It's interesting that you watched the news as well. I mean—'

'I didn't understand any of it though. I mean I couldn't even hear it.'

'Listen, Arman. I have some bad news but also some good news for you. Let me start with the good, shall I?'

Arman froze in his place. What could the bad news be? It could only be...

'But let me explain first. Those people were protesting because... Oh, no, that's the bad news. So let's...'

Arman waited, frowning, squinting at the Guard. How bad must it be that he didn't even dare to be direct? Was his claim rejected again? That must be it.

'You know, the good news is that they... I mean the protesters managed to force the government to accept a lawyer to take on your case.'

Arman took a step forward and put his hands on the glass,

peering into the Guard's eyes. Was that what they were celebrating last night?

'She's going to fight it. The decision. I mean there was a decision on your application. And this woman, I mean your lawyer... You know, a whistle-blower had apparently... Maybe one of the people working at the office, a man or a woman, no one knows yet, had told the media about you and the fact that they had rejected your application. I mean also your most recent one. So before I had even seen it, it was in the papers and on TV two days ago. So people got mad. You probably saw how they blocked me from—'

'I did. And I am sorry! They shouldn't have treated you that way.'

'Ah, never mind,' the Guard brushed away Arman's comment with a wave of his hand. 'It was worth it.'

'Was that the bad news?' Arman said calmly, his lips trembling. So they had rejected him. That was it. His last chance. Gone.

'Listen, Arman,' the Guard stood up. 'It doesn't mean there is no...'

Arman felt dizzy and leant against the glass, looking at him.

'Listen, I'm devastated too. Really. But what can I do? What can *we* do? Except for just hoping it will all turn out well for you. And I'm hopeful, I must tell you,' the man said, staring at Arman.

Arman put his head on the glass.

The Guard put on his coat. 'Arman, dear boy, I'm exhausted. You don't know how I spent the last two days. I need to go. The bus is coming. I came only to tell you the news. I had to. And here it is. Very short.' He picked up a paper from the desk and started reading:

Dear Arman,

We regretfully inform you that your third and final asylum claim has been rejected. We know that your country as well as your Region have democratically elected governments, with whom we have good relations. We support your country and the people and leaders of your Region. Although we acknowledge that sporadically some unrest can occur in your country, you have failed to deliver any evidence of the events with which you claim you were involved. You are, therefore, by no means entitled to refugee status, without which you will not be allowed to enter our country. Thus, the gate cannot be opened to you.

'Would you please stop? I know the rest,' Arman said, turning his back, leaning on the glass.

'I'm sorry, Arman. By law, I have to read the whole text for you,' said the Guard and continued:

You are advised to go back to your country of origin. However, our law...

Arman now heard only the panting of his own breath and the chaos in his head. He sagged down in front of the hut, staring at the desert that was blurred by the prisms of his tears. What now? Must he spend the rest of his life, if he were to remain alive, in this desert, waiting every fortnight for aid? What could a lawyer do for him if they hadn't believed him when he spoke for himself? How and from where could a lawyer get the evidence they requested? Evidence? What evidence? Are they crazy? Or stupid? He was the evidence himself. He *was* the evidence.

'Arman... Arman...' the metallic sound of the speaker, interpreting the Guard's voice, interrupted his rumination.

'Arman, boy, I'm sorry, my bus is coming in a minute. I have to go now.' The Guard pushed the paper through the slot in the glass door. 'Take it. But really don't worry too much. Let's wait until Monday and see, okay?'

Arman stood up lethargically and pulled the paper out, looking at the Guard with a shaky, forced smile.

'Listen, boy. My heart goes out to you. But we can't give up, okay? There is hope. This woman, the lawyer, she is one of the best. Really. So I wish you a good weekend. And let's see what Monday brings,' he said and rolled down the blind.

Arman turned and wandered off into the heat of the desert, under the rising sun. Weekend? What good weekend? What's this man talking about? Really. 'Are you kidding? You are joking, aren't you, old man?' What weekend in this hell of a desert? What difference does it make when all days are the same and every day is worse than the one before?

He tossed his baseball cap as far as he could, then kicked in the sand, and kicked until he was exhausted and knelt down, panting. He took off his T-shirt and started digging madly, scattering the sand all around. To bury himself. Just as the jackal did when digging in the sand. The bastard who never appeared again. But even deep down the sand was so hot that he couldn't dig anymore. His knees throbbed, burning in the hot sand. He threw himself on his back, facing the scorching sun, then when he could no longer endure the roasting sand on his back, he rolled on his front, his back to the sun.

In less than ten minutes, Arman was literally baking in the hot sand, under the glowing sun. He jumped up, grabbed his T-shirt, then walked to his cap, picked it up and rushed into the tent. He took off his shoes, then his trousers, sat in the middle of the tent and poured half a bottle water over this head. Then the other half.

'Oh, how much I wish I was home, Mother. You could smear my face and back with some Vaseline.' He closed his eyes, clenching his teeth. 'And if we had no Vaseline, you would smear it with yoghurt. I don't even have yoghurt here. Oh, Mother, not even...' He remembered the cream they had provided along with the Vaseline in one of the batches of aid a few weeks ago, which he then didn't know the purpose of. But maybe it was for sunburn. That made sense. What else could it be for?

He crawled to the corner and rummaged among the scattered groceries and utensils until he found the tube. He squeezed a mass of the cream into his palm, smeared his face with it, then his shoulders and chest. He squeezed another mass and smeared it on his back. It immediately began to cool down the burning of his skin and comforted him. But the suffocatingly heavy, hot air took his breath away. He sprawled over the mattress, trying to retain his normal breathing. 'Am I going to die in this damn desert, Mother? With no one around. Not even a savage jackal.'

That night, sitting at the glass wall, with his back to the City, staring at the empty desert, bluish grey under the dark sky, he smelled a salt-whiff of the sea brought by the chill breeze that brushed his face. He vomited.

32

The next day, early in the morning, Arman was jogging along the glass wall. The sand crumbled under his feet. Sweat dripped from his face. But his own huffing and puffing, his pounding heart inside his heaving ribcage and the rhythmic, muffled thuds of his feet hitting the sand soothed his uneasy thoughts. Going for a run, he had thought, might clear his mind; the dismay of losing all prospects of entry to the City. Except for maybe a small chance that a lawyer might be able to reverse the decision. But should he pin any hope on that? There was no silver lining whatsoever and he had to stop deceiving himself. How could a lawyer do anything for him if she didn't know him or even his story? Any of his stories. Or maybe she knew?

He had run a few hundred metres south. All the time, his head ached with simmering thoughts, trying to think of what his next step should be. But was there any possible next step at all? Or must he rot here in the rising heat of the desert? It was already getting hot, despite the morning breeze that brushed his face and bare arms.

He stopped, bent over and put his hands on his knees, staring at the frail legs sticking out of his shorts. He heaved his head and looked up. He was so small and insignificant in front of the colossal wall, under the bright sky, and in the vast empty desert.

The sand rippled in the breeze that was becoming stronger, combing the tops of the dunes, spattering him with sand. He looked over. A sandstorm was approaching, sweeping through the desert; a high, moving wall of sand, whirling, coming his way, sending its powerful wind as a herald to warn him. He ran back along the glass wall, enshrouded by the wind and sand. But he was already far from the tent.

With his hands in front of his eyes, he walked with his back to the wind, forcing himself through the storm, until he was exhausted and could move no further.

The sand wall reached him and hit the glass wall with a harsh thud, pressing Arman to the glass with such a mighty push, he thought it would break the wall or at least crack it, to send him rolling into the other world. Wouldn't that be amazing? But the wall remained standing there, as solid and lofty as it always was. And he was still pressed against it, sand pouring at him.

He sat down with his back pressed to the glass, curled up, hugging his knees tightly, with his head bent down. The sand, clattering against the glass, accumulated at the foot of the wall, and at his own feet.

After about ten minutes, when the storm calmed down and he moved the sand off himself, he could see his tent, still about two hundred meters off, just a small dot in the mass of sand. He stood up and wandered slowly towards it in the now low wind. He was walking back home. So that was it, wasn't it? This is home? He was going to rot in there, in his tent, to be buried under the sand. Or devoured by the jackals.

A few metres closer, he backed off, hunkering down. The tent was moving as if somebody was inside. He groped in his pockets, but both were empty. Oh, of course, the folding knife was in the pocket of the other trousers inside the tent. He looked round but there was nothing to pick up. He didn't need to though. He could just let them take all the food and water and beg them to leave him alone. Whoever was inside his tent. 'Just leave me a bottle of water, please,' he would ask politely.

He bent forward on his bare knees and waited a few minutes. The wind had now settled into a gentle breeze. There was someone inside, indeed; a shadowy figure floundering about, bumping against the sides of the tent, sounding as if they were looking through his belongings. It could also have been a large animal. But it wasn't the jackal, that was for sure.

'Hey there, what are you doing in my tent?'

The figure, who was leaning on the side of the tent, jumped off, probably to the middle, therefore Arman could no longer see it.

A few moments of silence.

'Listen, if you want my food and water, you can have them.' But would the person inside, if it was a person, understand his language?

The figure stuck his head out, looking round, then crept slowly out of the tent. A boy, around Arman's own age, with shorter hair and a thinner beard, stood at the opening. A knife in his hand. It looked like Arman's knife. But the boy's gloomy eyes reflected more fear than malice.

'Listen, man, I'm harmless,' Arman hollered. 'Just please come out of my tent and we will settle it. I hope you understand me. Do you?'

'I don't want to hurt you,' the boy said, in Arman's language, looking at the knife in his own hand.

Arman stood up slowly, looked at him closer and said, 'Hey, man, I'm glad someone—'

The boy was now smiling. So has he agreed to... Oh, no, wait! Was he not...?

'What the hell brought you here, man?' Arman yelled, opening his arms.

'I can't believe it either, Arman. Is that really you?' the boy shouted back. He closed the folding knife and tossed it into the tent. 'I thought you were dead. That's what they said. They said your boat had sunk.'

Arman smiled, stared at him for a moment, then strode towards him with open arms. 'Come, give me a hug, man!'

They hugged and caressed each other's hair, then stepped back and took a good look at one another.

'Hey, are you thirsty? Hungry? Look, that's my stash in there.' Arman bent and crept inside the tent. 'Oh, I see you've already helped yourself.'

They both laughed.

'Sorry! I was very thirsty. And starving. I was very lucky to have found this tent in that crazy storm. And it's yours too. Unbelievable!' the boy said, bending down, standing at the opening of the tent, looking at the wrappers of the nut bars he had eaten and an empty water bottle, tossed on the floor.

'Don't worry. We'll get more food and drink tomorrow,' said Arman, coming out of the tent again.

The boy looked at the glass wall as if he was noticing it for the first time. 'What is this? A wall?' he asked, walking over there, as though he were under a spell. 'That must be the City. How can we get to the other side?'

'You will get used to it,' Arman shouted at him from the tent. 'You just need some patience. Actually, lots of it.'

He watched the boy put his head to the glass. He left him for a few moments to take in the situation, then dawdled to the wall and stood beside him.

A car passed swiftly on the other side of the road, without being heard.

'So that's the City behind those hills? Where we need to go?' the boy asked calmly.

'Yup!' said Arman. 'It's even more beautiful when the lights are on at night.'

'And no one would even stop to see what's happening to us here behind this bloody glass?'

'They don't see us. It's mirrored on the other side. They see only themselves and the lake and their City behind their back. You can imagine it, can't you?'

The boy looked at Arman, frowning. 'What do you mean mirrored? They can't see us?'

'No,' said Arman, turning to lean with his back on the glass wall. He waited a moment to give the boy some time to imagine it, then grabbed his arm and walked to the hut, dragging the boy behind him. 'Come, let me show you.'

In front of the hut with the blind drawn down, Arman asked him to look inside the cubicle.

The boy peered into the hut through the slit at the edge of the blind.

'There's only one way to get in there,' said Arman.

'Where is it? So why don't you…?'

'It's this door,' Arman said, pushing the glass door with all his strength.

The boy rushed to it and examined the slit and the thin metal frame. 'What the hell is this? How is this possible?' said the boy, staring at Arman.

'This is the gate to the City. But you need a good story to be let in, as the Guard says,' said Arman calmly.

'The Guard?'

'Uh-huh,' said Arman, crouching down in front of the hut, observing the boy's confusion. 'He's a nice old man. But you need patience with him.'

The boy took a few steps away from the hut, dragging his hand along the glass wall, shaking his head. He peered attentively at the world behind the glass. 'And who is the fucker on that billboard over there?'

'That's the genius who invented this wall,' Arman said, turning his head to the desert. 'He's welcoming people into the City.'

'But not us.'

'Nope!'

Early in the afternoon, Arman was lying down in front of his tent, in the shadow of the glass wall, when the boy came out, after he had slept for about five hours. Arman lifted his head and looked up. The boy seemed still to be surprised at finding Arman here.

'What a long nap,' said Arman, staring at the boy's hands that were fumbling with something that looked like... oh, no, it was one... a smartphone.

'Hey, you have a phone on you?' Arman said, sitting upright.

'Ah, no signal,' the boy said, holding up the phone, moving it round. 'All the way here, there was no signal. Since we left, actually. Already in the sea.'

'I lost mine in the sea,' said Arman. 'Come, sit down. It'll get cooler in two hours, then I'll cook some rice and stew for us. You're now my refugee. In my shelter.'

The boy tossed the phone inside the tent and sat down beside Arman. 'The battery is dying anyway. So what's the use? I've got a charger as well. But here?' he sneered. 'Tell me, where do you get the food from?'

'I'm going to tell you how everything works here,' Arman said, looking at him. It was wonderful to at last have a companion. A compatriot, for that matter. From Arman's very own village. He had known him since they were kids, as he was only a year younger than Arman. Even after they moved to the city, Arman used to meet him with other friends whenever he visited the village. And they had met again at the harbour town before Arman managed to get on the boat and he had stayed behind.

Arman looked at him with a smile. The boy's sunburnt arms and face reminded him of his own first days. 'I'm going to give you some cream for your sunburn,' he said to the boy and stood up.

While preparing dinner, late in the afternoon, Arman explained to his young Refugee all that he needed to know about the wall, the asylum procedure, efficient ways to go about life in the desert and what to do not to go insane. Then when they sat to eat, watching the sunset behind the City at the other side of the glass wall, he told the boy about his own journey and what he had seen and gone through up to now.

The young Refugee, the plate of rice and tomato sauce with white beans on his lap, listening eagerly to Arman, seemed to have retained some strength. He was luckier than Arman to find the glass wall after a walk of only two days through the desert.

After dinner, Arman brewed some tea, using the last of the gas that was left in the stove. They went and sat by the glass wall, drinking their sweet black teas, staring at the twinkling lights of the City and their swaying reflections in the lake. Then the boy told Arman about his recent journey and how their boat had stopped about a mile from the coast and sent the refugees ashore in small groups of three or four in little dinghies. So there were more people, including some families, expected to arrive here if they were able to make it through the desert. It had been a dark night when they had arrived at the coast, thus the boy had lost the rest of his fellow travellers.

As the night went on, the desert breeze got stronger and colder. Arman went to the tent and brought both blankets. They wrapped themselves up and lay on their backs, watching the stars. And the slender crescent that was rising at the horizon.

'Don't tell them about your misery and true problems,' Arman said after a while, turning to the boy. 'Because they don't care. Invent something.'

'Such as?' the boy said, sitting upright. He tightened the blanket around his shoulders and leant back on the glass wall.

'I don't know, something that moves them; something harsh; something dangerous. I told them the story of my life and the history of my family and our country and our Folk, and yet they rejected me. All three times.'

'So what now?' the boy asked, lying down again, putting his elbow on the ground, his hand under his head, looking at Arman.

'Well, what then? I don't know,' said Arman, turning his head to look back at the stars. 'I think at some point they will even stop the care deliveries. Once this man came along and said he was wandering in the desert for longer than a year. He had even tried to enter the City at two other gates. It appears that there will be no other chance. I don't know. I really don't.'

'How long have you been here?' the boy asked.

'Once I started counting. It must now be forty-five or forty-seven days,' Arman said, still looking up at the dark sky. 'And three or four days on my way through the desert. So I don't know exactly how long. I lost count of some of the days.' He then sat up and stared at the boy, tightening the blanket around his shoulders. 'There's probably one tiny chance, but I have little trust in it.'

'How, please tell me,' said the boy, now sitting upright.

'Well, it seems that some whistle-blower has revealed my existence behind this wall. I suspect maybe the Guard himself. But how do I know? So then apparently a lawyer has taken on my case. She's trying to win it for me.'

'But that's great news, Arman, isn't it?' the boy gushed.

'I really don't give a damn anymore. What's your story anyway? I mean the real reason. You can tell *me* that. But let's go in the tent. It's getting cold.'

33

The young Refugee awoke to the pulsating loud whirr of something like the blades of a helicopter. Oh, but it was a helicopter, indeed! Its rumble could not be mistaken. He turned his head to left and right and realised that he was in Arman's tent. But Arman was not in his bed. And his blanket was missing too.

'Hey, Arman! Are you outside?' he shouted through the roar of the helicopter, sitting up, then crawled to the mouth of the tent.

A huge helicopter, only some thirty metres from the tent, hovered two metres above the ground, scattering the sand in a vortex that reached the tent, brushing the boy's face. When it was balanced, floating stable, its hatch opened and a uniformed man, helmet and goggles on his head, dropped a large wooden box that fell in the sand with a muffled thud. The man raised a thumb and shut the hatch. The young Refugee waved to him but was sure the man didn't see it, as he was inside again, sitting beside another man in helmet and goggles in the front pit.

The helicopter ascended so quickly that in no time it was above the glass wall, then veered with a swift turn, its noise fading gradually in the distance.

In the now overwhelming silence, the boy looked round for Arman, barefoot in the hot sand, the heat of the desert slapping his face. The sun was already approaching the middle of the sky. Almost midday. Where was Arman with his blanket in this sweltering heat?

Standing at the entrance of the tent, he held his head in his hands, eyes shut. Then lifted his head up to the sky. What should he do? Go open the box or wait until Arman was back?

A moment later, he ran to the box. The sand burnt his soles. He knelt in front of the box and grabbed the hasp. But it was in fact not for him. He stood up, looked round again, then ran back to the tent.

He put on his shoes and looked for his straw hat. It had gone. Arman must have taken it. He had left the baseball cap for him. Or maybe he had just borrowed it to go for a dump or something. Perhaps a walk? He had said that he would sometimes go for a walk or a jog. But it was too hot for that now. And with a blanket? Oh, and his own large rucksack was missing as well. The phone was in it too. It was dead anyway. And wait! Arman also had taken all the food and water. So he has gone. Maybe for good? Can't be true.

The young Refugee put Arman's cap on and ran out of the tent, into the desert, calling for his friend.

No response, nor any trace.

Now, he was among only little hillocks of sand with only a metre of the top of the glass wall in sight; its faint grey line cutting the blue sky on the horizon. He called for Arman and called again, hearing his own voice fading gradually. As if the muffled resonance of his voice was hanging around him for a second then being slowly absorbed by the sand. But no sign of Arman. And the heat was already becoming unbearable.

Back to the tent, the boy opened the box, staring at all the food and drink, not able to stop his grin, despite the loss of his friend. He rummaged through and was thrilled to find the water. He took out a bottle and drank half. Then picked up a small pack of orange juice and gulped down all of that. He dragged the box but could barely move it. So he took out armfuls of the groceries and carried them into the tent.

When he had dragged the empty box up to the tent, he arranged some of the food and drink indoors, covered it with the pans and pots or in their own packaging, then put back the rest into the large wooden box. He poured water over his head and face. But it was actually better to save the water. Arman had told him of the disaster when he had run out of water.

The young Refugee went back into the tent again and had a splendid breakfast. He had to watch Arman more closely to learn how to cook. Arman would have taught him if he had asked him to. But how could he have known that the bastard would disappear just like that? Now, he was going to have to go through all that Arman had gone through, all on his own. It was so incredible to have arrived at Arman's tent, as if fate had directed him here: his lucky star. And indeed, he was following a shiny star when he was walking the desert. But now the star had gone out. He shook his head. At least he wouldn't have to suffer from the hunger and thirst that poor Arman had had to endure.

He shouldn't have told Arman about his grandmother. It had

made him cry last night, when the boy told him that after he was left behind at the harbour and later had heard that Arman's boat had capsized, he had returned to the village for a short while. He had gone to visit Grandma before leaving the village again. She was now everyone's Grandma, and was so called by all the villagers. When the boy had told her that he was going to try the journey again and he might one day meet Arman, she had made him promise that he would hug her grandson, tightly for her. She had said she couldn't die before she heard news from Arman. And dying was what she was waiting for. It was her time, she had said.

Now, the young Refugee wished he had just kept all that to himself. Old grannies said these kinds of things. There had been no need to tell Arman. Would it have made any difference, anyway? Perhaps Arman was just tired of everything and had given up already. So maybe the boy didn't need to feel guilty about it. It was too late now anyway; he couldn't take it back. He could only hope that Arman would return, as there was even no possibility that Arman would ever be able to go back home. And that, of course, depended on him not getting lost. And on him surviving the desert again. That they both had arrived safely here from the coast did not mean they could make the journey back with the same good fortune. It was by no means an easy affair to come this far.

He started tidying and cleaning the tent. It seemed that Arman hadn't bothered very much. Breadcrumbs and apple cores everywhere. Even his mattress was scattered with scraps of nuts, biscuits and rice and apple seeds. The boy took off the cap and dusted the mattress with it. He lifted the pillow and found a notebook and a pen underneath. He looked into it, read a few lines, then leafed through. Arman had described his journey in it.

The boy turned more pages. Arman had also written about the time he had spent here at the wall and in the desert. Then about his family, and about his time in prison. So he had been jailed? For what? He had never heard that Arman had been arrested. But should he be reading this? It didn't feel right. What if Arman suddenly appeared? It would be very embarrassing. So he put the notebook back under the pillow.

He went out and stood by the glass wall, staring at the world behind it. It looked so peaceful and clean. Unsullied. If they hadn't let Arman in, how were they supposed to allow himself to enter this City? He had to have a good story. But he had none. What should he tell them? Arman had advised him to invent a strong story full of violence and danger. He had promised to help him think of one. But now he was gone.

Before his journey, at the harbour town where he was waiting to come over here, smugglers and other people who were also preparing for the crossing, were talking about all kinds of stories one could tell to be accepted as a refugee. If only he had listened more attentively. But he was then focused on getting away. It was his second time trying. And was it not enough to tell them how desperate his life was in a village without any job, working hard in the fields throughout the year, cultivating fruit and vegetables that could not be sold on the market even at cost price? Their lovely crops, of which they took care with all their sweat and blood, could not compete with the imported food. Arman had laughed at him last night, when the boy said that is what he would tell. Well, he didn't laugh, but had said, 'Amazing! That's exactly what they are waiting to hear. That's guaranteed rejection, my friend!'

The young Refugee looked closer. Across the wall, people were lying in shorts and bikinis floating in boats far in the lake—some even seemed completely naked. Some women lay down in the boats with bare breasts. But the details were not easy to make out. Not even the breasts of those who lay by the lakeside. Some were among the trees closer to the wall. Still, details of their bodies were not easy to recognise either. They apparently enjoyed the midday sun, while on this side, the boy was roasting, getting dizzy and dazzled by the blazing light that, though it now slanted down to the other side and he stood in the thin shadow of the glass wall, was agonising. He could no longer stand it, so he walked back to the tent.

He pulled out Arman's notebook again, lay down and read the diary entries. He was surprised by some, and saddened by others. Although it was chaotically written, jumping from one event to another, the boy enjoyed the read. His way of reading, in fact, meant he struggled to make out some words or understand a whole sentence. Not only because of Arman's untidy handwriting, but because of his own limited literacy. Wouldn't it have been fair if he had, at least, finished his primary schooling as Arman had?

Suddenly, he heard a thud. He hurried to the opening of the tent on all fours and saw an animal resembling a dog or a fox on the grocery box. Oh, it must be one of the jackals Arman told him about.

The jackal jumped off and ran a metre away, then stopped,

turning to the boy, staring at him.

'Hey, you must be... Oh, I forgot your name. Arman told me about you.'

The jackal lowered its head, bared its fangs and snarled, peering right in the boy's eyes, its furry tail wagging.

'Hey, don't get mad. Do you want some food?' the boy said, crawling back slowly into the tent, looking over his shoulder at the animal.

The jackal came closer, still snarling.

The boy ran outside and kicked the sand. 'Hey, you get the fuck away from me, okay?'

The jackal scampered away and stood on the top of a small dune, staring at him.

The boy ran a few steps towards it, looked round, but there was nothing to pick up. He took a handful of sand and threw it at the animal.

The jackal darted further away and stood at another dune, but still wasn't far from the tent.

The boy went back inside, grabbed a piece of bread and went out again. He tossed it as hard as he could. 'Now, get the hell out of here, little shit!'

The jackal snapped at the bread and ran away with it.

The boy went back into the tent and started reading again. It was getting hotter by the minute. He tore a piece of cardboard from a small box, started fanning himself with it, and continued reading.

Dark had fallen when the young Refugee came out of the tent. He had read half of Arman's diary and had fallen asleep. Now a heavy weight sat on his chest. What did his family do at this time of the day? They must be mourning his absence. But, actually, now he felt so much more energetic and rested, he might have a walk along the glass wall, as Arman had suggested. This would do him some good.

He took a few steps but walked back to the tent. His muscles still ached in his calves and thighs from his long walk coming here. He then went and sat at the glass wall, staring at the City. Arman came to his mind again. Wasn't it astonishing that a boy from his very own village had had so much experience and had seen and gone through so much? But the fact was, Arman was more a city boy. And the boy just learnt that he had even been born in the capital. And what a rich family history he had! Now, he understood why Arman's grandmother was so well respected in the village. The boy's own family was nothing special and his own life had been barely any different from that of his parents and grandparents, or from that of everyone else in the village. Farmers they were. That was all.

It was actually not true at all that his own family had achieved nothing special. He shouldn't be so contemptuous of his own family. Arman's family might have been part of the history of his Folk and Grandma was the oldest, wisest woman in the village, but the boy's own father was the person to consult about finding the best time to cultivate the soil for a certain crop. Even though they could get all the information from the weather forecast on the radio and television, they would still trust him more than any other source.

His father could predict the weather weeks before rainfall or snow or heat or the right time for anything just by observing the behaviour of birds and animals. He knew how the seasons each year were going to develop just by the arrival of some migrant birds or by some others departing the village.

Also his mother was respected in the village for being able to grow anything in her garden, even if it was out of season. She would build special glass boxes or grow vegetables indoors. She could also make the best dairy products from the same milk that everyone else had, but knew also what and how you should feed your cow and sheep and goats to get the best milk from them. She had invented new kinds of cheese and butter that no one else had dared to think of, taking the step to move on from the traditional ways of making things in the village.

As for himself, he should also be proud that he had now changed his family's destiny. That he was doing something different. He indeed felt proud of himself for undertaking this perilous venture. He was now equal to Arman, wasn't he?

He smiled and stared at the City where lights now twinkled in the buildings, over there in the distance behind the glass wall. But why not try to see if he could cook as Arman had done? He walked to the tent to get the ingredients.

The next day, the young Refugee woke up in Arman's bed to some strange voice yelling.

'Arman! Hey, Arman, boy, are you there?' a metallic voice shouted in the boy's language, sounding as if it came out from a megaphone.

'Arman! Are you awake boy? I've got good news for you,' the voice yelled again.

The boy jumped off and ran out. The sun had risen high, and

it was already getting warm.

'Hey there, where's Arman?' the voice came from the hut.

The boy looked over. The blind was rolled up halfway. Someone was there inside the small room. Must be the Guard. He walked slowly to the hut, barefoot, and saw a huge, bald old man sitting at the desk; his fat hands just reaching the keyboard, staring at the monitor that was reflected in his glasses.

'Hello. I'm new here,' the boy said in a low voice, not sure if the man would understand him, though Arman had explained how the interpreting system worked.

'I can see you are new, but where is Arman?' the old man said impatiently. 'And could you talk louder, please?'

'He's left,' the boy said more loudly, bending his head towards the circle of pinprick holes.

'Left? What do you mean left?' The man stared at him in surprise. 'What have you done with him? You didn't do him any harm, did you?'

'No, man. How could I?'

'Well, I have bloody good news for him. He is accepted. Here it is,' the old man said enthusiastically, pointing to the monitor. 'I just received it.'

'Really? That's amazing! I'm going to find him,' the boy replied, turning to the desert. 'I'm going to bloody find him. This bastard!' He started running round, yelling, calling for Arman, not knowing to which side he should go. But first he had to go to put on his shoes and Arman's cap. He ran to the tent.

'Wait boy! Wait!' he heard the metallic voice shouting behind him. But he was already inside. He put his shoes on and grabbed a small, shabby rucksack Arman had left behind, and filled it with water bottles and as much food as could fit. He put the bag on his shoulders, put on the baseball cap and ran out, looked over to the Guard, then walked hurriedly into the desert, shuffling through the sand.

'Are you fucking mad, dude?' the Guard cried. 'Come back, boy! Immediately! I am commanding you.'

The boy ran back to the hut, stood in front of the glass door, glowering at the Guard. 'You can't command me, old man!' he roared. 'You've imprisoned yourself behind that bloody glass, how can you force me to do anything?'

The Guard sneered. 'Easy boy! Easy! You're right. I can't even come out to your side.' He stood up and came towards the glass between them. 'But I still feel responsible for you. You've made it so far. You don't want to go in there again. So let's just wait for him. Hopefully he'll show up. Okay?'

'I don't think so,' said the boy, calming down. 'He was very upset by your treatment of him,' he added, then took the rucksack off his shoulders and put it down.

The Guard took off his glasses and squinted at the boy for a moment, then said, 'I understand! I'm sure he was.' He then went back to his desk, sat down in front of the computer and put his glasses back on.

'Arman was a very patient man. I'm so sorry that it's going to end this way. He has to come in within twenty-four hours before the code to open the gate expires. So we will wait for him. Okay?' He stared at the boy.

'Uh-huh! We have to, yes!' The boy took a step back from the glass and put his hands in his pockets, still looking at the Guard.

'As for you, listen to me, you can't help him. You should stay here, as this is the only gate. Believe me. And your only chance to be let in is a good story. Have you got one?'

'Of course!' the boy bellowed, took his hands out of his pockets and stepped forward again, his chin up, shoulders back and chest out. 'I'm—'

'But not today. I can't take it today. Let's try tomorrow. You had better go and think about a good story.'

The boy frowned and squinted at the Guard. What does he mean he couldn't listen to his story today? Does he have any compassion, this old man? Does he think that one day is just nothing? Doesn't he know how long one whole day is on this side of the wall?

'I'm sorry to make you wait, boy, but sometimes with patience things can take a good turn. Take it from me. I have to leave early today. My bus is coming in a minute. Would you tell Arman to be ready early tomorrow morning, if he shows up?'

The boy said nothing, watching the Guard turn off the computer, put his coat on, shove his glasses into his pocket, grab his large, black leather bag, and come to the glass with a smile on his lips, skirting the large turnstile. When he stood right behind the glass, he drew up the blind fully, waved to the boy, then winked and rolled down the blind.

The boy shook his head, picked up the rucksack and walked back to the tent. Before going inside, he turned and saw the old man lock the iron door outside his hut, then walk towards the bus stop, a few metres from the hut, right behind the glass wall. Exactly as the Guard reached the stop, a bus came along with colourful pictures and texts printed on its side, passengers looking out, staring into the mirror wall. The old man got on the bus, weirdly through a door on the left side of the vehicle. And the boy saw the driver sitting at the right side of the bus, exactly the opposite side of driver seats in his own country. How could they drive so on the wrong side of the road? Or was the glass-mirror wall playing a trick on him?

The Guard swiped a card on a device, the door shut, and the bus drove away. All in silence.

Early the next morning, the boy sat beside the glass wall, staring at the City and the lake. Just across the glass wall, now and then a car passed. On the other side of the road some people hurried. They looked as though they might be foreigners who were maybe tolerated in the world behind the glass wall. They must be going to the fields, as they had tools that were probably for farming.

He had finished reading Arman's diary and was on the warpath, now that Arman was going to miss his chance of a better life.

The boy must have sat there for an hour when a bus arrived at the bus stop on the other side of the road and when it moved away, the Guard crossed the road, his black leather bag in his hand. He opened the iron door to his office and went in.

A few moments later, the boy stood up languidly and went to the hut. The Guard had drawn up the blind halfway and already sat at his desk, glasses on. The upper half of his body was in the shade, while the sun shone on his hands on the keyboard, and on the desk and the lower half of the little room.

The speaker crackled and clicked behind the perforated circle of little holes. The boy heard the Guard's muffled voice saying something inside the hut, then the metallic voice said loudly in the boy's own language, 'Any news from Arman?'

'No!' the boy said, his voice cracking. 'I feel so awful about it. So sad,' he stressed.

'I know. That's such a shame! Really! I'm not allowed to say this. But oh, I loved this boy,' the old man said and even though the robotic voice did not reflect any emotion whatsoever, the boy saw the tears in the Guard's eyes.

The man took off his glasses, put them on the desk, then put his head in his hands, hiding his face. His shoulders started heaving.

The boy stood there, staring at him, stunned, not knowing what to do or say.

A few minutes of silence ensued, then the old man lifted his head, pulled out a handkerchief and wiped his eyes. 'Listen young man, do you promise to also be a good boy?'

The boy grinned. Should he feel humiliated or be hopeful that something good was to be promised to him? He nodded.

'Great then!' the Guard said. 'You actually look a bit like him. Certainly, for the people here you all look the same. Listen, when I took Arman's photo for his asylum application, he had almost the same beard and hair as you do now.'

The boy frowned. What was the man trying to explain?

The Guard took out a file from the drawer, pulled out a sheet of paper, came to the glass door and held the paper up to the boy. A photo of Arman was stuck to the top left side of the paper; indeed, very different from how he had appeared two days ago.

The boy stepped back and looked at his own reflection in the glass. He didn't see much similarity but didn't say anything as he now almost sensed what the Guard was about to say. Was he